ONE NIGHT IN WINTER

Also by Simon Sebag Montefiore

FICTION

The Moscow Trilogy:
Sashenka
One Night in Winter
Red Sky at Noon

NONFICTION

Catherine the Great and Potemkin
Stalin: the Court of the Red Tsar
Young Stalin
Jerusalem: the Biography
The Romanovs: 1613–1918
Written in History: Letters that Changed the World

CHILDREN'S FICTION
(WITH SANTA MONTEFIORE)

The Royal Rabbits of London series

ONE NIGHT IN WINTER

A Novel

SIMON SEBAG MONTEFIORE

PEGASUS BOOKS
NEW YORK LONDON

ONE NIGHT IN WINTER

Pegasus Books Ltd.
148 W 37th Street, 13th Floor
New York, NY 10018

First Pegasus Books cloth edition December 2018

ISBN: 978-1-68177-908-9

10 9 8 7 6 5 4 3 2 1

Printed in the United States of America
Distributed by W. W. Norton & Company, Inc.

To my parents, April and Stephen,
and my son Sasha,
the oldest and the youngest

Not a soul knew about it and . . . probably no one would ever know. He was leading a double life: one was undisguised, plain for all to see and known to everyone who needed to know, full of conventional truths and conventional deception, identical to the lives of his friends and acquaintances; and another which went on in secret. And by some strange, possibly fortuitous chain of circumstances, everything that was important, interesting and necessary for him, where he behaved sincerely and did not deceive himself and which was the very essence of his life – that was conducted in complete secrecy.

Anton Chekhov, 'The Lady with the Little Dog'

List of Characters

Major characters are underlined; historical characters are marked with an asterisk*

THE CHILDREN AND THEIR PARENTS

The Romashkin family

Constantin Romashkin, scriptwriter and poet, married to:
Sophia 'Mouche' Gideonovna Zeitlin, film star
<u>Serafima Romashkina</u>, 18, their only child
Sashenka Zeitlin, Sophia's cousin, arrested 1939, fate unknown

The Satinov family and household

<u>Hercules (Erakle) Satinov</u>, Politburo member, Central Committee Secretary, Deputy Chairman of the Council of Ministers, married to:
'Tamriko,' Tamara Satinova, English teacher at School 801
Mariko Satinova, 6, their daughter
Satinov's sons by an earlier marriage in Georgia:
'Vanya,' Ivan Satinov, pilot, killed 1943
David Satinov, 23, pilot
<u>'George,' Georgi Satinov</u>, 18

Marlen Satinov, 17, School Komsomol Organizer
Colonel Losha Babanava, Comrade Satinov's chief bodyguard
Valerian Chubin, Comrade Satinov's aide

The Dorov family

Genrikh Dorov, Chairman, Central Control Commission, and Minister of State Control, married to:
'Dashka,' Dr Daria Dorova, Minister of Health, cardiologist
Their children:
Sergei Dorov, 20, army officer
'Minka,' Marina Dorova, 18, schoolfriend of Serafima
Demian Dorov, 'the Weasel,' 17, Organizer of Young Pioneers
'Senka,' Semyon Dorov, 'the Little Professor', 10

The Blagov family

'Nikolasha,' Nikolai Blagov, 18
Ambassador Vadim Blagov, his father, diplomat
Ludmilla Blagova, his mother

The Shako family

Rosa Shako, 18, schoolfriend of Serafima
Marshal Boris Shako, her father, Soviet Air Force Commander
Elena Shako, her mother

The Titorenko family

Vladimir Titorenko, 17
Ivan Titorenko, his father, Minister of Aircraft Production
Irina Titorenka, his mother

The Kurbsky family

Andrei Kurbsky, 18, a newcomer to the school
Peter Kurbsky, his father, Enemy of the People, arrested in 1938, sentenced to twenty-five years 'without right of correspondence'
Inessa Kurbskaya, his mother

THE TEACHERS OF THE JOSEF STALIN COMMUNE SCHOOL 801

Kapitolina Medvedeva, Director (headmistress) and history teacher
Dr Innokenty Rimm, Deputy Director, political science/ Communist morals teacher
Benya Golden, Russian literature teacher
Tamara Satinova, English teacher (see Satinov family, above)
Apostollon Shuba, physical education teacher
Agrippina Begbulatova, assistant teacher

THE LEADERS

Josef Stalin,* Marshal, General Secretary (Gensec) of the Communist Party, Chairman of the Council of Ministers, Supreme Commander-in-Chief, the Master, the Instantsiya
'Vaska,' Vasily Josefovich Stalin,* 24, his son, Air Force officer, 'Crown Prince'
Svetlana Stalina,* 19, his daughter, student

Vyacheslav Molotov,* Foreign Minister, Politburo member
Lavrenti Beria,* secret policeman, Minister of Internal

Affairs (NKVD/MVD) 1938–45, Deputy Chairman of Council of Ministers, Politburo member
Georgi Malenkov,* Politburo member
Andrei Vyshinsky,* Deputy Foreign Minister
'Sasha,' Alexander Poskrebyshev,* Stalin's chef-de-cabinet
Vsevolod Merkulov,* Minister of State Security (MGB)
Victor Abakumov,* Chief of Military Counter-intelligence (SMERSH: Death to Spies), then Minister of State Security (MGB)

THE GENERALS

Marshal Georgi Zhukov,* Deputy Supreme Commander
Marshal Ivan Konev*
Marshal Constantin Rokossovsky*

THE SECRET POLICEMEN

Colonel Pavel Mogilchuk, investigator, Serious Cases Section, MGB
General Bogdan Kobylov,* 'the Bull,' MGB
Colonel Vladimir Komarov,* investigator, SMERSH/MGB
Colonel Mikhail Likhachev,* investigator, SMERSH/MGB

THE FOREIGNERS

Averell Harriman,* US Ambassador to Moscow
Captain Frank Belman, diplomat, deputy military attaché, interpreter

ONE NIGHT IN WINTER

Prologue

June 1945

Just moments after the shots, as Serafima looks at the bodies of her schoolfriends, a feathery whiteness is already frosting their blasted flesh. It is like a coating of snow, but it's midsummer and she realizes it's pollen. Seeds of poplar are floating, bouncing and somersaulting through the air in random twirls, like millions of drunken ballerinas performing dances of sublime but unpredictable lightness. That humid evening, Serafima struggles to breathe, struggles to see.

Later, when she gives her testimony, she wishes she had seen less, knew less. 'These aren't just *any* dead children,' slurs one of the half-drunk policemen in charge of the scene. When these policemen inspect the IDs of the victims and their friends, their eyes blink as they try to measure the danger – and then they pass on the case as fast as they can. So it's not the police but the Organs, the secret police, who investigate: 'Is it murder, suicide or conspiracy?' they will ask.

What to tell? What to hide? Get it wrong and you can lose your head. And not just you but your family and friends, anyone linked to you. Like a party of mountaineers, when one falls, all fall.

Yet Serafima has a stake even higher than life and death: she's eighteen and in love. As she stares at her two friends who had been alive just seconds earlier, she senses this is the least of it and she is right: every event in Serafima's life will now be defined as Before or After the Shootings.

Looking at the bodies of her friends, she sees the events of the day with magnified vividness. It's 24 June 1945. The day that Stalin reviews the Victory Parade. Yes, it's one of those occasions when every Russian remembers where they are, like 22 June 1941, the day the Nazis invaded. The war's over, the streets teem with drunken, singing crowds. Everyone is certain that a better, easier Russia will emerge from the war. But this depends on one man whose name is never uttered by sensible people except in reverent praise.

Serafima cares nothing for all this. She thinks only of love, even though her lover is a secret, and for good reason. Usually when schoolgirls nurture such a secret, they confide every detail to their closest girlfriends. This isn't Serafima's style: she knows from her own family that gossip can prove fatal in their age of witchhunting. She also knows that she's somehow different even if she cannot quite decide why. Perhaps it's growing up in her mother's shadow. Perhaps it's just the way she's made. She is convinced that no one in all of human existence has ever known such a passion as hers.

This morning, she is woken by the oompah rhythms of the military bands practising their Glinka down the street, the rumble of tank engines, the clip of cavalry hooves on pavements, and she gets out of bed with the bruised feeling that she has scarcely slept.

Her father, Constantin Romashkin, knocks on her door. 'You're awake already? You're excited about the parade?'

She goes to the window. 'Oh no, it's raining.'

'It'll stop for the parade.' But it doesn't. 'Shall we wake your mother?'

Serafima walks along the parqueted, chandeliered corridor to her parents' room, past the framed poster advertising the movie *Katyusha*, which is dominated by a statuesque woman in army uniform, toting a machine-gun against a military background. She has jet-black hair and smudges of gun oil on her cheeks like a Cherokee brave. Dramatic letters declare that the movie stars 'SOPHIA ZEITLIN' (Serafima's mother); and its script is written 'BY CONSTANTIN ROMASHKIN' (Serafima's father). *Katyusha* is the Soviet soldiers' favourite film by Stalin's top scriptwriter. Serafima has a strong impression that it was through such scripts that her papa romanced her mama – it's certainly the way he has kept her.

The bedroom. A heap of silk sheets. There lies 'Katyusha' herself. Long black hair, a bare plump arm. Serafima smells her mother's familiar aura of French scent, French cigarettes, French face cream.

'Mama, wake up!'

'God! What time is it? I have to look good today – I have to look good every day. Light me a cigarette, Serafimochka.'

Sophia sits up; she's naked; her breasts are full. Somehow though, she is already holding a cigarette in an ivory holder. Her father, anxious and fastidious, is pacing up and down.

HE We mustn't be late.

SHE Stop bothering me!

HE You're always late. We can't be late this time.

SHE If you don't like it, divorce me!

Finally, they're dressed and ready. Serafima unlocks the front door just as the doors of all the capacious parquet-floored, high-ceilinged apartments are opening in the pink wedding cake of the Granovsky building (otherwise known as the Fifth

House of the Soviets). The other élite families are coming downstairs too.

In the stairway: the voices of children tremulous with excitement; the creak of well-polished leather, the clip of boot-heels; the jiggling of medals, pistols clinking against belts with starred buckles. First, her parents greet the smug Molotovs – he's in a black suit like a bourgeois undertaker, pince-nez on a head round as a cannonball, his tomahawk-faced wife, Polina, in mink. Just ahead of them: Marshal Budyonny of the waxed moustaches as wide as bicycle handlebars is singing a Cossack ditty (soused? at 8 a.m.?), a pretty new wife preening behind him.

On the first landing: Hercules Satinov is in his general's dress uniform, red-striped trousers and scarlet shoulderboards with golden stars. Her mother embraces Hercules – a family friend since before the Revolution. The Satinov children nod at Serafima with the complicity of school conspirators. 'What's news?' asks George Satinov eagerly. He always says that. She saw them last night at the Aragvi Restaurant and this afternoon they are going to do what they always do. They're going to play the Game.

'Communist greetings, Serafimochka,' says Comrade Satinov. Serafima nods back. To her, he's a chilly, passionless statue, typical of the leaders. Granite and ice – and hair oil. She knows he'll soon be standing beside Stalin atop Lenin's Mausoleum.

'I think the rain will stop for Comrade Stalin,' says Mariko, the Satinovs' six-year-old daughter. She has braided hair and a toy dog under her arm.

'Probably,' laughs Tamara, Comrade Satinov's wife.

Out into the parking lot. Warm summer rain. The air pregnant with the closeness of thunder, the sticky aromas of lilac and apple blossom. Serafima worries that in the dampness, her hair is curling into a frizz of fair corkscrews, and her powder-blue dress with its white collar is losing its shape. For all the high heels, bell-shaped hats and the men's scarlet-visored caps, she can already smell the staleness of sweat and waterlogged satin.

Uniformed bodyguards wait, bearing opened umbrellas. The armoured limousines, headlights as big as planets, curves like showgirls, speed forward, one by one, to ferry them the short distance to the Great Kremlin Palace. A traffic jam curls almost twice around its red walls.

SERAFIMA Why are we driving?

PAPA It's only a hundred metres.

MAMA You try walking anywhere in such high heels! You don't know anything about women, Constantin!

Serafima thinks of her lover. 'Missing you, loving you, wanting you,' she whispers. Somewhere not too far away, is he doing the same?

The car deposits them outside the Great Kremlin Palace. The red crenellated fortifications, golden onion domes, ochre and white palaces, are so familiar Serafima scarcely notices them.

What she sees is her entire world as she walks through the Kremlin. She emerges beside the mausoleum, which resembles an Aztec temple. Made of red marble, mottled like an old lady's skin, it looks much lower than it does on the cinema screen. Behind barriers and guards, a wooden grandstand has been erected for the Bolshevik nobility. Serafima knows everything in their lives is secret but nothing is private. She is a 'golden child', and all the 'golden children' attend the same schools, holiday in the same resorts, and, when they grow up, they marry each other. Everyone knows their place and every word has several meanings.

Her best friend, Minka Dorova, kisses her. She is with her little brother, Senka, aged ten. Their father, Genrikh, also in uniform, gives Serafima a beige smile and a clammy handshake. He is the authority on what does or doesn't constitute 'Bolshevik virtue.' Minka once confided that when she was a toddler, her father placed a portrait of Stalin in her crib.

Her other schoolfriends are there too and just about every commissar, marshal, arctic explorer, composer, or actress she has ever heard of. And their children, most of them from her School 801. A general is bowing at someone. Serafima peers around his shoulderboards and there's Svetlana, Stalin's sturdy, freckled, red-haired daughter, who's not much older than she. She is with her brother, who is wearing an air force general's uniform, and swigging from a hip flask. Vasily Stalin smiles wanly at Serafima, and even when she looks away, she feels his surly eyes on her.

Long before 10 a.m., she, her parents and their friends are in their places in the stand next to the mausoleum. The vast crowds and bristling regiments go absolutely silent as one old man, bowlegged and duck-gaited in his marshal's uniform, climbs the steps up to the mausoleum, followed by his comrades-in-arms: Molotov, Beria and, yes, her neighbour, Satinov. Even though Serafima is close enough to see the rain pouring down Marshal Stalin's visor onto his face and to observe Satinov conversing with him, she doesn't care what they might be saying. She can scarcely remember a thing about the parade. She dreams of seeing her lover later in the day, of kissing him. She knows he's nearby and that makes her ache with joy.

The parade is over. It's time for the Game. Escaping her parents, Serafima pushes through the packed throng of dancing soldiers and ambling civilians to meet her friends on the Great Stone Bridge by the Kremlin. She searches for her friends – and there they are. Some are already in costume. For some of them, the Game is more than just a game; it's an obsession – more real than reality.

The rain stops suddenly; the air is packed with suffocating pollen, and Serafima loses sight of her friends as she is buffeted by the carousing crowds. The smell of vodka and blossom, the thunderous boom and the drifting smoke of a cannonade, a hundred impromptu street choirs singing wartime songs amidst the salvoes of that fifty-gun salute, surround and confuse her. Then two staccato gunshots, very close.

Serafima knows something's happened to her friends even before the sound has finished ricocheting off the Kremlin walls. As the crowd shrinks back, she walks and then runs towards the noise, bumping into people, pushing them aside. She sees Minka Dorova pulling her little brother into the protective warmth of her coat and staring at the ground as if transfixed. Around her stand a gaggle of her schoolfriends in an oddly formal half-moon formation. All are staring down at something; all are very still and silent.

Minka raises her hand to her face. 'Don't look, Senka,' she says to her brother. 'Don't look!'

Serafima is momentarily petrified by the unspeakable horror of what she sees. The girl is closest to her. She lies still, yet her entire chest, covered by the folds of her costume gown, glistens with scarlet blood that flows like a stream over a rock. She is dead, Serafima knows, but dead only seconds ago and her blood is still spreading across her, settling, soaking, clotting as Serafima watches. But her gaze stays there for only a second before it flits on to the boy beside her. One side of his face is pristine, but the other, shattered by the bullet that ripped into it, is gashed open to the elements. She registers shards of skull, flaps of pink flesh and white matter that gleams like moist new dough. One of the boy's eyes rests on his cheek.

She sees him twitch. 'Oh God! Oh Christ!' she cries. 'Look – he's alive!' She runs forward to kneel beside him, to take his hand, aware that the blood is soaking her knees, her dress; it's between her fingers. His chest . . . the cravat and velvet of his fancy-dress frock coat are still immaculate because they are burgundy, she notes absurdly. He pants very fast, groans, and then, most unforgettably, sighs – a long bubbling sigh. He quivers all over and then his chest is still. He is no longer a boy, scarcely a person, never the friend she knew so well, and in his present state, it seems incredible that he ever was.

Minka vomits. Someone is sobbing loudly now; another has fainted and lies on the ground. Strangers rush forward and retreat just as fast, horrified. And Serafima hears a loud and shrill scream very close to her. It is her scream. She stands up, backing away, but finds something sharp like a thorn under her foot, and when she lifts it up, she holds two bloody teeth.

Some soldiers and a sailor see what has happened and take the schoolchildren in their arms with the rough-hewn kindness of peasants who have been to war. They move them back, shield them. One of them gives Serafima a swig of his vodka and she grabs it back and takes another and gulps until she is almost sick. But the burn in the belly steadies her. Then the police – the *militsia* – are there. Red-faced, interrupted amidst their toasting and singing, they seem bleary and lairy but at least they take control of the crowd and move Serafima away from the bodies that she can't stop looking at.

She goes over to her friends, who cling to each other. But Serafima is smeared with blood and they draw back.

'Oh my God, Serafima, it's on you! It's all over you!'

Serafima raises her hands and they are caked with it.

Silver sparks whirl behind her eyes as she looks back at the bodies and then up towards the red-sapphired stars glowing atop the Kremlin towers. Somewhere in the Kremlin, very soon, she knows that Stalin will be told that two schoolchildren from School 801 have died violently – and that restless, wily, ferocious force will seek meaning in these deaths, a meaning that will suit his own high and mysterious purposes.

As the pink-fractured sky darkens, she is struck by the most unbearable certainty: that this is the last night of their childhoods. These shots will blast their lives and uncover secrets that would never otherwise have been found – hers most of all.

PART ONE

The Fatal Romantics' Club

Unbelievably happy have become
Every hour, study, and play,
Because our Great Stalin
Is the best friend of us kids.

Of the happy childhood we are given,
Ring forth, joyful song!
Thanks to the Great Stalin
For our happy days!

'Thank You, Comrade Stalin, for Our Happy Childhood,'
popular Soviet song

1

Several weeks earlier

The best school in Moscow, thought Andrei Kurbsky on his first day at School 801 on Ostozhenka, and, by some miraculous blessing, I've just made it here.

He and his mother were far too early and now they hovered in a doorway opposite the school gates like a pair of gawping villagers. He cursed his mother's anxiety as he saw she was holding a checklist and running through his paraphernalia under her breath: satchel – yes; white shirt – yes; blue jacket – yes; grey trousers – yes; one volume Pushkin; two notebooks; four pencils; packed lunch of sandwiches . . . And now she was peering into his face with a maddening frown.

'Oh, Andryusha, there's something on your face!' Drawing out a crumpled hankie from her handbag, she licked it and started trying to scrub away at his cheek.

This was his first memory of the school. They were all there, the threads that led to the killings, if you knew which to follow. And they began with his mother scrubbing him while he tried to wave her away as if she were a fly buzz-bombing him on a summer's day.

'Stop it, Mama!' He pushed her hand away and proudly rearranged his spectacles. Her pinched, dry face behind metal spectacles infuriated him, but he managed to suppress it, knowing that the satchel, blazer, shoes had been provided by begging from neighbours, appealing to cousins (who had naturally dropped them when his father disappeared), trawling through flea markets.

Four days earlier, 9 May 1945, his mother had joined him in the streets to celebrate the fall of Berlin and the surrender of Nazi Germany. Yet even on that day of wonders, the most amazing thing was that somehow, during the laxer days of wartime, they had been allowed to return to Moscow. And even *that* did not approach the true miracle: he had applied to all the schools in central Moscow, expecting to get into none, but, out of all of them, he had been accepted by the best: the Josef Stalin Commune School 801, where Stalin's own children had been educated. But this astonishing good news immediately sent his mother, Inessa, into a new spiral of worry: how to pay the school fees with her librarian's salary?

'Look, Mama, they're about to open the gates,' Andrei said as a little old Tajik in a brown janitor's coat, wizened as a roasted nut, jingled keys on a chain. 'What gates!'

'They have gold tips,' said Inessa.

Andrei examined the heroic figures carved on the two pilasters in the Stalin imperial style. Each pillar was emblazoned with a bronze plaque on which, in golden silhouettes, he recognized Marx, Lenin and Stalin.

'The rest of Moscow's a ruin, but look at this school for the top people!' he said. 'They certainly know how to look after their own!'

'Andrei! Remember, watch your tongue . . .'

'Oh, Mama!' He was as guarded as she was. When your father has disappeared, and your family has lost everything, and you are hovering on the very edge of destruction, you don't need reminding that you must be careful. His mother felt like a bag of bones in his arms. Food was rationed and they could scarcely afford to feed themselves.

'Come on,' he said. 'People are arriving.' Suddenly children in the school uniform – grey trousers and white shirt for boys, grey skirt and white blouse for girls – were arriving from every direction. 'Mama, look at that car! I wonder who's in it?'

A Rolls-Royce glided up to the kerb. A driver with a peaked cap jumped out and ran round to open the door at the back. Andrei and Inessa stared as a full-breasted woman with scarlet lips, a strong jaw and jet-black hair emerged from the car.

'Look, Andryusha!' exclaimed Inessa. 'You know who that is?'

'Of course I do! It's Sophia Zeitlin. I love her movies. She's my favourite film star.' He had even dreamed of her: those full lips, those curves. He had woken up very embarrassed. She was old – in her forties, for God's sake!

'Look what she's wearing!' Inessa marvelled, scrutinizing Sophia Zeitlin's checked suit and high heels. After her, a tall girl with fair curly hair emerged from the Rolls. 'Oh, that must be her daughter.'

They watched as Sophia Zeitlin straightened her own chic jacket, checked her hairdo and then cast a professional smile in three directions as if accustomed to posing for photographers. Her daughter, as scruffy as the mother was immaculate, rolled her eyes. Balancing a pile of books in her arms and trying to keep her satchel strap on her shoulder, she headed straight towards the school gates.

Inessa started to brush imaginary dust off Andrei's shoulders.

'For God's sake, Mama,' he whispered at her, pushing her hand away. 'Come on! We're going to be late.' Suppose his classmates first sighted him having his face cleaned by his mother! It was unthinkable.

'I just want you to look your best,' Inessa protested, but he was already crossing the road. There were not many cars and Moscow looked faded, scarred, weary after four years of war. At least two of the buildings on Ostozhenka were heaps of rubble. The Kurbskys had just reached the pavement when there was a skidding rush and a Packard limousine, black and shiny, sped towards them, followed by a sturdy new Moskvitch car. Braking with a screech, a uniformed guard with waxed moustaches leaped from the passenger seat of the Packard and opened the back door.

A man climbed out of the car. 'I recognize *him*,' Andrei said. 'That's Comrade Satinov.'

Andrei remembered him in *Pravda* wearing an entire chest of medals (headline: 'Stalin's Iron Commissar'), but now he wore a plain khaki uniform with just a single Order of Lenin. Arctic stare, aquiline nose: emotionless discipline, Bolshevik harshness. How often had Andrei seen that face on banners as big as houses, on flags aloft in parades? There was even a city in the Urals called Satinovgrad. His mother squeezed his arm.

'It's quite a school,' he said. The bodyguards formed a phalanx around Comrade Satinov, who was joined by a tiny woman and three children in school uniform, two boys who were Andrei's age, and a much younger girl.

Hercules Satinov, Politburo member, Secretary of the Party, Colonel General, approached the school gates holding his daughter's hand as if leading a victory march. Andrei and his mother instinctively stepped back, and they were not the only ones: there was already a queue at the gates, but a path opened for the Satinovs. As Andrei and his mother followed in their wake, they found themselves right behind the Satinov boys.

Andrei had never been so close to a leader before, and glanced back anxiously at his mother.

'Let's step back a bit.' Inessa gestured: retreat. 'Best not to be too far forward.' Rule number one: Don't be noticed, don't draw attention. It was a habit born of long misfortune and suffering in this flint-hearted system. Years of being invisible in crowded stations where they feared their IDs would be checked.

Torn between fearful caution and the craving to rub shoulders with his new classmates, the Golden Youth of Moscow, Andrei couldn't take his eyes off the nape of Comrade Satinov's neck, shaved military style. Before many minutes had passed, they found themselves near the very front of the line, almost between the two gold-crested pillars of the school gates, under a hot Moscow sky so cloudlessly blue it seemed bleak.

Around Andrei and his mother, the crowd of parents – well-dressed women, men in golden shoulderboards (he saw a marshal up ahead) and creamy summer suits, and children in the red scarf of the Pioneers – pressed close. Beside him, Inessa was sweating, her face made ugly by worry, her skin dry as grey cardboard. Andrei knew she was only forty – not that old – yet the contrast with the glossily coiffed mothers of the school in their smart summer frocks was all too obvious. His father's arrest and vanishing, their banishment from the capital, seven years' exile in Central Asia, all this had ground her to dust. Andrei felt embarrassed by her, irritated by her and protective of her, all at the same time. He took her hand. Her crushed, grateful smile made him think of his father. Where are you, Papa? he wondered. Are you still alive? Was their return to Moscow the end of their nightmare or yet another cruel trick?

Comrade Satinov stepped forward and a woman in a sack-like black shift dress, which made her resemble a nun, greeted him.

'Comrade Satinov, welcome. I'm Kapitolina Medvedeva, School Director, and I wish on behalf of the staff of the Stalin School 801 to say that it is a great honour to meet you. At last! In person!'

'It's good to be here, Comrade Director,' replied Satinov with a strong Georgian accent. 'I've been at the front and haven't done a thing with the children since the twenty-second of June 1941' – the day Hitler invaded Russia, as Andrei and every Russian knew – 'but now I've been summoned back from Berlin to Moscow.'

'Summoned,' repeated the director, blushing faintly because 'summoned' could only mean an order from Marshal Stalin himself. 'Summoned by . . .'

'Comrade Stalin has instructed us: now the war is over, we must restore proper Russian and Soviet values. Set an example. The Soviet man is a family man too.' Andrei noticed that Satinov's tone was patient and masterful yet never arrogant. Here was Bolshevik modesty. 'So you might be seeing too much of me at the school gates.'

Director Medvedeva put her hands together as if in prayer and took a deep breath. 'What wisdom! Comrade Satinov, of course we know your family so well. Your wife is such a valued member of staff and we are accustomed to prominent parents here but, well, a member of the Politburo – we . . . we are overcome, and so honoured that you've come personally . . .'

The boy in front of Andrei was shaking his head as he listened to this performance. 'Mother of God, you'd have thought Papa was the Second Coming!' he said aloud. Andrei wasn't sure whom he was addressing. 'Are we going to have this bowing and scraping every time he drops us off at school?' It was one of Satinov's sons, who had half turned towards Andrei. 'It's bad enough having a mother who's a teacher but now . . . oh my God. Nauseating.'

Andrei was shocked at this irreverence, but the dapper boy, with polished shoes, creased trousers and pomade in his bouncy hair, seemed delighted at the effect he was having on the new boy. He gave Andrei an urbane smile. 'I'm Georgi Satinov but everyone calls me George. English-style.' The English were still allies, after all. George offered his hand.

'Andrei Kurbsky,' said Andrei.

'Ah yes. Just back in the city? You're the new boy?' asked George briskly.

'Yes.'

'I thought so.' And the smile vanished. Without it, George Satinov's face looked smug and bored. The audience was over – and Andrei felt himself falling back to earth.

'Minka!' George was embracing a curvaceous girl with dark skin. 'What's news?' he was asking.

Andrei paled a little and felt his mother beside him again. They both knew what George had meant by 'Just back in the city?' He was tainted by exile, the child of a Former Person.

'Don't expect too much. They'll all want to be your friend in the end,' whispered Inessa, squeezing his arm sweetly. He was grateful for it. The girl called Minka was so pretty. Would Andrei ever be able to talk to her with George Satinov's confident, carefree style? Her parents stood behind her with a little boy. 'That must be her mother over there. I recognize her too. It's Dr Dashka Dorova, Health Minister.' Minka's mother, brown-skinned and dark-eyed, wore a cream suit with pleated skirt more suited for tennis than surgery. The most elegant woman Andrei had seen in Moscow stared momentarily at Inessa's darned stockings, scuffed shoes and the aubergine-coloured circles under her eyes. Her husband was also in uniform but tiny, with prematurely white hair and the pasty skin of the Soviet bureaucrat: the Kremlin Tan.

Andrei was just trying to regain his natural optimism when his mother pulled him forward.

'Thank you, Comrade Director.' Satinov had assumed a winding-up tone. 'We appreciate your work too.' Director Medvedeva almost bowed as the Satinovs processed inside, and then she turned to Andrei, her face a mask of solemn rectitude once again.

'Yes?' she asked.

As he looked beneath the lank hair and beetly brows into her severe eyes, he feared that she would not know his name or, worse, would know it in order to send him away. Inessa too shook her hand with an expression that said, 'Hit me. I'm used to it, I expect it.'

'Mama, how will we pay for this school?' he had asked Inessa only that morning, and she had answered, 'Let's live that long first.' Would he be unmasked as the son of an Enemy of the People and expelled before he had even started?

Director Medvedeva grudgingly offered a hand so bony the fingers seemed to grind. 'The new boy? Yes. Come see me in my office after assembly. Without fail!' She turned to the Dorovs: 'Welcome, comrades!'

Red heat spread through Andrei's body. Director Medvedeva was going to ask how he would afford the fees. He recalled how often the tiniest signs of hope – his mother finding a new job, a move into a larger room in a shared apartment, permission to live in a town nearer Moscow – had been offered and then taken away from them at the last moment. He felt his composure disintegrating.

The vestibule led to a long corridor.

'Shall I come in with you?' Inessa asked him. There was nothing so daunting as the first day at a new school, yet one moment he needed her warmth beside him, the next she metamorphosed into steel shackles around his ankles. 'Do you need me, darling?'

'Yes. No. I mean—'

'I'll leave you, then.' She kissed him, turned and the crowd swallowed her up.

Andrei was on his own. Now he could remake himself: reforging was a principle of Bolshevism. Stalin himself had promised that the sins of the father would never be visited on the son, but Andrei knew they were – and with a vengeance.

2

Andrei stood alone for a moment in the doorway that led into School 801's main corridor and took a deep breath that smelled of his new life: the bitter disinfectant of the washrooms, the sweet floor polish of the parquet floors, the scent of the glamorous mothers, the acrid whiff of vodka on some teachers' breath, and, stronger than anything, he inhaled the oxygen of hope. Then he plunged into the crowd, looking at the walls, which were decorated with framed posters of Young Pioneers on camping trips, cartoons of *Timur and His Team* on their wartime adventures, and lists of *otlichniki*, the 'excellent ones,' the highest-achieving children.

Yes, he was inside – and he felt his resilient cheerfulness vanquishing George Satinov's disdain and the director's sinister summons. There right in front of him was the film star Sophia Zeitlin, talking to Comrade Satinov. He could not help but stare. He had never seen two such famous beings making ordinary conversation. It was like a newsreel in real colour. He could hear their voices. Do they breathe like us mortals? he wondered; then he caught himself with a laugh. Of course they did.

Satinov's plainclothed bodyguards were peering at him contemptuously, and he turned, almost knocking into Sophia Zeitlin's daughter – and stopped, not sure what it was about her that caught his attention. Of course, the fact that she rode to school in a film star's Rolls-Royce explained some of it.

She moved heedlessly, with the long-legged, unregimented spirit of a much younger girl. Her curly fair hair was unbrushed, her face and skin clear of make-up, yet Andrei sensed a natural authority of the most elementally basic kind, the power of someone who expected admiration and whose expectation was self-fulfilling. Her green eyes met his for a second, and Andrei noticed that her long black eyelashes and wide sensuous mouth were so striking that they entirely overshadowed her laddered stockings and the white blouse buttoned up to the neck that she was wearing.

As Sophia Zeitlin and Comrade Satinov advanced down the corridor, greeting everyone, Zeitlin's daughter, noticing perhaps that Andrei was watching her, raised her eyes towards the heavens, a complicit gesture that seemed to say her mother embarrassed her too.

'Serafima!' It was Satinov's son again. 'Good holidays? What's news?' It seemed to be George's catchphrase, Andrei thought.

Andrei was following Serafima and George down the corridor when the bell rang. The parents started to retreat and the children headed for assembly. Serafima and George watched Dr Dashka Dorova and her desiccated husband pass.

'What an affinity of opposites Minka's parents are,' said George.

'He's just like . . . yes, an uncooked chicken cutlet!' said Serafima.

'That's exactly what he's like!' chuckled George. And Andrei smiled too. Serafima's wicked comment was spot-on.

The children flowed one way and the parents the other. When Comrade Satinov passed, he nodded brusquely at Andrei, who had no idea how to react (salute? no!) but was borne on down the corridor by the crowd.

In the school gymnasium, ranks of wooden seats had been placed beneath thick ropes that hung like giant nooses from the rafters of a high wooden ceiling. Exercise ladders ran up the walls and a wooden horse was stored near the back beside the Lenin Corner's white bust of Lenin. Seats for the teachers were arranged in two rows on the wooden stage. Director Medvedeva's stood in the middle: the only one with arms and a cushion. The school was a mini-Russia, thought Andrei. Every institution had its hierarchy just like the Party. Giant portraits of Stalin and the leaders hung from the walls behind (yes, there, fourth in order, was Satinov).

For a moment, Andrei panicked as the five hundred pupils found their friends. They were all greeting each other after the holidays – what if he couldn't find a seat? He caught George's eye for a moment but George looked away. 'Minka, I've saved you a seat,' he called out. 'Serafima, here!' Sitting between Minka Dorova (daughter of the Uncooked Chicken) and Serafima (daughter of the film star), George radiated the pinked-cheeked satisfaction of the boy who believes he is in his rightful place. A tall red-haired boy rushed to get the seat next to Serafima.

Andrei looked for a seat for what seemed like a horribly long time before sitting down with relief on one of the empty chairs opposite George and Serafima. A slim pale girl with fair hair sat down beside him. She looked at George and his friends, and then turned to Andrei as if she had just awoken from a dream.

'Oh, hello. You're new?'

'Yes,' said Andrei.

'Mmm,' she murmured. 'I'm Rosa Shako.'

She must be Marshal Shako's daughter, thought Andrei,

who'd seen the air force commander just outside the school. When they'd shaken hands, she gazed over at George's row as if she'd forgotten him again.

'Those are my friends,' she said. 'Didn't you meet George outside school?'

'Not really.'

'It must be hard arriving for the last term of the year,' she said. Andrei thought that with her blue eyes and flaxen ringlets, she looked just like an angel in a children's book. 'You see the red-haired boy?'

'The one who's sitting next to Serafima?'

A cloud crossed her face. 'That's Nikolasha Blagov. My friend.' She'd opened her mouth to say something else when – hush – everyone's voices sank to a whisper. The teachers entered, filing in order of importance down the aisle and up the steps to the stage in exactly the same way Stalin and the Politburo entered at Congresses.

'Do you know who they all are?' asked Rosa kindly.

'I only know her,' said Andrei as Director Medvedeva herself marched forward on to the stage, followed – presumably – by her deputy, a man whose greasy straggle of auburn hair, brushed over his baldness, had the texture of a woven basket.

'That's Dr Rimm,' whispered Rosa as he passed them. 'Serafima, who thinks up all the nicknames, calls him the Hummer. Listen.' Comrade Rimm was loudly humming a tune that was unmistakably 'May Comrade Stalin Live Many, Many Long Years.'

'Quiet, George,' said Dr Rimm in a high voice. 'Eyes straight ahead, Serafima. Sit up straight. Discipline!'

Then came the rest of the teachers. 'That's Comrade Satinov's wife, Tamara,' said Rosa. 'She teaches us English.'

A strapping old gentleman, whose wrinkly knees the colour of tanned leather were framed between flappy blue shorts and scarlet socks, entered next. 'That's Apostollon Shuba, our physical instructor. Do you think he looks like a sergeant major in the Tsarist army? Well, he was!'

'Really?' How on earth had this relic with the pitchfork-shaped moustaches survived the Terror? Andrei thought. But he was one of a generation of children brought up to believe that discretion was the essence of life, so he said nothing.

One seat was still empty. And then a teacher in a baggy sand-coloured suit and striped socks jumped nimbly on to the back of the stage. A murmur buzzed through the children.

'Always last,' said Rosa softly. 'Let's see! Look at that new canary-yellow tie! That's Benya Golden, our Pushkin teacher.' Andrei saw an agile, balding man with receding fair hair and a playful smile slip into his seat. 'Serafima calls him the Romantic. If you're lucky you'll be in his class; if you're unlucky, you'll get Rimm the Hummer.'

Another bell heralded a rigorous silence. Director Medvedeva tapped her baton on her lectern. 'Welcome back to the school in our era of the historic victory won by the genius of our Leader, Comrade Stalin.' She turned to Dr Rimm, who stepped forward.

'One question, Komsomolniki!' he piped in a voice that might, on the telephone, be mistaken for that of a soprano. 'If you had to lose all your possessions or your Komsomol badge, which would you choose?'

A boy with his hair brushed back in a slick wave like the Soviet leaders stood and led the reply: 'All our possessions!' he cried.

Andrei recognized him as the other Satinov boy.

'It's George's brother, Marlen,' confirmed Rosa in his ear. She smelled of rosewater. 'Are you a Komsomol, Andrei?'

Andrei wished he were – but there was no place for tainted children in the Young Communists.

'Young Pioneers! Rise! Young Pioneers, are you prepared?' shouted Dr Rimm. The red-scarfed Pioneers replied as one.

'*Always prepared!*'

'Bravo, Pioneers.' Dr Rimm scanned the gym. Andrei was too old to be a Pioneer now, but he would have given anything to wear the red scarf.

Director Medvedeva tapped her baton. 'Would Mariko Satinova come up to the rostrum,' she said. That family was everywhere, thought Andrei as a little girl with plaits and a red scarf appeared on the side of the stage.

Tap, tap from the director's baton: the sign to a young blonde teacher at the piano, who started to bang out the opening bars that Andrei knew so well.

'And who's the pianist?' he asked.

'That's Agrippina Begbulatova, the assistant music teacher,' answered Rosa as the little girl started to sing the first lines of the schoolchild's anthem, 'Thank you, Comrade Stalin, for Our Happy Childhood.' Andrei could sing it in his sleep; in fact, sometimes he did.

Director Medvedeva made announcements about the term: about the Pioneers camping at Artek in the Crimea; the second eleven football team would play the VM Molotov Commune School 54. Benya Golden seemed to regard many of these bulletins as faintly amusing, noticed Andrei as the teachers filed out, and the school term began.

Director Medvedeva was writing at her desk when Andrei was ushered in to see her. Her office was furnished with a single Bakelite phone, a small photograph of Stalin, and a tiny safe. (Andrei knew that the number of phones, and the size and quality of Stalin portraits and safes, were all measures of power.) A banner across one entire wall declared: 'Thank you, dear marshal, for our freedom, our children's joy, our life.'

She gestured towards a wooden chair. 'Welcome to the school. We forge new Soviet citizens, understand?'

Andrei waited miserably for the 'but,' which he knew from bitter experience would not be long in coming.

'But you have a tainted biography. Most of my colleagues here don't approve of your admission. I doubt it will work out, but it's only for a term. I shall watch you for the slightest sign of deviationism. That will be all, Kurbsky.'

He walked with heavy steps to the door as she too stood up briskly. 'You must go to your first class. Follow me!'

Andrei's mind whirred: should he ask about the fees? What was the point? It sounded as if she would get rid of him soon enough. Their footsteps echoed along the wooden corridor, which was by now deserted. Trying to keep up with her, Andrei thought her flaky skin and lank hair had never enjoyed the kiss of sunlight in all her life. At last, she stopped outside a closed door and gestured to him to come closer.

'You won't be paying school fees.'

Andrei opened his mouth to ask how, why? But she silenced him with a glance.

'Do not discuss this, Kurbsky. Understood? Here's your class.' She turned like a sentry and the march of her metal-heeled boots receded down the long corridor.

Andrei wanted to scream with relief, but knew he must not. *Tell no one. Reveal nothing. Analyse its meaning later.* Struggling to control his breathing, he steadied his shaking hands and knocked on the door.

* * *

His first lesson was Russian literature but he did not know if he would get Dr Rimm or Teacher Golden. Which would be more helpful? As he opened the door, twenty-five sets of eyes swivelled towards him – and Andrei immediately noticed with a mixture of thrill and anxiety that Serafima, the Satinov brothers and the severe red-haired boy named Nikolasha were in his class. Only Rosa nodded at him.

'Ah – a stranger!' said Benya Golden, who was sitting languidly in his chair with his feet on the desk. 'Come on in! We're just starting.'

'Am I in the right class? Is this Russian literature?'

'Some of it is, some of it isn't.' The class laughed at Benya Golden's insouciance. 'You wish to join our fraternity of dear friends, beloved romantics, wistful dreamers?'

'Um, I think so.'

'Name?'

'Kurbsky, Andrei.'

'Take a seat. Nikolasha Blagov, move up and make space.' The red-haired boy was again sitting next to Serafima, and, with much sighing, sulkily moved his books. Serafima in turn had to move up too. Nikolasha muttered to himself as Andrei sat next to him.

'Now, Kurbsky,' said Benya Golden. 'Where are you from?'

Andrei hesitated. 'Well, I was in Stalinabad, but I've just come back to Moscow—'

'Stalinabad! The Paris of Central Asia!' Nikolasha exclaimed in a deep voice that seemed to crack at the wrong moments. A boy with long black hair sitting right behind them sneered: 'The Athens of Turkestan!' They all knew why someone like Andrei had ended up living in a Central Asian backwater. It was his tainted biography all over again.

'Who asked you, Nikolasha?' Benya Golden snapped. Jumping to his feet, he walked across to the boy with the long black hair: 'Or you, Vlad? There's nothing less attractive than Muscovite snobbery. Your presence in this class is by no means a fait accompli. I hear Dr Rimm's classes are *much* more fun than mine!'

Nikolasha glanced back at Vlad, and both seemed to shrink at Benya Golden's threat. Andrei noted that Nikolasha was the leader and Vlad the henchman in a group of youths who seemed to take their long hair and intellectual tastes very seriously indeed.

'Let's welcome Andrei, you inhospitable bastards. If Director Medvedeva's put him in our class, there's a reason. This term we're doing Pushkin's *Eugene Onegin*.'

Benya Golden stepped back onto the platform where his desk stood and picked up a book.

'*Eugene Onegin*,' he said. 'Most of us know some of this text. What about you, Andrei Kurbsky?'

'God grant that in my careless art,
For fun, for dreaming, for the heart . . .
You've found at least a crumb or two.'

Andrei's reply earned a murmur of approval from the class. Serafima looked up, surprised – or did he imagine that?

'Good! I bet it feels good to be back in Moscow,' Benya Golden said, smiling at him.

Emboldened by Golden's enthusiasm, Andrei continued:

'How oft . . . forlorn and separated –
When wayward fate has made me stray –
I've dreamt of Moscow far away!'

'Now I see why the director placed you in my class, Kurbsky.' Golden climbed up to stand on his chair, holding his volume in one hand. 'Nikolasha, blow your bugle!'

Nikolasha had taken an instrument from its case beside him and, self-consciously shaking his red locks, he stood up and blew his trumpet as if heralding a medieval king.

'Your hair's even longer this term,' Benya Golden said to him. 'Is this new coiffure a romantic affectation? My colleagues won't like it. They might even think you were cultivating the un-Bolshevik image of a young romantic. Right! Now, welcome to *Onegin*. Prepare to be dazzled by the bard of Rus himself. There's such richness in its pages that it never loses the capacity to surprise and delight us. Is this an "encyclopaedia of Russian life"? Is it a tragedy, comedy or romance?'

As Golden talked, Nikolasha had sat down, replaced his trumpet and was earnestly writing notes in an exercise book with scarlet velvet covers. When he saw that Andrei was looking, he muttered, 'Mind your own business,' and moved the book as far from Andrei as he could.

'Is Onegin himself a dreary misanthropic narcissist or a victim of love and society? Is Tatiana a dull provincial, unworthy of such passion, or a paragon of Russian womanhood? Is this a guide how to love today? Yes, Demian Dorov?'

'Surely only the Party can guide our lives today?' Andrei recognized the pointy face and red scarf of the school's Chief Pioneer.

'And Comrade Stalin!' interjected Marlen Satinov.

'Comrade Stalin what?' Benya Golden asked, still standing on his chair on the platform.

'Only Comrade Stalin,' declared Marlen, 'and the Party can guide our lives. You're in danger of bourgeois sentimentalism.'

'Well, thank you for reminding us,' said Golden. 'But I'm just teaching Pushkin here. Now let us begin. Ready?' Benya Golden closed his eyes. 'Mobilize the senses, dear friends, beloved romantics, wistful dreamers. Remember: life is short. It's an adventure. Anything is possible! Breathe with me!' He inhaled through his nose, and the children did the same. All exhaled together. Andrei looked around the room to see if anyone was laughing or rebelling, but Nikolasha gave him a grave look, as if he were proposing blasphemy, while Serafima took a breath with just a hint of amusement on her face to tell him that she knew he was looking at her. So he joined in with the insanity and had just exhaled again when Golden, not even opening his book, declaimed the first lines, his right hand raised and open as if reciting a spell: '*My uncle, a man of firm convictions* . . .' And on he went, reciting the text with such grace that the children listened in silence – until George Satinov put up his hand.

'Yes?' said Benya Golden.

'I just wondered what Pushkin really means by the *mysteries of the marriage bed*?'

This sparked much sniggering from the back of the class.

Nikolasha turned round. 'This is about *love*,' he hissed.

'Grow up, George,' echoed his ally, Vlad, who seemed to support Nikolasha in everything.

'You're thinking of Rosa, aren't you?' teased George.

'No, he's dreaming of Serafima,' said Minka Dorova. More laughter. Rosa blushed while Serafima ignored Nikolasha completely; Andrei realized that she hadn't so much as acknowledged him all morning.

Benya Golden put his hands over his ears: 'George! Minka! How can you slaughter the poetry with your tawdry innuendoes?' Andrei had never seen a teacher who so relished, even encouraged, the mischief of his class. 'Back to the divine poetry!' Golden sat back on his chair. 'Serafima, are you with us this morning? Tell us how Onegin falls in love with Tatiana, an innocent provincial girl.'

As Serafima read, the class became quiet again. Andrei watched her, fascinated, and realized everyone else was watching her too. She wasn't as pretty as Rosa, nor as alluring as Minka in the back row, yet her startlingly green eyes were sprinkled with gold that glinted from under her black eyelashes. Was she agonizingly shy and simply unaware of her power? Andrei couldn't work it out.

'Well done, Serafima,' said Golden, stopping her at last. Serafima looked up at him and smiled. 'That's enough for today. Andrei, I want you to stay behind.'

The children gathered their books, chairs grinding on the echoing floors. As George Satinov passed their desk, Nikolasha showed him the velvet-covered notebook and whispered something.

'As you can see,' said Benya Golden when they were alone, 'my pupils are as serious about their little knots of friendship as they are about their poetry. But although some of them are the sons and daughters of our leaders, they're mostly good kids. Anyway, even they were impressed by your knowledge of Pushkin, as was I.'

'Thank you,' said Andrei.

Golden patted Andrei on the shoulder. 'Cheer up. You're going to be a success here.'

'I'm . . . I'm very happy to be here.'

'You'll end up being friends with Serafima's group, don't you worry. But I know it's not easy coming back.'

'You do?'

'Yes,' said Golden. 'Because I haven't been back in Moscow for long myself.'

Andrei looked up at the teacher, at his receding light hair, now greying, his dimpled chin, his lined face. His smile seemed genuine – but was it? Andrei knew it was better to say nothing more. Consulting his timetable, he hurried to find his next class.

At lunchtime, Andrei ate his sandwich of black bread with a gherkin at his desk, content to be on his own for a moment while Nikolasha and his friends Vlad, George and Rosa pushed some desks together to form an ink-stained table where they shared their fish, beef, cheese and tomatoes. It seemed that Nikolasha was never alone, never without an entourage of pale, floppy-haired creatures who looked as if they never took any exercise or ventured outside. Nikolasha was reading to them from his red velvet notebook and they whispered excitedly. Andrei felt pangs of disdain and envy – but he remembered his father and he knew neither of these sentiments was worthy of him. He finished his sandwich and as he walked past them, he saw Nikolasha giving his notebook to George.

'You can read it, George,' he was saying, 'but take it seriously and I want it back tomorrow. With your comments.'

'Of course, of course,' replied George jovially.

Afterwards, as Andrei was hurrying up the corridor to his next lesson, he heard the squish of plastic soles on the parquet floor behind him. He turned and a white, freckled face hove into view. Nikolasha Blagov was so tall that he hunched over as he walked. As always he was followed by the dark-haired cadaverous figure of Vlad, as well as the fey Rosa Shako.

'What do you think of Teacher Golden?' Nikolasha asked lugubriously. His voice was so deep that his words came out slurred, as if his tongue were a wooden spoon. Vlad and Rosa both leaned in to hear his answer.

Andrei hesitated, cautious of making some terrible mistake on his first day. 'Interesting,' he said finally.

Nikolasha shook his head as if disappointed. 'Is that all you have to say?' He leaned over as if about to impart a most perilous secret. 'You'd best be careful. Things are different here.'

'Has Serafima said anything to you yet?' asked Vlad.

'Serafima? I don't even know Serafima.'

'Serafima really understands poetry,' said Nikolasha solemnly. 'Well, you obviously haven't made the grade, even if you can pull a few Pushkin quotes out of the air.'

'What grade?'

'You'll see. Think on it.'

He and Vlad slunk off around the corner. Rosa lingered a moment and touched Andrei's hand. 'He takes it all very seriously but he's so clever and original, you'll see.'

Andrei's first day at School 801 was almost over. His last lesson: Communist ethics with Dr Rimm, a pedant compared with Benya Golden, Andrei thought. Rimm's sand-coloured Stalinka tunic was so tight that it only accentuated the lumpiness of his figure. The class stood to attention when he entered and remained standing until he moved his hand downwards in a silent gesture of command. After a turgid hour, during which Demian Dorov and Marlen Satinov competed with Dr Rimm to quote from the works of Stalin and Lenin, while the rest of the class yawned, wrote notes to each other and tried to stay awake, Andrei was the last out of the room.

As he left, he noticed Nikolasha's red velvet notebook on the floor next to George Satinov's desk. I'll return it to them tomorrow, he thought, and put it in his satchel.

3

Five p.m. at the Golden Gates. This, thought Andrei, watching the limousines picking up his schoolmates, truly was the age of new freedoms, new pleasures. Chauffeurs and army batmen leaned against the curvaceous flanks of their Packards and Lincolns, smoking cigarettes, sweating in the sun. There were some mothers waiting, but most Bolshevik women worked. The nannies, a tribe of florid Matryoshkas, peasant women in housecoats, stood separately, laughing at their own jokes. You couldn't mistake them for the mothers, thought Andrei, and the two groups never spoke.

He stopped between the gold-tipped pillars of the gates, looking for – what? His mother to turn up and collect him in a giant limousine? No chance of that, but he had half expected she might take time off work to meet him. Still, he was relieved that she wasn't there. Instead he was hoping that he might see Serafima and her film-star mother again . . . when she slipped right past him.

'You *do* know your *Onegin*,' Serafima said softly. 'I'll bet Nikolasha's jealous.' He noticed, all over again, her heart-shaped face, her white skin, and those amused green eyes. She did not stop to hear his answer, which was just as well because he could not think how to respond. Later, a host of witty answers would come to him.

The Rolls was waiting for her, the chauffeur leaning on the grille, cigarette between his metal fangs. There was no sign of her parents. But she did not seem pleased: 'Thanks for coming, Khirochenko,' she said. 'But I'll walk. Tell Mama I don't need the car.' The driver shrugged as she walked away from him into the balmy streets; the poplar blossoms whirled around her like a haphazard escort.

As the chauffeurs pulled away, Andrei yearned to be part of the lives of these golden children. Calm down, he told himself, you're in their school, you're in their lives. Soon you too will be in their group.

Holding his school satchel, he walked through the streets. He could feel the heat rising from the paving stones. Around him, the capital of Soviet victory looked like a defeated city. He saw crumbling buildings, their façades peppered with shrapnel, windows shattered, roads pockmarked with bomb craters. Everything – the walls, the houses, the cars – everything except the scarlet banners was drab, beige, peeling, khaki, grey. But the faces of the passersby were rosy, as if victory and sunlight almost made up for the lack of food, and the streets were crowded with pretty girls in skimpy dresses, soldiers, sailors and officers in white summer uniforms. Studebaker trucks, Willys jeeps and the Buicks of officials rumbled by (all gifts from their generous American ally) – but there were also carriages pulled by horses, carts heaped with hay or bedding or turnips, right in the middle of this spired city with its gold domes. Sometimes, when he closed his eyes in the heat and the world went a soft orange, Andrei heard laughter and singing and he was sure he could hear the city itself healing in the sunshine. Down Ostozhenka he walked, then round past the National Hotel and the Kremlin, and up Gorky Street, past the House of the Book on the right, and the City Soviet on the left.

When he peered through one of the archways, he saw goats and cattle in the yard, wrangled by an old peasant with a red kerchief on her head and a crook in her hand. Yet this was the city that had defeated the Hitlerites and stormed Berlin! What pride he felt in the greatness of his Motherland, what horror at its cruelties. The old hag squatted to piss, still with a cigarette between two stumps of teeth. Andrei sighed: he loved his Moscow. He was almost home.

He turned in to the next archway, walked into the courtyard through the vegetable gardens planted amongst the heating pipes, and then entered the doorway of a 1930s apartment block. He climbed the concrete stairs with its fermented vegetable smell of *shchi* soup and vinegary urine to the second floor, where he shouldered open the door of their apartment. A radio was on, Levitan was reading the news in his authoritative, sonorous voice and there was a row going on. In a corridor that had neither carpet nor paint, Ivanov, a middle-aged scientist from Rostov, was screaming at one of the skinny Goldberg children: 'You little cockroach, you drank my milk. I'll report you to the committee. I'll have you slung out of here . . .'

The door to the left opened and the stink of fresh human dung made Andrei's eyes water even before Peshlauk, an antique but indestructible colossus, staggered out, pulling up his giant-girdled trousers. 'I've delivered a veritable baby in there!' he boasted.

Another of the Goldberg children – how many were there: four, five? a plague of undernourished rats – shoved past Andrei. 'Hey, don't push me,' he said, but then he remembered that no one in the Soviet Union respected personal space. Everyone existed in a state of neurotic anxiety, but as his mother always told him: The key to survival is to be calm and save yourself. Never ask others what they did before and what they're doing next. Never speak your mind. And make friends wherever you can.

'Mama!' Andrei went into their little room with its two campbeds packed close together. It often smelled like a rabbit hutch, but it was in Moscow and it was theirs.

'Just close the door,' said Inessa, who lay on her bed, reading about the Japanese war in *Pravda*. The European war was over and now Stalin was in on the kill of Japan. She patted the bed next to her. 'Tell me about the school.'

'Have you got any food?'

'Of course, Andryusha. You must be so hungry. Cheese and black bread. Have a look in Aladdin's Cave.'

Andrei climbed over the other bed and, crouching down, edged a breeze-block out of the wall and brought out the cool cheese. Their apartment had no fridge. In winter they kept their milk fresh by hanging it out of the window, but in summer, this was the best way to preserve perishables, as well as keeping it out of the hands of the Goldberg children or Peshlauk's churning bowels.

Inessa smiled weakly as she watched him eat, and when he'd regained his energy, he beamed at her.

'Good news, Mama! I'm accepted into the school and my fees are paid!'

'Oh darling.' She hugged him and then looked anxious. 'Who by? What's going on?'

Andrei told her exactly what had happened, and watched as his mother's uneasiness cleared. Surely this was evidence of a new era? And a new era meant the return of Andrei's father.

'Andrei,' she whispered, moving closer to him. 'Do you think . . .'

'Don't think, Mama. How often have you told me that?'

'Yes, but . . .'

'Don't hope, because if we're disappointed again, it'll kill us one more time.'

She nodded, and dabbed her eyes. Quickly, to change the subject, he told her about the school: about the director, and Dr Rimm – yes, every school had a few of those – and then he described the literature teacher, Golden. 'I've never had a lesson like that. It was such fun. He brought it to life, and there was something in the way he talked about poetry . . .'

'A teacher like that in a school like yours . . . something's really changing,' she said.

'And, Mama, he said he'd only just returned to Moscow too.' She was about to ask more about Golden but by now, he was describing Serafima (her eyes, the way she dressed), the airy swagger of George, and creepy Nikolasha and his Gothic retainers, Vlad and Rosa.

'Be careful of these princelings,' Inessa was telling him. 'Factions are dangerous, Andrei. Remember whose children they are . . .'

But Andrei wasn't listening: he was already on his way to the bathroom with his satchel. No one was in there because no one in his right mind would visit it after Peshlauk – but he didn't care.

He locked the door. He could actually taste the shit in the air and he didn't dare look down into the bowl, but sat on the edge and, like a miner who has stolen a diamond, he pulled out his treasure, titled the Velvet Book of Love. It was just a plain exercise book with velvet glued on the covers. But it was new and Nikolasha had only just started writing in it.

Agenda for the Summer Term
Top Secret

Thoughts on our new literary movement: the Fatal Romantics' Club, founded December 1944 by me, Nikolasha Blagov. I shall record our meetings, rules and thoughts in this book.

So, thought Andrei, Nikolasha has a little club. Most schools had literary and theatre clubs, but this seemed different. He read on: *Membership: secret.*

Not that secret! Vlad and Rosa had to be members too, maybe Serafima, and certainly George.

Our inspiration: Pushkin

Our moments in history: just as for Christians, the Crucifixion of Christ is the moment. For us it is 1837, the death of Pushkin in a duel.

Our favourite teacher: Teacher Golden

A knock on the bathroom door made Andrei jump. He had forgotten where he was. The book showed that something, perhaps the war, perhaps their privilege, had changed these children, and allowed them the freedom to take a risk.

'Are you going to be long?'

It was Kozamin, the bus conductor.

Andrei gave a bovine groan, one of the repertoire of noises essential to communal living. 'Five minutes. Aaaagh!'

'Take your time,' said Kozamin.

We declare:

1. *We suffocate in a philistine world of science and planning, ruled by the cold machine of history.*

2. We live for love and romance.
3. If we cannot live with love, we choose death.
This is why we conduct our secret rites; this is why we play the Game.

The Game! Andrei smiled to himself but he narrowed his eyes and reread it. Could this have been written with a hint of cunning to conceal its real spirit? These days, everything – from the government announcements in the newspapers to the tedious ramblings of teachers – was in a hieroglyphic code. Nothing meant quite what it said – and sometimes it meant the exact opposite. But Nikolasha's target was obvious. *Science and planning*. That was the Communist Party. *The cold machine of history*. Communism. *Love and romance*. That was what Communists called 'bourgeois sentimentalism.'

Andrei put down the book. In the adult world, in a more oppressive time like 1937, this might have been dangerous anti-Soviet talk. But things had become much more easy-going in the war. No one could take Nikolasha's silly writings seriously, could they? Still, he remembered the wisdom of his father and his mother's warnings. These children were not of his world, and yet he longed to know them better.

4

'May I have a word?' Andrei said to George. They were in school a few days later, and the bell for lunch had just rung.

'A word?' George turned round as he followed Nikolasha and Vlad out of the classroom.

'It's private.'

'Private? How can it be?'

No grand duke of the old days, thought Andrei, could equal the sneering haughtiness of a Communist prince.

'You've lost something and I've found it.'

George frowned. 'Something containing mysterious scribbles?'

Andrei nodded.

'I'll be with you in a second,' George called over to Minka and Serafima, who were waiting for him, sandwich boxes in hand. 'Come with me.' And he pulled Andrei through the washrooms into the room where sports equipment was stowed, and school mischief hatched.

'Thank God you've got it,' George said, looking a good deal less confident than he had a minute earlier. 'Nikolasha makes such a big thing of it. He keeps asking for it back, but I keep telling him I'm still studying it with sacred passion.'

'Well, here it is,' said Andrei, drawing the book out of his satchel.

'You've rescued me,' said George. Andrei held out the book and George put his hands on it and turned breezily to go – but when he tried to take it, he found that Andrei was still gripping it. 'What are you doing?' asked George.

'Have you read it?'

'No, I didn't have time – but you obviously have. Are you offering to brief me?'

'It's a romantic manifesto that could be described as bourgeois sentimentalism . . .'

George hesitated for a moment. 'Thanks for the warning – but Pushkin is the Party's favourite poet. I'm just worried about Nikolasha finding out I lost it.' He waved it away genially. 'So let's keep this between ourselves and I'll find a way to say thank you. I'll see if I can get you in to the Fatal Romantics' Club.'

'I would like that,' replied Andrei, letting go of the book as it disappeared into George's satchel.

'It won't be easy to get you in,' George continued. 'Nikolasha's a fanatic. But you really should be a member – you know your Pushkin better than any of us.'

Andrei opened his hands, palms up, as his curiosity got the better of him. 'One final thing. What is the Game?'

George was already half out of the door but he turned back. 'It's Nikolasha's obsession. You'll find out. For now, we've got to eat lunch. Will you join us in the gym?'

The gym was usually empty for lunch and the children ate their sandwiches perching on its chairs and soft mats. But when George and Andrei found the girls, Minka was obviously upset. 'Look what's happening to my little brother,' she said.

The Director of Physical Education, the moustachioed

Apostollon Shuba, was standing with one hand on the wooden horse and a whistle in his mouth. His face was a deep shade of teak. A class of younger children in shorts and T-shirts stood to attention in a line on the other side of the horse. Alone at the far end of the gym was the frail figure of Senka Dorov, whom Andrei had last seen at that morning's drop-off with his father. Senka looked as comfortable in sports kit as he would in a deep-sea-diving outfit. He gave his sister a beseeching 'rescue me' look with his big brown eyes, but it was too late.

'Right, boy,' Shuba barked. 'Fifth attempt! No one leaves until you get over the horse!'

'But I never will,' said Senka in his high voice.

'Defeatism is not Soviet!'

'I'm not one of your strapping horse-vaulting heroes. Surely even you can see that,' Senka said.

'Hurry up, Senka! We're hungry!' cried one child.

'SILENCE!' Shuba ordered, pointing at the wooden ladders on the wall. 'Next one to speak must touch the ceiling twenty times!' He blew the whistle. Senka took a breath and then ran very fast towards the horse, jumped on to the springboard but then, like a racehorse refusing a jump, shied away.

'Do you call yourself a Soviet man?' Shuba yelled. 'AGAIN!' Another blast on the whistle.

'I can't do it, and I won't do it,' Senka shouted, bursting into tears.

'You'll do it if you die here!' Shuba bellowed back, at which Senka suddenly grasped his chest, fought for breath and then fell to the floor.

'He's collapsed!' cried a voice from the class. 'He's ill! He's dying!'

'He's faking,' replied Shuba, marching over. There was total silence in the gym.

'Oh my God,' said Minka, stepping forward.

'Is he OK?' asked George, taking her hand. 'Minka!'

'GET UP, BOY!' ordered Shuba. 'If you're scrimshanking' – he used old military slang – 'you'll pay for this.'

'What if he isn't?' asked one of Senka's classmates.

'All right, at ease,' said Shuba finally. 'Briusov, get me some water.' He leaned over Senka and slapped his cheeks a couple of times with a leathery hand. When the water arrived, he splashed it on Senka's face. Senka appeared to stir.

'Where am I? Am I at school?'

'Don't give me that,' Shuba growled, breathing heavily.

Senka remained lying down. 'Please don't make me do it again.'

'I knew it! You *are* going to do it again,' Shuba said, straightening up. 'And then you're going to touch the ceiling a hundred times!'

'I get dizzy up ladders, and might fall off,' replied Senka. 'I have blocked sinuses.'

'I've seen Russian heroes die in battle! How do you think we won this war? By fainting in the gym? I'm training another generation of warriors to defend our Soviet paradise. The Party demands sacrifice and hardness. Can everyone hear me? NO ONE MOVES UNTIL THIS USELESS BOY GETS OVER THE HORSE!' He blew the whistle, but Senka did not move.

'We need warriors,' Senka agreed, 'but we also need thinkers and I'm one of those. Comrade Stalin also said that "we must value our cadres," and even if I'm not a future warrior, I am a future cadre. I must warn you that if I die of a heart attack, Teacher Shuba, it will be all your fault.' Senka managed to raise his head and look around the class. 'And there are lots of witnesses.'

Shuba stood back, scratched his head and chewed the end of his moustaches. 'You'll pay for this, you little poodle! I'm reporting you and your lies to Director Medvedeva. Class dismissed!' He marched off and Minka ran up to Senka, who, thought Andrei, had made an astonishing recovery.

'Somehow,' Minka said as she rejoined him and George after Senka had gone off to change, 'the Little Professor always gets his way.'

'Little Professor?' asked Andrei.

'That's what we call Senka in my family,' explained Minka. 'My mother says it's because he's precociously precious.'

George put his hand on Andrei's shoulder. 'Minka,' he proposed. 'Let's get Andrei into the Romantics.'

'Teacher Golden will approve,' she said. 'You know he was quite famous once.'

'Golden? Never!' said George.

'Benya Golden . . .' Andrei said, remembering how his mother had reacted when he'd said the name the previous evening. It had taken him back to his childhood. Nine years earlier – another life. They had lived in Moscow, in a spacious apartment, then, and his father had presented his mother with a blue book entitled *Spanish Stories*. 'Inessa, you've got to read this book by Golden, it's spun gold . . .'

Two years later, his father had gone. Andrei remembered finding *Spanish Stories*, looking at its cover, embossed with a Spanish bull and red star, and going to the first page to begin reading. And Inessa taking it away quickly. 'No one reads Golden anymore,' she had said, and Andrei had never seen the book again.

* * *

Benya Golden was lingering in the school common room. He was late for his own Pushkin class but a man like him who had suffered so much and returned from the darkness only by a series of miracles should enjoy life, he thought. He was so lucky to be there, to be teaching Pushkin, to be breathing. No one quite knew what he had been through, but he, more than anyone in the room, knew how flimsy was fortune.

He lay full-length on the leather divan peering over the Leningrad satirical magazine, *Krokadil*, as the young piano teacher, Agrippina Begbulatova, known (to him alone) as Blue-Eyes, brewed the *chai* in a Chinese teapot, laying out cups and saucers for everyone.

Director Medvedeva, owl-shaped horn-rimmed spectacles on the bridge of her nose, groaned loudly as she marked papers at the long table – one of the signs, along with noisy chomping at meals, of a woman who has lived alone for too long. But, Benya thought, she had taken a risk by giving him this job, and he was truly grateful.

Her deputy, Dr Rimm, had been trying to get Benya sacked ever since. He was ostentatiously reading a copy of Comrade Stalin's *History of the Communist Party of the Soviet Union (Bolsheviks): Short Course* – as if anyone, even someone as slavishy drear as Rimm, could actually read that unadulterated gibberish. Rimm kept changing position with little preening sniffs and looks around the room to check that everyone had noticed his virtuous reading. And Apostollon Shuba had just come into the common room, cursing wildly about the laziness, cowardice and softness of the school's spoilt brats. Now he was studying the soccer scores in *Pionerskaya Pravda* while chewing a sprig of his magnificent moustaches.

'Tea's ready,' Agrippina said sweetly. Benya watched her

pour the *chai* for the teachers in order of seniority while reliving the way he had undressed her, opened her long legs and stroked her with his fingers, his tongue, his cock, just twenty minutes earlier, in his one-room apartment round the corner. They had enjoyed forty-nine minutes of dizzy pleasure and she had not even had time to wipe herself before rushing back – a thought that now thrilled him.

No one knew, of course. The secret particularly delighted Benya because his fellow teachers were perfect examples of the new generation of tight-arsed Soviet prigs. Agrippina was as pretty as she was pure, a Soviet virtue she liked to promote by saying 'I don't believe in gossiping about people' and 'I believe a Soviet girl must keep herself for husband and children,' sentiments she seemed to believe absolutely when she said them.

When Benya was not reading (he was a voracious reader) or talking, he was assailed by his epicurean passion for women, poetry, food, the senses. Once he had been a well-known writer who had reported on the Spanish Civil War and known Picasso and Sartre. But he had lost the two jewels of his life. He had lost contact with the daughter of his marriage when she and her mother emigrated to the West. And he had lost the only woman he'd ever truly loved, a woman whose memory caused a jolt of agony, even now. She had been an official's wife, a mother, an Old Bolshevik. In 1939, she had fallen into the abyss of 'Soviet justice' – and he had fallen with her. When, or if, she returned, he would be waiting for her. It was a promise he intended to keep.

Dr Rimm left to teach Communist history. Benya looked at his watch. He was now five minutes late for his favourite class. He finished his tea and hurried out, noticing, as he did so, a badly typed envelope in one of the pigeonholes. As he passed Dr Rimm's classroom, he peeped around the door. 'Comrade Rimm,' he said, 'you have a letter.'

He entered his classroom and was at once enveloped in the affection and respect of the pupils. Their vivacious chatter delighted him: Nikolasha was showing Vlad Titorenko some pages of his obsessional project in his velvet-covered notebook. Both boys sported Byronic hairdos as a tribute to their romanticism. It was surely only a matter of time, Benya decided, before Dr Rimm brought in an army barber. The new boy, Andrei Kurbsky, had turned out to know even more Pushkin than the others. And there was Serafima – listening to him with her head on one side, beautiful without believing it, drawing the eyes of the boys without being aware of it. Even now, Nikolasha was looking back at her; Andrei too. But there was another reason Benya appreciated her: she, more than anyone else, reminded him of his lost love, the woman who'd disappeared before the war.

He could not believe his own luck at landing this job, at teaching literature to children who loved it as much as he did. It was his Second Life and he'd been reborn. He could no longer write. That reed was broken yet he could teach – and how! But he was marked with the black spot: how long could it last? He wanted to share all he knew before it was over.

'Dear friends, beloved romantics, wistful dreamers!' He clapped his hands and opened his *Onegin*. 'It's the night of the fateful ball,' he said, 'that causes the duel. Just imagine the excitement. Everyone is waiting for Lensky the fiancé to arrive. How does Tatiana feel to see Eugene Onegin?'

'And paler than the moon at dawn,
She cannot raise her eyes to face them
And trembles like a hunted fawn.
Inside her, stormy passion's seething;
The wretched girl is scarcely breathing . . .'

Golden paused, and then cried: 'Oh, the agony of her suffering! But who can give us some idea of what she's going through? Andrei?'

'I'm not sure . . . Isn't love just a thing in novels and songs?'

'Who agrees with Andrei? Nikolasha?'

Nikolasha sat up. 'The absence of love means death,' he stated, his deep voice cracking. 'Like Romeo and Juliet. Antony and Cleopatra.'

Golden looked interested. 'So you are saying love reaches its apotheosis in death? Doesn't it perish when life is extinguished?'

'On the contrary,' replied Nikolasha. 'Death makes love immortal. Isn't that the lesson of Pushkin's duel? How to be a Russian, how to be a lover, how to live and die.'

'But love is just amorous obsession, surely?' blurted out George.

'Class is what matters,' said George's brother, Marlen. He had one of those Bolshevik names – a combination of Marx-Lenin – that were fashionable in the 1920s, thought Benya, and now mercifully assigned to the dustbin of history. 'The rest is just bourgeois sentimentalism, a very dangerous thing.'

'Whom do you agree with? Serafima?' said Golden. As he had expected, everyone turned to Serafima.

'I'm not sure I can say . . .' said Serafima.

'Have a go, Serafima Constantinovna,' Golden coaxed her. 'Illuminate our darkness.'

She put her head on one side. 'Well . . .' She spoke very softly, so that Nikolasha and Andrei had to lean over to hear her. 'I would say that in *Onegin*, Tatiana dreams of nothing else. She can't eat or sleep. She protects the secret in her heart. No one else has suffered or celebrated love like her. Love is *all* that matters.' She looked around. 'That's what I think.'

George Satinov and Minka pulled Andrei into the doorway as Dr Rimm waddled past and down the corridor. Both were shaking with laughter. George grabbed Andrei's cuff: 'Come here! Watch the Hummer.' They followed Dr Rimm towards the common room.

'He's looking back. Pretend to read the notices,' whispered Minka.

Dr Rimm had stopped outside the common room, where the teachers' post was placed in pigeonholes.

'Now – look,' said George as Dr Rimm picked up his mail, leafing through papers, until he suddenly held up an envelope. 'He's got it!'

Dr Rimm peered around, up and down the corridor, and then, stuffing all the other papers back into his pigeonhole, he hurried off with the envelope to the teacher's lavatory. When he came out, he was singing so loudly and tunelessly that he was almost dancing. As he passed them, they struggled not to giggle.

'What was that letter?' demanded Andrei.

'You can keep a secret, can't you, Andrei?'

'Of course.'

'He can,' agreed Minka. 'Let's tell him.'

They pulled him down the corridor and outside into the little yard by the science laboratory. No one was there.

'Read this,' said George, handing him a piece of paper. 'This is the next one.' It was typed in capitals:

TUNEFUL SINGER AROUND THE SCHOOL, SWEET 'ONEGIN,' I KNOW YOU LOVE ME, BUT YOU ARE ALSO LOVED FROM AFAR, AS ONLY TWO BOLSHEVIKS CAN LOVE.

KISS ME LIKE A TRUE COMMUNIST.

'TATIANA'

'Oh my God!' said Andrei. 'He thinks . . .'

'That's the fun of it,' replied Minka. 'Don't you love it? "As only two Bolsheviks can love"! That was my idea.'

'Who do you think he thinks wrote it?'

'Director Medvedeva, perhaps?' George was laughing so much that he could barely get the name out.

Andrei was amazed. This could happen only now, after the war. George's father was a leader, his mother was a teacher; and both Minka's parents were important. Andrei knew that only two such privileged children would dare to contemplate a trick like this, and on the First Secretary of the School's Communist Party Committee. That stuff about 'loving like a Bolshevik' was perilously disrespectful. In the thirties, people had received eight grams in the back of the neck for less . . .

'Kurbsky?'

Oh my God! Rimm was calling him. George and Minka vanished as the teacher summoned him from the doorway. As he went back inside to face Rimm, Andrei wished he had known nothing about the spoof love letters.

'Kurbsky,' said Dr Rimm jocosely, 'I hear your Pushkin is more than proficient.'

'Thank you, Comrade Rimm.' The title 'Comrade' meant Rimm was a member of the Communist Party.

'You might have heard of my class on socialist realism?'

'Of course.'

'I teach literature as it should be taught,' Rimm said, and Andrei knew he was referring to Benya Golden's class. Rimm hesitated, and then his eyes rolled as he checked they were alone in the corridor. 'Are you happy in Teacher Golden's . . . group, where Pushkin is taught, I understand, without class consciousness at all, merely as the cravings of bourgeois romanticism? Would you like to switch?'

'Thank you, Dr Rimm. I am content in whatever class the director places me.'

'Your answer is correct,' he said. 'But bear in mind that it is the Party that teaches us the only way to analyze literature. The non-Party path has no future. You're intelligent. I know your tainted file, but remember this is the school that Comrade Stalin chose for his own children. If things go well for you, there's Komsomol, and perhaps the Institute of Foreign Languages. Do you understand me?'

Andrei had dreamed of wearing the Komsomol badge. The cleansing of his tainted past would mean that he could join the Party and follow his heart into academia or the diplomatic corps. His mother had warned him; now Dr Rimm was doing the same thing. The antics of the Fatal Romantics could ruin his rehabilitation. But as Andrei hurried towards his next lesson, he sensed it was already too late.

5

'Kurbsky! Are you Kurbsky?'

A strapping security officer in MVD blue tabs loomed up in front of Andrei outside the school at pick-up a few weeks later. He was someone's bodyguard, no doubt, but Andrei's heart still missed a beat: he remembered the night, long ago, before the war, when the Chekists had come to arrest his father, when men in boots had tramped with ominously officious footsteps through the apartment.

'I . . . I am,' stammered Andrei.

'Are you a sissy like those floppy-haired friends of George? Do you read girlish poetry? Do you pick flowers? Do you fold your britches before you fuck a woman – or do you just rip 'em off, toss 'em aside and go to it like a man?' asked the security officer.

Andrei opened his mouth to answer, but then closed it again.

'Just joking, boy.' He introduced himself: 'Colonel Losha Babanava, chief of security for Comrade Satinov,' and Andrei's hand was crushed in a throbbingly virile handshake. Losha's accent was thickly Georgian, his barrel chest was covered in medals, and his red-striped britches were skin tight. Andrei noticed his ivory-handled Mauser in a kid-leather holster, and how his teeth gleamed under an extravagantly winged set of jet moustaches.

'George is waiting in the car with his brother and sister. You, boy, have been invited to tea with the Satinovs.'

The officer guided Andrei by the shoulders towards a ZiS limousine.

'Hello, Andrei,' said George through the open window. 'Get in.'

Losha opened the door and Andrei saw George, Marlen and little Mariko in the back seat, which was almost as large as his bedroom. George gave him a smile. 'You see the door and windows? Fifteen centimetres thick. Armour-plated! Just in case anyone tries to assassinate Marlen.'

'Why would anyone want to kill me?' asked Marlen, looking around.

'Because you're so important in the school. Our enemies will certainly know you're school Komsorg.'

'Really?' Marlen seemed pleased by this.

Losha slammed the door; then, whistling at the 'tail,' the small Emka car filled with guards behind them, he placed his hairy hands on the car roof and swung himself into the front seat as if leaping into a saddle. 'Foot down!' he barked to the driver. The cars accelerated together, the driver spinning the white leather steering wheel and manipulating the brakes to give unnecessary screeches of burning rubber that made passersby jump out of the way as the little convoy careered past the Kremlin.

'Your papa was up all night and he's been in the office since dawn,' Losha told the Satinov children, nodding at the red crenellated walls of the Kremlin and lighting up a cigarette. 'I'll be picking him up in a moment . . .' Then, with a creaking of leather and a whiff of cologne, Losha swivelled around and pointed at a girl on the pavement. The chauffeur, also in uniform, craned his head to look – and almost crashed the car. 'Hey, Merab, eyes on the road!' Losha turned back to the children. 'You see those Russian guys? No rudeness intended, Andrei, but most of 'em don't know how to handle a woman. Russian girls are always looking sideways. Do you know why?'

Andrei shook his head.

'They're always looking for a Georgian guy, that's why! You understand me, right?' He slapped his palms together. 'Kerboosh!'

The drive from Ostozhenka to Granovsky Street took only a few minutes. Soon they were turning onto a small street, and guards were waving them through the checkpoints into a car park.

'Welcome to the Fifth House of the Soviets,' said George as a guard from the car behind them jumped out and opened the door for them.

'Out you get, youngsters,' said Losha. 'I've got to get to the Little Corner and pick up the big man.' Banging his hands on the dashboard, he gestured to the chauffeur to drive on, leaving Andrei and the Satinovs standing amidst a collection of beautiful cars.

'Whom do these all belong to?' asked Andrei.

'Well,' explained George, 'most of the leaders live here. But these are ours – you've seen the big one, but then there's the Cadillac, the Dodge, and that open-topped Mercedes came from Berlin. It belonged to Goebbels. Or was it Himmler?'

'Do you use them all?'

'Of course not. Papa couldn't care about cars and stuff. But no one turns down a gift from the Central Committee.'

Andrei looked around him at the cars shimmering in the sunlight, then up at the pillared pink building above.

'Recognize that Rolls-Royce?' George asked. 'Serafima lives here too. It's the only privately owned Rolls in Moscow.'

A guard opened the back door of the apartment building, and Andrei and the Satinovs walked up a flight of wide marble steps.

George pushed open the door on the first floor. Inside, a dazzling corridor of parquet and crystal chandeliers beckoned. So this is how the grandees live, thought Andrei as the maid, a swarthy but cheerful girl in a white and black uniform, hugged each of the children, kissing them several times on the face and shepherding them down the corridor.

'Go on,' she called after them. 'I'm cooking up a Georgian feast. Oh, and your big brother's here. Hurry!'

The smell of spicy vegetables, melting cheese and roasted chicken curled through the airy spaces of the apartment. They passed through a reception room with a grand piano, Persian rugs, photographs of the children, a display case of turquoise china, an oil painting of Stalin – larger than life – at the front, holding binoculars (could it be an original by Gerasimov? Andrei wondered). Then they were in a small wood-panelled room filled with books and papers.

'This is Papa's study. We never look over there.' George pointed at the heap of beige files on the desk marked 'Central Committee. Top Secret.' Andrei glanced at them: were they signed by Stalin himself? George opened a wooden case, took out four discs and, placing them carefully on the turntable mounted in a laminated wooden cabinet, turned a knob. The turntable started to whirl, a long arm with a needle jolted into place, and the jazz songs of Utesov started to play.

'It's a gramophone from RCA, America,' said George. 'It can play the discs one by one – and isn't the sound beautiful?'

'It's not bad,' Andrei said, absolutely dazzled by what he was seeing.

'And this has just arrived.' George was pointing at a bizarre glassy tube set in another elegant wooden cabinet.

'What a weird contraption. What is it?'

'That', said George, 'is a machine called an iconoscope – or a television – and it shows a picture . . .'

'Really? But how—'

'Come on.' Andrei could hear the sound of laughter, sizzling food and clinking cutlery as they ran through into a huge kitchen where the Satinov family sat at a mahogany table while Leka, the maid, was juggling at least three steaming pans on the stove.

'Andrei Kurbsky!' His English teacher, Tamara Satinova, George's fine-boned stepmother, was shaking his hand. 'You're the new boy in my English class. Come on in and have some *khachapuri*.'

Andrei's eyes widened at the steaming Georgian dish, somewhere between a pizza and a cheesecake, and the sheer quantity of other food on the table in front of him.

'We eat a lot of Georgian food here. Here's *lobio* – bean soup – and this is chicken *satsivi* . . .' Andrei did not want to admit he had never tried such things, but Tamara seemed to understand this and made him feel so at home that he started to help himself.

A young man in an air force uniform with the gold star of the Order of the Red Banner on his chest sat at the head of the table. 'Aha, George's new friend,' he said, shaking his hand. Andrei knew this was Major David Satinov, newly returned from the war. He almost bowed before this heroic pilot who had been shot down and wounded.

Mariko, the six-year-old, was sitting on her mother's knee, holding a toy dog.

'Leka, would you make Mariko a hot chocolate?' asked Tamara.

Mariko was tiny and dark with her hair in braids woven over the top of her head. 'Meet my dog,' she said to Andrei, holding up the shaggy toy, a black Labrador. 'Stroke her fur. Isn't she silky? I run a school for female dogs called the Moscow School for Bitches. Today they're studying Pushkin, like all of you.'

'Ah, Andrei,' said Tamara. 'You should know that if you enter this home, you have to embrace Mariko's School for Bitches! But now, quiet, darling, I'm listening to your big brother.'

'Well, these new planes turn well,' said David, 'but there's a problem with them . . .'

'Don't say another word about that,' said Tamara with uncharacteristic sharpness.

There was silence. They were all aware that men had been arrested and shot for criticizing Soviet technology.

'But everyone in the air force is talking about it,' David protested.

Tamara glanced at Andrei, the outsider, as Losha Babanava strode into the kitchen. 'The big man's home!' he said.

The gaiety vanished, and the air changed, as it does when snow is imminent. All the boys stood up sharply: the power of the Soviet State had entered the room in tunic and boots, with a spareness of emotion and economy of movement. Taut as a bowstring, his hair razor-cut and greying at the temples, Comrade Hercules Satinov greeted the children as if reviewing a regiment.

Each of the boys kissed their father thrice: 'Hello, Father,' they said formally. Satinov took Mariko into his arms, lifted her high and kissed her forehead.

Andrei was captivated by his presence, and terrified. He imagined the deeds of Satinov's long years with Stalin: the struggle with Trotsky, the war against the peasants, the spy hunt of the Terror, the war. What secrets he must know; what things he must have seen. He personified *tverdost*, hardness: the ultimate Bolshevik virtue. Only when he kissed Tamara and rested his hands on her hips did Andrei glimpse the sort of warmth that he remembered seeing between his own parents.

'How was school, Tamriko?' Satinov asked her.

She sighed. 'As always, too many papers to mark,' she said. 'Do you need anything? Coffee?'

Satinov's grey eyes examined Andrei. 'And who's this?' he asked George, who took Andrei's arm and pushed him forward.

'Father, this is my new friend Andrei Kurbsky from school. He's just arrived.'

'Just arrived?' said Satinov sharply.

'From Stalinabad. For the last term.'

Satinov took Andrei's hand. The grip was tight and dry as a saddle. 'Stalinabad? What's the name again?'

'Kurbsky.' Andrei could almost hear Satinov's bureau of a mind flicking through an index of files marked 'Central Committee. Top Secret.' What if he asked questions about his father?

'You're always welcome here, Andrei,' said Satinov at last.

'Thank you, Comrade Satinov.'

Satinov looked him up and down. 'What do you want to do for your motherland?' he asked.

Everyone went silent.

'He's going to be a professor. He really knows his Pushkin,' George broke in. 'He's going to the top of the class.'

Satinov frowned. 'So he's another of your cloud-dwellers, George? At your age, I had no time for literature. I was a revolutionary. Pushkin's a symbol of our national greatness, of course, but why study him?'

'Because Pushkin teaches us about love,' insisted George. 'We need food and light scientifically – but none of it matters without love.'

'For God's sake, George! What nonsense. We created the first socialistic state. We fought our enemies in a battle of survival – and we've won. But the Motherland is ruined. Starving. We need to rebuild. We don't need poetasters but engineers, pilots, scientists.'

'Yes, of course,' agreed Andrei.

Satinov took out a cigarette – and Losha jumped forward to light it; he then saluted and withdrew. 'David, how's the new plane?'

'Flying well, Father.'

'Good. Well, I'll leave you to your poems, boys.' He nodded at Andrei, then he said curtly to his wife: 'Tamriko?'

She followed him out of the room, and the barometer in the room rose again.

'Father has something to tell her,' explained George as he led Andrei back to his father's little study with the gramophone. He closed the doors, restarted the jazz records and lay down on the sofa with his legs crossed. 'They whisper in the bathroom. He never tells us, of course. The less we know, the better. Now he'll have a nap for a few hours, and then probably he'll be summoned very late for dinner.'

'You mean—'

'Don't say the name, you fool,' said George, pointing heavenwards. Then he whispered, 'If you work for Stalin, you call him the Master but never to his face. In documents, he's Gensec, for General Secretary. The generals call him Supremo; in the Organs, it's the Instantsiya. And when anyone says "the Central Committee," they mean *him*.'

'So he'll be having dinner in the Kremlin?'

George sat up. 'Don't you know anything? *He* works at the Little Corner in the Kremlin but he really lives in the Nearby Dacha outside Moscow where my father and the Politburo meet late into the night over dinner. Then my father has to change and shave and be back in his office first thing in the morning. We hardly see him.'

'He was at the fall of Berlin, wasn't he?'

'Oh yes, and at Stalingrad,' said George proudly. 'Now the war's over, Father says he wants to see more of us – which means taking us to school, with all the bowing and genuflecting that entails. Pure hell! But no one tells my father what to do. No one except . . .' And he pointed towards heaven again: Stalin.

'I'd better be getting home,' said Andrei. 'My mother worries.'

George put his hand on Andrei's arm with all the warmth that was lacking in his father. 'Listen, Andrei, I know you want to get into the Komsomols and I've been singing your praises to Marlen. But it would be fun to have you join us in the Fatal Romantics' Club. We're planning to play the Game.'

Andrei felt a stab of excitement. This was what he really wanted – wasn't it?

'But there's a problem,' George continued. 'It's Nikolasha's club and he wants to make it harder to join than the College of Cardinals or the Politburo. And Nikolasha says he's not sure about you.'

Andrei swallowed. 'What do you mean?'

'He doesn't know you as well as I do,' George said. 'Anyway, he says Serafima has the casting vote.'

'Serafima? But Serafima doesn't know me either. And I'm not sure sure she cares about anything, especially not the Fatal Romantics' Club.'

'But Nikolasha cares about her, and that's the important thing.'

'But isn't he with Rosa? She adores him.'

George nodded. 'She does, but Nikolasha lives for Serafima. In fact, sometimes I think the entire Fatal Romantics' Club is really for her.'

Andrei stood up. He cared about this more than he meant to – and he had shown it all too clearly.

'You helped me out,' George said, standing too, 'and I know you're one of us. They're planning to play the Game right after the Victory Parade so you have to join before then. It's a special ritual.'

George led Andrei out of the study, across the corridor to his bedroom, where he pulled from under his bed an olive-green leather case, which he flicked open. There, lying in red velvet, were two nineteenth-century duelling pistols.

'Beautiful,' said Andrei. He closed his eyes, remembering his *Onegin*.

Now nothing else mattered –
A brace of pistols and a shot
Shall instantly decide his lot.

Andrei admired the pistols: the bevelled barrels, polished wood, burnished steel. 'Are they real?' he asked.

'I doubt it. We borrow them from the Little Theatre. They

use them in plays,' George said, laughing. 'And we're going to use them in the Game – you'll see.'

A few streets away, School 801 was not quite empty. The janitor mopped the floors of the empty corridors with the disinfectant that gives schools their characteristic pungency, and the director, Kapitolina Medvedeva, was alone in her office planning how the school would celebrate the Victory Parade on 24 June. It was getting closer. A few Komsomols and Pioneers would be chosen to serve in honour guards. And when she thought about this, she wished she could include Andrei Kurbsky, because she knew how much it would mean to a boy of tainted biography.

The report on her desk showed that Andrei was thriving in the school, and she was proud that she had overruled Rimm to let him in.

'I wish to register my disapproval of the acceptance of a child of an Enemy of the People,' Rimm had said. He believed Medvedeva was not Party-minded enough, and he wanted her job. She knew that every school, every institution, had a Rimm. They were usually cowards, so she'd stood her ground.

'Fine,' Rimm had surrendered. 'Let him in if you must, but a family like his won't be able to pay the fees.'

'Actually, comrade, they *can* afford the fees,' she'd responded, and smiled as she thought about the opportunity she was giving Andrei. He was her special project and she approved of his neat, reserved appearance, his parted brown hair and dark-framed spectacles. And he was already friends with George Satinov, Minka Dorova and Rosa Shako.

Kapitolina Medvedeva was a devout Communist who believed that loving children too much made them egotistical. She was proud to be the director of a school with pupils from such eminent Party families. She was not impressed by the clammy and rather menacing pallor of Comrade Dorov, but his wife, Dashka, managed to be both chic *and* a doctor. Marshal Shako, the commander-in-chief of the air force, was the very model of a Soviet commander. And as for Comrade Satinov, he was so impressive that, when she spoke to him, she stammered and over-egged her compliments. There was something about Comrade Satinov. Perhaps it was because he was the real thing: he had done time in the Tsar's jails, helped storm the Winter Palace in 1917, known Lenin, spent the winter of '42 in Stalingrad. And no one was closer to Stalin himself.

Kapitolina Medvedeva had taught Stalin's own children just before the war. Svetlana loved history – and came almost top of her class. But Kapitolina had failed to teach anything to his son, Vasily. The boy had been a delinquent scoundrel. Still, it must be hard to have the greatest titan in world history as your father.

She looked down at her desk to read Benya Golden's report on Andrei. The hiring of Golden was another decision she had made over Rimm's head, and he had turned out to be the best teacher she had ever known. Besides, how could any headmistress pass up the chance to employ the author of *Spanish Stories*?

She took off her glasses and rubbed her eyes. When she put them on again, she noticed that she could see herself in the reflection on her polished inkwell. Was it the distortion of the reflection or did she really look that frayed? What a sight she was! She had grey streaks in her hair, and her nose was more like a beak! There's not much one can do with a face like mine, she thought.

She was a spinster, living alone in one room in a *kommunalka* on the outskirts, her only luxury being a little set of antique Tolstoys in brown leather bindings. A woman had more important tasks in life than lipstick and dresses, she told herself. The school was her mission in life, and she had to be as hard and modest as a Bolshevik should be.

She had taken two risks in her professional life, but both were consistent with her mission: to educate and enlighten – even in an age of ice.

She looked at her watch. It was after seven, and she had nowhere else to be. She sighed, admitting to herself that she now groaned aloud when she got out of bed or the bath – or when she sipped at a particularly delicious soup. She was fifty-two. Getting older.

She closed her eyes, thinking about Benya Golden. She enjoyed having him around the school, and when he fixed her with his playful blue eyes, she actually blushed. Sometimes she dreamed of him at night. She knew he would be wonderful to kiss, and she felt that the touch of his hands would transform her. Her hair would grow thicker; her skin would become as rich and tanned as that of Minka's mother, Dashka Dorova. With him, she could become the woman she had always wanted to be.

She shook her head. Golden was a real gamble, not just because Dr Rimm had denounced his teaching style as 'a bourgeois circus act of philistine anti-Party hucksterism.' She didn't know the details of his case, of course; only the Organs, the secret police, knew that, but she knew that no one had expected Golden to return from prison or exile or wherever he'd been. The Organs hadn't stopped her from hiring him, so they must have checked him out and cleared him, but however charming and exuberant Golden was, he still had the power to destroy her.

'Don't you know what Golden is? He bears the mark of Cain on his forehead. He's like a leper!' Rimm had whispered to her. 'He's a "lucky stiff." He's come back from the dead.'

'He's alive now,' she'd replied. 'And that's what matters.'

She perused the report again, but thoughts of Golden and Andrei still filled her mind. Andrei was a safer bet than Golden, but he too was a liability who could harm her. Because what no one else knew – least of all Andrei himself – was that she had accepted him into the school not in spite of his tainted background but because of it. And she was paying his fees out of her own salary.

Yes, she thought now, I may be on my own and getting older, but I believe that everyone's capable of redemption, no matter who they are.

6

Andrei emerged from the Granovsky building into the blinding sunlight. On Gorky Street, Moscow's main thoroughfare, he passed soldiers, not much older than he, in uniforms, laughing with their sweethearts. Their careless happiness was infectious. He was convinced that his life had changed, and couldn't wait to tell his mother about how the Satinovs lived, about the glacial grandeur of Comrade Satinov, about George's hints concerning the Fatal Romantics' Club and their esoteric rituals. Then he saw her. A tall girl with blond hair crossing Gorky Street without looking in either direction so that cars braked around her. She wore her school blouse buttoned right up to the neck and long sleeves, even though it was a glorious summer evening. She turned purposefully in to the House of the Book, Moscow's best bookshop.

Andrei had no money to spend and he was already late for supper but he followed her inside. The books of Marx, Lenin, Stalin were displayed at the front alongside the romantic war poems of Simonov, the novels of Gorky and Fadayev, the screenplays of Constantin Romashkin (yes, Serafima's father). Where was she?

Immediately, Andrei was soothed and inspired by the smell of new books – by the acrid glue and the fresh leather as well as the mustiness of old ones that were almost rotting on the shelves. He scanned students and pensioners, spotted a titian-haired lady in a fuchsia trouser suit, a government *apparatchik* in a blue suit and peaked cap, but no sight of Serafima.

Andrei had no plan, no particular idea, just the optimism of a summer's day, and the boost of tea at the Satinovs', as he climbed the stairs to the second floor. Perhaps he had imagined her, he thought, as he surveyed the gorgeously bound special leather volumes on the shelves around him. He went deeper into the metal forest of the bookstacks. Then, as a hunter senses the quick breath of a deer in the woods, he knew she was there. He pulled out a book by Ernest Hemingway in English, and peering through the gap, he saw her. She was leafing through a book, intently, as if searching for a line. And her head was on one side, that winning mannerism that he had noticed in class.

'Serafima?'

She started. Green eyes speckled with gold looked at him questioningly. 'Teacher Satinova recommended Hemingway and I just found *For Whom the Bell Tolls* and you were just looking at . . . oh, Galsworthy. *The Forsyte Saga*. Isn't that about a bourgeois-capitalist dynasty in London?'

'What if it is?' Serafima asked.

Andrei saw the other book she was holding. '*The Age of Innocence*? Edith Wharton on the corrupt haut-bourgeois customs of robber-capitalism in old New York?'

She looked at the book, as though surprised she was holding it, and then up at him again. Her intense gaze made him feel he was being very tedious.

'If I was reading Fadayev, would it tell you something different about my character than if I was reading Wharton or Akhmatova? Are you analysing me by what I read?'

'No, of course not.' Feeling embarrassed, Andrei tried a different tack. 'What's Edith Wharton like?'

'Just like our own barons and princelings here. Our secret world is just like hers but with one crucial difference – it's Edith Wharton with the death penalty.' She smiled at him, and he felt the rays of the evening sun were shining right on him. He noticed she had one very pointed tooth to the right of her front teeth.

Then he glanced around, concerned; no one had overheard her. Things were different for people like Serafima, he told himself. She could say what she liked.

'I've got to go.' She replaced the books and headed for the stairs. 'By the way, why are you following me?'

'I wasn't . . . I happened to be looking for the same books.' Andrei knew that he needed to be a better liar to survive in this milieu. 'I'd heard about the House of the Book but I hadn't had time to pop in until today . . .'

Serafima looked back at him. They were now on the street outside, and he was about to be dismissed.

'I'm on my way to the Bolshoi to see Prokofiev's new ballet . . .' she began, but her words were lost in the skid of tyres.

An open-topped Packard had performed a U-turn on Gorky Street and swung towards them so recklessly that its wheels ground against the pavement.

Andrei pulled Serafima out of peril's way, conscious of the perfume on her neck.

'God, he almost hit us. What an idiot!' he exclaimed.

'Hey, Serafima!' called the driver. He had a cigarette between his teeth, and was wearing an air force colonel's shoulderboards. 'I've been meaning to come round ever since I saw you outside school. I was going to surprise you and pick you up at the gates. Wouldn't that be good for your standing? My sister and I were at School 801, you know. How's that lesbic witch of a director and that preening motherfucker Rimm?'

'Still haunting us,' Serafima said coldly.

Andrei sensed her distrust, her unease.

'I was just going to grab a drink at the Cocktail Hall. Hop in, darling.'

'Thank you, but I can't right now. I've got homework.'

'Your mother won't mind, I can tell you. She thinks I am a good thing. I love her movies. Come on!'

A diminutive man got out of the car, wearing skin-tight britches, shiny boots, an array of medals. His dark brown hair was brushed back in a wave. He kissed her hand, old-style. 'Are you going to make me – me of all people – beg?'

Serafima glanced at Andrei. 'I'm with my best friend, Andrei. He comes too.'

'Sure,' said the man. 'I get it. Best friend comes too! Get in, Andrei.'

He held open the back door and Serafima stepped inside. As Andrei got in beside her, the man ground the car into gear, backed it into the middle of Gorky, and accelerated into the path of a Studebaker truck that swerved to avoid them. A couple of militiamen watched, but did nothing to stop him.

'Do you know who he is?' whispered Serafima. 'He's Stalin's son, Vasily. Be careful, OK?'

After a couple of minutes, Vasily swung the car to the right, stopped, and ran round to help Serafima out. They were in a cul-de-sac. In front of them was a plain wooden door guarded by a muscle-bound Uzbek in a crimson blouse.

'You're not going in, you hayseed,' he was telling a cavalry lieutenant with his girl. The queue of people snaked around the corner. When he saw Vasily, he changed his tune: 'Good afternoon, Colonel!' he said, shoving the others out of the way and opening the door with a bow. 'Welcome to the Cocktail Hall. Go right in!'

Vasily and Serafima swept in, but Andrei hesitated.

'Not you, schoolboy. Scat!'

'But I'm with them! Serafima!' Andrei called out, hating the whine of his own desperation. Vasily Stalin raised a hand without even turning.

'Your lucky day!' The Uzbek opened the door, and Andrei caught up with Serafima in a crowded rabbit warren of booths and alcoves, all richly upholstered with scarlet silk and pine panelling.

Vasily knew everyone. He kissed the raddled hag at the cloakroom, and the moment he entered the little bar, he began holding court like a chieftain. He was embraced by a drunk pilot, a fat general and two girls in tight cocktail dresses with décolletages. But he seemed happiest to meet a bald toad with a squint who wore three watches on his wrist.

'Hail the King of Sturgeon!' he shouted. 'Send some steaks over to the dacha!'

Another man, dressed in a zoot suit like an American jazzman, with two-tone shoes, approached him.

'Fancy a Schiaparelli ballgown that once belonged to a Viennese princess?' the man asked in a Hungarian accent. 'For your lady? How about this ring? You can find anything in Europe these days if you know where to look.'

Vasily turned away and ordered cocktails from an Armenian waiter in a brocade waistcoat.

'Who are these people?' Andrei asked Serafima.

'These characters,' whispered Serafima, 'are the *styliagi*. Muscovites *with style*!' (She did a good American accent.)

The cocktails arrived. Andrei sipped his and it made his eyes water.

'Who's the schoolgirl, Vaska?' the man with the squint asked.

'Sophia Zeitlin's daughter. I'm on my knees begging her for a date, but she won't even look at me. Hey, Serafima, how do you like your cocktail?'

'It's vile,' said Serafima, looking haughtier than ever. 'I want to go home.'

'Good idea,' said Vasily. 'My home.'

Andrei could scarely remember the journey to Vasily Stalin's house. His head was spinning from the orange cocktail he had consumed too quickly at the Cocktail Hall. Leaving the city, they sped through pine woods dyed red by a sinking summer sun. Somewhere along the way, Vasily drew his Mauser pistol and fired it as he overtook a truck. 'That'll teach the fucker!' he shouted.

Now they were pulling in to a driveway. They were waved through a heavily guarded checkpoint, the barrier rising as Vasily put his foot down, throwing up clouds of dust. At last they stopped outside a white-pillared mansion in colonial southern style, and went inside.

'Bring drinks! Where's the food! Fetch the gramophone!' cried Vasily, his voice high, his eyes wild. 'Welcome to Zubalovo. My parents used to live here. Now it's mine.'

Minutes later, Andrei was next to Serafima at a table covered in Georgian snacks and bottles of exotic liqueurs Andrei had never even heard of. Vasily was at the gramophone playing records as guests arrived and started to dance. 'Listen – this is

American jazz, the music of the oppressed Negroes!' He cackled with laughter.

'Hey kiddo,' he said, his eyes in his pinched, sallow face narrowing at Andrei. 'You're not drinking. That's an insult! Don't forget my father's a Georgian. Or rather he used to be a Georgian. Now he's a Russian.'

'I'm not a great drinker,' confessed Andrei.

Vasily handed Andrei and Serafima shots of something disgusting called Fernet Branca. 'No heeltaps!' he said.

Andrei looked at his drink, feeling sick.

'Best to drink, dear,' said Serafima.

Vasily pointed at him. 'I'm watching you!'

Andrei downed his Fernet Branca shot. Around him, the party, the dancers and the sitting room seemed to twist and wave like a mirage in the desert. Two girls from the Cocktail Hall were dancing closely together, each holding a cigarette but somehow not burning each other. Rivulets of mascaraed sweat streamed down their faces so they looked like half-naked coalminers in the rain. A captain was doing the *lezginka* in just his boots and britches. And, at the centre, Vasily stood clapping his hands, checking the gramophone while drinking vodka, Armenian cognac, Crimean *champagnski*, Georgian wine and brightly-coloured liqueurs from a fleet of glasses and bottles.

Andrei looked at Serafima, who looked as alone and vulnerable as he was. How were they going to get away? He felt very far from Moscow; they had no car, no means of escape. His mother would be worried about him. And what would Serafima's parents think?

A dapper air force officer sat down at their table. 'What the hell are you two doing here?' he asked. It was David Satinov, George's older brother. 'Who brought you?'

Serafima pointed at Vasily Stalin. 'We didn't have much choice in the matter, actually.'

David Satinov shook his head. 'I might have guessed. This is no place for schoolgirls.'

Vasily had rejoined them. 'David, a toast to my father. To Stalin! To our brave pilots!' Everyone drank to this amidst a chorus of cheers.

'Tell me this, David, why do our planes keep crashing?' Vasily asked suddenly, leaning across the table.

'Soviet planes are the best in the world,' said David.

'If there are faults in our planes, I'll tell my father. We've got to find the criminals who send our boys up in coffins! Their heads will roll, David.'

'Yes, Vaska,' said David.

'You know why I'm celebrating?'

David shook his head.

'I've just been promoted to general. My father trusts me again. He's forgiven me.' Tears pooled in his fallow, wounded eyes.

'Congratulations.' And David embraced Vasily.

'Serafima! I'll take you flying in my plane,' cried Vasily. 'We'll dive so low, the peasants will hide in their haystacks. Let's celebrate. Come on, dance!'

'Hey, Vaska, go easy on her, she's young,' said David.

But Vasily Stalin pulled Serafima into the crowd. 'Let's foxtrot.' He took her in his arms, his hands cruising her hips, running through her hair . . . She stiffened as he squeezed her, and Andrei could see her discomfort. Several other girls started to gyrate around Vasily; while trying to dance with all of them, he loosened his grip on Serafima, who, somehow, a moment later, managed to slip out of the crowd.

David was waiting for her.

'Come on, you two.' He gestured towards Andrei. They trailed him through the party, out of the front door, down the steps towards the cars, where chauffeurs and guards stood smoking and chatting.

'Is it the poetry sissy from school?' boomed Colonel Losha Babanava. 'Not enjoying the party?' Then he saw Serafima. 'What's she doing? She's too young to be here!'

'We need to go home,' said Andrei. David Satinov stood behind them.

'Take the kids home, Losha. I'll square it with General Stalin.'

Losha Babanava sang a Georgian song as he drove Andrei and Serafima home through the warm darkness.

In the back of the car, Serafima rested her head on Andrei's shoulder. 'You're so dependable, Andrei,' she said sleepily. 'Thank you for not abandoning me. I don't think I'd have managed if you hadn't been there.'

Andrei dreamed that she was his girl. He would invite her to stroll around the Patriarchy Ponds and the Alexandrovsky Gardens. He'd hold her hands and recite a verse by Blok, Akhmatova, or even Pushkin. Dizzy with drink and the smell of her skin, he stroked her hair as he stared at the straight, empty road back to Moscow, guarded by an army of silvery birches, lit by the face of a full Russian moon.

7

'Andryusha,' George called to him the next morning as they rushed along the parquet corridor towards Mrs Satinova's English lesson. 'A word!'

Andrei turned and George pulled him into the changing room. He checked that there was no one in the lavatory by kicking open the doors of the two cubicles, and then turned on the tap. 'I heard from my brother David about last night. Don't speak about it to anyone, will you?'

'Of course not,' Andrei said, knowing that only a fool would ever gossip about anything that concerned the Leader.

'People could lose their heads over those faulty planes,' George said urgently. 'It never happened. Oh, and David said you acquitted yourself well. And Serafima . . . Well, Serafima says you were heroic.'

After school, Andrei walked to the Patriarchy Ponds. His head ached, and he felt sick. His mother had been distraught when he arrived home in the early hours of the morning; she'd taken him in her arms, mewing plaintively. It had irritated him enormously but there was nothing he could do to stop her. Now he should be feeling pleased with himself, he thought. He had met and survived the attentions of Vasily Stalin; he had shaken hands with Comrade Satinov; yet he was still alone, observing the tankmen and pilots buying their girls ice creams or iced lemonades. Old ladies sat watching the ducks. Mothers let their toddlers play on the grass. Nothing had really changed.

'Shall I buy you an ice cream?' The voice was soft as a kitten's but it still made him jump. It was Rosa Shako, daughter of the air force commander.

'Isn't it a beautiful day?' she said. 'Do you want to go for a walk in the Sparrow Hills, escape the traffic and everything else . . . ?'

'I don't feel very well today, Rosa. I think I should get home.'

'But I have Papa's car,' said Rosa, waving towards a limousine parked nearby.

'Can't we do it tomorrow?'

Her hand gripped his arm with a force that surprised him. 'You don't understand. Nikolasha's waiting at the cemetery for us. *He's* inviting you. It's his place. And he's never invited you before. You need to come.'

'But, Rosa—'

Rosa let go of his arm and placed her slender hands together almost as if she was praying. 'Andryusha' – she lisped like a child – 'please. If you don't come, it'll be my fault. Nikolasha's so unforgiving. I can't disappoint him.'

'In what way?' he asked, a little intrigued.

'Nikolasha says it's impossible to compromise in the way we live. If we compromise, it's not worth living at all.'

'And you believe that?'

Rosa appeared amazed that anyone could question anything that Nikolasha said. 'He's a true original, the ultimate romantic. He guides me. He's not like anyone else I've ever met – surely you can see that? I think one day he'll be famous, don't you, Andrei? So are you coming? They're all going to be there.'

'All?' Andrei asked. And when Rosa nodded, he knew he had to be there too.

It was already getting dark, and jagged splinters of scarlet zigzagged across the sky as Andrei opened the gate of the cemetery and then stepped aside to allow Rosa to lead the way.

Inside the cemetery, buzzing with mosquitoes, the gravestones were overgrown with green ivy; Andrei could see that rich families from the nineteenth century had built their tombs here: some were like little marble houses with pilasters and capitals and arches. It took him a moment to find his friends in the rosy graininess of a summer dusk, but then he saw the candles, their flames dancing in the still, sultry air.

Vlad Titorenko greeted him in a green frock coat and britches. 'Nikolasha's expecting you,' he said to Andrei. 'The Romantics are gathered.'

'Come here!' It was Nikolasha. He was standing beside an ornate tomb covered with candles and decorated with crosses, carved names, and embellished with moss and old beer bottles.

'Quiet, please. Everyone ready?' said Vlad. 'Let us begin. First everyone take one shot glass of vodka. Andrei, you stand there – and you may take a glass.'

Andrei, holding the thimble of vodka, was on his own on one side of the tomb, and on the other stood the Fatal Romantics. He could see Minka and George and Rosa, all of whom were dressed in nineteenth-century costumes; surely Serafima was also here somewhere?

The Velvet Book, an illuminated candelabrum and a dark green leather case lay on the tomb itself, and all around them, the dark cemetery flickered with scores of candles. Corny, certainly, but melodramatic, undoubtedly.

'Fatal Romantics,' said Nikolasha solemnly, his freckles buried deep in his white skin. 'This is the temple of the Fatal Romantics' Club. Let us welcome a neophyte: Andrei Kurbsky.'

'Do I . . . do I need a costume?' stammered Andrei, feeling self-conscious in his grey trousers and white shirt.

'Wait please!' mouthed Nikolasha testily. He cleared his throat. 'Fatal Romantics, I hereby declare that we are in session. I open the Velvet Book. Its words are secret; few names are inscribed in its sacred pages.'

Andrei glanced at George, who gave him a wink. Andrei looked away and Nikolasha continued, his unnaturally deep voice wavering a little as he chanted like a pagan priest.

'First, let us together declare our essential beliefs. Vlad, you may lead us.'

'Fatal Romantics,' started Vlad and then, all together, they chanted, 'WE BELIEVE IN A WORLD OF LOVE.'

'How will we live in this steely age?'

'LOVE IS OUR LODESTAR.'

'What is our choice?'

'LOVE OR DEATH.'

'Do we fear death?'

'WE FEAR NOT DEATH. IF WE LIVE WITHOUT LOVE, LET US DIE YOUNG!'

'And if we die?'

'OUR LOVE WILL BE IMMORTAL.'

'Let us drink to love,' Nikolasha declared.

The Romantics downed their vodka, but, troubled by the anti-Party talk of death and love, Andrei hesitated.

'You may drink, Andrei,' Nikolasha commanded. Feeling a

little as he had the previous evening, Andrei swallowed. The vodka was like a red-hot bullet in his belly.

There was a loud sigh and then a burp, and George started to giggle; Minka too fought back a laugh that travelled up her nose and emerged as a strangled sneeze that made George shake with laughter.

'George!' snapped Vlad.

'Don't spoil it,' added Rosa.

'Sorry,' said George.

'While we're here at a sitting of the Romantic Politburo, we can quite easily vote out a member,' explained Nikolasha with the weariness of a severely tried teacher. 'Now. Let us begin our meeting. Membership of our sacred brotherhood is select and secret. Andrei Kurbsky, what is your choice?'

'Umm . . . love or death?'

'Yes. Andrei, you have been called here to enter our Club of Fatal Romantics. Do you wish to be considered for inscription in the Velvet Book of Love?'

Andrei nodded.

'Andrei, I should explain that in our membership, there are two grades. The first is candidate membership, and candidates are welcomed to our meetings. But to play the Game, to wear the costume and bear the pistol, one must be a full member of our Politburo.'

Andrei understood this system perfectly because that was how the Communist Party worked: you first became a candidate member and then a full member – and the whole country was run by the Politburo.

'One day in the distant future you may be honoured by being considered for full membership but tonight you have been chosen as a candidate member of the Fatal Romantics' Club.

Step forward and place your hand on the leather case on the tomb. Now recite with all of us: LOVE OR DEATH!'

'LOVE OR DEATH!'

'Andrei, welcome to our society. I hereby write your name in the Velvet Book of Love.' Nikolasha scribbled portentously in the book. 'Toast our new candidate.'

Rosa refilled the glasses.

George swigged back two shots. 'Can we talk now?'

'Now for item two on the agenda,' Nikolasha said, ignoring him. 'We propose to play the Game in full costume after the Victory Parade on the twenty-fourth of June. On the far end of the Great Stone Bridge where the road will be closed.'

'Is that wise?' asked Minka. 'On such an important day?'

'Why not?' answered Vlad. 'We've played it in the street before. People love Pushkin.'

'So shall we vote?' asked Nikolasha.

They all raised their hands just like Politburo members at a Party Congress. Nikolasha counted them with his pen. 'Passed.'

'So what do you think of my costume, Andrei?' asked Minka, coming around the tomb. She struck a pose.

'You look lovely,' said Andrei, smiling at her.

'You may watch us play the Game although, as a candidate, Andrei, you may not participate,' continued Nikolasha, 'but you realize that the duel in *Eugene Onegin*, echoed later in Pushkin's own fatal duel, is the essential expression of our belief in romanticism.' He raised the leather case on the tomb and the members bowed their heads, all except Andrei, who looked at it – and George, who was pouring out another vodka shot. It was the case that George, had showed him at his apartment. Within lay the two antique duelling pistols borrowed, presumably with the costumes, from the Little Theatre.

Rosa said, 'Who dies tonight? Let's play . . .' Then she recited:

'The gleaming pistols wake from drowsing.
Against the ramrods mallets pound.
The balls go in each bevelled housing.'

She offered the case to Nikolasha, who chose one pistol, and then she handed it to Vlad, who took the other.

'Are you happy with your weapon, Mr Lensky?' Rosa asked Vlad. He nodded. She turned to Nikolasha. 'And you, Mr Onegin?'

'Are the pistols charged and ready to shoot?' he asked.

She nodded formally.

Vlad and Nikolasha held their pistols upright like crucifixes in church and proceeded ritualistically out into the graveyard, where a twenty-yard path was marked out by candles.

'*The duellists shed their cloaks and wait*,' said Nikolasha. He and Vlad shed their frock coats, George marked out thirty paces, and the boys stood facing each other. Their ruffled white blouses glowed in the moon-flooded twilight, and the oiled steel of the pistols glimmered.

Rosa's voice rang out: '*Approach at will*.' The boys walked towards each other.

'*Four fateful steps . . . Five paces more*.'

Nikolasha lowered his pistol slowly and, closing one eye, aimed the barrel at Vlad's chest, saying as he did so:

'Onegin then, while still not ceasing
His slow advance, was first to raise
His pistol with a level gaze.'

Vlad raised his pistol too and took aim. But Nikolasha, playing Onegin, was ahead of him: he started to squeeze the trigger.

Andrei found it hard to breathe. It was all very silly, this ritual of amateur dramatics, yet there was something enthralling about it. The black thuja trees, the candles casting long shadows over the graves, the swirling teenage emotions and the macabre drama of fatal duels touched him. They were play-acting, but every Russian had lived Pushkin's duels, the passion plays of the Russian soul.

The trigger clicked, and there was a deafening crack and an orange flash. Vlad held his chest, tottering. Red blood soaked his white shirt. He fell.

Nikolasha, narrating every movement with the correct words from Pushkin, ran to Vlad, knelt beside him, called his name and then, standing over his 'body,' the Fatal Romantics recited together:

'The storm has blown, the lovely flower
Has withered with the rising sun.
The altar fire is out and done!'

The Game was over, and Andrei could breathe once more. Half an hour later, as Rosa was collecting the glasses, she tripped and knocked one off the tomb.

'I'm so sorry,' she whispered, picking up the shattered glass from the ground.

'You're so clumsy, you spoil everything,' Nikolasha snapped in a spasm of cruelty that made Andrei wince for her. 'You just don't have the sensory talents for passion. But Serafima has it in spades. Serafima understands poetry. Without her, the Fatal Romantics wouldn't exist. Don't you agree, Rosa?'

Rosa's pale face flushed. 'At least I'm here this evening,' she said. 'Serafima's not. Where is she, Nikolasha?'

'She said she might come later,' he said.

'Well, I hate to tell you, but I don't think she's coming.' Rosa turned to Andrei. 'But that makes no difference. Even when she doesn't deign to join us, she's *always* here.'

And that was when Andrei realized why Nikolasha was so peevish. Serafima hadn't come and Rosa's devoted presence reminded him of her absence. Andrei understood how he felt. Ever since he'd arrived at the school, he had wanted to join the Fatal Romantics' Club. Now he was in – but without Serafima, he didn't give a kopeck whether his name appeared in the Velvet Book of Love or not.

8

A column of mechanical khaki dinosaurs, T-34 and heavy KV tanks, rumbled down Gorky Street the next morning as Andrei walked to school. One lurched to a halt, shook and broke down, spluttering black diesel smoke. Phalanxes of soldiers drilled on Red Square, horses clattered on the cobbles, and the roar of the machinery and bark of drill sergeants sounded louder, more urgent: a symphony of rising excitement. It was five days until the Victory Parade, and Moscow had become a stage with a vast cast of foreigners arriving each day: Chinese, Americans, even Fijians and Africans, filled the hotels. Women were on the streets too – peasants offering fruit and flowers and sometimes a knee-trembler in an alleyway. The roads were crammed with trucks and self-propelled guns; and one could not move at the Belorussian Station for soldiers in army green and navy blue, all arriving to march past Stalin.

At assembly in School 801, Director Medvedeva announced the Pioneers who would go on a special camping trip.

'I hate camping,' whispered Senka Dorov, who was sitting next to Andrei. 'It's cold and uncomfortable and the food's horrid. Why's everyone in the Soviet Union so obsessed with camping?'

But Andrei was looking for his fellow Fatal Romantics. There they were – all together a few benches away: Minka and George,

Vlad more cadaverously pale than ever, Nikolasha with Rosa Shako, her eyes as always seemingly half closed, at his side. But where was Serafima? Try as he might, Andrei couldn't find her.

At lunch break, Andrei bumped into George and Minka, who were running down the central corridor towards the lavatories. Dr Rimm was following them.

'Chin up, girl!' he cried at Minka. 'Discipline. The world's eyes are settled on Moscow. Five days until the parade. Long live Stalin. No smirking, Andrei Kurbsky – tuck your shirt in!'

As soon as he'd passed, George pulled Andrei into the cloakroom. 'Have you noticed anything special about Dr Rimm?' he whispered.

'He's excited about the parade,' said Andrei.

'No, silly, he's quivering with love,' added Minka.

'You haven't sent him another letter, have you? The more you send, the more dangerous it'll be if he ever finds out.'

'How can he?' George was laughing. 'We've been sending him special ones for the Victory Parade. We're going to post this to him right now.' He showed it to Andrei.

DEAREST PEDAGOGUE,

I DREAM OF YOU SINGING A PATRIOTIC SONG TO CELEBRATE THE VICTORY PARADE. IF YOU LOVE ME, OH BOLSHEVIK NIGHTINGALE, SING, SING LOUDLY!

YOUR 'TATIANA'

He didn't see Serafima until that afternoon at pick-up.

'I hear they let you in to the Fatal Romantics' Club.' She'd come up behind him. Andrei jumped a little and remembered the drive back from Vasily's.

'I'm sure you told them to.'

'Why would anyone listen to me?' She smiled as they walked through the Golden Gates.

'Will you be playing the Game?' he said, desperate to detain her. 'You'd suit the costumes.'

She stopped, her head on one side in that way of hers that made him feel he had her full attention – just for a moment. 'You mean I'm old-fashioned?'

'I like the way you dress.'

'You admire my Bolshevik modesty?'

'It just makes you even more—'

'A compliment from Andrei?' She cut him off. 'Don't we have enough romantics here already?'

'But you'll be at the Victory Parade?'

'I suppose so.'

'You don't sound very excited.'

'My parents are excited. I'm not very interested in howitzers and tanks.' She leaned towards him. 'But I'm looking forward to the Game afterwards.'

'Why's it all so secret?'

'Don't you see? In our age of conspiracy, *everything* is conspiratorial. Even having a picnic or reading poetry.'

They'd reached the street, and with a wave, she was gone.

Andrei hesitates for a moment or two – and then he follows her. She doesn't notice, so entirely is she in her own world. She pushes her hair back from her face, and when her head turns a little, showing the perfect curve of her forehead, he sees that her lips are moving: she's talking to herself, to someone, all the time. Up Ostozhenka she goes, past the Kremlin, Gorky Street, and into the House of the Book. Up the stairs to the Foreign Literature section. She looks at the same books. Then she's off again.

Often she looks up the sky, at trees, at ornaments on buildings. Three soldiers point and whistle at her. She walks down another street, and men look after her. She notices none of them. Several times, he wants to shout, 'Wait! Stop!'

He longs to know what she's saying and to whom. She skips up the steps of the Bolshoi Theatre and vanishes into the crowds waiting for curtain-up.

9

The Golden Gates resembled a parade ground the next morning. Comrade Satinov was in full dress uniform, boots, medals and braid. There was Rosa's father, Marshal Shako, with his spiky hair, snub nose and Tartar eyes, in jodhpurs and spurs that clanked on the flagstones.

'I'm rehearsing for the Victory Parade,' he growled at Director Medvedeva. Then he spotted Serafima, whose waist he tweaked as he passed. 'You're a beautiful girl. Just like your mother!' he bellowed.

'Behave yourself,' said Sophia Zeitlin, waving a jewelled finger at him. 'Men get more excited about dressing up than women,' she added, and Andrei realized she was talking to him. 'Are you Serafima's friend Andrei?'

He blushed. 'Yes.'

'Serafima told me how kind you were during your trip to the country house of a certain air force general.' She drew him aside confidentially and took his hands in hers. 'It's hard for a mother to say this but may I speak frankly?'

Andrei nodded.

'I'm concerned about her, and suspect she may be meeting someone after school. Her father and I know she has her admirers, but you probably know more than we do. If you do, dear, may I count on you to tell me?'

Andrei started to say something but stopped himself. Was she referring to the Fatal Romantics' Club?

'Oh Mama, leave poor Andrei alone,' said Serafima, coming to his rescue.

Sophia laughed. 'I was only inviting Andrei to dinner with us at Aragvi tonight, wasn't I, Andrei? I'll send the car for you.'

A summer evening in a street just off Gorky. Outside the engraved glass doors of the Aragvi Restaurant, a moustachioed Georgian in traditional dress – a long *cherkesska* coat with bullet pouches and a jewelled dagger hanging at his belt – stood as if on sentry duty. He opened the door for Andrei, who stepped hesitantly inside a panelled restaurant with tables on the ground floor.

Andrei looked around him. The place was crowded, every table taken. He felt the thrill of a famous restaurant, the sense of shared luxury, the glimpse into the lives of others, lives unknown and unlived. Where were Serafima and her mother? There, making their way towards some stairs at the back that led to the main part of the restaurant. He hurried to join them, and together they entered a space that contained more crowded tables as well as closed alcoves on a second-floor gallery where a moon-faced and very sweaty Georgian in a burgundy tailcoat sang 'Suliko,' accompanied by a guitarist.

Sophia Zeitlin embraced the tiny maître d', who wore white tie, white gloves and tails: his skin was so tautly stretched over his cheekbones that you could almost see through it.

'*Gamajoba*, Madame Zeitlin!' the man declaimed operatically. 'Hello, dear Serafima! Come in! And who's this? A new face?'

'This is Longuinoz Stazhadze,' said Sophia to Andrei. 'The

master of Aragvi and' – she raised her hand in mock salute – 'one of the most powerful men in Moscow.'

He's wearing face powder, noticed Andrei.

People from many different tables hailed Sophia Zeitlin, and then Minka appeared as if from nowhere.

'Andrei! Serafima! We're expecting you!' Minka led them to a table heaped high with dishes – *satsivi, khachapuri, lobio* . . . Waiters brought more, to form a precarious ziggurat of plates. Longuinoz crooked his fingers, and more waiters bearing chairs above their heads wove amongst the closely packed tables, laying out new places just in time for Andrei, Serafima and Sophia to sit down.

The whole Dorov family was there, Senka perched on his mother's knee.

'Andrei,' Senka called out, 'do you like my suit?'

'You look just like a real little professor,' Andrei agreed, laughing.

Their host, Genrikh Dorov, ordered Telavi wine Number 5. His wife, Dashka Dorova, embraced Sophia, and pulled up a chair next to hers.

'Have a martini,' she suggested in her rather exotic Galician accent.

'I'll have a cosmopolitan. American-style,' Sophia declared.

'Eat up, children,' said Genrikh, who seemed too puny to be a Party bigshot.

Andrei scoured the restaurant. In the far alcove, next to a table of American officers, sat Comrade Satinov and family. George, next to him, made frantic wing-flapping gestures while pointing at Genrikh Dorov. Andrei smiled back at him to signal that he understood. Genrikh Dorov, the Uncooked Chicken, was looking more uncooked than ever.

'There's a happy family,' joked Minka, who was next to Andrei. She was pointing at Nikolasha Blagov, sitting in silence with his parents at a poky corner table.

'I wonder if they're sending Nikolasha's father abroad as ambassador?' asked Serafima.

As they watched, Nikolasha sulkily pushed back his chair and stood.

'Uh-oh,' said Minka. 'He's heading this way!'

The two girls laughed at what happened next as Nikolasha became stranded in the middle of the restaurant while streams of Georgian warriors flowed around him, balancing plates of *lobio* for the group of Americans at one of the larger tables.

'You know the Game is just Nikolasha's way of seeing you, Serafima. *That's* what it's really about,' said Minka.

'I don't think Papa would approve of your game,' said Demian Dorov prissily. 'Papa would say it's un-Bolshevik.'

'Are you going to tell him?' asked Minka. 'You'd be a real creep if you did.'

Demian raised his finger. 'I'm just saying: be careful. There's something sinister about Nikolasha's obsession with death.'

Andrei looked up as Nikolasha loomed over them. 'My father's been sent to Mexico as ambassador,' he said dolefully.

'Surely you don't have to go too?' Minka was sympathetic.

'He says I must. It makes tomorrow night especially significant,' said Nikolasha. 'It could be the last Game!' He leaned down to whisper to Serafima and then Minka.

'I think we should invite Andrei to play it this time,' said Serafima suddenly.

'But Andrei's not a full member. He only became a candidate last week. He's not ready,' Nikolasha protested.

'It doesn't matter,' said Andrei. 'I can just watch.'

'Do you want *me* to come?' Serafima looked intently at Nikolasha, who shifted uncomfortably.

'Very much.'

Andrei saw her green eyes shine as she leaned forward.

'Then Andrei plays the Game. If you want me, you must include him too.'

10

The morning of the Victory Parade, and the rain was pouring down on the soldiers, tanks, horses and, amongst the throng of Muscovites on the streets, Andrei and his mother, Inessa. He was, he thought, the only one of his new friends not to have a seat in the grandstand on Red Square. Wearing hats, galoshes and anoraks, they'd got up early to find a good place at the bottom of Gorky Street to watch the show.

A roar. 'That's Stalin arriving!' said the woman next to Andrei. As the orchestra of fifteen hundred musicians played Glinka's 'Glory,' blasted out of giant but tinny loudspeakers mounted on the backs of trucks, Andrei and Inessa could just make out Marshal Zhukov, on a white horse, riding out of one of the Kremlin gates to meet Marshal Rokossovsky in the middle and take the salute. Tanks, howitzers and horsemen passed; flanks of steel and muscle glistened in the rain. They saw soldiers bearing Nazi banners, scarlet and black, like a Roman triumph, and heard their passionate '*URRAH*' as they tossed them at the feet of their leader, the Great Stalin.

Afterwards, the roads were clogged with tanks and jeeps, crowds of soldiers and civilians.

'What a shame it rained,' Andrei said to his mother. But he was not really thinking about the rain. 'Mama' – he turned to her and put his arms around her – 'do you think—'

'Do I think Papa will come home now?' she finished his thought perfectly. 'Hush.' She looked around, even though no one could hear in that din of singing and shouting, footsteps and rain. 'Lower your voice.'

'I'm sure they will all come back now, won't they? I feel it,' Andrei whispered. 'I so want him back.' It was something they had never said to each other, because it was so raw even after all these years.

'Darling Andryusha, don't wish for anything too much. They say you can't live without hope but I think hope's the cruellest trick of all. I survive by not expecting much.'

'But, Mama, there are so many out here today who must be like us. And I know they're all thinking like me. Surely there'll be an amnesty, and everyone will come back?'

Inessa closed her eyes for a moment to collect herself, and when he looked at her bone-weary face, he realized that she was steeling herself for him. 'Don't forget him. Never forget him. But go forward now, darling. Just look forward.'

Andrei felt a lurch of disappointment. He sighed and dropped his arms, stepping away from her. 'I'm meeting my friends on the Stone Bridge at five.'

'To read Pushkin? Are you dressing up?'

'Oh Mama, do you think I'd look good in a top hat and velvet coat? No, I'm too late to find a costume.' They laughed as he pushed his way into the crowds – and afterwards, when he had so many long nights to replay everything, he wished he had said goodbye properly, and told her that he loved her.

'Be careful, you're all I've got. Off you go then!' she called after him as she let him step into his new world.

* * *

Andrei fought his way up the steps. Soldiers, in cloaks and mantles and greatcoats, caps over their eyes, visors running with droplets, were singing on the bridge. Strangers hugged one another and swigged from vodka bottles handed through the crowd. It was hard to see far through the rain and the mist – he kept having to wipe his glasses – but as the crowd closed around Andrei, so closely packed that it took the weight off his feet, he looked back at the red walls of the Kremlin, the stars atop the towers, the gold of the Great Palace, the onion domes, streaked with light in the sheets of rain, and he thought that somewhere in there was Stalin himself, and with Stalin were Comrades Satinov and Dorov, and probably Sophia Zeitlin, famous people whom he now knew. He'd even dined with them at Aragvi. What were they doing at this moment? He knew Satinov, and Satinov knew Stalin, so he, Andrei, was just a few steps from the greatest man in the world.

'Andryusha!' It was Minka, and she was holding the hand of Senka, who was wearing a new suit under a yellow raincoat – just like a grown-up.

'Hello, Little Professor,' said Andrei. 'I see your mama let you out?'

'You're not wearing fancy dress either?' said Senka. 'I don't blame you. Minka isn't dressed up. Is it only those credulous imbeciles who take the Game seriously?' He pointed along the bridge, over the massed heads and bobbing caps, and there was Nikolasha, towering above everyone else in the crowd, at the other end where the road was barricaded to create a wide pedestrian walkway. He was resplendent in an olive-green frock coat and boots, his strawberry-red hair coarsened and rusted by the rain. Shoving through the crowd to get across the bridge, Andrei greeted George and Marlen Satinov, who had their little sister Mariko with them, and nodded at Vlad, who was also in costume. But where was Serafima?

'She'll come, don't you worry,' said Nikolasha. 'See?' He smiled triumphantly.

And there she was, in a blue dress and Peter Pan collar, soaked by the rain, which had frizzed her hair into uncontrollable curls. Andrei couldn't stop looking at her. He scarcely paid attention as Nikolasha clapped his hands and Vlad handed him the Velvet Book.

'Comrade Romantics,' Nikolasha declared formally, 'I am recording the first attendance of Andrei Kurbsky as a full member qualified to play the Game.' The crowd was so noisy that Andrei could barely hear him, and it was hard to stay with the others, such was the shoving of the crowds. But everyone was in a good mood that day, and when George and Minka began to pour out shots of vodka and hand round the glasses, a spotty sailor grabbed one and quaffed it and soon it seemed as if they were providing drinks for the entire Baltic Fleet.

'Are you a theatre troupe?' asked one of them, pulling on Nikolasha's frock coat.

Rosa, in a purple cloak over a red dress with golden appliqué, fought her way through the mass of passersby. 'Sorry, Nikolasha, I couldn't get through. Here they are!' She handed him the pistols in their little green case. She bowed before Nikolasha, who nodded back.

'Comrade Romantics . . .' he started in his solemn high priest's voice. 'We're here as always to celebrate poetry over prose, passion over science. What is our choice?'

'LOVE OR DEATH,' replied Vlad and Rosa. 'WITHOUT LOVE, LET US DIE YOUNG!'

'Let the Game begin!' said Nikolasha, but his incantation was drowned out by the sailors singing 'The Blue Shawl' and then 'Katyusha' – for it was a song as well as a movie.

'Get on with it or we'll lose each other!' George shouted, swigging the vodka.

'What? I can't even hear myself!' shouted Nikolasha, nodding at Vlad, who held up the case and showed them the two duelling pistols. As he chose his pistol, Nikolasha stowed the Velvet Book in the pistol case – out of the rain.

'Who dies today? Let's play . . .' said Rosa, but her little cooing voice was lost in the roar of the crowd.

No one saw what happened next. They were separated by the currents of the crowd, which carried Andrei so far from the others that he lost Serafima altogether and could only just see Nikolasha's head in the distance when the two shots rang out. Amidst the sudden hush that followed, the rain stopped and with it time itself. Slow steam arose from the sweating, damp crowds, the sticky air congested with white poplar pollen instantly, mysteriously unleashed, and that red head was nowhere to be seen.

When he found them again, standing startled and horrified around the bodies, Andrei looked at his friends, at the other Fatal Romantics – and across the bodies, his eyes met Serafima's in a kind of horrified complicity. And then time speeded up again.

In front of him two army medics were working on the bodies, and a clearing had opened up in the dense pack of people. Policemen were running from both directions. And he saw the duelling pistols on the ground, one shattered into pieces, and the Velvet Book, splayed open on the wet ground, its covers all muddy. The police were holding people back, placing barriers around the scene and asking questions.

'Are you friends of these two?' a police officer asked, a burly fellow with a Stavropol accent and a paunch. 'Pull yourselves together. Say something!'

'Yes we are.' Andrei stepped forward, conscious that Vlad beside him was shaking in his bedraggled frock coat.

'Are you actors or something? Do you dress up like this all the time?'

'We're not actors,' Vlad said and began to cry.

'Christ! What about you, girl?' said the policeman, pointing at Minka, who was hugging her little brother, Senka.

'Come away, Senka, I'm taking you home.'

'But look at that pistol – it's in pieces – and the Velvet Book's all torn,' said Senka, crouching down to look.

'Leave all that; the police will need them,' said Minka.

'No one's going anywhere yet,' ordered the policeman, turning to Serafima. 'You there! What's your name?'

'I'm Serafima Romashkina.' Andrei could tell she was struggling to hold her nerve by being icily calm and formal. Yet she had blood on her hands – she must have got to her friends first.

'Like the writer?'

'He's my father.'

'You're kidding. So your mother's Sophia Zeitlin?'

'Yes,' said Serafima.

'I'm a fan. I loved *Katyusha*. What a movie! But you don't look like her at all.'

'Look, our friends are lying there and you're just—'

'So what were you doing here, Serafima Romashkina?' The policeman was now brandishing a little notebook and pencil that seemed too small for his thick fingers.

'We were all meeting here. After the parade. Just for fun.'

'M-e-e-ting,' said the policeman, trying to write this down.

Andrei realized he was drunk. Most of Moscow was drunk and several of the policemen at the scene were struggling to stand up at all. 'Why the hell are you in fancy dress?'

'We're in a dramatic club,' said Serafima.

'What the fuck is that?'

'They're playing the Game,' blurted out little Mariko Satinova from the back of the group. Andrei noticed Marlen was standing in front of her so she could not see the bodies or the blood.

'Give me your name and address and you can take the little ones home.'

'Satinov,' said Marlen.

'Satinov? Like the Politburo member?'

'Yes, I'm Marlen Satinov.'

'And I'm Mariko, his sister,' added the little girl.

'Mary mother of Christ!' said the policeman, pushing back his cap and wiping his forehead. 'GRISHA, GET THE FUCK OVER HERE!' he yelled, turning around.

A pimply policeman who did not look any older than the schoolchildren ran over, looking anxious. 'Yes, Captain?'

'Run fast as you can over to the guardhouse at Spassky Gate' – he pointed towards the Kremlin tower – 'and ring Lubianka Square. Tell them we have a double killing with special characteristics. It's for the Organs. Tell them to send someone down here fast. Go!'

Andrei watched the young policeman running; just as he reached the sentry box with its telephone link to the MGB, the Ministry of State Security, he jumped as the sky boomed and a galaxy of fireworks exploded above the Kremlin.

The roar of the crowd spread from the bridge along the packed embankments and bridges of the River Moskva, but

Andrei had eyes for only the policeman gesticulating as he told the guards to ring their superiors. He imagined phones ringing from guardhouses up the vertical hierarchy – captains to colonels, generals to ministers – all the way to Lubianka Square and thence to the Kremlin itself.

Around him, the fireworks made the night into a daylight that turned the two bodies on the bridge red and white and green as those supernovas flashed above them in crescents and stars and wheels.

Serafima stood beside him. In the dazzling, bleaching light he saw her tears, and, for a moment, it felt as if they were quite alone. Then he took her in his arms as a stab of sheer dread pierced his innards.

'It's begun,' she kept saying. 'It's begun.'

It was only much later that he'd understand that she was crying not just for their dead friends and the pasts they shared, but for their futures. And for the secret that she cherished more than life itself.

PART TWO

The Children's Case

Children in ages to come will cry in bed,
Not to have been born in our lifetime.

'We Have No Borders,' popular Soviet song

11

A few hundred metres away, in the room behind the Lenin Mausoleum, an old man smiled, honey-coloured eyes glinting, his face creasing like that of a grizzled tiger.

'You're looking like a Tsarist station manager in your uniform,' Stalin teased Andrei Vyshinsky, his Deputy Foreign Minister, a pink-cheeked, white-haired man who stood before him in a grey, gold-braided diplomatic uniform with a ceremonial dagger at its belt. 'Who designed this foolish rig? Is that a dagger or a carving knife?'

'It's the new diplomatic uniform, Comrade Stalin,' replied Vyshinsky, almost at attention, chest out.

'You look like a head waiter,' said Stalin, his eyes scanning the leaders who formed a semi-circle around him. Golden shoulderboards and gleaming braid, Kremlin tans and bulging bellies. 'What a collection,' he said. 'Some of you are so fat, you hardly look human. Set an example. Eat less.'

Hercules Satinov, who stood to Stalin's right in a colonel general's uniform, was proud to stand beside the greatest man in the world to celebrate Russia's victory. Stalin had promoted him, trusted him with challenging tasks in peace and war, and he had never disappointed the Master. Stalin's restless scrutiny of his comrades-in-arms was sometimes mocking, sometimes chilling – even Satinov had experienced it – but it was just one of the many methods Stalin had used to build Soviet Russia and defeat Hitler. Virtually the entire leadership was in this room. Every single man was pretending to talk – but actually they never took their eyes off *him*, and Satinov knew that Stalin was always aware of this. Now he felt Stalin's gaze upon him.

'Now look at Satinov here. Smart! That's the ticket!'

'He's no more a soldier than me,' Lavrenti Beria objected.

'True, but at least Satinov has the figure for it, eh, *bicho*?' Stalin gave everyone nicknames and he often called Satinov *bicho* – 'boy' in their native Georgian. 'He looks like a Soviet man should look. Not like you, Vyshinsky.' Stalin beamed at the sweating courtier, enjoying his discomfort – especially when Alexander Poskrebyshev, his chef-de-cabinet, a bald little fellow in a general's uniform, crept up behind Vyshinsky, slipped the dagger out of its scabbard and replaced it with a small green gherkin.

'I think Vyshinsky needs to drink a forfeit, don't you, comrades?' asked Beria, the secret-police chief. Satinov did not like this bullying of Vyshinsky even though he was a craven reptile: sycophantic to superiors, fearsome to inferiors. He observed how Beria played up to Stalin, however. Beria's glossy, braided Commissar-General of Security uniform ill suited his glinting pince-nez, grey-green cheeks and double chin.

'But I have to be careful, I have a heart condition,' pleaded Vyshinsky.

'Comrade Vyshinsky, might you deign to join us in a toast to the Soviet soldier?' said Stalin, as flunkies in dark blue uniforms filled all the glasses.

Stalin had drunk several vodkas earlier and Satinov could tell that he was slightly drunk – and why not? Today was his supreme moment. But the stress of the war – four years of sixteen-hour days – had visibly aged him. Satinov noticed that his hands shook, his skin was waxy with red spots on his cheeks, the grey hair resembled a spiked ice sculpture. He wondered if Stalin was ill but put that thought out of his mind. It was unthinkable; Stalin's health was a secret; and the Master distrusted doctors even more than he distrusted women, Jews, capitalists and social democrats.

'To Comrade Vyshinsky,' Stalin announced. 'And to our diplomats and our gherkin-growers who supplied our brave forces!'

The leaders guffawed at this and Vyshinsky, still wearing his scabbarded gherkin, joined in with oblivious enthusiasm, unsure what the joke might be.

Stalin was still smiling but he immediately noticed when the State Security Minister, Merkulov, who ran the secret police Organs, tentatively joined the outer edges of the circle.

'Comrade Merkulov, welcome,' said Stalin. 'Haven't they arrested you yet?' He winked. It was a running joke.

Merkulov bowed but was hopelessly tongue-tied around Stalin. 'C-c-congratulations . . . C-c-comrade Marshal Stalin.'

A silence inside, the hum of crowds and engines outside.

Stalin narrowed his eyes. 'Are you reporting something?'

'Yes, but n-n-nothing important . . . Should I report to Comrade Beria?'

'Haven't we shot you yet?' teased Stalin, since it was Merkulov's ministry that was responsible for *chernaya rabota* – the black work, his euphemism for blood-letting. Stalin was not shy about that: killing was the quickest, most efficient way to accelerate the progress of history. 'We must never lose our sense of humour,' said Stalin with the tigerish grin, 'eh, Comrade Merkulov?'

Merkulov mopped his brow and tried to laugh, but hurried across to brief his boss, Beria. Satinov had been waiting for just this gap in the conversation. He nodded at Marshal Shako, the stalwart air force commander. But the marshal hesitated. Even brave warriors were nervous around Stalin, and with good reason.

'Go on,' Satinov prompted him. The gruff commander saluted.

'Permission to report! Comrade Marshal Stalin,' Shako blurted, 'I propose on behalf of the marshalate of the Soviet armed forces that you be promoted to the rank of generalissimo and receive the gold star of the Hero of the Soviet Union.'

'No, no.' Stalin waved this aside with his good arm; the other he kept stiffly by his side. 'Comrade Stalin doesn't need it. Comrade Stalin has authority without it. Some title you've thought up!' Stalin, who had started to refer to himself in the third person, cast a black glance at Satinov and Beria. 'Who cooked up this pantomime?'

'The people demand it,' replied Satinov.

Stalin suddenly paled and raised his hand to his forehead. He was having one of those dizzy spells that had become frequent at the end of the war. He stumbled forward and leaned against the wall, but it passed, and he dismissed the concerned frowns of his comrades. 'I'm tired, that's all. I'll work another two years then retire.'

'No, Comrade Stalin, that's unthinkable!' cried Beria.

'I will let Molotov and Satinov run things,' insisted Stalin.

'No one could replace you,' said Molotov urgently. 'Certainly not me.'

'Nor me. We need you!' added Satinov. His comrades, whether in marshal's stars or Stalinka tunics, repeated this, outdoing each other in enthusiasm. 'You're everything to us! Indispensable! Retirement is out of the question!'

Stalin's honey-coloured eyes scrutinized them, but he said nothing. He pulled a pack of Herzegovina Flor cigarettes out of his pocket. '*Bicho!*'

Satinov lit it.

'Generalissimo?' murmured Stalin. 'It makes me sound like a South American dictator. Comrade Stalin doesn't need it, doesn't need it at all.'

'The people demand you accept this rank,' insisted Satinov.

'Ten million soldiers insist,' said Marshal Shako. Marshals Zhukov and Konev, the most famous army commanders, forming a bull-necked human rampart of shoulderboards and medals behind him, nodded gravely.

'What liberties you take with an old man!' Stalin said, almost to himself, closing his eyes as he inhaled.

'We have to do something,' said Beria. The courtier knows when the king wishes him to disobey, Satinov thought. Stalin was weakening.

'It's not good for my health at all,' said Stalin. 'As for the gold star, I've never commanded in battle.'

'But I have the gold star right here,' said Satinov, drawing a little box out of his pocket. 'May I present it?'

'No!' Stalin held up his hand, the cigarette between the fingers. 'That, I won't accept.'

Satinov looked across at the other leaders, Molotov and Beria. What to do? He put it back in his pocket.

'Fuck it! He'll accept in the end like he accepted the generalissimo title,' Beria whispered.

'We'll find a way to give it to him,' Molotov, formal in his dark bourgeois suit, agreed.

Beria stepped closer to Stalin. 'Josef Vissarionovich,' said Beria, 'may I report?'

'What, even today? Can't you decide anything without consulting me?'

'We all wish we could, Comrade Stalin, but it's something a little out of the ordinary.'

The wily old conspirator inhaled his cigarette wearily. Satinov wondered what it was. It was often better not to know the black work Stalin discussed with Beria. Yet even as the two stepped back slightly, Satinov could still hear some of their conversation.

'There's been a strange event on the Kammeny Most. A schoolboy and schoolgirl have been killed. Just thirty minutes ago.'

'So?'

'They are both pupils at School 801.'

'School 801?' replied Stalin, a degree more interested. 'The finishing school for little barons? My Vasily and Svetlana were there.'

'Some of them were in fancy-dress costume, Josef Vissarionovich.'

'What on earth were they doing?'

'We'll find out imminently. We haven't identified the dead yet but initial reports mention the involvement of the children of "responsible Party workers."' Satinov took a quick breath. 'Responsible workers' was the euphemism for the leadership.

Stalin focused like a diving hawk. 'Who?'

'Some of the parents are in this room. Comrade Satinov, Marshal Shako, Comrade Dorov . . .'

Stalin shook his head. 'Fancy dress, you say? We let our guard down during the war. This could be the work of our enemies abroad – or of the children themselves.' He held up a single finger as straight as a tallow candle. 'No little princelings are above Soviet justice. Everyone knows how I demoted my Vasily for behaving like a spoilt aristocrat. Solve the case. If it's murder, heads must roll.'

'Right, I'll get to work,' said Beria, backing away from Stalin and leaving the room.

Satinov felt the hand of fear clutch his heart: what role did his children play in this? What if George or Marlen or Mariko lay dead on the bridge?

But Stalin was strolling back towards him and Satinov saw that he was bristling and bushy-tailed again, a satyr refreshed by the macabre excitement of conspiracy. His eyes twinkled roguishly.

'How's your family?' Stalin asked. Satinov concealed his worries with all the arctic expertise of a veteran of Stalin's world. There would be time later to find out what happened on the bridge.

12

Just before seven p.m., Sophia Zeitlin and her husband, Constantin Romashkin, climbed the steps to the Georgievsky Hall. The dinner to celebrate victory would be her moment to shine and be admired – but that depended on her table placement. The fifteen hundred guests crowded nervously around the table plans on boards outside; a seat near Stalin endowed the lucky ones with an almost visible halo; those seated furthest away could scarcely hide the shadow of disappointment.

'Darling, that dress will dazzle everyone,' said Dashka Dorova, kissing Sophia and Constantin. Many were quick to criticize Sophia for un-Bolshevik vulgarity but she knew that Dashka was a real friend who wished her well.

'I have to give the public what they expect.'

'Well, your dress certainly does that,' said Dashka.

'I love your dress too. That cream colour really suits you, and the pleated skirt shows off your curves,' said Sophia, who also meant it. 'I have to tart myself up a bit, but you always look so chic and professional. You are our most glamorous minister!' She hesitated, and then gave her deep throaty laugh. 'But that's hardly a compliment when you see the rest of them!'

'Don't be ridiculous!' Dashka laughed away the compliments and started to peruse the table plans. 'Ah, there I am. Not too bad. I'm on the Council of Ministers' table.' She looked at her husband. 'How about you, Genrikh?'

Genrikh looked pasty and irritable. 'I'm nowhere near the Politburo,' he said glumly.

'No one will notice, dear,' Dashka said, patting his arm. But Sophia knew that everyone noticed such things, and she certainly liked her own placement. Her husband was placed with the editors of the Red Army newspaper, even further away than Genrikh, but *she* was at the Politburo table.

The leaders hadn't arrived yet and she could feel everyone looking at her as she put a cigarette in her holder and Marshal Shako lit it.

A hush; then a collective intake of breath: Stalin had entered with the Politburo. The entire Georgievsky Hall jumped to its feet and shouted, '*Urrah! Urrah!*' and cheered for so long that Stalin himself first waved at them to sit down, then clapped back at them and finally became cross, ordering them to stop. But no one would stop. Stalin sat down at the table next to Sophia's between Marshal Shako and Molotov, and, shrugging modestly, looked a little embarrassed until the cheering subsided.

Sophia could not take her eyes off Stalin. As an actress, she noticed how he seemed to change before her eyes, walking sometimes with quick little movements, occasionally like a clumsy goose, often more like a stealthy panther.

She was sitting between Satinov and Mikoyan, the most courteous and elegant of the leaders, who were, as a rule, uncouth and dreary. When she looked around, she saw most of them sported the telltale archipelago of red spots on their cheeks, the signs of alcoholism and arteriosclerosis. She noticed the gruesome Beria making eyes at her across the table.

'I wish he would look at someone else,' she whispered to Satinov.

'You are dressed to be admired,' replied Satinov, who seemed to Sophia to be uncharacteristically tense. 'Wasn't Serafima meeting with her Pushkin club friends tonight on the Stone Bridge?'

'I think so, but I never know where she goes these days,' Sophia said with a sigh.

'We know less about our children than we think,' Satinov agreed. 'It worries me.'

'And they know even less about us! Thank God!' And Sophia laughed huskily.

Twenty stodgy courses – blinis and caviar, borscht with cream, beef Stroganoff, sturgeon, suckling pig, Georgian wines and Crimean champagne, brandy and vodka – were served by the waiters Sophia recognized from the Aragvi as well as the Metropole and National hotels.

Stalin stood. Silence fell. He spoke in his Georgian tenor, surprisingly high and soft, toasting the Russian people 'without whom none of us marshals and commanders would be worth a damn!' Then he turned to the generals, starting with Marshal Zhukov, whom he invited to come and clink glasses with him. Sophia noticed that Stalin downed his glass of vodka at each toast, and guessed that his carafe was full of water.

When he toasted Admiral Isakov, Satinov whispered to Sophia: 'How's Isakov going to walk all that way?' – Isakov had lost his leg in the war – but Stalin seemed to know where the admiral was sitting, for he threaded through the tables to the far end of the hall and clinked glasses with him there.

'That's so touching!' Sophia said.

Ten, twenty, forty toasts were drunk, and she lost count until suddenly, surprisingly, it was *her* turn.

'Sophia Zeitlin!' The breath left her body and she felt quite alone in the magnificent hall. 'Your beauty inspired our soldiers in dark times!'

Somehow she walked over to him, fifteen feet that seemed like a mile. Stalin kissed her hand: 'Katyusha!' he toasted. 'An example to all Soviet womankind.' How he had aged during the war, she thought as he stood before her. A paunchy old man, grey, grizzled, his skin yellow with pinpricks of red in his cheeks. But what a fine, noble head, what eyes.

When the toasts were over, Stalin and the Politburo filed out, but Sophia realized she would never be able to sleep after so much wine, vodka and excitement. She couldn't go home. She wanted to go on for a nightcap. Marshal Shako winked at her. And then she remembered Satinov's tension, his question about Serafima, and, as a woman who listened to her instincts, she called for her driver and told him to hurry home.

Serafima was still in her blue dress with the white Peter Pan collar when Sophia and Constantin came in.

'Mama!'

'Aren't you going to ask who toasted your mother tonight?' Sophia started, but then she saw her daughter's face. 'What is it?'

'Sit down and tell us,' suggested Constantin, joining Serafima on the sofa and taking her hand. Sophia had to admit he was good at moments like this.

Sophia poured herself a cognac and lit a cigarette: 'Come on, darling,' she said, 'you know nothing shocks me! I'm an actress, for God's sake.'

'Let her speak, Sophia,' Constantin told her.

Then out it came – the Game, the bridge, the gunshots, the

two dead children, and the parents suddenly realized the spatter on her dress was blood.

'Oh my God,' said Sophia, shocked yet relieved that Serafima was safe. 'I always thought Nikolasha Blagov was a maniac. But dear Rosa, and her poor parents. What on earth were they doing?'

'The Organs are investigating,' Serafima said, wiping her eyes. 'I just can't believe that Rosa—'

'Don't worry, darling,' said Sophia, looking at her husband to see if he was as worried as she was. She leaned over and put both her hands on Serafima's face as if to keep her safe, and then straightened up and started to pace the floor. 'I'm so sad about sweet Rosa but . . . Stalin kissed my hand tonight. You will be safe. No one would dare touch Sophia Zeitlin's daughter!'

'I wish that were true,' said Constantin, kissing both Serafima's hands. 'How I wish that were true.'

Satinov didn't get home until four a.m. the next morning. Stalin had invited him back to the Nearby Dacha after the dinner. The drinking had seemed interminable. All the time he'd been worrying about the children and Tamara.

She was waiting for him as he opened the front door. 'You know what happened, don't you?' she asked.

He nodded.

'Those poor children,' she said. 'And oh, their mothers! I can't bear to think what they must be going through.'

'Tell me what you know,' he said, and listened carefully. 'Tamriko, I fear our boys have been foolish.'

Tamara sank wearily on to the divan. 'I noticed the clique at school; we all did. And I warned George not to get mixed up with it. But, oh Hercules, they're just children.'

'It will probably be fine,' he said, looking down at her in his serious way.

Tamriko – he always used the Georgian diminutive – was blonde with green-brown eyes and the most perfectly delicate bone structure. When he held her body in his arms, she felt vulnerable and soft as a little bird. Bolshevik wives were expected to work, and he admired her career as a teacher at School 801. When he had wanted to bring his four grown-up sons by his late first wife up from Georgia, she had agreed, treating them as if they were her own. He couldn't do without her and the cosy household she'd created in her own image.

'Hercules, what will come of this?' she whispered.

He looked at her with unwavering vigilance in his cool grey eyes that she understood meant that the apartment was probably bugged. But he could imagine a number of different scenarios, including one in which everything was fine. 'Can you speak to the children now? They're terrified of what you're going to say to them.'

'It's the middle of the night.'

'But they're still wide awake.'

He sighed and stood up. 'Boys!' he called out.

Seconds later, George and Marlen were standing in their pyjamas, almost at attention, in front of their father, who, still in his general's uniform, himself stood rigidly upright, framed by the martial portrait of Stalin behind him. He was exhausted but, as he now examined his sons, flushed with the night and very anxious – the cheeky, genial George and the conventional, serious Marlen – he saw they were still really children, shocked by this tragedy, mourning their friends. He felt such love for them that suddenly it was all he could do not to take them into his arms.

'You've been very stupid, you little fools,' he said, knowing he had to be stern. It was his way, and he knew no other. 'Tamriko's told me what happened. If you've anything to do with this mess, I'll strangle you myself. Now: bed and sleep!'

'Thank you, Papa,' said George.

'Good night, Papa,' said Marlen, who appeared to be fighting back tears.

Tamara followed them to their rooms, and making a calm sign with two open hands, she let them each know that it was over and their father was no longer cross. Then she kissed them both on the forehead as if they were still little.

When she came back to Satinov, he was sitting on the divan. He lit a cigarette and she sat next to him and patted her knee. 'Come on then,' she said, and he raised his legs onto her lap and she helped pull off his boots, unclicked his holster, unbuttoned his tunic.

When they went to bed, she went to sleep quickly, for she found sleeping easy, and it had been quite a day and an even more stressful night. But he lay with his eyes open, playing out the possibilities, until the first birdsong of dawn.

13

'Children, please!' said Director Medvedeva the next morning, tapping the rostrum with her baton after the singing of 'Thank You, Comrade Stalin.' Tap, tap. 'As you all know, the school has suffered a tragic incident. We've lost two of our pupils. However, we Soviet people are strong. We have suffered much in the Great Patriotic War but the Great Stalin has taught us that toughness is a Bolshevik virtue. We are no different here at School 801. We are agreed' – and here she looked down the row of teachers, and Dr Rimm, Teacher Golden and Miss Begbulatova nodded vigorously – 'there'll be no wailing here, no bourgeois sentiment. The self-indulgent folly of misguided youth is nothing compared to the sacrifices of our Soviet peoples.'

She was about to dismiss her pupils to their classes when the doors at the back of the gym swung open.

'Can we help you, comrades?' she asked, acutely aware of the slight tremor in her voice.

With the sound of dropped satchels and dragged chairs echoing on the gym's wooden floor, the children turned around too, and their eyes grew wide. Three men in tidy blue suits stood at the back with the air of purpose, urgency and fearlessness that they all recognized. Absolute silence fell as the men walked down the aisle of the hall, looking into the faces of the children until they reached Vlad Titorenko, instantly recognizable with his white face and long black hair.

'Titorenko, Vladimir?' asked one of the men.

Vlad opened his mouth and tried to say yes but no sound came.

'Come with us!' But he could not move so the men lifted him under his arms and dragged him out. As they left, one of them turned back towards the teachers on the raised platform. 'Carry on, Comrade Director,' he called, and then they were gone down the corridor. Everyone could hear Titorenko's sobs.

The children rushed to the windows and there, outside the Golden Gates, they saw Vlad being pushed into a grey Emka car, which drove off with the skidding of tyres.

There was an ominous calm in the staff common room during lunch break. Antique Dr Noodelman dozed in the deep armchair, but everyone else was only pretending to read their newspapers and mark their essays.

Golden looked over the top of his copy of Pushkin's stories at Agrippina Begbulatova, who was, as usual, brewing the *chai* in the Chinese teapot. He was not considering the silkiness of her thighs and the intoxicating taste of her excitement on his lips *in spite of* the deaths and Vlad's arrest that morning but, on the contrary, even more intensely *because of* them.

Agrippina had the essential gifts for achieving happiness in life, and there was none greater than her boundless capacity for pleasure. Benya had long since realized that in sex, as in life, intelligence and technique counted for nothing; the capacity for pleasure was everything. She always said: 'You're old' – Benya was forty-seven – 'and I'm young, so I must marry soon. But when I'm married, will you still fuck me once a month?'

Once again, the darkness had stepped closer to him. Golden, who had known unbearable torments already, knew that he had to enjoy the proximity of sensual joy while he still could. But actually he needed no excuse. He found himself entangled in delicious flirtations wherever he went, and since even at the best of times he suffered from Jewish fatalism and rampaging hypochondria, always believing death was imminent, he seized every opportunity with boyish enthusiasm.

When he heard the humming of 'Comrade Stalin, thank you for . . .,' he turned towards the door. Dr Rimm came in, sat at the table and started to smooth out the crumpled pages of *Komsomolskaya Pravda*. Then he threw it down and said: 'Comrades and citizens, if I may have your attention. I need to say something.'

Do you? thought Benya Golden. I wish you wouldn't.

'In the light of the arrest of our pupil, I propose a vote – a unanimous show of support – for our esteemed director, Comrade Medvedeva, for the way in which she has run the Josef Stalin School 801.' All the teachers raised their hands in agreement.

As Golden passed Agrippina in the corridor afterwards, he whispered: 'Unanimous vote of support from Dr Rimm – now we know Director Medvedeva is in trouble.'

And she whispered: 'Later, Benochka?'

That afternoon: frantic knocking on the door of the Satinovs' apartment. When Leka the maid answered it, Irina Titorenka almost fell into the lobby and ran straight into the arms of Tamara Satinova. She was crying hysterically and seemed to be trying to get to Hercules Satinov's study.

Tamara stopped Irina before she could burst through the

double glass doors and led her into the kitchen, sitting her at the table and offering her some Georgian delicacies. Like Jewesses, Georgian housewives regard food as the best cure for unhappiness, and the sweetmeats earned Tamara a respite – but not for long.

'I saw everyone at pick-up,' Irina sobbed. 'The children came out. But not mine. Then I'm told by Director Medvedeva: Vlad's been with the Organs since nine a.m. No one rang me. No one knows where he is, or what he's done. No one knows anything. What can I do? Comrade Stalin loves children. Comrade Stalin will put things right.' Shouting now: 'Tamara, I must ring Comrade Stalin!'

Tamara was sitting next to Irina. 'Have you called your husband?'

'Yes, yes, he's distraught. He's trying to ring Comrade Beria, anyone, but no one will take his calls. That's why I came here. Comrade Satinov is my husband's boss: no one is closer to Comrade Stalin than he is. Comrade Satinov will speak to Comrade Stalin, won't he? Say he will!'

Tamara chose her words carefully: 'The Organs only act with good reason, and the good reason in this case is that they are simply investigating the deaths of poor Nikolasha Blagov and Rosa Shako. That's all. Your boy will tell them what he knows and then they will release him. You must calm down, Irina.'

'No, no, they'll beat him. He's very sensitive and vulnerable. Anyone can see that. He could kill himself. They could kill him.'

'No, that couldn't happen.'

'But they're capable of anything. We both know this. I must speak to your husband. I know he's here. *He* must call Comrade Stalin!'

Tamara took both of Irina's hands and squeezed them hard. 'Stay here. Quietly. I will speak to my husband now.'

As she said it, Tamara's voice almost cracked. Hercules himself had gone to pick up the children that day. He planned to do so every day until the case had blown over. He'd told her that pick-up at the Golden Gates was buzzing with the news of Vlad's arrest and gossip about Nikolasha's weird games. But there was nothing particularly sinister about the Organs' questioning of Vlad, he'd said. The deaths had to be investigated and Vlad was Nikolasha and Rosa's best friend. There was nothing to worry about.

'Hercules?' Tamara said, softly knocking on the door and coming in.

'I'm working, Tamara.'

'Irina Titorenka is here. She's hysterical. She wants your help to appeal to the . . . the highest authority.'

Satinov raised his eyes from his papers and shook his head very slightly. 'Take her for a walk in the yard and give her some advice. Tell her to trust in Soviet justice. That's all.'

Tamara kissed the top of his head and was hurrying back to the kitchen when she saw George and Marlen peering down the corridor at Irina Titorenka, who was blowing her nose.

'What's going on, Mama?' demanded George.

'Is that Vlad's mother?' asked Marlen.

'Hush! To your rooms – or your father will have something to say.' And they were gone.

A few minutes later Tamara led Irina Titorenka downstairs to the yard. Losha Babanava and the other bodyguards were down there smoking. A couple of old people, Molotov's aunt and Politburo member Andreyev's father, in shorts and a string vest, were sitting in the sun playing chess. They knew. All of them whispered to each other when they saw the distraught mother.

When they could not be overheard, Tamara placed her hands on Irina's shoulders. 'Now listen to me,' she said. 'I know this is worrying. But you must say nothing of this to anyone. Do not ever mention Comrade Stalin. Never try to call him or any other leader. That will only delay Vlad's release. The Organs will inform you of Vlad's whereabouts when they're ready. Take your younger child to school. Everyone is watching you. My husband says you must put your faith in Soviet justice. Do you understand me?'

But when Irina was gone, Tamara noticed that her own hands were shaking.

14

'What was your role in the criminal conspiracy to murder the two schoolchildren Nikolasha Blagov and Rosa Shako?'

'Conspiracy? Murder? I don't understand.' It was early the following morning, and Vlad was sitting in a grey room at a table with a single light.

'Let's start again shall we? Your name?'

'Vladimir Ivanovich Titorenko.'

'Age?'

'Seventeen and nine months.'

'I am Pavel Mogilchuk. Special Case Section, Ministry of State Security, understand?'

'Yes.'

'Come on, Vlad, stop crying,' Mogilchuk said, handing him a handkerchief. Vlad looked at him, at his round spectacles and reddish hair with a touch of grey. He looked a little like a teacher. 'I know it's been a tough couple of days and you're worried but I want to reassure you.'

'But I want to see my mother. Does she know where I am . . . ?'

'Do *you* know where you are, Vlad?'

Vlad's romantic locks had been cropped, and without them, his face seemed long and forlorn. He shook his head.

'It's a state secret, boy, but I'll tell you: you're in Lubianka

Inner Prison, Dzerzhinsky Square. Was it very frightening arriving?' Vlad nodded. 'It's scary being processed here, stripped and searched inside and photographed. But it's just routine. How did you sleep?'

'They wouldn't let me sleep. They kept the light on; they woke me up; they made me put my hands on top of the covers. I couldn't sleep. Where's my mother?'

Mogilchuk leaned forward across the plain table and redirected the light so it was not shining into Vlad's eyes. 'Come on, boy. Show some Bolshevik toughness! I'm going to ask you questions and you'll answer everything in full. Don't lie about anything. If you lie, that will be worse for you. If you tell the truth about everything, you'll go home soon. OK?'

Vlad nodded.

'What was your role in the conspiracy to murder Nikolasha and Rosa?'

'What conspiracy?'

'Let's start from the beginning, shall we? Or you'll never go home.'

Vlad took a sharp breath, and looked at his hands. 'Nikolasha Blagov had a club and he liked to play something called the Game.'

'The Game? What was that? Whites and Reds? Cossacks and Tartars? Soccer?'

'No, we dressed up in costumes.'

'So it's a theatre group?'

'Yes, we pretended to be Pushkin . . .'

'Go on,' said Mogilchuk. 'I understand. I'm a writer myself. We Russians love poetry, do we not?'

Vlad nodded. 'We played characters from *Onegin*.'

'What could be more normal than that?' Mogilchuk opened his hands. 'Where did you meet? At school?'

'No. We usually met in the graveyard in the Sparrow Hills.'

'The graveyard? Why?'

'Because it was a secret club.'

'And did this club have a name?'

'Yes, the Fatal Romantics' Club.'

'And what did you do at these secret meetings?'

'We talked about romanticism. Poetry.'

'And politics?'

'No.'

'There's something missing here. Come on, think!' Mogilchuk clicked his fingers. 'How did it go from poetry play-acting to the shooting of two children?'

Vlad gave a loud and unexpected sob. 'I just don't know.'

'You were Nikolasha's deputy in the club, weren't you? So what did you debate?'

'Love. Death. Nikolasha said that if you could not live with love, it was better to die. Like Pushkin.'

'Did Rosa mention death?'

'No.'

'Would you say it was likely that they'd agreed to a suicide pact?'

'No. Never!'

'Would you say it is possible that Nikolasha killed her and then himself?'

Vlad's face was in his hands. 'I don't know.'

'That evening on the Stone Bridge, did you see them close up?'

'No.'

'You're lying.'

The door flew open as if kicked in, and a lieutenant general of State Security entered the room. The word 'swagger' might have been invented for this bull of a man, thought Vlad miserably. He seemed too bulging, too bright, too big to be real. An array of precious rings sat on fingers as fat and hairy as grubs. And Vlad thought that the muscles of his arms, let alone his legs in their striped britches, seemed as thick as his waist.

'Comrade Kobylov!' Mogilchuk stood to attention.

'Sorry to interrupt your gentle chat.' Kobylov brought his fleshy, olive-skinned face very close to Vlad. He was wearing an eye-wateringly strong cologne and smelled of cloves. 'I warn you, if you lie to me, you may never get out of here. No matter who the fuck your parents are!' He smashed his fist on the table, and Vlad jumped with fright.

'So Nikolasha shot Rosa?' Kobylov said.

'If you say so, maybe. Yes.'

'Where was the gun?'

'I never saw it!'

Kobylov rolled his eyes at Mogilchuk. 'He never saw a gun!' he imitated Vlad in a girlish intellectual voice. 'You'll spit it out in the end.' He ruffled Vlad's hair and chuckled. 'Mogilchuk, a word!'

The two MGB officers stepped outside. General Bogdan 'Bull' Kobylov was Beria's right-hand man, and Colonel Mogilchuk, standing to attention in his blue shoulderboards and tunic, hurried to light Kobylov's cigarette.

'Comrade Colonel,' Kobylov said, 'remember Comrade Beria's orders?'

'A murder. A conspiracy. To be solved without regard to rank or position. The very words of the Instantsiya.' Mogilchuk paused. 'But they're just kids.'

'You milksop! You're getting soft. There are two children with gunshot wounds on Professor Schpigelglaz's slab right now down at the Kremlevka. And not just any teenagers either. Did you ever hear about the Lakoba case in Georgia?'

Mogilchuk pretended that he hadn't.

'Well, I've got some experience of working with kids,' said Kobylov modestly. Comrades Beria and Kobylov had killed the Abkhazian leader Lakoba and then they had inflicted unspeakable torments on his young sons, but they couldn't be executed until they were twelve, so they were kept alive. On the day they celebrated their twelfth birthday, Kobylov shot one and beat the other to death. 'Comrade Stalin says, "You can't make a revolution with silk gloves,"' he went on. 'But so far the order is: no French wrestling, and that suits me. I don't want to hurt a bunch of kids either.'

'So what do you suggest, Comrade General? Should we wait for Schpigelglaz's post-mortem?'

'The Instantsiya wants this solved fast, Mogilchuk. It's obvious what happened. Let's just tie it up quickly and get on with some real work.' Kobylov took a drag on his cigarette and then kicked open the interrogating-room door.

Vlad, startled, recoiled, knocking his chair over backwards and crouching in the far corner.

'Hey, easy now! Not so jumpy, eh? Come on. Sit down again.' Kobylov coaxed Vlad back into his chair. 'Who else was in this poetry-reading, transvestite, cock-sucking, arse-licking, Pushkin-duelling strip club?'

'It wasn't like that at all, I promise!'

'Look, just cough up the names and you can go home. Who helped Nikolasha plan the murder? Or did he do it alone?'

Satinov's bodyguard, Losha, collected George from the football game later that evening.

'What's news, Losha?' George asked anxiously as he got into the car.

'On the shooting case? Nothing yet. Chinese saying: Never worry worry until worry worries you!'

George nodded. 'How are you, Losha?'

'Sizzling, son. Now, have you kissed that girl yet?' He accelerated through the traffic in the Packard.

'Which girl?'

'Minka Dorova, you sissy. She's your girl, ain't she?'

'Well, I suppose so, but I haven't kissed her.'

'What are you, a sissy or a man?' Losha boomed. 'She's longing for a Georgian man. You can tell by the way she's always looking around under those long black eyelashes. It's time you kissed her. Now you've got to kiss her tonight. Or I'll . . . shave off half my moustaches in protest!'

'You're joking, Losha!'

'No, I swear. Everyone will say, "Losha, where're your whiskers," and I'll tell 'em what a sissy you are. Ask her for a walk in Sokolniki Park. Give her a full meal. With girls, a full stomach goes straight between their legs. Kerboosh! Like a train when you put coal in the furnace. The train builds up steam and, kerboosh, it toots its whistle! Add a few shots of cognac. Losha knows. Call her now.'

George thought for a few moments. Losha was right. He did like Minka. He dreamed of her. It was now or never. 'Drop me off at the House on the Embankment.'

'Kerboosh! Attaboy!'

George, still in his Spartak football strip and white shorts, watched the limousine speed away across the bridge. He peered up at the eighth floor of the eastern wing of the modernist complex beside the Moskva. The lights burned in the Dorov apartment. He prayed Minka's father, the Uncooked Chicken, wouldn't answer: with any luck he would be at Old Square bullying his staff as usual. And surely her mother, Dr Dorova, was at the Kremlin Clinic? Ludmilla the housekeeper would be cooking supper for Senka, Demian and his own adorable Minka. He picked up the phone in the public phone booth, listening to it ringing, then he dropped the kopeck in.

'I'm listening.' Victory! Minka's voice, soft as the buzz of a bumblebee.

'What's news? It's George. My parents are driving me mad about . . . about the case. What about you?'

'Same here. Papa says the club was un-Bolshevik, a bourgeois heresy. He thinks everything's a conspiracy. But Mama says that's nonsense. The school's seething with rumours. It's ridiculous! Shall we ask Andrei and Serafima to join us somewhere? I called Andrei earlier, and said we might . . .'

George panicked suddenly. Losha would have to shave off half his moustaches. Courage!

'No, let's just be the two of us tonight. There's so much to discuss.'

A pause. Had she guessed? 'Oh, all right. Are you inviting me to supper?'

George made a thumbs-up: Kerboosh! A full stomach! 'I'm at the phone on the embankment. Looking up at your window. How about meeting in the usual place?'

'Give me ten minutes. I'd better put on a nice frock. See you soon!'

With his back against the phone box, George settled down to wait. Not long now.

* * *

Minka came out of the lobby of the House on the Embankment in a red summer dress that she knew she looked good in. But as she stepped into the breezy evening air, two men in suits took her arms with such smooth momentum that she found herself sitting between them in the back of a boxy Volga, the car of the middle bureaucracy, before she even had time to say anything.

'What's this? Who are you?' she whimpered as the car sped into the night.

The man in the passenger seat turned round. 'Just a few questions,' he said. 'You'll be back for your hot date before you know it.'

Across the street, the boy in the Spartak soccer strip standing next to a public telephone had seen it all.

'Minka! *No*,' said George, as he too was almost lifted off his feet and guided into a little Emka car. As it accelerated into the traffic and crossed the river, he kept saying to himself: Losha will have to shave off his moustaches . . . This was just about the deaths on the bridge, he told himself a few minutes later. He had nothing to hide. The Organs had to investigate it, and he would answer all their questions.

But if it was so straightforward, why was he so afraid? Why was his football shirt soaked with sweat? And why was he worried for Minka too? Surely his father would get him out soon enough. Then he remembered overhearing his father say to his stepmother: 'At this rate, I'll have to take them and pick them up every day until this blows over.' George had often heard them whispering behind the doors of the bathroom, and though the main part of the conversation was always inaudible, it virtually always ended with the words: 'Say nothing to anyone. Carry on as normal.'

His heart was thudding in his ears. This could mean only one thing: his father would do nothing.

High in his *kommunalka* apartment, Andrei was planning the evening. Losha was on his way to pick him up, and then he would meet up with George and his friends.

'Have fun,' said his mother. 'But be careful too. Watch your tongue.'

'Don't be silly, Mama. See you soon.'

But when he went downstairs, it wasn't Losha at the wheel, but another driver entirely.

'Hop in, boy,' said the driver. 'We'll have you with your friends sooner than you think.'

'But this isn't the way to Granovsky Street,' said Andrei five minutes later, as the car swept into Dzerzhinsky Square, where the buildings seemed like colossal granite tombs.

'You're not going to Granovsky Street,' replied the driver.

Andrei closed his eyes for a moment and experienced the terrifying feeling of falling into an abyss without end.

'You're not surprised, are you, kid?' asked the driver.

Andrei shook his head. He was not sure he could have spoken even if he had wanted to. He felt the joints in his arms and legs were made of jelly and his blood ice cold.

'My . . .' He could not say it.

'Your mother? She'll be fine. After all, she's used to this, isn't she?'

The Aragvi Restaurant that night. Maître d' Longuinoz escorted Sophia Zeitlin and some of her friends from the Mosfilm Studios to her favourite table just below the band. He held her wrist a second longer than necessary: he knew something important.

'Go right ahead to the table,' she called to her friends. 'Order me a cosmopolitan.' As she lingered beside the maître d', Longuinoz whispered: 'More on holiday. Up the hill.'

'Up the hill? How many? Who?' she replied breathlessly, her mouth close to his ear with its pearl earring.

'One Yak fighter plane. Second model. Check-up at the local doctors. Two o'clock appointment.'

Her heart raced: 'Oh God,' understanding his code instantly.

On holiday meant arrested. Up the hill was Lubianka Prison. Yaks were the brand of fighter plane built in Satinovgrad. Therefore 'Yak' was Satinov. 'Second model' meant second son – George. 'Local doctors' – Dr Dorova. 'Two o'clock': second child, i.e., Minka.

Sophia guessed that Longuinoz knew this because he performed discreet favours for the Chekist 'responsible workers,' favours no doubt involving food, girls and information. He was safe provided the information went only one way.

Longuinoz raised two hands as if to say: Sorry, but it's routine. As he showed her to the table, he whispered, 'A bit of advice, Sophia. Pull your horns in, darling!'

That night, Sophia could not eat her food. Would this touch her Serafima? she thought. They say I'm Stalin's top actress and he loves Constantin's scripts. Or am I believing my own publicity? Comrade Satinov is Stalin's favourite, and that hasn't protected George. Stalin demoted his son Vasily and disowned his other boy Yakov when he was captured by the Germans. The lesson? The shooting would be investigated, whoever was involved. And she could not help but remember those terrible years at the end of the 1930s when her beloved cousin Sashenka had vanished with her husband and children, vanished off the face of the earth.

She thought about her own life: her love affairs, her wartime movies, her hotbloodedness inherited from her incorrigible father, her addiction to those intrigues that made bearable the daily grind of the worthy institution that was marriage. But what if they arrested Serafima? Could she bear it?

15

The school run: eight fifteen the next morning. In the car park at Granovsky, Sophia Zeitlin got into the Rolls with Serafima.

'Why do you have to come? I hate you coming.' Serafima frowned at her mother. 'It's embarrassing enough to be in this car.'

'I'm just doing my maternal duty,' answered Sophia. She was dreading the scene at the school gates. 'Look! There're the Satinovs.'

They watched Hercules and Tamara Satinov get into their car with Marlen and Mariko. Tamara looked terrible. She had black circles around her eyes, her skin seemed tight across her narrow cheekbones – and the poor woman now had to teach classes in which her own stepson's chair was empty.

Serafima looked at her mother urgently. 'Where's George? Mama, you know something, don't you?'

'Good morning, Khirochenko,' Sophia said loudly to their chauffeur. They drove on in silence.

At the Golden Gates, Sophia read the parents and the missing children in a glance. The other parents moved too quickly, too skittishly, looking around but afraid of what they might find. Whose child had vanished into the maw of the Organs? The small crowd outside the school gates, formerly so fashionable and sociable, seemed suddenly despondent and doom-laden.

She met Hercules Satinov on his way out, Tamara having taken the children in with her.

'Hercules!' said Sophia. 'Aren't we good parents, dropping off our children so dutifully!'

'Duty. My second name,' replied Satinov.

The Titorenkos passed them, greeting Sophia and Satinov.

'Yes, comrades, a beautiful day, isn't it?' Satinov responded.

Sophia tried to imagine how the Titorenkos must be feeling, and realized that their apparent warmth was a mixture of solidarity and relief. Now that the Satinovs and Dorovs were in the same boat, their Vlad was no longer alone.

Sophia stood in the queue to shake hands with Director Medvedeva. The Dorovs were just ahead – with Demian and little Senka but no Minka. Dashka wore no make-up and her black hair was pulled back in a bun but she still looked lovely in a loose flowery blouse, and she had the chutzpah to chatter frivolously as if nothing were wrong.

'Doesn't the banquet seem an age ago,' said Sophia.

'Several lifetimes,' answered Dashka, bustling around her children. 'Now, did I remember all those textbooks? Every day there's more and more to remember! They want me to organize a charity quiz night. They seem to have forgotten that I have my own work to do. Oh, Demian, did I forget the maths homework? Right, off you go.'

Dashka usually just gave Demian a peck but today she hugged him.

'Get off, Mama.' The seventeen-year-old wriggled out of her arms. 'You're like a boa constrictor.'

'Oh dear,' sighed Dashka. 'I got that wrong.'

'You can kiss *me* as much as you like, Mama,' said Senka. Being a little boy, and therefore in love with his mother, Senka gave himself to Dashka, closing his eyes with a beatific smile – until Genrikh poked his wife's shoulder.

'Don't throttle the child,' said Genrikh sharply. He was paler and more shrivelled than ever. 'I've told you before. You indulge that boy too much. That's not how we Bolsheviks do it.'

'I can't get anything right today.' Dashka shrugged, smiling bravely.

At the front of the line, Director Medvedeva offered her hand. 'Good morning, Comrade Dorov, Dr Dorova, I see not everyone's in today. Summer colds are the worst, aren't they, Doctor?'

'Let's hope it doesn't spread,' agreed Dashka.

'Oh, Madame Zeitlin, good morning,' Director Medvedeva greeted Sophia. 'We do have a full turnout of parents today. It must be the sunshine.'

But Sophia was not listening. She was watching her daughter disappear down the school corridor.

Serafimochka is safe, she was thinking. So far.

In the interrogation room at Lubianka Prison, Kobylov leaned over the desk to smell Minka's thick hair.

'You even smell sweet. Like honey. What shampoo do you use? I want to tell my girls what to use. They could use a lesson from a little princess like you.'

Minka shrank from him, afraid of this bull of a man with his rings and his cologne so strong that she could taste the cloves on her tongue.

She had no idea who else was in prison being interrogated.

At first, as she lay awake all night in the cell that stank of detergent and urine, she had worried about George: had he waited for her? Had he thought she had stood him up? But then she realized that her arrest had been planned. Either the Chekists had been listening to her parents' phone or George had lured her out to be arrested. But surely he couldn't have done that. Not George.

By the morning, by the time the warders collected her slops bucket and then doled out the watery *kasha* and the thin tea with half a sugar lump, her date with George seemed a century ago. And then there were her parents. Did they know where she was? They seemed far away too. Even after a few hours of Lubianka, she was becoming a different person.

A warder opened the eyehole in her cell door that prisoners called 'the Judas port,' and then the locks ground open and she was marched along the corridors, up the stairs, down some metal steps, through a padded door with more locks, into a new building without the smell of urine and detergent and the room where she was now sitting in front of a desk with a single light. Moments later, the door had opened and this giant with general's stars on his shoulderboards and kinky oiled hair had appeared to stand, hands on hips, looking at her.

'Minka,' he said now. 'Help me tie this up. Tell me about Rosa and Nikolasha.'

'They were together.'

'As a couple? Did they fuck?'

'Oh no, no one does that sort of thing. But they were together.'

'Did they love each other?'

Minka looked down at her shoes: she was still wearing her pink sandals. 'Sort of,' she said, feeling a kind of betrayal.

Kobylov got up and left, kicking the door shut, swaggered

down the corridor to the next door and opened it. Inside another child sat on his own.

George Satinov looked up, startled.

'The girl named Rosa Shako loved Nikolasha Blagov?' asked Kobylov. George blinked at him as if slightly disorientated. He still wore his football strip. Here was a boy who breathed privilege, Kobylov noticed, a right little baron's son.

'Yes.'

'What sort of love? Puppy love? She wanted to marry him?'

'Real love. Yes. She was so sweet, so romantic about him.'

'I didn't ask for her biography. Was it a crush on her part or the real thing?'

'She probably wanted to marry him but—'

'Just answer the questions. She loved him. He loved her. Case closed.'

George's eye twitched and Kobylov could see that he was concentrating, choosing his words carefully. 'Well . . .'

'Good boy. That Minka's a right beauty. Your girl?'

'No.'

'Have you kissed her?'

'No.'

'Have you fucked her?'

'No, of course not.' George raised his hands to his face, blushing.

'What are you, a sissy?' Kobylov smiled, relishing his power over the boy. 'You see? I know all about you. Losha's my old buddy. Oh yes, we've had some moments together, I can tell you.'

Kobylov got up, slammed the door, and went into the next interrogation room, where Andrei Kurbsky was being interviewed by his keen subordinate, Mogilchuk.

'Rosa adored Nikolasha,' Andrei was saying. 'She'd do anything for him.'

'How did he treat her?' asked Kobylov, taking charge.

'He shouted at her. He belittled her. He was a real bully. He had to be in charge.'

'Is this one cooperating?' Kobylov asked Mogilchuk.

'I am,' said Andrei.

'You'd better be,' said Kobylov. 'Because we know who you are, and you're not like the others. We don't have to wear silk gloves with you, Kurbsky. You're the son of an Enemy of the People who's wormed your way into that school, into the golden youth. And what we're asking ourselves now is: Did you set up the murders?'

Andrei's face went white. 'No!'

'If you turn out to be connected to this murder, you'll receive the *Vishka*.' Kobylov used the acronym for the Highest Measure of Punishment: death. 'Eight grams in the neck.' He turned to Mogilchuk. 'Do you believe him, Comrade Colonel?'

'I'm not sure I do, Comrade General,' said Mogilchuk.

'Me neither. So Rosa and Nikolasha were love's young dream. Tell us what changed, Andrei?'

'I wouldn't say Nikolasha was . . .'

'What changed? What made him kill her? Tell me or I'll grind you into camp dust.'

Kobylov saw that Andrei was clasping his hands to stop them shaking.

'I think . . . I think Nikolasha heard about his father's posting to Mexico.'

Kobylov clapped his hands: 'Of course! The posting! Nikolasha was going away!'

He grabbed Mogilchuk's puny arm, heaved him out of the

room and down the corridor. The prospect of a case solved in a matter of hours made his nostrils flare.

Minka looked up as the two men came into her interrogation room. One was the bejewelled giant with the kinky hair, the other the ginger-haired colonel in spectacles, dull enough to be an accountant.

'Minka,' said the giant. 'When did Nikolasha find out about the posting to Mexico?'

'A day before the Victory Parade.'

'Was he happy about it?' asked the ginger man, leaning over her. She felt nauseated suddenly.

'No. He said he would refuse to go.'

'Good!' said the giant, clapping his hands. 'Comrade Mogilchuk, let's have a smoke.'

Out in the corridor, the two men huddled.

'What do you think, Comrade General?' With grandees like Kobylov, thought Mogilchuk, one should use their titles and ranks whenever possible. 'Are we getting close, Comrade General?'

'It was worth pulling 'em all in,' replied Kobylov. He rubbed his hands together. 'Let's go and report to Lavrenti Pavlovich Beria. He's going to be pleased with us, isn't he?'

16

Dr Dashka Dorova donned her white coat absentmindedly, shut the door of her surgery on the top floor of the Kremlevka, the Kremlin Clinic – and sat down on her velvet divan.

It was a cosy room decorated in old-style comfort with Persian rugs overlapping each other, oil paintings of dachas and woods from the turn of the century, an umbrella stand in brown leather, two soft leather chairs, the divan. To the right was a medical couch with a white curtain round it.

She usually sat behind an old desk with green leather on top and two Bakelite telephones on the side desk. The portrait of Stalin – always a guide to an official's importance – was medium-sized, not an original Gerasimov, and not an oil, but her safe was a large one because the medical records of the leaders were a state secret.

Finally alone, she found she was breathing fast. Keep it together, Dashka, she told herself. The pressure of her different roles – mother, wife, doctor, minister – was suffocating, and there was more. It was too much and something, however precious, had to be sacrificed. Even at home, she had to be careful: Genrikh believed the Party and its 'fearless knights,' as he called the secret police, could do no wrong. There was a Bolshevik way to behave and he, as the Party's conscience, its enforcer, would decide what it was because

Comrade Stalin trusted him to know. Genrikh decided every detail of their life. He had to. He was a Bolshevik leader and nothing – neither the décor of their dacha, nor the recipe for lunch, nor the rules for their children – was too small for him to pass judgement on it. And that made Dashka feel safe. Only her love of fashion had somehow been allowed outside Genrikh's control.

But now Minka had been arrested, her adorable Minka. Dashka's outer personality was sunny and exuberant, but within she was a tangle of emotions and anxieties. Minka, darling, where are you? Are you safe? she whispered. Answer their questions and come home. Thank God, her other children were safe.

She loved all four of them passionately, of course, but Senka, the fourth, the baby of her thirtieth year, the last, that miniature of herself with his long face, his full lips, the sprinkle of freckles across the nose, the olive skin, was her delight. Nothing else, no ambition, no other passion, however cherished, counted for more than her Senka, her Little Professor.

She closed her eyes. A drum beat behind them; her temples pounded. If only Genrikh would talk to her; if only he could bend his rules, checks and regulations a little. As it was, she felt utterly alone.

Her internal phone rang. 'Comrade Doctor, you have an appointment in five minutes,' her assistant announced.

Dashka had two offices: one was in the Ministry of Health and one was here at the Kremlevka, the place where the 'responsible workers' were treated by the finest specialists. When she started working there, the Kremlevka had been in the Kremlin itself, but now it stood in a new home on Granovsky, near the building where many of the leaders lived.

The daughter of a cultured Jewish family in Galicia (twelve

generations of rabbis, her mother claimed), Dashka had studied medicine in Odessa. After years of working as a cardiologist, she was promoted to the Kremlevka, where she had become the trusted doctor to many of the leaders. Most of them suffered from hypertension, arteriosclerosis and other complaints associated with overwork, a fatty diet, stress, lack of exercise, obesity and alcoholism.

Comrade Andreyev: headaches. Treatment: cocaine. Comrade Zhdanov: heart disease and alcoholism. Treatment: total rest and no alcohol. Comrade Beria: overweight. Excessive drinking. Treatment: vegetarian diet.

Then in late 1944, Comrade Molotov had summoned her to the Sovmin – Council of Ministers – in the Kremlin. 'Sit down, Comrade Doctor,' he said in that robotic voice of his. Dashka noticed his spherical head with its pince-nez was connected to his torso without much of a neck. 'Let me cut to the chase. How do you feel about becoming Health Minister?'

Dashka recoiled in surprise – shock, even. 'I'm a doctor,' she had protested. 'Even running the Kremlevka is not ideal. I've never worked in government.'

'Comrade Stalin wishes you to start tomorrow.' He looked down. In front of him on the desk was a note scrawled in red crayon. During their short meeting, she managed to see that it read: *Com. Molotov. Health Minister works poorly. Remove him and appoint lady cardiologist from Kremlevka. J. St.*

Comrade Stalin had not even remembered her name, she realized, but she had never met him. She was not particularly ambitious and had never sought such a promotion, so someone must have recommended her. Zhdanov or Beria?

Dashka had a powerful vocation: she adored medicine, loved to help people and had always aspired to be a doctor. Yes, she enjoyed the fine things in life, especially fashion (preferably imported from Paris), but she lived for her family, more specifically for her children.

Now, at nine thirty a.m., she had an appointment that normally would not have concerned her. But she could not stop thinking of Minka and worrying about the other children. She had not slept and the worst of it was that she could do nothing to help them. Nothing at all.

She knew the leaders. She had seen them without their shirts on. She knew their medical secrets and often more, because even Bolshevik grandees felt the need to confide in their doctor.

She was waiting for her next patient, surely a powerful man who could get Minka released. But even asking for special help was against the rules.

No, she must continue as if her darling Minka were not a mile away in a cell in the most dreaded prison in Europe. She raised her hands to her face. She would not let herself cry. She must not!

One of the phones on her desk rang and, shaking herself free of the silent tears running down her face, she rose and answered it.

'Comrade Doctor, the comrade is waiting for you.'

Dashka looked at herself in the mirror. She wore a little mascara to hide her tired brown eyes and her black hair was pulled back in a strict bun but she looked presentable. Her mother had taught her that the greater the challenge, the better you should look. Dashka knew she was a beautiful woman.

She pulled back her shoulders, clipped her stethoscope around her neck, opened the door and gave her dazzling smile. 'Comrade, come on in.'

* * *

'Comrade Beria is not in his office,' said the aide who ran Beria's complicated schedule. 'Please wait.' He nodded to Kobylov to take a seat at the far end of the otherwise empty ante-room.

Kobylov grunted and shifted his considerable weight on the leather sofa as he resigned himself to a wait.

After ten minutes, one of the Bakelite phones on the aide's side desk rang. 'Comrade Kobylov, Comrade Beria is on the phone for you,' said the aide.

Kobylov seized it hungrily: 'Lavrenti Pavlovich,' he said. 'We've solved it. Yes, I'll tell you. We've closed it! Well . . .' Here Kobylov grinned triumphantly at Mogilchuk, who was still in awe of Beria. 'It's like this: Nikolasha Blagov loves Rosa Shako; she loves him. They want to get married. He's a fucking degenerate who talks about death all the time; she's a droopy, simpering rose petal – but he loves her to death. Literally. He hears his father's being sent off to Mexico. He's going to lose Rosa. Perhaps never see her again. So he kills her and then himself. Solved!'

A hush except for a tinny voice blaring faintly out of the earpiece. Kobylov straightened up by degrees until he was standing to attention. 'Right. Of course. We'll be right down there, Lavrenti Pavlovich!'

Kobylov banged down the phone, feeling his heart racing and his hands sweating.

'You idiot!' Grabbing Mogilchuk by the arm and heaving him out of Beria's antechamber. The moment he was outside, he punched him in the face: 'This is far from solved and you've made a fool of me in front of Comrade Beria!'

'But I . . . aah!' Mogilchuk stepped back and felt his cheek. Stalin had once recommended Management by Punching. It was Bolshevik leadership. But his lip was bleeding. 'Your rings cut me!'

'You want another smack in the kisser, you pansy? Come on!' boomed Kobylov, marching down the corridor and out into the courtyard where a group of drivers waited.

They rode in a Packard down the hill around the Kremlin and up towards Gorky, turning left on to Granovsky. They did not stop at the building where the Satinovs lived, however, but drove on.

At the end of the street, the car turned left in to a new building with no name. Two checkpoints waved them through. Kobylov and Mogilchuk, who was by now holding a handkerchief to his mouth, jumped out and hurried up the steps. Nurses in pinafores and a doctor in a white coat were smoking in the lobby of the building where four bodyguards in blue MGB tabs kept watch brandishing PPSh machine-guns.

At the end of the hall, Colonel Nadaraia, Beria's chief bodyguard, a small sturdy man with fair hair and slightly bulging eyes, was expecting them. He kissed Kobylov with the camaraderie of drinking partners. 'Hurry up, Bull,' he said in their native Georgian. 'And who's your ginger friend with the bleeding lip? Hurry up. He's ready!'

One of Nadaraia's men was holding open the lift even though a handful of doctors and nurses were waiting to get in. They rode down two levels and when the doors opened, they found another two bodyguards waiting.

'This way!' said a third, leading them down a corridor with a blue-tiled floor and through two double swing doors. Kobylov noticed that the deeper they went into the building, the colder the air became, the more acrid the stench of formaldehyde and carbolic soap. Finally, they entered a chilly white-tiled room with channels set in the concrete floor, like an abattoir. One entire wall of steel doors faced the men.

'Ah, there you are, Sherlock Holmes! What kept you? Solving more cases, you fat fool?' Lavrenti Beria, wearing a summery cream jacket, a flowery Georgian shirt open at the neck and baggy linen trousers, stood between two white slabs. 'Don't you think I've got better things to do? My wife's away in Gagra and I've got a new fourteen-year-old girl waiting for me at the dacha.'

'I apologize, Lavrenti Pavlovich,' said Kobylov, bowing slightly.

'Comrade Stalin will want a report tonight. But don't rush so much, Bull. That's how we make mistakes. Things take as long as they take.' Beria glanced at Mogilchuk. 'What happened to your lip?'

'I banged it on a door.'

Beria laughed. 'I can see the imprint of Kobylov's rings. But don't blame your subordinates, Bull. It was your theory, right? Professor Schpigelglaz, where are you?'

'Here!' trilled an adenoidal voice with a Yiddish accent. 'Stwaightforward, very stwaightforward, comrades.' Beria stepped aside to reveal Professor Schpigelglaz, whose angular glasses with huge black frames dwarfed his beaky face. He had a white coat and a cloud of frizzy white hair to match.

The professor was such a wraith that he had been entirely concealed by Beria's paunchy bulk. 'Gentlemen, I have something to show you.'

'Get it right,' Beria said, 'and you go back to your cushy *sharashka* laboratory. Get it wrong and you'll be hauling logs in the Arctic.'

'Ach, no danger of that!' Professor Schpigelglaz seemed

delighted to have such an interesting case. 'May I pwoceed? Now, let's roll out our young overnight guests. That's what we call them here – overnight guests.' He gestured to a hollow-eyed young man who looked as if he had spent too much time in the company of the dead. The assistant opened the steel doors to pull out a metal platform on which lay the waxy naked body of a male red-haired teenager. As the platform came out, wheeled legs dropped down from it, enabling the hollow-eyed young man to push the trolley alongside one of the slabs. Then he and another assistant lifted it on to the slab.

'Let's see now, gentlemen.' Kobylov enjoyed being addressed as a gentleman – the professor talked as if the Revolution had never happened and he and Beria were a pair of aristocratic generals. 'Who are our overnight guests? *Ach ya*. Blagov, Nikolasha. Eighteen years old,' said the professor, reading from a label tied to the big toe.

The body looked to Kobylov as if it had been filleted: jagged red lines – like railways on a map of flesh or a zip made of skin – ran around the hairline of the head and from the throat down the centre of the chest to split at the waist. All was clean and neat – except the jaw and mouth. All the cleaning in the world could not put that together again. The assistants then returned to the steel doors. This time a naked female body was laid on the other slab. Again, a label on the toe.

'Shako, Rosa. Eighteen years old.'

Beria whistled through his teeth, looking at the teenage girl. 'Shame we didn't get to her when she was alive, eh, Bull?'

'Not my type,' said Kobylov, grinning. 'A little dainty for me.'

Beria turned to the professor. 'Start with the boy,' he instructed.

'Ach yes, Lavrenti Pavlovich. Well, it's quite obvious when you examine the wounds. The boy has a diwect bullet wound fired from a Mauser service revolver. One shot.' He leaned over Nikolasha's face. 'There's the entwy wound in the mouth which shattered the jaw and passed through the cwanial chamber, causing catastwophic twauma.' He twisted the boy's head with its slicked-back red hair. 'And here's the exit wound, back of the head. Death instantaneous.'

'And the girl?' said Beria.

'Ach yes, the girl.' He crossed to the other slab. 'Here on the right breast, gentlemen, we see a single shot to the heart. Vewy neat. We dug out the bullet. Here it is. You may keep it, dear Genewal, as a memento of me, ha ha. Yes, a standard service revolver was used. Mauser. Death also instantaneous.'

'There it is,' said Beria.

'So *he* shot her and then himself? Like I said?' said Kobylov.

'Please enlighten my blockheaded comrade, Professor,' Beria said.

'All right, gentlemen. Nikolasha Blagov was killed by a shot fired at about seven metres. You see the wound.' He leaned over the slab until he was very close to the shattered mouth. 'No powder burns. Now look at her wound.' He switched to the other slab with surprising agility. 'Look! Hers is blackened quite clearly awound the edges. Her wound is point-blank. It was *she* who killed him and then herself. She made a mess of him, but as is typical of a female suicide: one shot to the heart. A lady likes a tidy house, yes? Her face is immaculate. You see, stwaightforward, all very stwaightforward.'

'Thank you, Professor.' Beria looked at Kobylov and Mogilchuk and opened his hands. 'You got it the wrong way round, you imbeciles. Remember, the dead are a marshal's daughter and a deputy minister's son. Remember whose children we've arrested. Get a move on or you'll find yourself guarding scum in Kolyma. The Instantsiya is impatient.' He turned away from them, rubbing his hands. 'Now, I've got a girl waiting who's good enough to eat! Fresh as summer strawberries. And then a game of netball with the guards.'

He swept out of the morgue, followed by Colonel Nadaraia and the other bodyguards.

'What energy Comrade Beria has,' murmured Kobylov. 'And what a brain. Every moment of every day is organized as precisely as a Swiss watch. We are pygmies beside him. Come on, Mogilchuk, let's return to our school games.'

17

Tamara had scarcely spoken to Hercules in their apartment. Was it bugged? He thought so. She couldn't speak to him in the car because of the guards; nor at the Golden Gates.

So, most unusually, after drop-off at the school, she said, 'I need to talk to you.'

'Do you have time to walk with me to Alexandrovsky Gardens?' Satinov asked her.

Tamara did not have a class until ten so they walked towards the Kremlin in silence. That day Hercules was not in uniform but a summer suit, with a white fedora low over his eyes, and Tamara thought what a handsome man he was.

Two guards walked ahead, Losha behind, and their car purred twenty metres behind them. The summer blizzard of gossamer seeds swirled around them. Young soldiers, a girl in naval uniform, pensioners in cloth caps walked the streets, eyes half closed, cushioned by the soft, easy air. Tamara noticed how sometimes these sleepwalking members of the public were jolted awake with the spark of recognition. 'Wasn't that . . . ?' they asked their companions as they passed Satinov.

If only they knew that our life isn't as easy as it appears, Tamara thought.

Having checked everyone was out of earshot, she put her

hand through Satinov's arm. Ever since George had disappeared, she had longed to talk to him.

She adored her Hercules. Amongst those coarse, hard-drinking leaders, with their fat, depressed wives and spoilt, disturbed children, Tamara's friends would often say, 'If only I had a husband like Satinov. Tamara, you're so lucky,' and she would reply, 'He's a wonderful husband but I just wish he talked to me more . . .'

Despite their years together, she found it hard to breathe around his coldness, his detachment. Why didn't he cuddle her? Why couldn't she be with a man who talked to her and told her about his day? It had been the same when his eldest son, Vanya, was killed. She wanted to shriek and tear her clothes – but he just seemed to *absorb* it. She wondered if he really wasn't that deep, if he was simply uncomplicated or, worse, flinthearted. He had cried once, but afterwards he just said to her, 'The whole Motherland is weeping, Tamriko. We're no different.' And he had returned to the front, leaving her to comfort the other children. Now his son was in prison and still she could not reach him.

'Hercules, is there any news of George?' she asked now.

'Nothing.'

'But you saw . . . *him* last night?' She meant Stalin, of course.

'Yes.'

'Did he say anything?'

Satinov shook his head. 'He's exhausted.'

'Did Beria say anything?'

'No.'

'I do hate that man. He's repulsive, Hercules. How can you work with him?'

'The Revolution needs people like him. He's our most capable Bolshevik manager, whatever his faults.'

'He's a rapist, a criminal.'

'Tamriko!' He sighed. 'Let's be grateful that I am friendly with him now, of all times.'

'Oh God!' So George was in Beria's hands. Her eyes filled with tears. 'I can't sleep, Hercules, I'm so anxious. Usually I love my classes but the school is like a hornets' nest. I look at George's seat . . . and Andrei, Vlad, Minka – all absent! And sweet Rosa. I want to cry. The children can't concentrate either; some are terrified, some are queuing up to denounce their friends. The common room feels . . . like it did in the thirties. Dr Rimm is up to something . . .' She hesitated to share the petty intrigues of the common room with her husband, but she couldn't stop herself, and out it all came.

'How very familiar,' he said afterwards with a thin smile. 'It's like the Politburo in miniature.'

'I miss George bitterly, and he's not even my son. How are you finding it?'

'I don't sleep a lot. For once, Stalin's schedule suits me.'

'You were so strong about Vanya . . .'

'Listen, Tamriko,' said Satinov tersely. 'You must hold the line. Especially at school.'

'But Mariko is asking for George, and Marlen too.'

'You must tell them not to. George and his friends will be well treated and home soon. They are simply witnesses. Two children are dead. They have to investigate. Find out what happened. That's all.'

'Then why is it so secret?'

'It's the way we Bolsheviks do things.'

'But you're one of the most powerful men in the country, so why can't you speak to someone? Find out when George is coming home?'

'Stalin is dead set against any favouritism.'

And that's supposed to make me feel better? Tamara thought. 'Of course,' she replied.

'Look, we built Lenin's state, we won the war. When you chop wood, chips fly.'

Not that damn slogan again! But she nodded submissively.

Satinov stopped. 'I've got to go.' He kissed her forehead and she watched him enter the Kremlin through the Spassky Gate.

Sometimes, she thought, it's a lovely thing to be married to an iron hero; sometimes, it's just too painful for words.

Beria collapsed wheezily by the side of his new girl, his green-grey man-breasts hanging pendulously like an old camel's humps. What a session! Then the *vertushka*, the special Kremlin line, rang. Doesn't a man get a moment's peace? he thought, picking it up.

'Comrade Beria?'

'Speaking.'

'Comrade Stalin expects you,' said the expressionless voice of Poskrebyshev. The line went dead.

It was five past midnight but in Stalin's world, it was the middle of the day. Beria dressed quickly in his usual garish Georgian shirt and loose jacket but then turned to look one last time at the fourteen-year-old girl lying naked on his bed, the skin of her flat belly a little flushed and creased by his weight.

'Colonel Nadaraia will drive you home,' he said softly, sitting beside her for a moment. Thank God he had managed to get his pox cleared up before he found this treasure. But he had to lose weight! Leaping around with a girl this age tired a man out. Memo to Comrade Beria: eat more salad! His hand actually trembled as he stroked her long hair, the satin of her lower back. 'But first Colonel Nadaraia is going to show you the apartment I've chosen for you and your mother.'

'Oh Lavrenti, thank you! How amazing. Mama will be so happy.'

'She will,' he agreed. He knew her mother. *She* had been his mistress first.

'You're pleased with me, aren't you?' she asked, frowning sweetly.

'Yes, yes I am. See you tomorrow.'

I am really very taken with her, he thought as his Packard raced through the Spassky Gate in the Kremlin and round to the Little Corner of the triangular Yellow Palace. Yes, this perfect girl is melting the heart of one of the hardest men in our carniverous era.

Beria took the lift to the second floor, showed his pass to two sets of guards (even he was not exempt) and hurried down the interminable corridors with the blue carpet held in place by brass rings set in the parquet. Two more checkpoints, and finally he was handing in his Tokarev pistol to the guards outside Comrade Stalin's office.

Two man-sized globes stood by the doors. A couple of ministers and several generals were waiting stiffly in the ante-room, grown men holding their papers on their knees like frightened schoolchildren. Quite an appropriate analogy, thought Beria, as schoolchildren were one of things he had come to discuss.

He was no longer so impressed with the Great Stalin, though. He had seen Stalin's dire mistakes in the early weeks of the war, his obstinacy, his panic, the waste of millions of lives; yes, Stalin would not have won the war without his help. Didn't Stalin realize that he, Beria, and the Organs had held the state together? Beria saw himself not just as a Chekist but as the most capable statesman in the entire leadership.

The old sot doesn't appreciate my talents, he thought, although *he* now thinks himself a genius and never stops boasting!

'The Master will see you now,' said Poskrebyshev, the livid red skin on his face wizened as if he had been burnt. The two men did not like each other: Poskrebyshev was a lowly cringing ink-shitter who hated Beria, and blamed him for the execution in 1939 of his beloved young wife after which he continued to serve Stalin loyally. Beria couldn't tell him, of course, that although he had brought Stalin the evidence that his wife had Trotskyite connections, it was Stalin who had ordered her killing.

As Poskrebyshev, in tunic and britches, escorted him through the short corridor that led to the double doors, Beria asked quietly, 'Is it a good evening?' He meant: Is Stalin in a good mood?

'It's a beautiful summer's night,' replied Poskrebyshev, meaning: Yes, he is. 'He's going to look at his new uniforms. Here they are!'

Three strapping young men, athletes all, entered the antechamber wearing flamboyant cream, braided, golden uniforms that wouldn't have been out of place in an Offenbach opera. One even had a golden cloak. In their wake shuffled Lerner, the tailor, his nimble white-tipped fingers a-twitch with tape measure and chalk.

'Very smart,' chuckled Beria.

'Stand over there,' said Poskrebyshev to the youths. He then lifted one of his many phones and said: 'Comrade Stalin, Lerner's here. The uniforms.'

Sometimes life was just too absurd, Beria reflected as the

double doors opened and Stalin emerged, drawn in the face, his grey hair standing on end as if razor cut. He was wearing a plain tunic with just his marshal's shoulderboards and a single Order of Lenin.

'Who are they?' he asked gruffly, looking at the youths. 'What are these peacocks doing here?' The three models saluted. Lerner bowed.

'The generalissimo's uniforms for your approval, Comrade Stalin,' said Poskrebyshev. 'Lerner's here to show you the finer details.'

Lerner, who'd started work sewing the Tsar's uniforms, bowed again.

'Comrade Stalin is grateful to you, Lerner,' Stalin said, always polite to 'service workers.' But to Beria and Poskrebyshev, he snarled: 'Whose idea was this? Yours, Lavrenti? Well, they're not right for me. I need something more modest. Lerner, do you want me to look like a doorman or a bandmaster?' He turned and went back into his office.

'You're designing for Comrade Stalin, not Hermann Göring!' hissed Beria to Lerner. 'It's back to the drawing-board!'

Lerner wrung his hands and backed away into the antechamber.

As Poskrebyshev closed the doors behind him, Beria entered Stalin's spacious room, with its ruffled white blinds covering most of the windows. On the far wall were portraits of Marx and Lenin and the latter's death mask. A long table with twenty seats, each with notebooks and ink blotters, filled the centre. At the far end was a desk with an extension holding about eight Bakelite telephones and a small table at right angles that formed a T-shape. The desk was very neat with scarcely anything on it except a blotter, an ashtray with a pipe that contained a lit cigarette smoking in its bowl, and a glass of steaming tea. Behind was a grey safe as large as a man and a small door whence Stalin now appeared, bearing a bottle of Armenian cognac. He sat down at the desk, poured two teaspoons of the spirit into the tea, which he stirred, and then looked up.

'*Gamajoba.*' He often spoke Georgian to Beria when they were alone. 'What have you got for me?'

'Much to report, Josef Vissarionovich.'

'What's the plan for the German trip?'

Beria opened the leather portfolio and brought out some papers. Even after all these years, all their shared schemes, triumphs of war and construction, and their little secrets of 'black work,' murder and torture, Stalin still treated Beria like a trusted servant who specialized in dirty jobs. Yes, there had been family holidays on the Black Sea – Stalin liked Beria's wife, Nina, and trusted his son, Sergo – but still Beria felt under-appreciated. Just in January, at one of the dinners in Yalta, Stalin had introduced him to President Roosevelt as 'my Himmler.' It was at that moment when he started to hate Stalin. The drunken braggart! Where would Stalin be without him?

'The meetings with the American President and British Prime Minister are set to begin on the seventeenth of July,' said Beria.

'I'll arrive last. Let the others arrive first,' Stalin said.

'Understood.'

'I miss Roosevelt. This Truman's not a patch on Roosevelt. As for Churchill, he'll reach into your pocket to steal a kopeck; yes, even a kopeck.'

'Everything is ready for you in Berlin,' Beria told him. 'The route to Potsdam is 1,923 kilometres. To provide proper security, 1,515 MVD/MGB operatives and 17,409 MVD troops are placed as follows: in USSR, 6 men per kilometre; in Poland, 10 men per kilometre; in Germany, 15 per kilometre. On the route, 8 armoured trains will patrol. Seven MVD regiments and 900 bodyguards will protect you. Inner security by the 6th Department will function in three concentric circles of 2,041 men and—'

'All right,' said Stalin, waving his hand. He relit the pipe, puffing clouds of smoke and watching them waft up, his eyes moist slits, almost closed.

'It's all in the memo here.' Beria handed over some typed sheets.

'I don't want honour guards and brass bands when I arrive. I mean it. I'm tired.'

'Understood.'

'Anything more about the new American weapon?'

'The nuclear device. Our agents in the British Foreign Office report that it is almost complete. It is possible America will use it against the Japanese. It has astonishing destructive power.'

'Keep me closely informed. Now, what about the schoolchildren?'

'We have made some progress . . .'

'Some of them are with you?'

Beria knew that 'with you' meant in his prisons. 'Yes, four of them,' and he gave their names.

'One of Satinov's boys, eh? What were they playing at?'

'We've investigated, and discovered that it was the girl – Marshal Shako's daughter – who shot the Blagov boy, Nikolasha.'

'Ah – Romeo and Juliet, is that it?'

'She was in love with him. But he was infatuated with another girl, Serafima Romashkina – you know, the actress's daughter?'

'As I thought. A love triangle.'

'You were right. When Rosa Shako found out Ambassador

Blagov was being posted abroad and the boy with him, something snapped and she shot him.'

'And then herself?' Suicide was a sensitive subject with Stalin: his wife, Nadya, had shot herself. A long silence. 'Nadya would be forty-three now.' Stalin sighed and then collected himself. Silence. Just the mellow puckering of an old man puffing on a pipe.

Beria waited. He knew Stalin was thinking about the Children's Case. Beria had no wish to interrogate teenagers. It was messy, too close somehow to his own beloved son, who had also attended School 801. 'They're just harmless children. Let's release them,' he was tempted to say. But he and Stalin knew better than anyone that there was no tool on earth as powerful in the management of men as a threat to their children. He raised his cloudy colourless eyes to meet Stalin's remorseless gaze.

'You said they were in fancy dress?' A tigerish grin.

'Correct,' said Beria. Stalin tapped his pipe. Now he was waiting. Beria shuffled his papers and read from Kobylov's report. '"Both dead children were members of a secret group named the Fatal Romantics' Club. Covert chosen membership. Clandestine meetings in graveyards. Obsession with romance and death."'

'Were they reading *Dracula*?' Stalin asked, puzzled.

'Pushkin.'

'At least they were studying good literature.'

'As you saw at once, it's a teenage love story. An old chestnut. Should we release the children now?' Immediately Beria regretted his words.

'Do you know what they were doing?'

'Kobylov says they were playing something called the Game.'

'And Kobylov didn't think to find out what this Game was?

And where did Rosa Shako get the gun?' Beria knew that Stalin had never forgiven his brother-in-law for giving his wife the pistol that she used to shoot herself. 'There's more to do in the Children's Case.'

Stalin leaned back in his chair and pressed a button that rang a bell outside.

Poskrebyshev opened the door and stood to attention, notebook raised, pencil at the ready. 'Yes, Josef Vissarionovich?'

'Sasha, let's invite some comrades to watch a movie and have a snack. Call Comrade Satinov and the rest of the Seven.'

It was already half past midnight. From Vladivostok in the east (where the Soviet armies were massing to attack Japan) to Berlin in the west, the Russians and their new subject peoples slept, but not their leaders. In Moscow, ministers, marshals and Chekists waited at their desks for Comrade Stalin to leave the office. Now that Stalin had summoned the Seven for dinner, Poskrebyshev would let a few favoured friends know that they could go home too.

'Are you busy later, Comrade Beria?'

'*Didi madlobt*, thanks so much,' said Beria in Georgian. Busy later? Who dared be busy later? Not him, that was for sure.

18

At one in the morning, the Judas port on George Satinov's cell door clicked open. He was sleeping properly for the first time because he was sure the interrogations were over. His interrogators had seemed satisfied with his answers and then he had been taken back to his cell and given a meal. Now suddenly he feared there was more. The clink of keyrings, the clip of boots on concrete, and then, moments later, the locks were grinding.

'Get dressed. Now.' He heard other doors opening, other locks turning and wondered who else from his school was there. As he was escorted along the corridors, he heard another prisoner coming behind him. Was it Vlad? Or Minka? He prayed that Minka was all right and that no one else was in trouble: not Serafima, not Andrei. He longed to see Minka, so that she would know he was nearby and that he had not betrayed her. I wonder if I am in love with her? he asked himself. How does one know?

Lines of cell doors, detergent vying with sweat, metallic stairways. 'Eyes straight ahead! No talking!' snapped one of the warders.

'Prisoner, step inside the box,' said the other, and George was forcefully guided into a metal box like an upright coffin: its door was closed, a lock turned. Short of breath, George started to sweat. He heard another prisoner coming the same way, and that prisoner too was ordered: 'Eyes straight! No talking!'

In the gait of the steps, in the breaths of the prisoner, he imagined it was Minka. For a moment he tensed his vocal cords and prepared to shout: 'Minka! Is it you? I know you're here!' But soon the corridor was empty again, the coffin unlocked, and he was free to breathe. Up stairways and down, through more sealed doors. As he was marched towards the interrogation rooms, he thought of his father's fury: 'I'll strangle you myself,' he'd warned George and Marlen if he found they were involved in the shooting. And now George was. What would his father say?

Inside the room, George found not just the gingery, bespectacled Mogilchuk but the giant Kobylov too. Both were tense, focused. There was going to be no more playing around.

'We're almost ready to send you home,' Mogilchuk said. He held out a cup of coffee. 'For you!' and he placed it in front of him.

'Thank you,' said George. He sipped the coffee. 'Do you always work at night?'

'You know how it works from your father,' answered Mogilchuk.

'Now,' said Kobylov, his bejewelled fingers drumming like cockroaches with diamonds on their backs. 'Just tell us: what was the Game?'

'The Game?' George said, surprised.

'We want the details,' explained Mogilchuk.

'It was a pantomime, really.'

'Who ran it?'

'Nikolasha and Vlad.'

'And you wore fancy dress?'

'Yes, but why does that matter? It has nothing to do with what happened.'

'Let us be the decider of that,' said Kobylov. 'Continue.'

Minka shook her head. 'I never took it seriously. I thought it was absurd.'

'But what was the Game *about*, Prisoner Dorova?' Kobylov asked. Mogilchuk sat beside him, writing.

'It was a re-enactment.'

'Of what?'

'Of literature or history.'

'You're losing me, girl, just spit it out. We need this fixed by dawn.'

'Sometimes it was the death of Pushkin himself. We'd re-enact the duel in which he was killed—'

'—and sometimes,' continued Vlad in the third interrogation room, 'it was the duel from Pushkin's *Onegin*.'

'Who decided?' asked Mogilchuk.

'Nikolasha.'

'Then what?'

'We borrowed the costumes and turned up at the graveyard where Nikolasha led our rituals.'

'Rituals?' repeated Kobylov, who was by this time leaning against the wall, chain-smoking.

'We would chant things.'

'What things?' Kobylov leaned over Vlad, breathing smoke in his face.

'You're frightening me,' said Vlad.

'I'll really frighten you if you don't get on with it.'

'Well, first . . . Nikolasha checked who was there in his Velvet Book of Love and he'd say something like, "Comrade Romantics, we're here to celebrate passion over science. Without love let us die young." And everyone repeated: "Without love let us die young!"'

Kobylov shook his head, and exhaled a lungful of smoke with a sticky cough. 'Sounds to me like voodoo!'

'That's what I thought,' Andrei agreed. 'I only went once to this secret club. It worried me. It was un-Soviet. But no one took it seriously except Nikolasha, Vlad and Rosa.'

'Did she chant with the others?'

'Yes, and then she said, "Who dies tonight?"'

'This is dark stuff,' Kobylov said. 'Carry on, Prisoner Kurbsky.'

'Then Nikolasha decided who would play Onegin and Lensky. Onegin kills Lensky in the duel.'

'Then what?'

'We played out the duel, reading the poetry.'

'Using which guns?'

'The duelling pistols from the theatre.'

'And the duelling pistols fired blanks?'

'Yes.'

'So there were no real guns?'

'Not that I ever saw.'

'So they would choose their pistols from the cases and then, holding them up, they would take the steps,' said George.

'Like a real duel?' said Mogilchuk, looking interested for the first time that night.

'Yes, sometimes I did the counting.'

'Count what?'

'The steps in the duel. I had to say: *"Approach at will!"* That night, Nikolasha was playing Onegin, and Rosa was playing Lensky, and they started to take the steps at the far end of the bridge. In their costumes. It was crowded, but we always followed the poem exactly.'

'What did they say?'

'I can't remember exactly.'

'Dammit, prisoner, I'm not here for a literature lesson.'

'Lensky tried to aim, but Onegin – that's Nikolasha – was quicker.'

'So you saw the pistols?' asked Kobylov.

'Yes. Just the duelling pistols from the theatre,' said Minka.

'And what did they look like that night?'

'Like they always did. We weren't paying that much attention, General.'

'What were you doing?'

'We were drinking vodka. And laughing. George, Andrei, Serafima . . .'

'You weren't watching?'

'The bridge was packed with people so I kept losing sight of George and Rosa and . . . Anyway, we thought it was a joke.' Minka started to cry.

'I took it seriously,' admitted Vlad. He rubbed his eyes, fingers jiggling compulsively, and Kobylov could tell he was still in shock. 'Some of the others were mucking around and ruining the evening. But the Game was a serious tribute to Pushkin. Nikolasha got angry when the others fooled about.'

'Concentrate, Prisoner Titorenko. Tell us what happened.'

'Because Rosa was Lensky, it meant she was the one who was going to die.'

'How do you all prepare for your roles?'

'I had the costume: frock coat, boots, tricorne hat. Whoever played Lensky, in this case Rosa, had fake blood from the theatre ready.'

Fake blood, wrote Mogilchuk.

'They took the steps. Nikolasha cocked his pistol.'

'And Rosa levelled hers?'

'Yes.'

'Nikolasha aimed his?'

'Yes, and he recited the verses from Pushkin that recount the duel: *And that was when Onegin fired!*'

'I don't want your fucking poetry!' Kobylov banged the table. 'Just get on with it!'

'It was very dramatic. Nikolasha would fire his pistol and then Rosa would fall as we'd recite:

'No earthly power
Can bring him back: the singer's gone,
Cut down by fate at the break of dawn!'

Mogilchuk leaned forward. 'But he didn't fire his pistol, did he?'

'No,' said Andrei. 'Onegin was meant to kill Lensky. Then they were supposed to put:

'The frozen corpse on the sleigh, preparing
To drive the body home once more.'

'But that didn't happen?'

'No, because some drunken sailors kept interfering, and the bridge was so crowded that most of us got separated . . .'

'But Nikolasha and Rosa were still holding the pistols?'

'I think so. We were looking for them. We'd all drunk vodka and we were fooling around. But I couldn't see them and then I suddenly heard two shots.' He put his hands to his ears, and looked at Kobylov, stricken. 'I can still hear them. Boom! Boom! Even now!'

'*That* was the Game?' Kobylov scratched his kinky hair. It was four a.m. and they were taking a break outside the interrogation rooms. 'That's *all* it was?'

'Ludicrous children,' agreed Mogilchuk.

'And they died for this childish pantomime.' Kobylov rubbed his face wearily. 'Come on, comrade. Before we report, we need one more piece of the puzzle.'

'Now, George,' persevered Mogilchuk. 'We're nearly there. But I need to ask you about the murder weapon. It was a Mauser service pistol and we found it on the ground. Now we know who killed who—'

'Nikolasha killed Rosa, the bastard,' George replied eagerly.

'Just answer the fucking question, boy. Did Nikolasha have a pistol?'

George leaned back in his chair. 'I have no idea. I'm sure his parents have guns in the house.'

'I'm sure they do too. But suppose it wasn't Nikolasha who fired the Mauser at all. Suppose it was Rosa.'

'Did you see Rosa with a Mauser pistol, prisoner?' Kobylov asked Minka.

'No. Nikolasha was the one obsessed with guns and death.'

'So did you see Nikolasha with a pistol?'

'Yes.'

'A duelling pistol?'

Minka put her head in her hands to think. When she looked up again, Kobylov could see that she was so tired she wasn't focusing properly.

'No,' she said slowly. 'It was a real pistol.'

Kobylov smiled. At last they were getting somewhere. 'Where did he get that?'

Minka looked worried suddenly. 'I don't know.'

'So how did *you* see the Mauser?'

'I was watching Nikolasha as he took the duelling pistols out of their case before the Game started. He put the real pistol in their place.'

'Did he plan to use the real pistol – but changed his mind at the last moment?'

'Possibly. He believed all sorts of stupid things. He said the duel was the front line between ordinary life and extraordinary romance.' Tears began to run down Minka's face again. 'He used to say things like that. Perhaps a real gun would have made it even more real.'

'Don't hide anything from us, Andrei,' said Mogilchuk. 'You know that your mother is all alone. She is worried, Andrei. You're all she has left.'

'How did Nikolasha get hold of that pistol?' asked Kobylov.

'After the dinner at Aragvi, in the car park, Nikolasha asked if any of us had a gun.'

'Why would he ask that?'

Andrei shrugged. 'He said silly things all the time. He said, "Death is better than routine." Total nonsense.'

'And did anyone have a gun?'

Andrei hesitated, staring down at the table.

'I'd hate to see your mother on the trains for Norilsk,' insinuated Mogilchuk. 'Most people never arrive in the camps. They die on the way and when the train slows down, the other prisoners throw out the bodies. Did you know that, Andrei?'

'No.' He was shaking.

'Think, Andrei – who is more important to you? Your mother or those brats?'

Andrei sat up and looked directly at Mogilchuk. 'Nikolasha asked George, who said he didn't have a gun. But his father's bodyguards did.'

Kobylov sat down beside Vlad Titorenko and put his arm around him. 'You see? This can be fun. Now, where did Rosa get the gun?'

'Rosa? I never saw her with it.'

'But you saw her open the gun case?'

'Yes.' Vlad was whispering.

'Which Rosa picked up. *That* was how she got the gun,' said Kobylov slowly.

'But Rosa loved Nikolasha,' said George. 'She was never interested in guns. She never hurt a fly.'

Kobylov and Mogilchuk were facing George. 'Leave the detective work to us, George,' said Kobylov, twirling the rings on his fingers. It was early morning and somewhere above the ramparts of Lubianka the horizon was glowing with light. Soon they'd have him and they could go home. 'Who gave Nikolasha the Mauser in the first place?'

A twitch. Like the first bite of a fish at the end of a line. Kobylov glanced at Mogilchuk and noticed his swollen jaw.

'I don't know.'

Kobylov leaned forward on his elbows so that George could almost taste his spicy breath – and feel his power.

'Did you give Nikolasha that gun, prisoner?'

George was sweating. His confidence, his entitlement, his very will to exist seemed to have melted away. He was just scared, a scared child in serious trouble, and Kobylov was pleased.

'But you said Rosa shot Nikolasha. I never gave her a gun. I swear it!'

'We know where Rosa got the gun. From the case. And we know how the gun got in the case. Nikolasha put it there. So how did Nikolasha get it?'

George doubled up and began to sob. Kobylov leaned in for the kill.

'Oh my God! My father's going to kill me.'

'Forget your father, George. We don't care who your father is. He could be the King of England for all we care. We have orders from the Central Committee to grind you to camp dust if we have to. Now, let me ask you again: did you give—'

'Yes,' George shouted. 'I gave Nikolasha that pistol. He asked for it and I thought nothing of it. My father has a pistol. My brother has a pistol. Half Moscow has them, I thought. He could have got one anywhere.'

'But he didn't get one from anywhere, did he, George? He got one from you.'

George nodded, his face swollen from weeping.

'And where did you get it? Did you go into your father's office and take it? Does the Mauser that killed two children belong to him?'

George sat very still, then he leaned across the desk and vomited.

19

From the moment he arrived at Stalin's Nearby Dacha earlier that night, Satinov could think only of his son.

Stalin, the Seven leaders and Poskrebyshev sat at the long table in the gloomy wood-panelled dining room. They were discussing the coming war against Imperial Japan, but all Satinov could think about was what George was doing. Sleeping? More interrogations? George, his impertinent son; his undutiful, un-Bolshevik son; yes, his favourite son.

'May we come in?' Valechka Istomina, Stalin's cheerful housekeeper, and her assistants, plump ladies in white smocks like nurses, wheeled in the dinner: a Georgian feast with *shashlik* kebabs. They laid out the dishes on the side table. Valechka waddled right over to Stalin. 'It's all ready for you, Josef Vissarionovich,' she said indulgently. She was right at home with him. 'Just as you like it!'

'Thank you, Valechka. Go and pour yourself a glass of Telavi. You deserve it.' Stalin treated the housekeeper like family, and Satinov sensed their bond was closer than anyone knew. 'Come.' Stalin raised his hands to Satinov and the others. 'Help yourselves!'

The leaders followed him to the sideboard.

'Is everything well, *bicho*?' Stalin was right beside him, ladling out the *lobio* and then soaking it up with bread.

'Yes, of course,' he replied – except my son is in prison, as you very well know, he thought drily.

'Tamriko's on good form? Still teaching English?'

'Very much so.'

'The family?' Stalin gazed right into his eyes, challenging him to mention George, to beg for forgiveness, to intercede and break all the rules, to reveal some bitterness that would taint the whole family and bring about their total destruction. Don't hesitate in a single answer, Satinov told himself. Don't evade his eyes. You have nothing to hide from Stalin, not even a whisper of resentment.

'Everything is as it should be,' he answered steadily.

Stalin's hazel eyes did not leave him. 'Good! Help yourself to dinner.'

Satinov exhaled. Stalin's cold, compressed ferocity never ceased to awe him.

After food: toasts. Stalin mocked Beria for not eating the *shashlik*s: 'Still eating that grass? You're turning into a breed of cow.' Then he teased the triple-chinned Malenkov: 'Eat less! I suggest calisthenics with Satinov.'

'Or dancing?' suggested Nikita Khrushchev. Satinov observed this squat confection, the warts on his face, teeth like a horse, his suit as baggy as a sack. He was a real peasant. 'Isn't Comrade Satinov an expert at the *lezginka*?'

Stalin swivelled towards him. 'I thought *you* were the great dancer, Nikita.'

'Me? I can hardly take two steps.'

'I think we need to see you dance, don't we, comrades?' suggested Stalin, eyes glinting.

'I've heard that Khrushchev is the best dancer we have!' cried Beria.

'The very best!' added Malenkov.

Zhdanov hiccuped. He was deathly white. He never joined in such horseplay. He was a serious man.

'Show us,' ordered Stalin.

'I can't . . . I mustn't . . . Not after such a banquet!' said Khrushchev anxiously.

'I think you'll survive,' laughed Stalin. 'Comrades, let's vote on it. Who wishes to see if Comrade Khrushchev can dance the *gopak*?'

Satinov raised his hand. Beria, Poskrebyshev, Zhdanov, Molotov copied him.

'Unanimous!' declared Stalin.

'Dance!' shouted Beria, who'd already begun to clap.

'It's a Politburo order!' teased Stalin.

The others – everyone except Stalin – also clapped in time, chanting: 'Khrushchev dance! Khrushchev dance!'

Khrushchev looked at Stalin, who shrugged apologetically and opened his hands. Khrushchev got to his feet and, raising his hands and bending his knees, started to dance the *gopak*.

'You're like a cow on ice!' Stalin tapped out the tune. 'No sense of rhythm at all, Nikita. Sit down now!'

Khrushchev slumped, panting, into his seat.

Beria, who was serving as the *tamada*, the toastmaster at a Georgian feast, raised a series of toasts to dancers male and female – especially female.

Stalin was focusing on Zhdanov. 'You're sitting there very virtuously like Christ himself but you didn't drink much.'

'He should drink a forfeit shot,' said Beria. Satinov knew Beria hated Zhdanov, Stalin's companion in intellectual matters. Stalin's choice as successor.

Streams of sweat ran down Zhdanov's face, and Satinov

could see he was ill. 'The Kremlevka says I have to refrain. It's my heart,' he explained.

'The Kremlevka? The lady doctor there?' asked Stalin.

'Dr Dashka Dorova.'

'Taking orders from women, eh? Well, you obey your lady doctor,' said Stalin with a grin. 'Women with ideas are like herrings!' He hated independent women.

'Comrade Poskrebyshev also didn't drink that last toast properly,' sneaked Beria.

'Is that true, Sasha?' asked Stalin.

'I did. Didn't you see?'

'The rules are that Comrade Poskrebyshev must drink a forfeit: three shots in one!' said Beria.

Stalin raised his eyebrows, smiling. Beria filled a tumbler with vodka, and Malenkov, his sidekick, delivered it to Poskrebyshev, who stood up. Taking a breath, he downed it: gulp gulp gulp. Flushed, he tottered. A hiccup convulsed his body, and he ran for the French windows, threw them open and vomited into the fish pond outside. Beria started to chortle.

'Sasha's got the hardest head I ever knew,' said Stalin, trying not to laugh. But then his expression suddenly changed. 'I think you're overdoing it, Beria. Stop bullying people at my table. I don't like it. You're lowering the tone here!'

'You're right,' said Beria. 'I apologize.'

'Go and check he's all right.'

Beria pulled himself up and followed Poskrebyshev outside into the grey light.

'I think it's bedtime.' Stalin stood up, slightly unsteady on his feet. Leaning on the doorframe, he went out onto the porch at the front. Guards in white suits stood like statues in the illuminated gardens. The sun was rising over Moscow.

The leaders staggered onto the porch, stiff-legged, bleary-eyed and as pale as a plate of *kasha*. Satinov thought he had never seen an unhealthier gaggle of middle-aged men outside a hospital ward.

He looked back and saw Beria trying to heave Poskrebyshev down the corridor from the dining room. 'Bring the bodies out!' Stalin shouted.

Together they dragged Poskrebyshev outside, past Stalin, down the steps and pushed him into the back of his car.

As they did so, Beria took Satinov's hand, squeezed it tightly and whispered so close to his ear that he wet it with his saliva: 'George is fine. The children are coming home.'

'What are you saying?' called out Stalin.

'I'm telling him that Poskrebyshev's going to vomit again,' said Beria.

'Pah!' said Stalin hoarsely.

Satinov felt weak with relief. The Organs had investigated the shooting, and that was that. He would not reprimand George again, he decided. The boy had been punished enough.

The road was a deep mauve, the sky, lilac with shards of pink: a perfect Russian summer dawn. The sweet scent of flowers and resin emanated from the woods. A peacock in Stalin's garden trilled a high-pitched leee-at! Leee-at! A nightingale cooed its last notes.

Stalin picked a rose, smelled it with his eyes closed and handed it to Satinov. 'For Tamriko,' he said.

Satinov understood. It was for George.

20

At seven twenty that morning, Dr Rimm, the Deputy Director of School 801, nicknamed the Hummer by the children, was waiting in the janitor's storeroom. He felt in his waters that he was about to receive a revelation. There had been no love letters from the enigmatic 'Tatiana' for a while, not since the shooting. But he wasn't thinking of this. He was thinking of the note that he'd been sent two days earlier.

He had been in his classroom preparing for Communist ethics when he'd noticed the envelope peeping out of his copy of the *History of the Communist Party of the Soviet Union (Bolsheviks): Short Course*. When he saw it, his heart had leaped: was it another love letter? Those letters had kept him alive for the last term. Rimm was long divorced from a Communist Party instructor whom he'd met on a Pioneers camping trip to the Crimea – and he had not had a girlfriend since. But surely he deserved happiness like anyone else. (Why did women so adore Benya Golden? What did that effete, skirt-chasing smooth-talker have that Rimm didn't? Didn't they know he was tainted?) The feeling that someone – he was sure he knew who it was – loved him had restored his battered pride. He knew their passion was impossible, at least for now, but this aura of love gave him confidence in his ambitions.

The envelope had been addressed in a childish hand.

'Tatiana's' love letters were always typed in capitals. But the disappointment had passed swiftly. The school was on the rack: two children dead, more arrested, all of them the scions of Bolshevik grandees. Out of the tragedy, he was convinced, the rottenness of Director Medvedeva's headship would be exposed. She had made mistakes, allowing bacterial heresies to spread through the school. He had warned her about the peril of employing Golden as a teacher and allowing the Fatal Romantics' faction to indulge in bourgeois romanticism. And he had been proved right in the most terrible way possible. Only he could cleanse the school of her un-Bolshevik, unpatriotic mistakes. He opened the note. *I need to speak to a person in authority. May we meet by the janitor's storeroom 7:30 a.m.? A young comrade.*

'Tra-la-la Stalin . . .' he burst out singing his favourite song. He had known instantly with a surge of sap in his gut that this note heralded his moment.

So now he was waiting there. He had woken at four a.m., heart palpitating, walked around Moscow since dawn, taken a coffee at the Moskva Hotel, just to celebrate. He had not served in the war (too old, and the problems with his hips), but he longed to be a spy or a leader. He knew people in the Organs and they appreciated him. And now, he was the only honest and vigilant Communist at the school, ready to do his duty. What time was it now? Seven forty and no one had come. Inside the storeroom, he began to hum.

The door opened and he jumped. It was the janitor, that hoary Tajik in brown overalls.

'What are you doing here?' the janitor asked.

Rimm hadn't thought how it would look: an important teacher like him skulking in a cupboard full of bleach and lavatory paper.

'How dare you!' he barked. 'Get on with your work! And not a word to anyone! Or you'll be on the next train home to Turkestan!'

'Yes, boss,' said the janitor, backing away quickly.

Five minutes later, Rimm opened the storeroom door to get some air – and there he was, a small dark boy approaching with the tentative steps and lithe vigilance of a night creature. When he saw Rimm, he froze.

The covert craft of a spy comes naturally to me, Rimm thought, as he led the way into his classroom. Closing the door, he sat at his desk and pointed to the front row of desks. The boy sat.

'Demian Dorov, why did you write me that note?' he asked.

Demian seemed terrified as he stared at Rimm.

'If anyone asks, we can say I was tutoring you on Stakhanovite poetry,' Rimm said more gently. 'Now, you've been very brave coming to see me.'

Demian nodded and relaxed a little, but still he didn't speak.

'What have you got?' Rimm asked again.

Demian shook his head. 'Nothing,' he said. 'I . . . I was just joking.'

Think like a Chekist, like a Bolshevik, Rimm told himself. Analyse your informant and his family. The key will lie there.

The Dorovs. The father Genrikh was the Chairman of the Party's Control Commission, an admirable enforcer of discipline and morals; the mother, that comely doctor and Health Minister. They had four children. After a son in the army, the daughter Minka had her mother's looks but was un-Party-minded, frivolous and impertinent. The Organs had been right to pull her in. The little boy Senka was clever but sickeningly spoilt by his mother. So Demian Dorov, who resembled his father and tried to emulate him by leading the school's Young Pioneers, was stuck between the two favourites. Rimm suddenly warmed to him: Demian too was unappreciated. The other children nicknamed him the Weasel but perhaps he too had seen the poison of bourgeois romanticism seeping into the rotten school . . .

Rimm came down from his seat on the platform and sat at the neighbouring desk to Demian.

'You've been noticed by the Party and I've always known that you will go far.'

'Thank you,' said Demian. Rimm could see he was blushing a little.

'I don't think your parents have really respected you enough. They're too busy with their important work – or in your mother's case, with your younger brother, her favourite. Am I right?'

Demian nodded slightly.

'If you did something for the Party, I think we could change that,' continued Rimm. 'Let me help you.' But Demian had begun to fidget nervously again. 'You have a choice,' Rimm said slowly. 'You can either be a hero, just like the schoolboy Pavlik Morozov, who denounced his wicked parents, and tell me everything – or you can hold back a secret. But if you do, and we find out, you could destroy your family.' He paused, giving his words time to sink in. 'Tell me what you know. The highest authorities in the Party are interested. Now!'

Demian's eyes blinked quickly. Rimm put his hand on the boy's narrow shoulders. 'I know what righteous Bolshevik deeds you are capable of.' Finally, reluctantly, Demian reached into his satchel and pulled it out. An exercise book with velvet covers.

'I recognize this book. It was Nikolasha's. Where did you get it?' asked Rimm.

'Senka found it on the night of the deaths and he took it home.'

'He hid it?'

'Under the mattress in his room.'

'He must have taken it right under the eyes of the Organs. Have you read it?'

'No.'

Rimm didn't believe him. He opened the book up and for a moment, he was disappointed. 'The Velvet Book of Love.' A schoolboy's scribblings. But as he glanced at its contents – lists of names, chronicles of meetings, strange rituals – he sensed there was treasure here.

'Demian, you've done a wonderful thing for the Party. Rest assured this will be our secret. You were right to bring this to me. Now go on with your day. And tell no one of this.'

Demian scuttled away, leaving Rimm with the book. Thoughtfully, he walked over to the new Lenin Library and sat at a desk in one of the remotest stacks. Should he show the notebook to Director Medvedeva? Possibly, but she might refuse to take it further. Or she could inform on him for being a meddler in an official investigation. She had every reason to suppress this for her own ends. Besides, he, Dr Rimm, was the secretary of the school's Communist Party committee, while she was a mere member.

Furthermore, if he kept the exercise book within the school, it would remain a school matter, while this case surely concerned higher authorities. Should he take it to Demian's father, Genrikh Dorov, Chairman of the Central Control Commission? In normal circumstances, yes, but his daughter, Minka, was under investigation, and Demian's role in procuring the book might compromise Comrade Dorov's ability to pass judgement.

Perhaps he should take the information to Comrade Satinov himself. Comrade Satinov would say, 'Comrade Rimm, someone wants to see you, to hear it from your own lips,' and a door in a Kremlin office would open, and there would be the Great Stalin himself, smoking his pipe. 'Comrade Rimm, we meet at last. I've heard so much about you,' Stalin would say. But no, no, Satinov's wife was a teacher and his son George had also been arrested.

So it was clear. Rimm would have to handle this himself. In short, this was a case for the Knights of the Revolution.

Stalin lay on the sofa in the wood-panelled little study of the Nearby Dacha, feeling weary, hung-over and liverish. It was early evening. He listlessly opened a Zola novel, then read the script for the movie *Ivan the Terrible Part Two*. He did not like it. It must be rewritten. Who should do it?

A knock and that soft lullaby voice: 'Coffee for a weary man who never gets any peace!'

It was his dear housekeeper, Valechka Istomina. She poured him a cup, just as he liked it, with two sugars. He looked around his study. Every surface was covered with piles of books and literary journals that he loved to read. But now, wearing his favourite old tunic (darned by Valechka in three places), soft kid-leather boots, baggy canvas trousers like an artist, and smoking a Herzegovina Flor cigarette, he tried to rustle up the strength to go into the Kremlin. Soon he must leave for the conference at Potsdam. Do I have the strength? he asked himself.

The *vertushka* rang. It was Poskrebyshev. 'Comrade Abakumov wants to see you. He says something new has come up.'

Something new. Stalin relished a fresh gambit in the game of shadows that was counter-intelligence. It was his natural habitat. Even before the Revolution, even in the underground, he had mastered the game of agents and double agents, of cash in envelopes, shots in the night, daggers in the back. The Organs were the only part of government, except foreign and military policy, that he would never relinquish.

A car drew up. One of the bodyguards knocked. Abakumov had arrived.

Stalin stood up, his knees unsteady. He felt dizzy; his vision blurred and there was a frightening tightness in the back of his neck. He had to steady himself by grabbing his desk. 'Send him in,' he said.

Victor Abakumov stood in the lobby in a general's uniform, looking the other way. Stalin could tell he was expecting him to come from the big office across the hall. It was always good to keep the security people on their toes.

'Come on in, Comrade Abakumov!'

'Oh.' Abakumov turned, startled. 'Good day, Comrade Stalin.'

Stalin led him into the bigger study, where there was more space. He nodded at one of the divans and took his own seat behind the desk. 'What have you got for me?' he asked. 'How's the cleansing and filtration of traitors in the Baltics?'

'We've arrested and deported thirty thousand Estonians this week,' said Abakumov. 'But I came about the Children's Case.'

'So you're sticking your snout into Comrade Beria's trough again?'

'That is not my aim.' Abakumov knew that Stalin was delighted that he was interfering in Beria's ministries. The MGB reported to Beria, but Abakumov, Chief of Military Counter-intelligence, SMERSH (Death to Spies), reported directly to Stalin. And Stalin had added his name to the distribution list for documents on the Children's Case. 'Thank you for your trust, Comrade Stalin.'

'But I don't think this one's for you. The young hooligans are about to be released. I think we should forgive them.'

'That's what I've come about. My operatives have discovered an aspect of the case that has been hidden from the Central Committee.'

'What aspect?' If there was anything Stalin hated, it was to have important matters concealed from him.

'The political aspect.'

'Go on.'

'Comrade Kobylov reports that the children's romantic club was harmless. But I believe it was more serious than that. Much more serious.'

Stalin was now very awake, and feeling much better. His vision was clearer, and the pain in his neck had vanished.

'You base this on what exactly, Comrade Abakumov?'

'This.' Abakumov opened his briefcase and took out what appeared to be a school notebook with red velvet glued on the front and back.

'I haven't seen one of those since I last signed Svetlana's homework,' Stalin said.

'It belonged to Nikolasha Blagov, the boy shot on the bridge.'

'And how have you got it?'

'It seems that Comrade Kobylov' – Stalin knew that when Abakumov named Kobylov, he really meant Beria – 'may have deliberately ignored this piece of evidence. It came to us because apparently Comrade Kobylov' – Beria again – 'was uninterested.'

'What do you mean?'

'The two Chekists appointed by Comrade Beria to investigate

the Children's Case were slack and reduced their vigilance. They allowed this vital piece of evidence to be pilfered from the murder scene, obviously in order to conceal it from the forces of Soviet justice. The extraordinary intelligence-gathering of SMERSH operatives uncovered this a few hours ago via an informant – a teacher named Rimm within School 801 – and I have brought it straight to you.'

'What's in it?'

'Comrade Stalin, permission to approach to show you a page that I think is relevant?'

Stalin raised an almost feminine hand and beckoned him to the desk. Abakumov bowed slightly as he handed over the notebook open at a certain page. Stalin read:

Meeting of the Politburo of the Romantic Central Committee

Agenda
Election of Council of Ministers

I, Nikolasha Blagov, First Secretary of the Fatal Romantics' Politburo, seconded by Vlad Titorenko and George Satinov, propose that the following be appointed ministers in our new government . . .

Stalin put down the book in some surprise. 'The Satinov children are involved?'

'I am afraid so,' said Abakumov sombrely. 'It seems that we've uncovered a conspiracy to overthrow the government.'

21

The children were coming home; Tamara Satinova was so happy.

'Is that you, Losha?' she called out from the kitchen.

'It is,' replied Losha Babanava. 'May I come in?'

'Do. How are you?'

'Sizzling.' His smile was all sunburn, moustaches and white teeth. Losha had guarded Hercules Satinov since he was in Tbilisi as the First Secretary of the Transcaucasus. He had seen Hercules married in the 1920s; he had guarded him on grain-collecting expeditions into Ukraine during collectivization; he had been at his side on sunny, relaxed holidays with Stalin on the Black Sea when they ate *al fresco* and sang Georgian songs; he had witnessed Hercules widowed and lonesome, and then happily meeting and marrying Tamara; he remembered the Terror when Hercules's friends were arrested and vanished; and in the darkest days of 1941, he had accompanied him to the front when the armies were being routed by the Nazis. So Tamara knew he was as anxious as anyone to see George come home.

'Is there any news?' he asked, looking at his watch.

'No,' Tamara said. 'But surely it can't be long now. It's seven p.m. after all . . .' Hercules was sure George would be home soon, and Hercules was always right about these things.

In the kitchen, Leka was making George's favourite meal,

beef Stroganoff, and Mariko was playing with her friend Raisa, the only other girl who enjoyed her game, the Moscow School for Bitches.

'I've got to stay here, Losha, in case the phone rings,' Tamara said. 'Please could you pick up Mariko? She's at the Bolshakovs'. Just off Pushkin Square.'

'Done,' said Losha. Losha knew where everyone lived, where anything could be procured, all the secrets. He left, and Tamara looked at her watch for the umpteenth time.

On the other side of the Moskva River, in the House on the Embankment, Dashka Dorova was not watching the clock because Genrikh had told her that the MGB bureaucracy was always slower than you might expect, so the call would probably come first thing in the morning. She thought: One more night! For Minka a night might be an eternity. At least Demian was dependable – and she had her Senka.

'Let me see how you look!' said Dashka, clapping her hands. She had a way of throwing back her head when she laughed. 'Turn around.'

Even in his pyjamas, Senka Dorov looked every inch a little professor. While other ten-year-olds sported pyjamas with pictures of bears or rabbits, Senka's were dark blue with stripes and red piping, made of Chinese silk.

'Do you like them, Senka?'

'Yes I love them, Mamochka.' He circled her, dancing round and round. 'They're so smart I think I could lecture in them, don't you think, Mamochka?'

'Oh, you're so sweet, darling,' cried Dashka, pulling him towards her and wrapping him in her arms. 'If you give me your matinée-idol face I'll have to kiss you.'

Senka focused his big brown eyes on the distance and tilted his head a little, knowing very well that, to her at least, he was adorable.

Dashka showered his face in kisses. Then he raised his hands around her neck and pulled her down to kiss her cheeks. 'I really love you so much, Mamochka!'

Dashka looked down at her youngest son, at his long eyelashes and the dimple in his chin. She buried her nose in his hair and inhaled the smell of him. Boys smelled stronger than girls. 'You're so handsome, my Little Professor. And so original. And such a charmer. One day a girl is going to be very lucky to be married to you.'

'I don't want to marry anyone but you!' he said.

'You won't want to be with me when you're a teenager and I'm a wrinkly old lady.'

'Mama, you'll always be the most beautiful woman in the whole wide world.'

'Rubbish,' she laughed. 'I wish!'

Senka frowned. 'Why are you so happy when Minka's still away?'

'I can't tell you that.' But she smiled.

'Ohh,' he cried out. 'I understand – Minka's coming home!'

'Hush,' said Dashka. 'Never talk about such things.' But she was certain Minka was coming home: the clues were all there. At dinner at the Aragvi the previous night, Longuinoz the maître d' had taken her hands and said, 'Dr Dorova, let me show you to your table.' He had moved so close she could see his mascara. 'Some of my favourite guests had colds in the last few days. Summer colds. But today, everyone is better, and tomorrow, completely cured.'

'Tomorrow?'

'Tomorrow. Here's your table. Enjoy your meal.'

Ever since Minka's arrest, Dashka had not enjoyed a moment's ease. Even her surgery, which she loved, had barely distracted her. She worried every second: was Minka sleeping? Was there a lavatory in her cell? What was she eating? What if she got her period in there? Were they being kind to her? Oh please, let them be kind to her: I beg you, Comrade Beria or whoever is in charge of her, don't crush her love of life. Dashka knew that Genrikh was in pain too, even though he had lectured her about Bolshevik justice. In a flash of temper, she had shouted at him: 'I want my daughter back, Genrikh! You can keep your Bolshevik justice!' But now that Minka was coming home, she could enjoy her family, and this meant enjoying her Little Professor.

'Mamochka?' Senka was holding her face in his hands and shaking her a little. 'Wake up at the back of the class!'

She had been dreaming of going to Lubianka to collect Minka. When would the call come? How would they celebrate? I will cook her pancakes with strawberry jam, her favourite, and she can have pancakes every day, she decided, forever!

'Mamochka, did you know I caught Demian in my room the other day, looking through my things? He was plundering my room.'

She shook herself back to the present. 'Plundering, was he?'

'Or it could have been looting. Or a deed of opportunistic piracy?'

'Good words, Little Professor. But Demian's too old to play with your toys, darling. I'm sure he didn't take anything.'

'But it's vexing.'

'I'll talk to him, I promise.'

'Thank you, Mamochka.' Another kiss. 'Can I pop next door and borrow a book from Lulu Nosenko's daddy? For homework.'

'What book are you borrowing?'

'*Tchaikovsky's Music and Librettos in Opera and Ballet.*'

'Well, that's essential reading.' Dashka smiled indulgently. 'Put on the matching dressing gown, and off you go. Papa will be here any minute and then we'll have supper. Hurry up!'

Dashka went into the kitchen. Demian was in his room. The maid Luda was stirring Genrikh's favourite spicy borscht with extra chilli. A few minutes later, she heard the door shut on the latch. Genrikh was home.

He kissed her, and as he did, she whispered, 'Is the news still good?' and he said, 'So far. Luda, pour us both a glass of wine.'

Dizzy with excitement, Dashka kissed her husband, and even Genrikh had to smile.

Soon their supper was ready. 'Demian! Senka!' called Genrikh. Demian appeared and sat at the table. Dashka noticed the dirty hair and pimply skin of her teenage son. What a surly phase he was going through. He was the image of his father, not like the other children, who were all her.

'Get Senka,' she told him.

'He's not in his room.'

'No, he went next door to the Nosenkos'. Will you fetch him?'

Demian left slightly sulkily but was back in a moment. 'He collected the book ten minutes ago.'

Dashka looked at Genrikh – and in that moment, she felt as if her stomach were falling, falling for ever, through her body, the floor, the earth, eternity. Then she bolted out of the kitchen.

'Senka! Senka!' she shouted, going from room to room. She

ran back into the dining room, where Genrikh and Demian were still sitting at the table in silence. 'But he was still in his pyjamas. Where could he be? Genrikh, what the hell is going on? Help me look for him, for God's sake! *Senka!*'

It had been a long and confusing day for George Satinov. As soon as he had revealed where he got the gun, he'd known he had done something terrible. Everyone in Lubianka was suddenly being kind to him and that made him even more worried.

After breakfast, he'd been taken to the interrogation where Mogilchuk chatted to him about football and Kobylov popped his head around the door as if to wish him luck. Back in his cell, he'd paced up and down. Perhaps I'm going home, he'd thought in a delirium of hope. The lunch was lamb cutlets and potatoes, a special feast, not the usual Lubianka fare.

But the hours passed, and nothing happened. And by the time it was supper, he was rattled. Then the food arrived: the thin gruel with a few knuckles of fat floating in the grease and the tiny square of bread and butter. No one came to fetch him, to collect his things and free him. Night fell. The light stayed on. He could not sleep, but as he began to doze, the Judas port clicked. 'Hands on top of the blanket. Wake up!'

The lock groaned open and he was marched down the corridor back to the interrogation room. 'No talking – or the punishment cell!' he was told. 'Eyes straight ahead.'

He was in the same room but a new interrogator was waiting for him.

'Sit down, Prisoner Satinov,' said a man who had a sharp face, sheer, flat cheekbones and a mouth and jaw that protruded like the muzzle of a dog. Prisoner? The words 'prisoner' and

'Satinov' did not go together at all. Satinov was usually mentioned with 'hero' or 'Comrade Stalin's closest . . .'

'Answer the questions directly and truthfully. Hide nothing from us.'

'But I've told you all I know.'

'Me? You haven't told *me* anything. I am Colonel Likhachev and we're starting again, boy. When did you plan to seize power, Prisoner Satinov?'

'Please, I'm confused. I'm a schoolboy. I'm not even interested in politics. I leave that to the Party.'

'Insolence is not tolerated here, prisoner.' Likhachev slapped him across the face with the back of his hand. Stars flickered behind George's eyes; his mouth stung.

'What are you doing?'

'Don't footle with me,' Likhachev said, 'or I'll reduce you to a puddle of fluid on the floor.'

George's stomach seized up. He was suddenly very afraid.

'You were a member of a conspiracy to overthrow the Soviet Government, kill members of the Politburo and install a new ministry,' Likhachev stated.

'I want to answer but I don't understand. I am utterly loyal to Comrade Stalin and the Soviet Government. I'm a Komsomol.'

'What was your role in Nikolasha Blagov's provisional government?'

'Oh my God, that was a joke.'

'Be careful, prisoner. A conspiracy against the Soviet Government is not a joke.'

'But it wasn't a conspiracy. It was Nikolasha's idiotic game.'

'Do you recognize this?'

'Yes. Yes, it's Nikolasha's Velvet Book.'

'Let me read you something: *Today I, First Romantic Secretary Nikolasha, will meet the members of the Central Romantic Committee to discuss the appointment of a new government*. You read this and agreed with it, did you not?'

'No!'

'But you signed it. Look – there's your signature.'

'I didn't take it seriously. I thought Nikolasha was mad and ridiculous. We all did!'

'You're in deep trouble, boy. This is treason.'

'I'll tell you anything, anything at all. Just ask!'

'Why were you to be Minister of . . .' Likhachev looked down the list of appointments. '. . . Sport?'

'That shows I wasn't serious. Sport's not important. I said I'd do it because I'm more into football than literature.'

'You could be shot for this, prisoner.'

'I'm only eighteen. Please, I don't understand any of this.'

'Whose idea was it to form an anti-Communist government?'

'It was Nikolasha's idea. It was all him.'

Likhachev cleared his catarrh. 'That's convenient since he's dead. Who was behind him? Forget your father. Forget your fancy friends. Forget the Aragvi. Now it is just you against the almighty power of the Soviet State.'

George was exhausted. He wiped his face, tried to focus. 'Vlad Titorenko was his best friend but I don't think Nikolasha even showed him the notebook.'

'But reading his notebook, it is clear that one person had to approve his ideas, his conspiracy, his government. Who was it?'

The shock was making George feel leaden. His eyelids were heavy and he wanted to yawn. 'Sorry, I'm so tired . . .'

'Concentrate, prisoner. It is clear that someone else was the brains behind this treason. Let me read you this: *NV has approved my ideas.* Or here: *NV must approve the government.*'

'It was not about politics. It never has been. It was about love.'

Likhachev punched George in the mouth, throwing him across the room.

'We have the written evidence of his notebook. And it is quite clear that this "NV" is the grey cardinal of his conspiracy. Who is "NV"?'

'Prisoner Minka Dorova, the punishment for conspiracy under Article 158 is death. Were you a party to a terroristic conspiracy?' asked Colonel Komarov. Soft-spoken with the habit of running his hands through his light brown curly hair, he focused on Minka sitting opposite him. His forehead, she decided, had the rumpled frown lines that marked the sincerity of the truly stupid.

'No.' Minka closed her eyes. She never thought she would miss Kobylov and Mogilchuk, but now each question made her feel sicker. She fought waves of panic and told herself: Keep your head!

'Then why is your name in the government as Minister of Theatre?'

'But that's a joke. Surely you can see from the title of the ministry?'

'We believe that you and Nikolasha Blagov and your other friends were pawns in this vile plot. Someone is behind it. Someone important.'

'I don't know whom you mean.'

'Answer the question. Who is really behind this conspiracy to form a new government?'

'No one.' Minka was conscious of the tears running down her cheeks.

'In his notebook, Nikolasha says that "NV" approves all his decisions. Who is this "NV"?'

Concentrate, Minka, she told herself, confess nothing, and you will get through this. She shook her head.

Komarov lit a cigarette. 'Come with me, prisoner,' he said and pressed a button on the desk.

Two warders entered and took her by the arms.

'Where are you taking me? What are you going to do to me?'

'We're going to show you something to concentrate your mind.'

She was marched into a room with a glass wall through which she could see an empty interrogation room, just like the one she'd been in. Table, lamp, two chairs.

'You can see in but no one can see out,' said Komarov. 'And no one can hear you.'

The door opened into the neighbouring room, and a small boy with tousled hair and large brown eyes walked in, wearing blue silk pyjamas with red piping.

'Senka!' she cried, throwing herself against the glass. '*Senka!*'

22

Andrei Kurbsky lay in his cell. He now knew he would never escape the curse of his tainted biography; he'd always be the son of an Enemy. But there was one consolation: he felt closer to his father.

His father must surely have been through the same registration, the same cells, perhaps even this one. Andrei looked at the marks on the walls: drawings, words, scratches. He read out the names, dates, messages. Some must have died here; some must have been shot in the cellars and they wrote their names here to be read. He searched for his father's name and dreamed that he too would be sent out to the Gulags – and that one day, in a snowy forest clearing, he would meet his father chopping logs . . .

The night was lonely. Someone was shouting; someone was coughing. Andrei was tired and so afraid. It was the uncertainty that was the hardest thing. Who else was in the cells here? What had they said? What was it safe to say?

The clip of boots outside. Locks turning. The door opened, and he was on his way to the interrogation rooms but this time he found a new officer was waiting for him. One look at Colonel Likhachev's sunken, broiling eyes and little yellow teeth and Andrei knew that the case had taken another twist.

'Prisoner Kurbsky, you were a party to an anti-Party conspiracy with Nikolasha Blagov.' Likhachev took a book from a beige folder – a book Andrei recognized all too well – and began to read: '*We in the Romantics' Club are no longer interested in that nonsense of the progression of history, the dialectic, class struggle: the passion of the individual is supreme.* How do you regard his views?'

'They are un-Leninist, un-Marxist: I was profoundly disgusted. As a Communist I reject it. Nikolasha was a clown, but a dangerous one nonetheless.' It was a relief, thought Andrei, to see the book, and know how he should respond to these questions.

'But you did nothing about this?'

'I did do something . . .'

'Don't lie. Let me continue. *Serafima is appointed Minister of Love. NV must approve all appointments. Meet NV for instructions.*'

Andrei struggled to sit up straight and focus. 'Look, I don't know any "NV" but I was the last to join the Fatal Romantics' Club. This is really nothing to do with me.'

'I'm interested in this "Minister of Love." It says here that Serafima Romashkina was elected to this position by the Politburo.'

'I didn't know.' Andrei did not want to discuss Serafima at all. Don't mention Serafima, he told himself. Stay awake! 'You couldn't take Nikolasha Blagov seriously about anything. He was unbalanced.'

Likhachev leafed through the notebook. 'Even so, here he writes: *Minister of Love is supreme because love is supreme, higher than Gensec.*'

Andrei shivered. 'Gensec' was the acronym for 'General Secretary' of the Party, and there had only ever been one Gensec: Stalin himself. This was treason.

Likhachev leaned across the desk, and Andrei was struck again by his bloodshot and yellow eyes, which reminded him of an egg with blood in the yolk. 'You need to tell me who NV is.'

'I think NV is imaginary.'

Likhachev slammed his hands on the table. 'Don't dare to misdirect this investigation. We know that you, Prisoner Kurbsky, know who NV is. And you will tell us. Even if I have to scrape it with a scoop from the inside of your dead skull.'

Minka had lost all track of time. She was back in her interrogation room and trying hard not to panic. But the sight of her small brother had rattled her, especially as she now knew that if she fell, she would drag Senka and her parents to perdition with her. She closed her eyes, picturing herself and Senka being shot in the back of the head. What should she do? What should she say?

'Why is Senka here?' she asked. 'He's ten. Please, I beg you, send him home. My mother must be frantic.'

'Tell us about Nikolasha Blagov's notebook. The one you call the Velvet Book of Love.'

'I never knew what was in it. If I had known that he was doing something so evil, something against our great Soviet State, I would have informed against him. But I promise: I knew nothing of any conspiracy. Nothing.'

'Who is "NV"?'

The walls seemed to lean in on Minka as she thought of Senka, her little brother. What was NV? *NV?* She must come up with something to free Senka, to free all of them. NV had to mean something. Perhaps she should invent a code, plant a red herring, a distraction to direct the Chekists away from herself and Senka, from George and Serafima. She presumed that because a code did not exist, they would not find it – and therefore nothing would come of it. Already an idea was ripening in her mind, taking shape at the tip of her tongue until the experienced Komarov could see it was coming.

'Tell me,' he coaxed.

'I've never heard of NV. But can I suggest something it might be? Could "NV" stand for "New Leader"? *NV. Novi Vozhd*. Someone that none us knew about?'

'Go on?'

'Perhaps it was Nikolasha's candidate for a new Romantics' leader?' proposed Minka.

'So you're confirming that this was a conspiracy? For there can only be one Leader, the Father of Peoples, the Head of the Soviet Government.'

'Well, no, I was just suggesting something . . .'

'There are no suggestions here, girl. There is just evidence. We will find the so-called New Leader of this conspiracy.'

'I was guessing,' Minka said, beginning to feel unsure of herself again.

'Are you telling me lies? Are you wearing a mask?'

'No, of course not . . . I'd never lie to you.'

'Good, then explain this. Here in the notebook, Nikolasha writes this: *Serafima and NV. NV and Serafima. Meeting to approve the Romantic government*. What was Serafima's relationship with Nikolasha?'

'There was no relationship. She didn't even like him.'

'So if Serafima Romashkina was not having a relationship with Nikolasha, who was she with?' Komarov settled back in his chair. 'She was with NV, wasn't she? NV is Serafima's lover.'

'No! She had no lover. I'm her best friend and I'd know if she did.'

Komarov opened his arms wide and stretched, like a diver leaping into a pool, and then he ran his hand through the fluffy hair that seemed alien to his uniform, his job, his lifeless eyes. 'We're going to have to start again. Tell me about Serafima and her relationship with NV.'

Minka felt the sweat start to shimmer through her skin; her jaw clenched, her shoulders tensed. She had meant to protect Senka, and Serafima. Now she realized that the sight of her little brother had distorted everything. To save him, she had made a terrible mistake and had placed Serafima at the centre of a conspiracy that had never even existed.

Too late, she saw that in this world, every breath had consequences.

23

'I'll be honest, Madame Zeitlin, I'm a fan. So I had to come myself,' said Victor Abakumov in his deep baritone. 'I'm a movie buff. I watch everything. Of course I have some of Goebbels's movies from Berlin. I have a movie director's eye. But you in that movie *Katyusha*. I'd call it a masterpiece. Your husband's script contributed to its success but your performance . . .'

It was early morning, and Serafima could hear Abakumov talking as she quickly packed a little bag under the eyes of the two uniformed Chekists who had already searched her bedroom and taken away books and letters.

'Well, Comrade Abakumov, you are very kind but I wish we had met under other circumstances,' her mother was saying. Her actress's voice lacked its usual vigour but Serafima was grateful her mother was not howling in hysterics. She too hoped that if Sophia was civil to the Chekists, it would somehow help her.

'Is that a poster from the movie I see over there?'

'Yes, it is.' A silence. 'Would you like it?'

'I would and I'd like it signed: "To Victor, with love." Yes, that'll impress my friends.'

'You flatter me, Comrade General.'

'I'd like to discuss the art of movies with you.'

'I'd like that too – but couldn't you question Serafima here? Do you really need to take her in?'

'Perhaps we could meet sometime later. Just you and I—'

The Chekist's trying to seduce my mother, thought Serafima, but didn't every marshal or *apparatchik* flirt with her, regardless of the feelings of her long-suffering papa?

Serafima felt the joints of her body prickling like pins and needles: It is fear, she told herself. Two of your friends have died; the incident has to be investigated; that's why your other friends are in prison. There is nothing to fear! Yet when the Organs investigate, they always find something more, and that is what I must hide at all costs.

Still wearing her school uniform, Serafima had finished packing her bag. Toothbrush. A sweater. Pyjamas. A couple of books: Hemingway and Pushkin.

'Are you ready?' said one of the Chekists.

Serafima nodded. She wanted the packing to go on forever. She wished Abakumov would keep talking to her mother eternally. She sat down on her bed again. Her legs were weak. She put her face in her hands and started to cry, and the next thing she knew, her mother was with her, and had taken her in her arms.

'There, there, Serafima, you'll be back soon, just answer their questions . . . You're not the only one, so don't worry. Darling, I love you so much.' But this only made the goodbye even worse. Her mother was trying not to cry herself but her voice petered out, and now Serafima was weeping so hard she couldn't stand. She wished her papa were there too but he was away, covering the war against Japan. Yet there was something worse than that, far worse. She couldn't say goodbye to the man she loved.

She had always known she might be arrested. She had felt

the shadow over her ever since the day on the bridge because she realized (and she had always known) that Nikolasha's ideas were tinged with madness. She saw clearly how the members of the Fatal Romantics' Club were roped together: when one fell into the abyss, the rest would surely follow.

'She'll be back soon,' said Abakumov jovially, as if he were taking her on a camping expedition. 'We're talking to all the children and then we'll release them soon enough. It's just a formality.' He filled the doorway like a slab of Soviet manhood. Wiping her eyes, Serafima looked up at his thick black slicked-back hair, his heavy eyebrows, his general's uniform with its rows of medals and his sportsman's barrel chest. Looking bored, he crossed his arms and leaned on the doorpost.

Finally she managed to stand up. If you love someone, she thought, you can endure anything. Slowly – unbearably slowly – her mother walked with her to the door, and gave her the overnight bag.

'Time to go!' Abakumov said breezily. 'Madame Zeitlin, it's been an honour,' and he took Sophia's hand and kissed it. '*Enchanté!*'

He mispronounced the French, but the humanity of the hand-kissing broke something within Serafima's mother.

'Please, Comrade General, please . . . Do you have to take her? You don't have to. She's done nothing. She's a child! Take me instead!'

The two Chekists flanking Serafima took her arms, and together they walked down the wide steps of the Granovsky building; then they stood back as Abakumov strode past them, his gold-braided hat on his head, his dark eyes straight ahead under the visor, and the movie poster under his arm.

'Get in with me, Serafima,' said Abakumov, gesturing at the

open door of his car, a white Fiat sports car, once the toy of an Italian general. 'Few girls resist a ride in this machine.'

The creamy leather creaked as he manoeuvred himself into the driver's seat next to her. 'I like to drive myself,' he said, slipping on his driving gloves and gripping the beige calf's leather of the wheel. 'You'll be more comfortable than in a "black crow."' He looked at her as she sat mutely in the passenger seat.

Throwing the gearstick into first, he accelerated out of the courtyard of Granovsky, followed in convoy by one of the secret police vans, known as 'black crows,' and a little Zhiguli full of guards. As they sped through the streets, Abakumov saw that Serafima was still crying. Fuck it, why did I transport her in my car? he thought. Because of the mother, of course. Weeping girls were tough for a man to see, even for him, whose rise had been oiled with the blood of men, women and children, those he had beaten to pulp with his own fists, or despatched with his own sidearm – and those hundreds of thousands more he had never met but whose lives he had destroyed. He suppressed a spasm of anger at her tears: didn't the little fool realize how kind he was being to her? She could have been in the cage in the back of a 'black crow.'

'And I thought it was just a love story,' Abakumov repeated Stalin's words to him from the previous day. Stalin had been implying that the Children's Case was a serious conspiracy that Abakumov must investigate vigorously. Well, he had arrested the children – even the ten-year-old Senka Dorov – but these were VIP kids. Silk gloves were called for. Stalin was preparing for the Potsdam conference but what did he really want Abakumov to do with them? Stalin spoke in hieroglyphic codes and Aesopian fables, and even Abakumov was often bewildered by the obscurity of his intentions. Abakumov needed another clue.

The high steel gates of Little Lubianka Street were opened by guards, and the car swung into the courtyard. The gates closed behind and the car doors were opened by two Chekists.

'Take her down and register her,' said Abakumov.

He watched Serafima Romashkina get out of the car as if in a trance and look around, unsure which way to go, at the high walls with the tiny barred windows and, to the side, at the rank of waiting 'black crows.' Placing his hand on her shoulder, he pushed her gently towards two figures in long brown coats who looked like laboratory assistants. 'That way! And don't worry, girl. You'll be home before you know it. It's just routine – you know that. Don't cry.'

The stench of detergent, distilled urine, compacted sweat – the perfume of prison life – made his nose twitch even though he knew it so well. He saw her face as it hit her for the first time. She staggered a little on her long legs and fear shadowed her green eyes. Well, prisoners were meant to be afraid, and this prison had been designed to frighten them because the power of the Knights of the Revolution had to be beyond the imaginations of the Enemies they had to break. But the main thing for him was that he was always on top. He always won. Stalin trusted him, and he believed absolutely in his own invincible destiny.

Holding her little case, Serafima walked down the steps into the lobby of the prison and stood before the counter. Its varnish was cracked, its surface greasy from the hands of thousands upon thousands of prisoners, and there were two slight indentations formed by their elbows as they leaned forward, just as this new prisoner was doing now.

'Surname, first name, patronymic and age?' said a brown-coated woman.

'Romashkina, Serafima Constantinovna. Eighteen.'

She was pretty, this Serafima, thought Abakumov, but it was the mother, the film star, whom he wanted. He wondered what else Serafima was saying, but weren't the words, like the tears, always the same, and hers were lost in the cacophony of doors slamming, cars arriving, locks grinding, orders barked and the crack of his boots on the stairs worn smooth by decades of unsteady feet entering the lost world for the first time.

'Sign here, prisoner,' said the warder. 'Go through that door. Body search.'

The registration section worked like clockwork, thought Abakumov, who had perfected the stages that reduced a free person to a prisoner with a number: register, surrender belongings, body search, photograph. It did not matter who they were before. They might be a Polish prince, a German general, a Communist bigwig or a film star's daughter, but that was the glory of the Soviet State and the Party.

I am the servant of this all-powerful state, I am the sword of the Party, thought Abakumov, and I can reduce anyone to a number, to a smudge of grease on the floor. He was sorry to see this girl fed into his machine – but she had been very unwise.

He walked further into the gigantic building, and now it was quiet. He had left the registration section far behind; here the doors were no longer opened by men with keys on their belts. Now his boots sailed over blue carpet as he was saluted by men in shoulderboards and striped trousers. A secretary opened the doors of his office. He tossed some genial words at his assistant: he prided himself on his lack of formality with subordinates.

A wood-panelled office. Persian rugs, six telephones (plus

a *vertushka*, the special line to the Kremlin), a man-sized safe, a life-sized oil painting of Stalin. The chief of SMERSH lay down for a moment on the divan, crossing his legs and admiring his shiny boots.

Tonight, once he had read the interrogation reports on the children, should he watch Dynamo play football? Or go jazz dancing? He was proud of his nickname in the Dzerzhinsky Club's dance hall where the MVD Jazz Band played the new songs: *Vitya-foks-trotochnik* – Victor the foxtrot-dancer. Or the theatre? Sometimes he even chatted with ordinary people during the interval.

That's the man I am, he told himself. Unlike Beria, I have interests beyond sex and power. He had learned how to work from Beria, but now they were nearly equals. And Beria hated him.

He congratulated himself for stealing the Children's Case off Beria. But success raised the stakes. The phone buzzed on his desk and he called out: 'Send them in.'

It was his two chief interrogators, Komarov and Likhachev, who saluted stiffly.

'Easy. Sit.' He waved at them from the divan and they sat in the leather chairs. 'Comrades, before we get on to our new prisoner, I want you to work the other brats tonight. We must have names by morning.'

They left, and on the divan, Abakumov closed his eyes. Serafima Romashkina was the key. Did she have a secret life? The Chief of Military Counter-intelligence grinned: I know something about secret lives. Everyone has one.

24

Senka Dorov was the first to be called for interrogation that day. Even though he was ten and small for his age, he had spent the previous night in an adult cell. Twelve-year-olds could be shot and he was younger so they couldn't shoot him but suppose the rules had changed and . . .

Every other second he whispered to himself aloud: Mama, where are you? I'm here. Please come and find me. I'm frightened. I love you. Do you know where I am?

These words had sustained him ever since last night, when, at home (a radiant place that now seemed far away), he had tried on his new silk pyjamas, navy blue with red piping, made in China specially for him. His mama had loved the pyjamas, she even clapped when she saw him in them, and she had kissed him again and again. She always laughed with her head thrown back, making a high sound as if she were singing. Even though she was so busy, being a minister and a doctor, she always took him, Demian and Minka to school and often picked them up too.

I think I'm her favourite even though she says she loves the other three equally, he thought now. She kisses me more than them, especially Demian. Yes, they're older but still, she says I'm irresistible. She's the most beautiful mummy in the world, and when I'm grown up, I can marry her. (But she's married to Papa, of course. Would Papa mind? He's often very grumpy and gloomy, so I think not. Surely Papa would step aside?)

Last night, he'd decided to borrow a book from the neighbours so he went out onto the landing and down the stairs, still wearing his incredibly smart pyjamas and a little red and blue dressing gown to match. Minka said he was a dandy. Was that bad? 'I'm merely a flamboyant academic,' he'd told her.

He'd knocked on the neighbours' door and his friend Lulu answered. Her mother was behind her.

'Hello, Little Professor,' said Lulu's mother.

'May I please borrow a book: *Discussing Music, Choreography and Libretto in Tchaikovsky's Opera and Ballet*.'

'For your parents to read?'

'No, for me to study,' said Senka quite seriously.

'Don't you like Marshak's stories? *Terem-Teremok*? Or *Timur and his Team*?'

'Those are for babies!' he said indignantly.

'What a character you are, Senka,' said Lulu's mother.

The book was very heavy but Senka was carrying it upstairs again when he saw four men, two in suits and two in uniform with blue tabs.

'You're Senka Dorov, aren't you?' said one of the men, who had a bald head the shape of an onion dome.

'Yes. Who are you?'

'That book looks most interesting. Can we have a look at it downstairs?'

'I've got to get back for supper. Mama's waiting.'

But the man had taken the book and was perusing it in a very puzzled way. 'Opera, eh?'

'Which is your favourite Tchaikovsky?' asked Senka. 'Don't answer *Swan Lake*. That's too predictable.'

'You're a funny lad,' said the man as he steered Senka into the lift.

'Hey! Hang on,' cried Senka, but at that moment, his arms were held behind his back and one of the other men put a cloth over his face and he went to sleep. And when he woke up (he didn't know how long afterwards), he was between the same two men in a car approaching Dzerzhinsky Square.

'Where are you taking me? Who are you?' he asked sleepily.

And the domed one said: 'We're taking you to play Reds versus Whites with your friends. There's nothing to worry about!'

'You must think I'm very stupid or was born yesterday,' said Senka fearlessly – though as the drug wore off, he was beginning to feel fear rising up his tummy and into his throat, where he could taste its bitterness, a sensation he had experienced only once before, when one of Demian's horrid friends had held his nose at school and he thought he was suffocating until he remembered that he could breathe through his mouth.

He found he was still holding *Discussing Music, Choreography and Libretto in Tchaikovsky's Opera and Ballet* on his knee. He looked out of the windows: I know this building, he thought as they drove into the grey granite mountain of Lubianka. He had heard his parents mention it as they passed, and he had not missed the awe, even the dread, in their voices. Before he could say another word, the steel gates swung open and the car accelerated into a courtyard, the doors were opened and he was being frogmarched down some steps and up to a filthy counter which he could not see over.

'Where is he?' barked an old woman in a brown coat. 'I can't even see him. Little blighter, isn't he?'

'Are you taking me to see my sister?'

'Surname, name, patronymic.'

'Ring my mama. She'll come and get me. She doesn't know where I am.' Then he remembered something important and reassuring. 'Is my sister Minka here? Maybe I'm here to collect her?'

'No talking, prisoner,' snarled the woman. 'Answer the questions!' But Senka was so relieved that he had remembered this and so accustomed, at home and even at school, to being treated with indulgent love that he ignored her.

'Because Mama says Minka's going home soon. Now I understand why I'm here.'

'Another word out of you,' shouted a man in uniform, 'and you'll get a thick ear, if not a beating! Do you understand me?'

'Yes,' said Senka, now shocked and deeply worried. 'Please can I ring my daddy. He works on the Central Committee.' He thought mentioning his father might frighten them, but they did not seem to care. They took away his book and gave him a receipt that he didn't know what to do with. Then a fat warder in a brown coat led him through a door: 'Body search. Medical,' she said. 'Take all your clothes off and hurry up about it.'

Senka felt shy. 'Even my pyjama bottoms?'

'Move it! You collect your clothes after.' She pushed him through another door.

'But I've got a terrible tummy ache. Mama makes me lie down when I have it and then it goes. And I have asthma.'

'Come here,' said a man with a wen on his nose and a stethoscope and a white coat. He was sitting in an old metal chair beside a plain hospital trolley, its mattress stained a faded brown. Senka could tell he was a doctor but he was not a doctor like his mother. 'Stand!'

Senka sensed danger: 'No!' He bolted for the door. But the doctor had pressed a button on the wall and the door flew open and in came three warders, a man and two women. Senka was crying now, sobbing: 'I want my mama. I want to go home, my tummy is really hurting!' But they held his pale naked body and carried him to the trolley, where they dumped him roughly.

'Let me check you, or they'll hold you down,' said the doctor, who was wheezing heavily. 'And it'll be worse than a stomach ache, I can tell you.'

Senka stopped struggling but he found he was shaking with fear and foreboding. The doctor told him to open his mouth. Then the wen-nozzled medic pushed in his fingers, which tasted of metal and rubbish simultaneously, and felt Senka's teeth and his tongue. 'Turn over,' he said. 'Take a breath!'

Senka felt something in his bottom and he started to fight again and cry out, but it was over quickly, and soon he was back in the first room and in his pyjamas and dressing gown again. Another room: a greasy-haired old man beside a camera told him to sit in the chair but he was too small, so the photographer placed a cushion on it before disappearing under a black blanket: 'Look at the camera' and boom: there was a flash and a fizzing sound. 'Well done, son.' The photographer ruffled his hair.

Senka saw an opportunity. 'Please can I call my mama? I so miss my mama!'

'You're young to be in here,' the photographer whispered quickly. 'You'll get out, son, unlike me. But my advice is to let the current take you. Don't fight it.' Then he cleared his throat and called out: 'Prisoner for transfer.'

Senka was given back to the warders in their brown coats, who handed him over to two uniformed guards. Each held one of his arms. Keyrings holding many keys jingled from belts next to their pistols. 'No talking. Eyes forward. Let's go.' Steel stairways, down, up again, through locked doors. Senka felt tiny in this enormous hidden world. Every time one door closed and another opened he was in yet another towering hall filled with metal landings, each of which held row upon row of enforced steel doors.

The place stank of wee, poo, sweat, detergent, dampness. Repulsive. Repellent. Revolting. Rebarbative. Nauseating. Egregious. Emetic. The thesaurus of words comforted him but his heart was beating like a train travelling at speed.

When he heard some more footsteps getting closer, his heart raced. 'Is it Minka?' he said, his voice quivering. But they pushed him into a box like an upright coffin, and locked the door. Senka thought he might suffocate and his tummy cramp returned but he heard the steps go past and then they took him out and finally they opened a cell number 235 and pushed him inside.

'Someone's weed in my bed,' Senka called when he saw the thin mattress on the metal bed: it bore a yellow stain in the shape of the Crimea. He wanted to go himself but there was no lavatory. He did not know what to do. Then the Judas port opened and closed, the locks turned and a warder looked in.

'I'm hungry and I need to go to the lavatory,' he said.

'You've missed that time,' said the warder. 'Use that slops bucket.'

'I don't think I can use a bucket.'

'Save it up till morning then, your majesty. Rations soon.'

'Please call my mama,' said Senka, bursting into tears. Soon he was crying in spasms, the tears running down into his mouth and even down his neck. 'Please!'

The door slammed again, and the eyehole was opened and closed repeatedly, but no one came, so Senka spread the blanket over the mattress. The pillow had a red-brown mark the shape of Africa, he noticed.

Finally, he had to use the repugnant slops bucket; afterwards exhaustion forced him to lie down and he started to cry again. The door opened and this time it was a lady with a trolley. She gave him a bowl of soup (which was really just grey water with two chunks of straggly yellow fat floating in it), a square of black bread and a tiny rectangle of butter. He was so hungry but the soup stank and the fat was horrid so he just ate the bread.

'May I have an extra piece of bread?'

'Against the rules. That's your allowance.'

She gave him a cup of tea with a tiny piece of sugar; then the door was shut again and he lay on his bed, terrified by the sounds of the vastness of the Inner Prison of Lubianka. The symphony of prisons, he decided, is more percussion than strings: slamming doors, tinkling keys, grinding locks, coughing, spluttering, spasming, howling, sobbing, shouting, the clank of boots on metal landings and stairs. All was harsh and all he had known until this moment had been gentle.

Who were all these heaving, grunting, hacking strangers in the cells nearby? Was there anyone his age? Were the other children from the school close to him? Where was Minka? He closed his eyes and dreamed of his mama, of his home, of his brothers and sister. Mama, I'm here. *Please* come and find me. Do you know where I am?

He cried and cried but even when the tears ran out, the fear remained. How had this terrible mistake been made? Surely they didn't know he was ten. If only he had told them that, they'd have realized they had the wrong person. He could not believe they didn't know who his mama and papa were.

He replayed the night of the shooting on the bridge in his head: he was in the prison because of those deaths; he knew that. But had George and Andrei been arrested in *their* pyjamas?

Senka realized that he had nothing to cuddle and no one had kissed him tonight: how could he sleep without his toy bear, Aristotle? He had never slept without the bear. At home, he would lie on his bed with the cover pulled up to his neck, feeling like a warm prince at the very centre of the entire world. His mama would sit on his bed and tell him stories and take his face in her hands and kiss his nose and his forehead and his cheeks and sometimes even his eyes and he would look up at her and sometimes he gave his matinée-idol look, lowering his face and raising his eyes, and his mama would say: 'Oh! Who could resist those brown eyes? One day, you'll get married and she'll be a lucky girl!' And then she'd throw back her head and laugh.

This made him cry again but at least he was beginning to realize why he was there. When Minka disappeared, his mama said, 'Two of her friends were killed, so of course they have to investigate. Then she'll come home.' But Mama and Papa said Minka was going to come home tonight. So why was he in prison too? And why couldn't he sleep? The eyehole kept opening, and the electric light was on. When he curled up, a voice said: 'Hands outside the blanket!' He was desperate to sleep. 'You're such a good sleeper,' Mama always said. He closed his eyes but just when darkness was beginning to close in around him, the door was thrown open abruptly and he was shaken out of bed, marched down the corridor, up a metal stairway, down, up again through several doors.

A bright room. Two metal chairs. A man with a grotesque face dotted with thousands of little red spots, a jutting chin that resembled the muzzle of a dog and hands like lobster claws faced him.

'I'm Colonel Likhachev,' said the man. 'We've treated you children too gently, but now we know that you are criminals and enemies, we'll deal with you just the same way we punish adults. I don't care if you're ten or eighty years old: you answer my questions and you tell the truth. If you lie or withhold anything, I'll knock your teeth in. Do you understand me?'

Senka looked at this vicious myrmidon and gave a loud sob, and the man brought his fist down on the table so hard that the lamp jumped and Senka recoiled, knocking his chair over. The man rose fast and grabbed Senka by the chin, his claws squeezing him so that his mouth was all squashed.

'Don't you ever fucking move a muscle without my permission. And don't cry either.'

Senka started to pant fast and faster until he was struggling for air.

'Answer me this one question and you can go back to your cell.'

Senka nodded.

'Do you know Serafima Romashkina?'

'Yes,' he whispered, still breathing very fast.

'Do you know her well?'

'She's eighteen but . . . well, she's very nice to me.' Senka felt as though he might faint but knew he must not. He took a few quick breaths. 'She's my sister Minka's friend.'

'Now think carefully. Don't say no. Don't protect anyone. We find out everything and if you lie, you'll go to the camps and you'll never see your parents again. But if you tell the truth, you'll go home very soon. We are investigating the deaths on the Stone Bridge. You were there, were you not?'

'Yes.'

'What did you see there?'

'Two of my sister's friends were dead on the ground.'

'But you noticed something?'

'Yes. The notebook. Nikolasha's Velvet Book. And I picked it up.'

'You know when you picked it up, you committed a serious crime by purloining evidence of a murder?'

'I didn't know that.'

'Then why did you act like a traitor?' asked the livid, pimply man who Senka now realized was really a lobster masquerading as a human. 'Why pick it up? Why hide it?'

'I didn't think. Is my mama coming soon?'

'Not until you tell us the truth. What did you do with the book?'

'I put in my room and hid it.'

'Why?'

'I thought it would be interesting to read. I didn't know it was a crime, I'm very sorry.'

'Did you tell anyone you had it?'

'Only my brother. Demian. Later I found him opening my desk drawers and I was so cross I told my mother, but the notebook was gone.'

'You never read it?'

'No. I promise I didn't.'

'Did you know it contained plans to form a government and assassinate our leaders?'

Senka shook his head, trying to think back to his parents' conversations. His earliest memories were of the lifts in the

House on the Embankment groaning at night as the secret police arrived to arrest another person. On one occasion his mother had glanced tensely at his father: 'What floor?' she had asked.

'Eleventh.'

'The Larins. They aren't Enemies, Genrikh.'

'The Party never makes mistakes, Dashka. Better to kill a hundred innocents than miss one Enemy. We're in a life-and-death struggle to prepare for war against Fascism and there are Enemies everywhere. Let's not discuss this in front of . . .' And his father had looked at him.

'Senka's too little to understand,' Mama had said. And he hadn't understood then, but he did remember how the Larins had been taken away and never returned.

After the shooting on the bridge, Senka's mama had taken them all for a walk in the woods near their dacha and said, 'If you're ever asked about this, tell them what you know. But nothing extra. Don't gossip; stay off politics. Secrets are like a minefield: you don't know the mine is there until you tread on it. Chatter can destroy a family.'

'This comes from the highest authority in the Soviet Union,' said the Lobster now. 'Search your memory: things you've seen, things you've heard. Did Serafima have a boyfriend?'

'Of course not. If she did have one, it would be *me*!'

'Christ!' The Lobster bent his hands back and clicked the bones. 'A special friend then?'

'But Serafima was always on her own.'

'Did anyone pay her special attention?'

Senka hesitated. He sensed danger, knew somehow that his words could hurt people. But where could the danger lie here? Was it a crime for a boy to admire a girl? He wasn't at all sure.

'All boys liked Serafima,' he said. 'Me most of all.'

The Lobster was writing on a piece of paper. Now he pushed it across the table. 'Do you confess to stealing this evidence of conspiracy from the crime scene?'

'I don't understand,' Senka said.

'You can't deny you took the notebook and hid it. Your brother Demian found it.'

'Oh!' Not only had Demian found the notebook, but he'd also given it to the secret police. That's why he was free. And he was jealous of Senka and obsessed with rising up the Pioneers and Komsomol and becoming as important as their father. Demian was a snitch and a weasel.

'If you ever want to see your mother again, sign this now,' the Lobster said, pushing it to Senka, who signed it quickly.

'If you were twelve, this piece of paper could sentence you to the Highest Measure of Punishment: death by shooting to the back of the head. But as you're only ten, you face ten years in the camps under Article 158,' the Lobster said.

Senka's head spun and he held on to the edge of the table.

'But if you help us about Serafima . . .'

'Minka said she had . . . admirers . . . suitors . . . chevaliers.'

'Name them now before I punch you.'

Senka loved Serafima and would do anything rather than get her into trouble but how would this harm her? How would it harm anyone? Beware the mines! He racked his brains for something about Serafima's admirers. Hadn't he heard Minka and Serafima laughing about the Crown Prince? They thought he didn't understand this code name – how stupid did they think he was? But he knew not to mention Vasily Stalin. Anything to do with Stalin was perilous. He had to find something that wasn't dangerous but it was hard because Senka did not know what the Lobster wanted. The mines were invisible. Senka's stomach started to churn and his breathing became laboured again.

'I think I'm going to be sick,' he said.

The Lobster stood up, his chair grinding against the floor, and he started to count: 'At three, I'll beat the answers out of you.' He pulled out a thick rubber bullystick and banged it on the table. 'I've smashed in a man's skull with this little friend,' and Senka could see that the club rested happily in the Lobster's claws as if he was accustomed to using it. 'One, two . . .'

'Well, yes, yes, there was a time . . .' Don't get Serafima into trouble, Senka told himself. Don't mention Vasily Stalin. Don't involve Mama or Papa. Don't harm Minka. There was so much to consider. He ran through the possibilities: *This* is nothing, *that's* secret; *this* won't satisfy him, *that's* dangerous. His mind was overheating with responsibilities, ambuscades, minefields, unspeakables, unmentionables, all of which were balanced against his own confession of taking the notebook and the ten years awaiting him in the Gulags: the train journeys, the snowy tundra, the threat of never seeing his parents again.

'There was one time . . .'

'When?' The Lobster put down the club and took up a pen.

'It was a few weeks ago . . . Minka and I were walking on Gorky Street and . . . and . . .'

The truncheon came down hard on Senka's hand. It hurt desperately and he started to cry, holding his wounded right hand in his left. The tears blurred his eyes until he couldn't see. 'I'll tell you, I'll tell you!'

But he still hadn't decided *what* to tell.

'Please don't hurt me again. I want to see my mama . . . Once Minka and I were walking down Gorky and we saw

Serafima and . . .' He tried to remember and then he had it. Yes, this was perfect – and it hurt nobody he loved. 'Behind her, a hundred metres behind her, we saw *him* following her.'

The relief was intoxicating as Senka settled down and began to tell his story.

25

Kapitolina Medvedeva was in her office waiting for Innokenty Rimm to speak. In the last few days, that witch-hunting hypocrite had pranced the corridors like a broad-hipped conquistador. Something – nothing good – had happened to give him this spurt of confidence. What was it? Kapitolina Medvedeva had studied Dr Rimm as a zoologist does a rare and poisonous spider. His bluster had to be connected to the Children's Case, she knew this.

Director Medvedeva was a strict disciplinarian, a Party member of many years, but what she really cared about was teaching and the children. This case had ruined her term – and she knew it could ruin her life too.

At night, she couldn't sleep. By day, she sat at her desk but she couldn't work. The parents (had Comrade Satinov ever visited the school gates so often?) brought the children; the children attended lessons, which the teachers taught, but all were pretending. They weren't really there. They were in the dungeons of Lubianka. If she was lucky, the children would be released quickly and the case would blow over, but she knew such crises were often exploited by busybodies with axes to grind, overweening Party-minded pedants like Rimm who could turn harmless scandals into tragedies. I must be strong, she resolved, I must be like steel. *Tverdost* – hardness – is a Bolshevik virtue.

Rimm hadn't knocked; he had just barged in. Now she was scrutinizing his nose – it was like a duck's beak – and his hair, the colour of rusty wire.

'I wish to call an extraordinary meeting of the School Party Committee,' he said.

'Why?'

'To examine if any mistakes have been made in your leadership of the school.'

Kapitolina sat back in her chair. I'm in charge here, she thought. Not him. Not the Hummer. 'I veto that idea, Dr Rimm.'

'You cannot do so, Comrade Director. I am its secretary.'

'There are three members of the committee and I have already spoken to Comrade Noodelman, and he is against.'

Director Medvedeva could see that Rimm was prepared for this. 'You may remember that the rules allow for me to convene an extraordinary meeting of the School Party Committee *with the attendance of all school staff* to read Party announcements. Such as this one on mathematics teaching textbooks from the Central Committee Education Sector.'

He raised his eyebrows, and Director Medvedeva could see the gleam of victory in those watery red-rimmed eyes. 'I shall see you there, shall I?'

The common room was full for Dr Rimm's special meeting of the School's Party Committee. The teachers were pale, tense, worried – and Director Medvedeva remembered the tragic meetings during the late thirties when two teachers had disappeared off the face of the earth and they had voted unanimously that 'Enemies of the People should be shot like hyenas.'

Now only one teacher, Benya Golden, was relaxed enough

to recline on one of the sofas with his legs crossed and a world-weary grin on his face.

She opened the meeting but Rimm immediately interrupted her. Since he was secretary, it was his meeting, and he moved fast to pass a series of resolutions – that the committee should examine whether the Children's Case exposed any mistakes by the director of the school; that during this process, he, Dr Rimm, should take over the school . . .

Silence greeted these proposals.

'Is this a coup d'état, Dr Rimm?' said Benya Golden at last. 'Do you wish to be the Napoleon of School 801?' There was quiet laughter from somewhere, and then silence.

'I'm surprised you joke! Your bourgeois and un-Party-minded teaching, particularly in your Pushkin lessons, has played a role in this tragic case, Teacher Golden.'

'All right, Dr Rimm,' Golden said, sighing and stretching. Director Medvedeva knew how hard Golden had taken the shootings and the arrests, and she sensed he had more experience of men like Rimm than she did. 'Have your vote but I will only vote for you if you promise that your singing of "May Comrade Stalin Live Many, Many Long Years" will improve dramatically. In fact, are you singing it *deliberately* badly? That may be a subversive act of musical sabotage.'

A gasp of surprise and, from someone, an attempt to fight laughter greeted this, but Rimm's officious demeanour, laced with hints of powerful connections, bewitched the frightened staff, who voted for him unanimously.

Afterwards, Kapitolina Medvedeva, who felt herself growing smaller and more insignificant with each step, walked slowly back up the corridor to meet the parents at the Golden Gates. She could survive this. Such intrigues occurred all the time.

But her worry about the arrested children compounded by this blow made her limbs heavy as lead. At the gates, she greeted the first parent, Dr Dorova. Demian was at her side but where was Senka? Director Medvedeva glanced at her face and the answering look of sleepless despair revealed the unthinkable. They had taken a ten-year-old! Whatever next?

She heard the ominous humming get closer, and Dr Rimm stood right in front of her, his womanly hips in his Party tunic blocking her way. 'I'll greet the parents and hold assembly this morning,' he said. 'This place is riddled with rotten elements and a fish rots from the head.'

She stepped backwards just as Dashka Dorova left and Comrade Satinov arrived.

'Esteemed Comrade Satinov,' she heard Rimm declare in his breathless soprano. 'I'm delighted as acting director to greet you at the gates of our school! Long Live Comrade Stalin!'

It was early morning but the good humour of the Chekists, even though their eyes were tired and their chins covered in stubble, showed Andrei Kurbsky that they were making progress, and that meant someone had sung. Andrei knew he was the only outsider amongst the children, and he simply could not bear to go backwards, to exile, to penury. He was determined to survive this. I still have cards to play, he reminded himself. I can still get out of here.

Andrei knew that Colonel Likhachev would beat him, but in that knowledge lay strength, for violence is at its most potent when it is unexpected. Andrei distilled all his fears down to two concerns: first was his mother. She would know by now where he was. She might even have been to the prison, having queued outside so many jails for his father. While the other parents could probably ring Comrade Beria himself, she alone had no one to turn to.

The bullystick struck him so hard in the face that it did not hurt. He felt a blackness with a heartbeat and pumping blood that turned the light into a night sky speckled with red sparks instead of stars. He was on his back on the concrete floor when Likhachev and another guard picked him up.

'That's just to wake you up, scum. To show you that here you're nothing. Whatever you say, you might never see the streets of Moscow or your mother again.' Andrei could feel his face pulsating as if it were a creature with its own life. He tried to wipe away the blood.

Be calm, he told himself, return to your mother, protect those you love. Above all, Andryusha, survive this to reforge yourself. Play chess with these brutes, even if your eyes are blind with blood.

Likhachev placed the truncheon glistening with Andrei's blood beside his notebook and pen. 'Nikolasha Blagov's conspiracy against the Party was inspired by a mentor known as NV. Your friends have already told us this stood for *Novi Vozhd*. New Leader. We know this snake was connected to Serafima Romashkina.'

'I don't think so,' Andrei said quickly. A smirk crossed Likhachev's face. 'No one was close to her.'

'Even after a smack in the chops, you jump when she's mentioned,' said Likhachev. 'Perhaps *you're* her lover. Are *you* NV?'

'I don't know what you mean.' But Andrei did, because protecting Serafima was his second priority.

'We know how you followed her around like a puppy, and that you conspired avidly to overthrow the Soviet Government.'

'Not true.'

'That's not what your friends say.'

'Well, they didn't know that I watched her sometimes.' There. He'd said it. Played his ace card. Now the question was: How would it be picked up?

Likhachev twitched. 'What do you mean?'

'I know it sounds . . . strange, obsessional . . .'

'Why did you watch her?'

Andrei blushed, even there, even on the edge of the precipice. 'I liked her . . . I wanted to know where she went.'

'Another lovesick puppy! Didn't you have better things to do? So you saw everything. What did you see? The conspirators?'

'Surely you can testify that Nikolasha was planning a coup?'

'I didn't realize he had gone that far.'

'You were concealing evidence from the Organs?'

'No, he didn't show us his scribblings.'

He saw Likhachev sit forward as he tried a different tack. 'Serafima Romashkina. You think you knew her well? The one thing we Chekists know is that no one knows anyone well. You can be married to a woman for twenty years and not realize that she is an Enemy, a traitor, a whore. Let me share with you that we know from Nikolasha Blagov's notebook that Serafima Romashkina was central to the conspiracy.'

'I know that's not true because I was watching her.'

Likhachev smiled. 'Your friends have already told us name after name of her lovers. All were devoted to her. Young and old. What was her trick? Who taught her? The geishas of Japan? She must be quite a girl.'

Andrei was trying to keep his footing in a landslide. He church-steepled his fingers to concentrate. Save yourself, your mother and Serafima, he repeated. He had to give them someone else. But who?

'Serafima's a decent, honourable Soviet patriot,' said Andrei. 'She didn't have a lover. I saw who she met. Yes, she met people like anyone does. Maybe she had mentors like we all do. But no lover.'

Likhachev was caressing his bullystick. 'Now you're fucking boring me. You mentioned a mentor, did you not?'

Andrei touched his face. His right cheek and mouth were numb and swollen. And he was tired. He felt he would die if he didn't get some sleep. The answer was obvious: Vasily Stalin. Perhaps there was something between Serafima and him? Vasily Stalin had picked her up, and she knew him. If NV – New Leader – was Vasily Stalin, wouldn't they see this entire case as a harmless joke, instead of a conspiracy? But George Satinov had warned him: never mention Vasily Stalin, and he had left him out of his reports to the Organs. Anyway, who would believe him, the son of an Enemy? And what gruesome Caucasian vengeance would the Great Stalin himself take on a boy who dared to mention the Name in vain? Yet despite it all, the word Vasily danced on his lips.

Likhachev leaned over and put his jaw so close to the wounds on Andrei's face that he could taste the sausage on his interrogator's breath. 'Come on, lover boy,' he said. 'Prove to me that Serafima's whiter than white.'

At lunchtime, the inspector from the Education Sector of the Agitprop Department, Central Committee, arrived to hear Dr Rimm's accusations.

'Comrade Director.' Inspector Ivanov licked his finger as he turned some papers. 'In the light of the Children's Case, we have received four anonymous complaints about the direction of School 801.'

Kapitolina Medvedeva looked miserably at Rimm, who beamed jubilantly back at her. Who cares if she knew it was *he* who had written all four denunciations? he thought. Whoever had written them, they told the truth.

'Therefore, I have been deputed to consult Comrade Rimm, who has confirmed some of the accusations. Is that right, Comrade Rimm?'

'Yes, Comrade Ivanov. But most reluctantly and with sincere sadness.'

Dr Rimm was delighted at the way things were going. It turned out he had quite a talent for undercover work. Demian had given him the Velvet Book and he had given it to an officer whom he knew in the Organs. Yes, Senka Dorov had been arrested thanks to him, but Comrade Stalin often said, 'You can't make an omelette without breaking eggs,' and, besides, the Chekists had promised no harm would come to Senka and the shock might teach the runt some respect.

'Good,' said Ivanov, licking his fingertips repeatedly as he turned more pages. 'Shall we take these one by one, Comrade Director?'

Kapitolina Medvedeva nodded.

'Who accepted Andrei Kurbsky, the son of an Enemy of the People, into the school this term?'

Kapitolina looked a little surprised. 'I did.'

'Why?'

'Comrade Stalin said we must not visit the sins of the fathers on to the children,' she said.

'True enough.' Ivanov made a note. 'Who is paying the fees?'

'I am. Out of my own salary.'

'Comrade Director, did you permit' – two licks of the fingertips – 'the teaching of Pushkin against Communist ethics with a romantic-bourgeois sentimentality?'

'If I suspected any teacher of bourgeois philistinism I would have dismissed them.'

He noted this.

'I fear these petty accusations are wasting your time, Inspector,' Kapitolina continued. 'In recognition of this, I propose that Comrade Rimm, with Comrade Noodelman, should investigate this and report in one month.'

This was a clever move. Even Rimm had to admit this, although he could see she was playing for time.

'That seems a good idea,' said Inspector Ivanov. 'Perhaps for the moment that is the best solution, don't you think, Comrade Rimm? The Central Committee would be satisfied with that.'

'Thank you, Comrade Ivanov,' said Rimm. The director had foiled him – cunning bitch. Now he would have to prove his own accusations, which would be much harder than sending anonymous denunciations.

But he had held back his gravest accusation.

'I have one question, Comrade Ivanov. You are doubtless aware of Teacher Golden's biography and the role he played in the tragedy.'

Inspector Ivanov looked interested. 'Pray tell us, comrade.'

Rimm leaned forward. 'Golden created the poisonous ideology that inspired these children to kill. I propose you investigate why this two-faced mask-wearer is teaching at this school? Who hired him? And even more importantly, who is protecting him, even now?'

26

When George was young, an aquaintance of his parents named Mendel Barmakid, a famous Old Bolshevik, had been arrested. His parents had whispered about it in the bathroom as parents did in those days – with the taps running.

'Can he be guilty?' asked Tamara.

'Read this,' answered his father.

Tamara quietly read out: '"Protocols of Interrogation of Mendel Barmakid . . ." But they could have used excessive methods,' she said. 'Excessive methods' meant torture in Bolshevik language.

'I doubt it,' answered Satinov. 'Look. He confesses everything and every page is signed by him. See? That's convincing. If he wasn't guilty, he wouldn't confess. Confession is the mother of justice. The lesson is to tell the truth but never confess anything!'

George Satinov was repeating this to himself now.

'Who is NV?' Colonel Likhachev was asking. 'And what was his relationship to Serafima Romashkina?'

George thought of Vasily Stalin. He recalled his brother David saying, 'Vaska's crazy about Serafima, and he always gets what he wants. When the rogue takes girls flying, they fall into bed with him out of sheer terror!' What if Likhachev found out George had not told him about Serafima's partying with Vasily Stalin? What if Andrei had told them already, and they were testing him? George kept his nerve and held back.

Likhachev stood up abruptly and banged on the door, which opened almost instantaneously. 'Major,' he rasped, 'bring in Prisoner 72.'

George's heart beat faster as terrible thoughts rushed through his mind. Would this be Minka? Or Serafima? And he prayed that if it was any of his friends, they would not be harmed. He hoped that they had not punched Andrei or Vlad as they had punched him and he prayed too they had been as strong as he had and had not incriminated themselves. And then for a moment, the nightmare: could it be his father? But that was simply unthinkable. He could hear the clip of footsteps getting closer. For the first time, George, so confident, so brash, experienced the most elemental fear. His belly contracted. Amidst the martial marching of guards, he sensed dragging: the shuffling of another presence barely walking at all. Then two guards pulled in a figure whom they deposited on the chair opposite. There was a bump like a sack of grain and a big head fell forward, but Colonel Likhachev seized the hair and held it up like a primitive warrior with the scalp of a fallen enemy. George gasped. At first it was just the atrocious wounds that shocked him: the face was smashed into pulp, swollen to twice its normal size, the nose crushed, teeth missing, the lip gashed to the nose, the hair caked with blood.

His head spun, his jaw clenched, his belly tightened and he vomited in the corner of the room. The face was scarcely recognizable but when he wiped his mouth and looked again, Colonel Likhachev said, 'Don't you remember your dear friend? Look more closely!'

The man seemed barely conscious. He was muttering to

himself, and one of his eyes was totally closed, with blood seeping out of it. He wore a uniform, though the tunic was missing half its buttons, the chest was torn where the medals had been ripped off and the shoulderboards had been cut away. George half covered his eyes. Even like this, the man was all too familiar.

'Losha?' he said. 'Losha – oh God, what have they done to you?'

'Ssssizz!' The sound came from Losha Babanava's mouth but it was incomprehensible. He opened his good eye, which somehow almost seemed to twinkle at George. 'Ssshhhzz.'

'Sizzling?' said George.

The head nodded.

George collapsed back into his chair. He thought he might vomit again. After his father, Losha Babanava was the man George most loved and respected. He had known him all his life. Whatever happened, whatever he needed, Losha had been able to fix it. Now Losha, this prince of men, was the bloodied ruin before him, flanked by two guards, in this godforsaken prison. If Losha was broken, anything was possible. His father could be here too.

'George, George, calm down,' said Likhachev. 'You can see what happens when you don't tell us all you know. No one can stand in the way of the state, however strong you are – isn't that right, Prisoner Babanava? Losha's as strong as an ox but we broke him, didn't we?' He paused, and then smiled at George, his face shining with sweat. 'We should thank you, George. How else could we have known where you got the gun that Rosa Shako used to kill Nikolasha and herself?'

George was almost overcome with the shame of it, and angry too. There was no shortage of guns in Moscow. Nikolasha could have got that gun anywhere. Yes, he, George, had borrowed it from Losha and given it to his schoolfriend, but it had not occurred to him that Losha would get into trouble. And now he realized that this ruin of blisters, blood, bruises, was his own doing.

But Losha was shaking and trying to say something. 'Don't blame yourself,' he thought Losha was trying to mouth. 'Do whatever you have to do.'

'Silence, prisoner,' shouted Likhachev. 'Or we'll finish you off!'

Losha slurred one more word until George recognised it: 'Family!' Family was everything to a Georgian, and Losha loved their family. George buried his face in his hands.

'Let's get on with this,' said Likhachev. 'Losha says there's something you haven't told us, George.'

George could barely hear him. He felt the fires of hell were screaming in his ears.

'If you want to earn Losha a visit from the doctor, tell us who was the important man who chased Serafima. Focus, George. Losha might die without a doctor.'

George looked at Losha and the caked head nodded. He was right. It did not matter. He must tell or Losha would suffer more.

'I'll tell you, if you get him a doctor. It was Vasily . . .' Losha nodded. 'Vasily Stalin.'

Likhachev stiffened when he heard the name. 'Vasily Stalin and Serafima?'

George read in Likhachev's face that no one else had mentioned that name in connection with Serafima. Well, now he'd said it, and it didn't matter, because Vasily Stalin was untouchable.

Likhachev rubbed his narrow brow. 'Vasily Stalin, you say?'

'Yes.'

Likhachev called out to the guards: 'Get Colonel Komarov.'

Komarov joined them, and Likhachev turned to George again.

'General Vasily Stalin was courting Serafima?' he asked.

'Yes,' said George.

'Did they have an immoral relationship?'

'I don't know.'

'Can you confirm this, Babanava?'

Losha nodded and George told the story that he had heard from his brother about the night Vasily had gone out with Serafima. The two interrogators looked at one another in silence for what seemed like an age while George understood that they, like George, were running through all the possible consequences of his revelation – but from a very different angle. All George could hope was that he had won Losha a medical visit. The interrogators would have to report to their superiors and George wondered if the magic name might stop this crazy investigation altogether. Surely if Comrade Stalin were told, if Vasily complained to his father, then the schoolchildren would be released . . . But this was George's last burst of optimism: he was so drained that, whatever the consequences to himself, all he wanted to do was sleep, to escape this hell.

'Let's return to the New Leader,' said Likhachev. 'If you still want to help Losha, that is?'

George rubbed his eyes. 'I don't think NV means New Leader. Nikolasha may have been referring to someone in *Onegin*. You need a Pushkin scholar . . .'

As the guards were dragging Losha towards the door, he looked back at George trying to say something again. 'Sszzy . . .' And then George understood it: '*Sissies*.'

George wept. For himself. For Losha. For sissies everywhere.

* * *

Innokenty Rimm had never been happier. In the past, he had often felt himself handicapped by his figure, by the bottom that looked big in whatever suits or tunic he chose. (He replayed the pain of his schooldays, thanks to the trousers that made his hips look ungainly, however tight or baggy they might be! What tantrums he'd had when his mother bought him trousers and he looked in the mirror!) When he had received those love letters from 'Tatiana,' he had often wondered what such a Helen of Troy had seen in him. But now power had lightened his chunky midriff, now he felt snake-hipped with the headiness of success. If she liked him then, when he was merely deputy director, she must love him so much more now. He expected the next letter to acclaim his new status.

He was at the Golden Gates, greeting the parents with bon mots. How natural: they all treated him as if he had always been in charge.

Assembly. School, stand! A simple gesture to sit. A merry song. A pointed homily.

Afterwards: 'Morning, Teacher Golden. A word, please?' he said, buttonholing Benya as the children pushed back their chairs. The children were watching him inconspicuously, wondering if he was reprimanding Golden, interested in his every act now that he was (acting) director.

'Yes, Innokenty,' said Benya Golden. 'I'm all ears.'

'Your Pushkin classes are suspended while the school is under such scrutiny and while we are rethinking the literature syllabus. Understood?'

Benya Golden had opened his mouth to make one of his facetious comments when Rimm spotted four strangers in suits who were obviously plain-clothed officers of the Organs. Now that he was in charge, he hoped they were not here to arrest any of his pupils. He was quite sure that the children in custody would be released very soon. If the Party believed Kapitolina Medvedeva had committed crimes, well, he would not dream of challenging the Party. 'Morning, comrades!' he said to them masterfully. In fact, he knew why they were here: to arrest Benya Golden after his denunciation.

The agents marched purposefully down the central aisle. The children too recognized them as the comrades who had arrested Vlad Titorenko on the day after the shooting, and shouldered their satchels more slowly, scared but still curious. The teachers froze in their seats. Rimm smiled as they approached, knowing why they were there, ready to guide them. Sure enough, one of them gestured slightly towards where he and Golden stood. So he had been correct. He always was.

Rimm looked at Golden and he was amazed to see that, while he was pale, he was calm. A courage of sorts.

Rimm stepped forward towards the Chekists. Now that they were close, he could not help but take control (as acting director and advisor to the Organs). He gestured a little towards Golden, to guide them to the right place, and they were grateful because they placed their hands on Golden's arms, lightly but firmly.

'Would you come with us?' said their leader. 'It won't take long. We just have a few questions.' They turned Golden around – he glanced back at Agrippina Begbulatova – and were just about to march him out when the chief agent said, 'You are Innokenty Rimm, are you not?'

'No, I'm not,' said Golden.

'I'm Dr Rimm,' Rimm said. 'But surely . . .'

'Apologies,' said the chief agent, patting Benya Golden on

the arm in an entirely different way than a second earlier. 'Do carry on and have a good day.'

Then, moving with the robust agility of men who live in the realm of physical force, they laid their hands on Rimm in such a way that they instantly assumed possession of him. He felt cumbersome, as if made of clay. He could not move his legs, and his face seemed to burn.

'Innokenty Rimm? Come with us, please. Just a formality. A couple of hours and we'll have you back in class. Nothing to worry about . . .'

As he was frogmarched out of the hall, Rimm glanced back, expecting to see a smirk of triumph from Benya Golden – but instead he saw only deep sympathy, and this from a man who had every reason to despise him.

And he wondered in that fearsome moment of freefalling if he had been wrong about Golden, about the headmistress, about *everything*, all along.

27

Was it morning or midnight, midsummer or the dead of winter? The days and nights were blurred together: interrogations that started in the middle of the night seemed to last into the afternoon. But the very fact that Senka had settled into the almost reassuring routine of the Grey Granite Mountain proved that a great deal of time had passed. More than a week. Maybe even two weeks. How could he tell? All Senka Dorov knew was that he was very tired and very hungry, and back in the interrogation room that had become his entire world, facing Colonel Likhachev.

I am cleverer than you, you ugly old bully, he thought as he looked at the Lobster. Senka had confessed to taking the Velvet Book but in innocence. When he saw the notebook, there on the bridge, he had grabbed it. When he read all that nonsense about the Romantic Politburo and Minister of Love after lights-out in his bedroom, he grasped that he must hide the book. But he had made two grievous mistakes: the first was not destroying it, and the second was telling his snitch brother. But in that all-important session, he had managed to find something to give the Chekists a new strand of investigation: 'Once we were walking down Gorky and we saw Serafima, and a hundred metres behind her, we saw Dr Rimm following her.' Yes, he'd offered up the grotesque Rimm as Serafima's secretly besotted admirer, and wondered if they had arrested him too.

The stench of Likhachev brought him back to earth. Senka analysed the Lobster (after all, he had spent hours with the horrible man). He identified: cologne, sweat, salami, garlic, too much vodka, and wee – yes, not unlike the odour of the school lavatories. However, he felt a tremendous urge to please this thug, to win his favour. This man had absolute power over him and his family, yet he was determined that he would not tell anyone anything, not anything important anyway. He remembered that his papa often said, 'Discretion is one of the cardinal Bolshevik virtues.' Comrade Genrikh Dorov was a clever and important man (if lugubriously solemn – did he never laugh?). Yes, even his mama admitted with a laugh that Papa was a curmudgeon. And how he loved his mama. Even here, he could will her presence: her lovely scent (it came all the way from Paris, she said), which he could identify quite separately from the sweet way her skin and hair smelled. But his daddy understood Bolshevism and politics better than his mama: Genrikh Dorov had been one of Stalin's own secretaries and Papa said, 'The Party is always right.' But why did his parents whisper things if the Party was always right? There was an inconsistency there, thought Senka, an inconsistency that could not be explained, not even by his parents.

One thing was clear amidst all the esoteric mysteries of the Lobster's questions: he would be a lot more comfortable in his professorial suit than these pyjamas. And now his chance came.

'So,' said the Lobster in a new amused tone. 'I hear you wear a suit all the time and sweep up leaves instead of doing school gymnastics. A weird little boy, aren't you?'

'Comrade Colonel,' Senka burst out, encouraged by this lugubrious affability, 'when my mama comes, please can you ask her to bring my suit?'

The smirk hovered around Colonel Likhachev's mouth. 'A Soviet child should wear socks and shorts.'

'Yes. But my dignity depends on a suit.'

'Your dignity? A suit?' Likhachev pulled out his bullystick and thumped the table.

Senka lowered his head, his eyes fixed on the truncheon. He was afraid, of course, but he was clever enough to *appear* even more afraid, and he saw that his fear pleased the Lobster.

'Quick question for you tonight, Senka. Which of you really knows Pushkin's *Onegin*?'

Senka sighed. Could it be part of a code? There were often codes within ordinary things: he liked to read the fables of Aesop, and Papa had explained to him that the Party leaders often used a special secret language that was Aesopian, with lots of double meanings, so Senka was always aware of the Aesopian language when he read the newspapers or listened to the news on the radio, and here in Lubianka he constantly examined each question with the diligence of a cryptographer.

So Senka turned the Lobster's literary question over in his mind: how could that hurt his mama and papa? He could not imagine that it would. How could it hurt his sister Minka? No, he could not see that either. He was puzzled. It appeared to be a question that he could answer, but what was its meaning in Aesopian language? Was Pushkin, in this case, national poet (good) or romantic nobleman (bad)?

'Get a fucking move on, boy, or you'll feel this across your face.' The Lobster brandished the bullystick. 'Who knows *Onegin* best of your sister's friends?'

He chose the boy whom he hoped would do the least harm. 'Andrei Kurbsky. You could ask him.'

* * *

Kapitolina Medvedeva was suspended. Even though her chief accuser, Rimm, was under arrest, her decisions on Andrei Kurbsky and Benya Golden were under investigation. At home that night, she wondered if she was going to be destroyed. She was being called before a judgement tribunal of the Education Sector of the Agitprop Department, Central Committee, at Old Square. Most likely, she would be sacked and then arrested. She would never teach again. The Gulags were likely. Even execution was possible. At the very least: exile. It was time to make a plan. A plan for survival.

I know who I am, Serafima told herself as Likhachev interrogated her. I know I love and am loved. Nothing else matters. And she touched her scar, the mark she called her snakeskin, with her hand, and heard his voice reciting their poem. But Likhachev was asking her something again.

LIKHACHEV Who was your lover, you whore? Who was NV? Name the New Leader.

SERAFIMA There was no New Leader and I don't know what NV means.

LIKHACHEV Don't play the saint with me, girl. You prostituted yourself to a counter-revolutionary conspiracy and your hot tail attracted tomcats from all over town. Now answer the questions or you'll be sorry. Was George Satinov your lover? Vlad Titorenko? Or Andrei Kurbsky?

SERAFIMA No. Andrei wanted to protect me. George is a friend. I don't know what you're talking about.

LIKHACHEV Kurbsky is the son of an Enemy of the People. Was Innokenty Rimm your lover?

SERAFIMA No! Dr Rimm is really old. He's about forty! I don't think any girl could be in love with Dr Rimm.

LIKHACHEV A degenerate traitor who is capable of conspiring to overthrow the Soviet Government is capable of sexual intercourse with Dr Rimm. Don't lie to the Party! We have the letters! We found them in your bedroom. Let me read this one: *My darling 'Tatiana,' I know it is you, Serafima Constantinovna – your letters have reached the throbbing heart of this Bolshevik lover, your handsome pedagogue. In my Communist ethics lessons I gaze upon you. I sing for you in the school corridors! Your 'Onegin' (yes, of course it is I, Innokenty).* Prisoner, your friends have told us that they saw Rimm following you in the streets. Confess this teacher seduced you. What depravity did he demand? Sodomy? If you lie to me, you'll rot in the camps! Confess!

SERAFIMA No. He sent me those letters but I was bewildered. Then I laughed. That's all.

LIKHACHEV Why didn't you report them?

SERAFIMA I wasn't sure what to do. If I reported him, would I be blamed? He was important at the school, and I'm leaving soon. I thought it best just to keep them and ignore him.

LIKHACHEV You are a lying prostitute. When we searched his home, we found *your* love letters to him! Look, read this one. *Tuneful singer . . . sweet Onegin . . . Kiss me like a true Communist. 'Tatiana.'* You're lying to the Organs of the Communist Party. Take this!

SERAFIMA Please don't hurt me. God, I'm bleeding.

LIKHACHEV Confess or I'll smash your teeth in. You'll be like a toothless hag, sucking your gums. Are these your letters to him?

SERAFIMA I've never seen these before. I didn't write them, I swear to you. Someone was playing a prank on Dr Rimm. You know everything and I'm sure you even know who was teasing Dr Rimm. Perhaps one of his pupils?

LIKHACHEV The Organs know everything. What about Teacher Golden? Was he your lover too?

SERAFIMA No!

LIKHACHEV You were his favourite pupil?

SERAFIMA Why are you asking me these questions?

LIKHACHEV Because you're a pretty girl and he's a fornicator. [Pause.] I have to ask you a question that is sensitive because of its relation to the Head of the Soviet Government. You were acquainted with General Vasily Stalin? Did you and he ever have immoral relations?

A stark white villa in Babelsberg, Berlin. Stalin lay on a divan identical to the one in his Dacha in a library filled with the same books and journals. His first meetings with Churchill and Truman were set for later that day and he wore his new generalissimo's uniform: a white tunic with a single star and golden epaulettes, creased blue trousers with a red stripe, and laced bootkins, instead of the baggy trousers tucked into high boots that he generally favoured.

Outside the room, he heard the hum of the headquarters of an empire: motors revved, phones rang, boots clipped on marble floors, young officials bustled, typewriters clattered.

He was not quite alone, however: his son Vasily stood before him in full uniform, almost to attention, as if he were not family at all but a lowly air force general.

'Sit, sit,' said Stalin.

Vasily sat nervously.

'How are you, Vaska?' Stalin said softly. He was about to ask how Vasily's poor wife and child were doing but it seemed a waste of time. He knew exactly how they were, and they were not happy.

'Fine, Father.'

'As you can see, I'm busy. No one can do a thing on their own, you know. You tell them what to do and they either ignore you or screw it up.'

'Of course, Father. Only you can decide anything.'

'You can see I'm weary. Not quite well.'

'You look very well to me, Father. Congratulations on the new rank, generalissimo.'

'Pah!' Stalin waved this aside disdainfully. 'We've got a lot to do here.' He knew from his British agents that Truman would tell him in the next two days that America had its nuclear bomb and that they would now drop it on Japan. He would pretend that he knew nothing about it. If its awesome power was not exaggerated, he would have to accelerate the Soviet nuclear programme to get his own bomb at breakneck speed. A titanic endeavour. Only his best organizer, Beria, could pull it off . . . Stalin had won the war; sometimes, in the early crises, sleeping on a campbed in his office for days on end. But now he had defeated Germany and conquered half of Europe. And just when he had triumphed, the Americans had got this new bomb and he would have to start all over again. His enemies were still strong and he would have to be harsher, stronger, more vigilant than ever. No one must find out how ill he was.

'Father . . .' Vasily started, and Stalin, whose mind had been far away, focused on the sickly grey face of his son. It was the face of an alcoholic. Like Stalin's father.

'Vaska,' said Stalin, suddenly colder and businesslike. He didn't have much time and the boy bored, shamed and irritated him in equal measure. What would his late wife, Nadya, have thought of this pathetic ne'er-do-well? She'd have blamed him, of course. 'You've been mentioned in connection with the Children's Case. The Chekists say you were chasing Sophia Zeitlin's daughter. You're a general now, and a married man. I've already cashiered you and demoted you once. Stop chasing skirt, stop drinking. You're making a fool of yourself and me. They'll ask you some questions. Answer them properly so I don't have to hear about this again.'

Vasily hung his head. 'Yes, Father, I promise. But this case involves Marshal Shako's daughter, Rosa, and I wanted to talk to you about him.'

'Go on.'

'It's about our fighter planes and how they crash far too often.'

Stalin sat up abruptly: 'What are you saying?' Military technology was his own speciality, so if things went wrong, it meant either incompetence or sabotage. Both were crimes.

'Our planes, specially Yak and MiG fighters, crash seven times more frequently than American Hurricanes or British Spitfires. Many pilots have been killed and there is considerable anger in the air force.'

'Why haven't you told me this before?' Now Stalin was paying Vasily his fullest attention, and Vasily, who seconds earlier had been no more than a delinquent weakling, now basked in the blazing sunlight of his focus.

'I reported this in full to Marshal Shako and Aircraft Production Minister Titorenko.'

'Their reaction?'

'They basically suggested that I conceal the evidence from you. To push ahead with production. To sacrifice more machines and pilots.'

Stalin was furious – he was thinking about those patriotic young pilots crashing in those faulty planes, and the criminals who had sabotaged them. He took a breath. He had to keep calm, preserve himself for his sacred mission in world history.

'You're not blackening the name of a Soviet hero like Shako just because he complained to me about your behaviour? That would be unforgivable in my son, Vaska.'

'No, this is sabotage,' replied Vasily. 'Something must be done.'

Stalin immediately saw how this revelation dovetailed neatly into one of his most urgent concerns. Perhaps the boy wasn't such a fool after all.

He padded to the desk and lifted the special phone to Poskrebyshev, who sat outside the door: 'Get Abakumov back in here.' He turned to Vasily. 'Wait outside, boy.'

When Abakumov entered, he bowed to Stalin and slightly less obsequiously to Vasily, who passed him on the way out.

'Have you visited Hitler's Chancellery?' asked Stalin.

'Yes, Comrade Stalin.'

'I was planning to take a look but then I changed my mind. Leave that to Churchill and Truman. Comrade Stalin doesn't make tours.'

He told him about Vasily's allegations. 'Check out Shako and Titorenko. Do whatever you need.' Abakumov knew that when Stalin said 'Check out,' he meant 'Arrest.'

'Their children are mixed up in the Children's Case,' said Abakumov.

'Oh, those poor children.' Stalin lit a cigarette and the fingers of blue smoke curled themselves around him. 'But they have to be punished. Their families could well be rotten to the core.'

'Comrade Stalin, Comrade Satinov is in charge of the aircraft industry. Should I check *him* out?'

'No. Find out what you can. A bit of pressure won't do any harm. Do we have Comrade Satinov's attention? If he's guilty, he'll answer to the Central Committee, but he's a hard-working comrade.' Stalin paused, deep in thought. 'You know, some of our generals behave as if they won the war on their own.'

'You won the war, Comrade Stalin,' said Abakumov.

Stalin scowled at him. 'Don't talk nonsense, Abakumov. The people won the war, the people.'

'Yes of course, Comrade Stalin, but many of our generals are corrupt. Their heads have been turned by titles and applause. Their apartments are filled with paintings, rugs and furniture brought in trains from all over Europe.'

Stalin grunted his agreement. 'We Bolsheviks don't tolerate corruption. Get back to Moscow and take off the silk gloves. Check out the generals and mount your prisoners at once. Vasily says pilots barely dare fly their planes at present. A crime.'

Stalin half closed his eyes. Abakumov was a blockhead, but this time, he seemed to have understood his coded semaphores. Didn't all the heroes of history – Genghis Khan, Ivan the Terrible, Nadir Shah, Napoleon – talk in riddles?

Abakumov saluted. 'I'll report, Comrade Stalin.' He headed for the door.

'Oh, and Comrade Abakumov?' The Chekist turned back. 'When I was a boy at the seminary, I was always curious about my friends, so I studied their parents. I could learn everything about the parents by talking to the children. Remember this, won't you, when you're back in Moscow?'

It was late in the evening when Hercules Satinov got home, but as soon as he opened his door, Tamara threw herself into his arms as if she had been waiting for him. She was so distraught that she could scarcely speak, and her skin was mottled with weeping. In the background he could hear Leka the housemaid sobbing too.

'You've got to do something. You've got to talk to Stalin!' Tamara cried.

The Name made Satinov's cheeks tighten and his eyes keen. He took his wife's hands and led her into his study. George had been in the Lubianka for weeks now, and long days had passed since they had thought he was going to be released. And still no word.

'Call Stalin!' she was shouting. 'Now! I'll call him myself!'

It had to be the children – or was it . . . no: had something happened to George? He had lost one son already. Could he bear the loss of another?

'Tamriko, calm down. Tell me what's happened.'

'They've taken Mariko! She's six, Hercules. Get her released! How will she survive in there?'

Oh my God: little Mariko, his only daughter, the jewel in his crown. A pulse started high on his cheek, and the fury rushed through him. The humiliation stung him. Analyse what this means, he told himself. Put together the pieces of the jigsaw in a game where there are no coincidences.

Stalin specialized in surprises, and Satinov spent his time predicting them if he could. Earlier that day, Marshal Shako and five other generals had been arrested. He knew this concerned the planes. It was aimed at him as the boss of the aircraft industry. But Mariko! This was unworthy of a Bolshevik, unworthy of Stalin.

The phone rang. Both of them jumped. Satinov answered it. 'Satinov. I'm listening . . . Comrade Abakumov, thank you for calling.' He looked at Tamara and gestured reassuringly as he listened. As he held the phone, Tamara stood up and pressed herself against him, laying her head on his shoulder; he wrapped his other arm around her. 'Yes, naturally we're worried . . . Yes, Tamara is upset. Mariko is only six, Comrade General, she'll be terrified and—'

'Tell him Mariko doesn't eat eggs,' said Tamara. 'She's allergic and if she doesn't have a biscuit at eleven, she feels faint. She doesn't have her toy dogs, and she can't sleep without them. Tell him, Hercules!' But Satinov held up a finger for quiet.

'Comrade General, I know Mariko was on the bridge that night and I appreciate that it is the Organs' Communist duty to investigate. If Mariko is essential, then yes, she must be questioned.' He listened. 'I appreciate that . . . Tamara will be there twice at eight a.m. and eight p.m. Thank you, Comrade Abakumov . . . Bolshevik greetings to you too.'

When he put the phone down, he gripped Tamriko firmly and told her that she would be allowed to visit Mariko in the Lubianka first thing in the morning and twice a day as long as Mariko was being questioned, and she could take a food hamper.

'How can they do this?' said Tamara. 'What kind of men are they? Tell Stalin! Call him!'

She did not know that Stalin was at the Potsdam Conference, his movements a state secret. Satinov held Tamara very tightly, her hair and the nape of her neck against his face, with their sweet smell that reminded him of home and children.

'The Organs act only with the highest authority,' he said, and this she understood. Abakumov never would have dared to arrest a Politburo member's little girl without Stalin's permission.

'Hercules,' she said softly, 'how am I going to get through this? I just don't know if I can. I feel I'm dying inside. I love her so much . . .' She was weeping in his arms and she seemed so fragile, so exquisitely tiny, that he felt as if he could count every bone in her body. 'How are we to survive?'

'We will,' he whispered back, 'because we have to.'

'Don't fuck us around any more, Andrei. We think you're being very stubborn for the son of an Enemy of the People,' Colonel Komarov told Andrei later that evening. 'My boss is getting bored with studying Pushkin so either we beat this shit out of you, or you just answer the question.'

'On Pushkin?'

'Yes. They say you're the scholar on *Onegin*.'

What are the Organs up to now? he wondered. Are the Organs setting up a course on poetry? After all, they had departments for everything from tailoring to medicine and gold-mining, so why not Pushkin too? More likely, it was a trick of some sort.

'I don't know it half as well as some people,' he said.

'"NV." What's it stand for?'

'You said it meant New Leader.'

'Now we think it's something to do with *Onegin*.'

Andrei nodded slowly. 'I think you may be right. My feeling is that NV may have been some codename for Rosa Shako.'

'That's convenient,' chuckled Komarov. 'She being on the slab with eight grams in her breast.'

'It's just what I think.'

'Let me help you with your thinking,' and suddenly Komarov moved very quickly, twisting Andrei's arm and dragging him by it so that the chair went flying. The door opened and two warders rushed in. They grabbed him as Komarov kicked away his knees, leaving him gasping in agony. 'Let's go.'

Across the corridor and into the room with the two-way mirror they went, the warders holding him so that his arms hurt. In the next room, a woman was reading aloud from a newspaper. When Andrei looked through the glass, he groaned. It was his mother, right here in Lubianka.

'Oh my God, Mama! What are you doing here?' he called to her.

'She can't hear you or see you. We're sick of you brats and our boss has told us to solve it tonight, whatever the cost. If you help us, we'll let you see your mother. But if you hold back, she'll get ten years in Kolyma.' Komarov shrugged. 'But you know she won't survive. She's skin and bone.' He pulled down a beige blind, stained with dark brown specks. 'So, Andrei?'

He turned to face Komarov. Before him stood an uneducated popinjay, insignificant in every respect except that he had the power of life and death over him and his mother.

'NV can only be one person,' he said. 'It's Nina Voronskaya.'

'Nina Voronskaya. Is she at the school? We'll arrest her right away.'

'No, respected investigator, she's a fictional character in *Onegin*, a beautiful society hostess in Petersburg.'

Komarov frowned. 'But she can't be,' he reasoned. 'Why would Nikolasha Blagov put her in the notebook if she wasn't real?'

Andrei saw how the progress of this case resembled a play in the theatre. None of it was true, and he had no idea how the plotline would conclude. Yet this deadly fantasy could be tilted one way or the other by a word too many here, a piece of bad luck there.

'Hurry up, boy, or the same thing will happen to you that happened to your father. Twenty-five years, remember?'

'Without right of correspondence.'

'Oh, of course,' Komarov sneered. 'Without right of correspondence.'

His laughing sarcasm opened Andrei's eyes with crystal-clear clarity. His father was no longer amongst the living. He had died right here in Lubianka.

Andrei had never known why his father had been arrested, but he knew that in 1937–38, thousands of comrades like his father had been executed. He had always presumed that his father had committed some political crime – but it occurred to him, after his own experiences with 'Soviet justice,' that his father could have been completely innocent. He had probably done nothing and been shot for some fabricated crime – treason or spying or Trotskyism – based on a false denunciation. These revelations, accompanied by the sight of his mother, almost broke him for the first time.

But tears can lie too. Because for Andrei, survival was all. He had one more option – to play his last card, the one that he hated himself for playing.

28

Midnight in the Lubianka. In the middle of darkened Moscow, the lights burned in every window as if it were the hull of a gigantic ship. Victor Abakumov hurried into the Inner Prison, moving with the stiff gait of the profoundly weary. The electric lights burn brightly here, he thought, and no one sleeps soundly in my night kingdom.

A blue-tabbed officer waited and saluted. 'She's here, Comrade General!'

'Let me take a look.' The officer opened a door in the long sterile corridor. Abakumov looked through the window into the interrogation room at the young schoolgirl, still in her school uniform, who sat at the table. Likhachev, smoking a cigarette, was pacing up and down, shouting at her: 'Come on, you whore, who are you fucking? You little bitch, I ask you again—' Abakumov flicked off the volume.

The single desklight lit up the gold threads of her hair. Serafima Romashkina was waiting, playing with her curls, and she looked tired, and too thin. Her lip was cut and swollen – one of my boys went too far, reflected Abakumov. He shook his head to see this glorious creature sitting so forlorn and dejected. He had meant just to take a look before he went in, but now, leaning on the wall, lighting up a cigarette and relaxing for the first time in his gruelling day, he was free to stare at her intensely – as both a connoisseur of female beauty and a manipulator, sometimes even a butcher, of men, families, villages, nations.

She wasn't as brazen as her famously alluring mother, but even so, he admired the perfect crescent of her white forehead, the heart shape of her face and her arrestingly green eyes with their lush dark eyelashes. This simply adorable girl was in his power, waiting for him and no one else. No wonder those stupid, spoilt schoolfriends had done foolish things to win her favour. But she possessed the last key to their case, a key he needed to unlock without delay.

Abakumov walked straight into Serafima's interrogation room. Likhachev sprung to attention.

'I'll take over here, Comrade Colonel. Shut the door as you leave.' Likhachev saluted and vanished; the door closed. Abakumov sat, smoking his cigarette, boots on the desk, eyes fixed on Serafima. She said nothing but something about her made his power seem futile. Yes, he could beat her to pulp, he could rape her, but he still wouldn't possess her.

'I was in Berlin a few hours ago and I had a chance on the flight home to think about you and the case.' Abakumov sighed huskily.

'You did?' said Serafima, looking bored.

'There's lot to think about.' Abakumov was still mulling over Stalin's riddles, which were becoming ever more obscure and gnomic. He had not been allowed to arrest Satinov – whom Stalin respected – so he had devised a way to 'get the attention of Comrade Satinov,' as Stalin put it: he'd arrested Mariko.

Stalin had also said the children 'have to be punished.' What did he mean? They were already in prison. Extra homework? A good thrashing? Eight grams in the back of the neck? I'll be damned if I guess wrong! But Abakumov was sure of one thing: Stalin's real targets were arrogant generals and smug bosses.

Serafima touched her lip and looked at her finger: still bleeding.

'We're all struggling with the truth here, Serafima, Colonel Likhachev most of all. I'm sorry about your lip. It's nothing serious, I hope?'

'No. Thank you,' she said softly.

'Did you get any sleep? You look tired, dear girl.'

'I'm fine.'

Silence. Abakumov thought about the Children's Case once again. A play-acting club, which was a front to conceal passions of adolescence, had led to the death of two kids. The investigation had uncovered a puerile game. If they hadn't been élite brats, Stalin never would have heard about it. But now that he had, he would use the children in any way that suited his manoeuvres of the moment. He, Abakumov, had applied pressure to the children to discover the mastermind behind the conspiracy but it was clear that none of them knew who it was. He could torture Serafima, but it was possible that even she didn't know. While the other children awaited Stalin's judgement, he decided, right there and then, to play a special game with her. And the only way it would work was if he freed her.

'Now, you will tell your mother how kind I was, won't you? You'll say, "Abakumov really looked after me!" eh?'

'I will, General.' Hope rose in her face and he saw how she suppressed it. But when she put her head on one side, that charming mannerism of hers, he couldn't help but smile.

'Go and get your things,' he said. 'There's a bath ready for you. Stand up, come on . . .' and he took her hands and helped her up.

The door of the room opened and two warders stood ready to escort her to a meal and, yes, that bath.

Serafima stood and he saw her relief, her exhaustion; her skin flushed from her neck upwards and she set her jerking lips, as if she was trying not to lose control. But she was hesitating.

'But what about the others? My friends – Minka, George, Andrei – are they coming home too?'

Abakumov was suddenly angry with the arrogance of these children when he had so much on his mind. He banged the table with his hands and saw her flinch. 'That's none of your business, girl. Get out before I change my mind.'

Tears running down her cheeks, she walked out of the room, and Abakumov sat listening to her footsteps disappearing down the long corridor.

Now it's my turn, he thought. Now we play *my* game.

Still suspecting that it might be a trick, Serafima walked down the prison corridors. The warders no longer held her but touched her elbow to guide her into a new section of the prison and into a room where there was a meal laid out. *Pirozhki*. Hot *shchi* vegetable soup. A sturgeon steak, newly grilled and served with potatoes. She sat and feasted on this, eating too fast, washing it down with Borzhomi mineral water. Next they gave her a bath, letting her lie in it for a time, and then told her to hurry up and dry herself. She was to be collected.

As soon as she was dressed, she waited in a wood-panelled waiting room, alone, until the door opened and her mother came in. Sophia was caked in make-up and dressed in an army uniform, having come straight off the set of her latest movie. Speechless with relief, Sophia held her in her arms; then she walked her to the waiting car. It was time to go home. Time to sleep.

When Serafima awoke the next day, she thought she was still in prison. Then she remembered that she was at home, that all was how it should be once more. She got up, to find that she had slept away almost the entire day. Her mother was out at Mosfilm Studios but the maid cooked a meal, which she ate thinking of *him*. She had a bath and then put on a yellow dress – and she went out. Down the steps of the Granovsky building and, looking behind her to check that no one was following her, out into the streets, towards the House of the Book.

'You look even more lovely amongst all these old books,' said Benya Golden to Agrippina Begbulatova.

It was the lunch hour, and Benya stood naked in his tiny one-room apartment just off Ostozhenka. He was showing her a new book. Vellum binding, antique. Agrippina lay on her back with her stockinged legs crossed, beautifully setting off the collage of book covers: some of pale kid leather, some of expensive black lacquer, many of greasy, torn, modern paper.

'All your favourite things in one place!' she laughed. 'Books, food and girls. I know you so well, Benochka. You're a Rabelaisan and Epicurean. It must be confusing trying to work out which to consume first. But choose me while I'm here. We can eat together, and make love; then you can read after I'm gone.'

In just a couple of years, Benya had managed to amass quite a collection of first editions and prints from the early nineteenth century. Wartime meant that a poor man with a good eye had many opportunities to buy refined rarities for next to nothing. The books closer to the sink and oven doubled as kitchen tables for black Borodinsky bread, goat's cheese, a half-empty bottle of wine. He looked around him. The picture – books, food, lingerie, the pale curves, tousled curls and fair pubic hair of the young teacher – would have worked well as absurdist art.

'I can take a hint,' said Benya. He started to kiss her feet. 'But how long are you here for?' His laugh was exuberant and frequent: there was much that amused him, and nothing delighted him as profoundly as Agrippina's sweetness. She was so cultured, so intelligent, and had such a promising future ahead of her, while he had been to hell and back, and it showed.

He worked his way up her body, kissing her. She gradually brought her knees up and around him until her ankles were on his shoulders. He kissed her there very slowly, absolutely delighted by her pleasure, by the taste of her, the heat; the sinews in her thighs were the most lovely he had ever seen in his life.

'I love being fucked by you,' she said.

'I love fucking you.'

Afterwards, they lay silently, until she cleared her throat. 'Benochka,' she started in a tone he had never heard before, but knew immediately what it meant. His heart pounded in bursts and a sliver of ice chilled him from the inside. 'Benochka? I have a bad feeling.'

'Agrippina, let's not spoil this.'

'Benochka, are you listening?'

'I'm trying not to.'

'Benochka, if something happens . . . I want to tell you that I . . .'

'I know. You don't have to say anything. Remember where I've been . . .'

'You never told me.'

'In our world, what you don't know can't hurt you.'

'I think you're the best teacher I've ever seen.'

'Teacher?' He laughed. 'Fuck my teaching! What about my lovemaking?'

They were laughing and he was kissing her again as the knock came at the door.

She turned away from him. 'They lied to me. They promised not to come now . . .'

He heard the fear in her voice. But he was eerily serene as he grabbed his underwear and trousers and pulled them on. 'I'm just opening the door,' he called out.

As a drowning man reviews his entire life compressed into an instant, Benya relived the happiness of the two years he called his Second Coming: his Pushkin classes – the best job of his life, the sharing of his love of literature with young people; his wanderings through bookshops and flea markets; the pleasure in finding a volume, and being able to afford it. Even Genghis Khan as he plundered another rich city filled with gold and jewels could not have enjoyed a prize as much as Benya bearing home a new book in triumph. And then the hours of lovemaking with Agrippina.

He opened the door. Agrippina, quite forgetting she was naked, had covered her face with her hands as the Chekists in blue uniforms poured into the apartment. Benya gathered his few possessions in the carpet bag he already had packed. He could see that the plain-clothed chief investigator was fascinated by Agrippina, and quite honestly, who could blame him?

'Get dressed, girl!' said the bald-headed Chekist. 'Where's your Bolshevik modesty? You've done your bit. Now scram!'

'Benya, I had to—' But Benya, now fully dressed and ready to go, waved her away. He could imagine the pressure the

Organs had brought to bear on her. The threats they'd made.

'Agrippina, I wish you luck. Never let this hold you back. Promise me that.'

Her eyes lowered, she dressed quickly, and was gone.

Golden stood alone in the cage in the back of the 'black crow' van (on which was written 'Eggs Milk Groceries'), freefalling into the abyss, normal life ending. Something occurred to him: Agrippina had managed to come twice even though she must have been anxious. Even Judas hadn't managed that! In the rumbling half-light of the van, he smiled admiringly as he remembered her brazen hunger for pleasure even under stress. What nerve! Then he shook his head with a maudlin fatalism. He knew what lay ahead, and how a man who has risen from the dead once could not count on pulling it off again.

29

Early morning in the Lubianka. A delicate, fair woman sitting stiffly, alone and silent in a room of plain wooden chairs, a glass wall, damp patches on the yellow wallpaper, paint peeling stiffly like oversized flakes of dry skin. She looks at her watch. She has been here for forty minutes already but she will happily wait here all day.

She has a bag on the seat beside her and she opens it several times, checking and rechecking obsessively that everything is there. With every creak, echo, footstep, she turns to look at the door, tenses, twitches, listens, and then subsides again, face in her hands.

The door opens. A plump female warder enters in a brown coat.

Tamara Satinova stands up, terrified that they've changed the plan. But then, after a moment, there's Mariko, dazed, pale, and still in her school uniform.

'Mariko!' cries Tamara, rushing towards her.

'Mama!' Mariko runs into her mother's arms.

Don't cry, don't cry, Tamara tells herself. Don't make things worse.

Tamara sits down. Mariko is on her knee; two warders stand watching, arms crossed; a guard in blue tabs at the door. Tamara kisses Mariko on her face, her forehead, her temple, her hair. Her hands are shaking.

'Mama, when can I come home?'

'Soon, Mariko. Soon. But I can come and see you twice a day.'

'But, Mama, what am I doing here?'

'We cannot know about the investigations of the Organs but they know what they are doing and as soon as they have finished, they will send you home.'

One of the warders blows her nose.

'I want to come home now. I'm frightened.'

'Papa sends his love. He says you must treat it like an adventure, like *Timur and His Team* – but answer the questions truthfully, won't you?'

'I don't want to stay here. It's horrible.'

'I know,' said Tamara. 'I know – but you must be brave. Now . . .' She is trembling with the effort of not weeping. She sets her jaw to stop the spasm of tears.

'Mama, you look funny. You're shaking.'

Tamara nods as she turns to her string bag. Just concentrate on practicalities, she tells herself. 'Are you warm enough?' she asks.

'No, I'm cold in my room. And the bed is horrible.'

'Right, so first here is a dressing gown, pyjamas and a sweater for you to wear and stay warm. Do you want to put on the sweater now?' She helps Mariko put it on. 'You must be hungry, darling.'

'The food was vile. I couldn't eat it.'

'Here's bread, your favourite cheese and biscuits, and yogurt. And fruitcake. All from Gastronom One.' They shop there often. Mariko opens the cake and starts to eat a piece.

'I won't be able to sleep, Mama.'

'You must try, darling.'

'I'm missing my dogs and my School for Bitches.'

'Well, look who I've got for you! Hello, Crumpet!' She pulls out a black-and-white dog.

Mariko smiles for the first time and grabs the toy.

'And who's this?'

Mariko takes the next dog and hugs it with the first.

'And hello!' Tamara pulls out another.

'Oh Mama, they're all here!' Mariko says their names: Crumpet, Bumble, Pirate.

Tamara packs the food and the clothes into the string bag.

'Time's up,' says one of the warders. 'Prisoner to be returned to her cell.'

Prisoner! The word hits Tamara hard and a fit of sobs well up again. Stop! You mustn't cry!

But Mariko, trying to hold on to her toy dogs, throws her arms around her mother. 'Mama, don't go!'

'I have to,' Tamara whispers. 'But I'll be back tonight with all your favourite things, and more dogs.'

'You can't go. I won't let you go,' cries Mariko. She drops the dogs and Tamara puts them in her bag, which she gives to one of the warders.

'It's time,' says the warder. She and another guard approach them, and as they come nearer, Tamriko feels their shadows, smells the cheap Red Square perfume and detergent, sweat, perhaps vodka.

She hugs Mariko and then she, herself, starts to pull back. 'Now I have to go. Be good. Don't worry. I love you so much and soon you'll be home. I'll see you very soon. What would you like me to bring?'

But Mariko throws herself against her mama, as if trying to burrow into her, and Tamara clutches her.

'Mariko!' Tamara is fighting for control, but she is not sure she can manage it. Her entire body is telling her to hold on to her little girl.

'Mariko, you must let go of your mother,' the warder says sternly.

'I won't!'

'You must or we'll separate you.'

Tamara loosens her grip on her child, but Mariko holds on. Feeling as if she is in the midst of a whirling tornado of debris and dust that darkens the world, Tamara buries her nose in Mariko's vanilla-milk-and-hay hair and inhales as if it is oxygen.

'Mariko, let go or they'll force you and it will be horrid. I'll . . . I'll be back so soon!'

'I won't let go. Don't go, Mama!' Mariko is sobbing, shaking, struggling to breathe, winded by her own desperation. Tamara closes her eyes as the guards prise open the child's fingers and lift her and take her away. She hears the door close and Mariko's screams as they carry her down the corridors. Tamara finds herself on the floor of the empty room, on her hands and knees like an animal, howling with anger and heartbreak. She thinks for a moment that she might just die right here. The walls of her heart feel paper-thin, her lungs shallow, her stomach is lined with gravel and she wants to die.

There is something beside her. One of the dogs has fallen out of the bag, and she picks it up. It smells of Mariko. She hugs the toy, and rocks herself, amazed that she, wife of a leader, respected teacher, proud mother, is lying on a floor, holding a toy, weeping.

She lies there for a long time. Finally, holding the dog to

her like a baby, she staggers out, so broken that she isn't sure she will ever be able to put herself back together again.

The rays of a sinking sun – gold and purple and white – soothe Serafima. How gorgeous the light is after her prison cell. She raises her face like a flower following the sun, noticing as if for the first time the blizzard of gossamer seeds that dance in the beams. She is free, she has preserved her secret, and now she is overwhelmed by the beauty of this evening.

Up Gorky Street to the House of the Book she goes. Upstairs to the Foreign Literature section. Hemingway? Galsworthy? There it is. Edith Wharton. She opens the book hungrily, reads what is inside; then she runs downstairs and out into the streets again.

It is seven p.m. and crowds of smartly dressed Muscovites and some foreigners are waiting to go into the Bolshoi to see Tchaikovsky's *Swan Lake*. Serafima goes inside to the ticket office. There's a queue. When she reaches the front, her ticket is there in an envelope.

Serafima is one of the last to take her seat in the stalls, and when she's sitting, with an old grey man on one side of her and a young girl like her on the other, she feels her face is flushing. She is happier than she's ever been in her life – but it is more than this. His eyes are on her and she can sense the love in them. She looks up at his box and there he is. Waiting for her, loving her, as he has been since the days before the shooting and her imprisonment in Lubianka.

Later that night, Satinov is in his study at his apartment, which, with just one child at home, is much quieter than it should be. Tamara is in his arms as she tells him about Mariko.

Satinov closes his eyes. His little Mariko with her brown eyes and braided hair, hay-sweet. A spasm flutters from his stomach to his throat and spreads to his eyes and mouth, to his whole being for, in spite of his being the Iron Commissar, in spite of his being Comrade Satinov, he is out of control.

He blinks. In the mirror on the far wall, he sees himself, holding Tamara, her hair in a bun, her long neck, her jerking shoulders. And he looks deep into his own eyes and sees they are full of a terrible betrayal. Shocked, he looks away, at the photographs lined up on the desk. But instead of his children and Tamara, he sees only one woman's face.

Yes, he is weeping for Mariko, for George, for Tamriko, but he is also weeping selfishly. For himself. And for the woman with whom he has fallen desperately in love.

PART THREE

Four Lovers

A loving enchantress
Gave me her talisman.
She told me with tenderness:
'You must not lose it.
Its power is infallible,
Love gave it to you.'

Alexander Pushkin, 'The Talisman'

30

Six months earlier

He first saw her in January 1945 just after the Red Army broke into East Prussia. He remembers the day, the hour, the minute. They were far from Moscow on the First Belorussian Front. As the Front's commissar, he and its commander, Marshal Rokossovsky, had fought all the way through Belorussia, and then through the wasteland of Poland to break into Germany itself. Even Germany's humblest cottages had larders filled with sugar, bread, eggs and meat, soft beds and white pillows. Most farmers had fled from the Russians, but the few who stayed were ruddy-cheeked and well dressed. They even wore wristwatches.

The sky had been growing chalkier all day but when the snowstorm came, it took them all by surprise. Sitting in his Willy jeep, with Losha Babanava at the wheel, Colonel General Satinov watched the army pass. Howitzers pounded Nazi positions a few kilometres down the road. They were, he thought, a Mongol horde in the age of machines: the mud-streaked tanks were now covered with bright rugs on which crouched filthy infantrymen in tattered uniforms dark with machine oil, wearing rabbit hats, shaggy sheepskin coats, and often several wristwatches, brandishing guns wrapped in white rags like bandages, swigging at bottles, singing songs that were lost in the rattling screech of machinery.

Next came the gun crews, who bounced along on their caissons softened with cushions embroidered in silk, playing German accordions inlaid with jewels. Tanks, howitzers, American Willy jeeps, and Studebaker trucks: all moved past in a slow inexorable line. Then: what was this? An antique Berline carriage with swinging lanterns, pulled by horses, and a glimpse inside of an officer's shoulderboards and a girl's glazed kohl-smoked eyes.

A blizzard at dusk in a deserted village, dense snow quickly settling on the surrounding fields and the roofs of the cottages of Gross Meisterdorf. The soldiers sheltered nearby in whichever cottage was closest. Still in his jeep, Satinov leaned wearily forward as an NCO saluted.

'Comrade General, the medical corps's setting up a hospital in the church hall. They're ready for you to inspect.'

Outside the church hall, Satinov saw soldiers carrying stretchers from a truck. Two of their soldiers were already dead. Not wounded by the Nazis, but poisoned by moonshine: alcohol made from antifreeze.

Inside a wood-panelled hall, lit with oil lamps swinging from the rafters, men were lying on the floorboards. Satinov smelled the fug of so many wartime bunkers: damp cloth and body odour, here mixed with iodine. Nurses in white smocks worked on the new arrivals. A little to his right, a female army doctor was crouched over a soldier. She was on her knees, massaging and pummelling his bare chest. 'Come on, come back, breathe!' she was saying. The boy spluttered and his chest lurched into movement like a rusty engine. The doctor, who wore the red cross on her arm, listened to his chest for a moment and then stood up. 'All right, he'll make it. Who's next?'

Satinov watched her approach a second poisoned soldier.

Again she managed to resuscitate him, but afterwards, when she was standing up, she wiped her forehead and said to no one in particular: 'Two saved; three stable; four dead.'

She saluted Satinov. 'Welcome to the Gross Meisterdorf Hospital, Comrade General. It's not much, as you can see. They die quickly of antifreeze. Every second counts.'

She was still wearing her white sheepskin coat. A pistol rested in her belt, a stethoscope was clipped round her neck, and she wore a blue *pilotka* beret. She hasn't had time to take it off, Satinov thought, noticing that her face was long and oval, and her straight high nose and cheeks lightly speckled with a few freckles. Even here, at the front, when she was putting all her energy into saving a life, he noticed that she had altered her uniform a little, and taken up her khaki skirt a few centimetres, to reveal her American nylons, which were dark and against regulations.

A nurse brought a tray of mugs of *chai*, very sweet, steaming. 'Glad you're here for these boys,' said Satinov.

'Are you inspecting us or just passing?' she asked. She had a fetching accent, he realized, certainly Galician, probably from Lvov, with a Mitteleuropean touch of Yiddish.

'Just passing. I'm on my way up to headquarters.'

'Of course you are.' Her eyes aglint with feisty intelligence were slightly mocking. She surely recognized him; most people did. 'Since we have a general here, could you find us some mattresses – on your way up to headquarters?' She gave a slightly crooked smile.

'I'll do my best,' he said, feeling somehow abashed, as if she was challenging him to justify his rank.

'Thank you, comrade,' she said, getting up and heading over towards the next wounded soldier. Her nurses followed.

Satinov opened the door. The snow had stopped. He felt the countryside was slumbering under the white blanket and that somewhere deep beneath it, nature was breathing.

Losha drove on slowly through the dark night, no headlights, the chains on their wheels clanking, their route periodically illuminated by arching tracers and explosions that dyed the sky as bright as day. Satinov looked out of the window. Sometimes the sky up ahead flashed scarlet for a moment as the howitzers fired their barrages. He thought of the doctor. Remembered her nose, its sprinkling of freckles and her brown skin. He had never asked her name.

31

January 1945 in Moscow: long fingers of ice reached down from the eaves of the houses but Serafima felt that springtime was close.

'Let's go to the Bolshoi tonight,' suggested Minka. They were walking down the corridor towards the Golden Gates for pick-up. Because it was still wartime, and all their fathers were at the front, the chauffeurs, mothers and nannies did the collecting. 'Say you will, Serafimochka!'

'But, Minka, we only went yesterday,' Serafima replied. 'Is there a new production?'

'No, it's *Romeo and Juliet*, but I love it.'

'Never mind Prokofiev, you just like dressing up, Minkushka,' said Serafima with one of her rare laughs. 'But I hate it. I always loathe the way I look.'

'You look so lovely in that green dress of yours. All the boys think so. Everyone was admiring you – even the officers in their boxes.'

'Really?' Serafima was sure she was too tall and too plain; she didn't feel at all attractive compared to her beautiful mother and her generous, confident friend. 'I know you want to go again,' she said. 'Those officers were looking at you, not me. You're such a flirt.'

'I plead guilty,' Minka said with a giggle. 'I loved the way they were looking at us both. But that's all!'

'Oh, I wasn't saying . . .' Serafima knew that Minka would never go beyond the prudish limits of Soviet morality. The military fronts these days resembled Babylonian bacchanalia, but for the schoolchildren anything more than a kiss and a few lines of poetry was unthinkable.

'Besides, dressing up is such fun,' Minka was saying. 'Say you'll come tonight. You always enjoy it when you're there. I think you like the officers' attention too. And I already have tickets.'

And so it was that at seven p.m. that night, Serafima, Minka and their friend Rosa Shako arrived by Metro at the Bolshoi to see *Romeo and Juliet* for the seventh time. The sky was bleached white, the air just changing to warn snow was coming. Moscow had been battered by three years of war, the Kremlin was still draped in khaki netting, its red stars dark, and Gorky Street was marked by bombs and ruined houses. The shops were rationed and people in the streets looked diminished and shabby. But victory was close, everyone knew that. All the ministries, embassies and theatres that had been evacuated to Kuybishev on the Volga were back. The nights were no longer illuminated by Nazi air raids and flak guns but by the salvoes of victory salutes from entire parks of howitzers, ordered by Stalin.

And, as Minka had predicted, the moment they pushed their way into the theatre, they started to receive attention – and they had not yet even taken off their furs and shapkas. Knowing that it matched her big brown eyes, Minka had borrowed her mother's mink coat. Rosa was wearing her best winter fox fur, but typically Serafima, whose mother possessed the best collection of furs in Moscow, was wearing her cheap rabbit furs. Inside the lobby of the theatre, the heating, the one and only

Soviet luxury, was blazing. Garlic, vodka and the smell of cabbage seemed to ooze out of the people squeezed together, but never had there been a happier crowd of Muscovites. Everyone, even the grumpy ticket collectors, even the elderly, even the drunken soldiers and sailors, was cheerful. Victory was imminent; good times were coming.

The girls, giggling as they were pushed and pulled this way and that, queued to leave their coats at the cloakroom, and then they could breathe again and the passing officers could admire their dresses. Minka Dorova was looking the most sophisticated. She was wearing a pink frock copied from *Bazaar* magazine at the couture atelier of Abram Lerner and Kleopatra Fishman, where the élite wives and the leaders had their clothes made.

'You're outrageous!' exclaimed Serafima, looking at Minka's glossy, half-bared shoulders and arms. 'No wonder you wanted to come to the ballet!'

'Your mother's the best!' Rosa said enviously to Minka. 'My mother would never take me to Lerner's atelier.'

'Mine's always asking me to go,' admitted Serafima, 'but I can't bear shopping with her. She's a despot, swans around like an ageing ingénue and makes me feel awful.'

'And yet you still look irresistible,' Minka said, trying to work out why Serafima's dress, done up to the neck and with cuffs to her wrists, looked so alluring.

'Oh, nonsense.' Serafima elbowed Minka, who tickled her while Rosa scolded them for embarrassing her at the ballet. They were not schoolgirls on an outing, she reminded them, but eighteen-year-olds on the verge of womanhood in their finest dresses.

'Shall we have a glass of *champagnski* before we go in?' suggested Minka, always the bon viveur of the three.

In the bar, they caught the attention of some American

airmen. Joshing, toothsome, young, they were so smart in their uniforms, and their skin was as unblemished as a baby's – and what teeth, Serafima noted, compared with the weathered complexions and golden fangs of Russian men. They possessed a lightness that she admired, even as she stood back a little awkwardly. She was happy for Minka and Rosa to flirt, and the men did not seem to notice her at all.

One of the Americans, an air force captain, a broad-shouldered athlete with a buzz cut, asked Minka for her telephone number but she did not give it to him, her refusal making her even more desirable. The other Americans teased him, 'Oh, he don't often get turned down! There's a challenge, Bradley!'

Sensible Minka, thought Serafima, however much fun this might be. The rules had loosened in wartime but her father had warned her that the Party would reinforce them again afterwards. Bradley, spurred on by his friends, not only insisted on buying them four rounds of drinks but offered them some tickets in a box. 'We've got some extra seats,' he said.

'Why don't you need them?' asked Minka in the perfect English she had learned in Tamara Satinova's class.

'We can't stay for the show, so please take them,' Bradley said. 'The box will just be empty if you don't.'

'You're just here for the drinks?' said Minka.

'And the dames!' cried one of Bradley's friends.

'We're going out to eat as soon as the play starts,' said Bradley.

Filled with uniformed foreigners and Russian girls, the Bolshoi was the centre of all social life in Moscow, so it didn't surprise Serafima that Bradley and his American friends were not remotely interested in Prokofiev. Even she, Rosa and Minka had seen it so often they could have danced it themselves.

'Hey,' Bradley continued, flashing his amazing American teeth, white and clean and big as icebergs. 'Wanna join us for dinner?'

'I'm sure you'll find some girls who aren't here for the ballet,' replied Minka, now suddenly haughty and mock-serious. 'But we are.'

32

Satinov was still in East Prussia a week later. It was evening and he was in the baronial hall of a country house that was now the headquarters of the First Belorussian Front. The first Soviet troops to break in to the *schloss* had urinated and defecated on the count's four-poster bed (once slept in by Frederick the Great, according to a gardener who showed them round) and fired at the oil paintings of bewhiskered Junkers, and although the house had since been cleaned up, Satinov could still see the bullet marks on the walls.

'I think the full staff can join us for dinner tonight, don't you, Hercules?' said Marshal Rokossovsky. They were friends, even though Rokossovsky was a real soldier, and he, Satinov, was a Party man, a member of the State Defence Committee, and Stalin's representative.

'Why not?' answered Satinov, who understood by 'full staff' that Rokossovsky meant the generals could invite their PPZhs (it stood for *pokhodno-polevaya zhena* – a field campaign wife, a pun on the Soviet machine-gun the PPSh). 'It's time everyone relaxed. We've earned it, after all.'

He looked across at Rokossovsky and raised his eyebrows as they both acknowledged the sounds of shooting and cowboy whooping outside. Losha and the bodyguards were culling dinner in the deer park from their jeeps. They too were in good spirits.

Coming down for dinner that evening, Satinov relished the delicious aroma of roasting venison, the sweet smoke of apple-tree wood in the fire, and, he thought, the scent of the women present. Rokossovsky, elegant descendant of Polish nobility, enjoyed female company but disliked any hint of debauchery in his decorous headquarters. This suited Satinov, who was happily married, hated drunkenness and disapproved of womanizers.

In the hall, Marshal Rokossovsky and his staff were at the table. Young female orderlies in khaki were serving plates of steaming venison piled with vegetables and pouring glasses of wine for the officers. Rokossovsky's batman was fanning the fire in the great open fireplace, and Satinov's guards were carrying up boxes of wine from the cellars.

Rokossovsky was sitting beside the young telephonist who was his PPZh. Satinov took his place at the other end of the table.

'Comrade Satinov,' Rokossovsky called down the table, pointing to a pale man. 'You already know Comrade Genrikh Dorov from the Central Committee?'

'I certainly do. Comrade Dorov, welcome!' said Satinov. He smiled, remembering that George and his friends called Genrikh the Uncooked Chicken. How right they were, he thought, feeling an unexpected stab of longing for the company of his sons (and the one he'd lost).

'Thank you. I'm here to inspect food supplies and root out wreckers and profiteers,' said Dorov.

Ah, that made sense, Satinov decided, recalling how, in 1937, Genrikh Dorov had metamorphosed from an inky-fingered, hero-worshipping assistant in Stalin's private office into a demented executioner. The more executions, the whiter his hair, the paler his skin became. In the first year of the war, his shootings (sometimes using his own pistol) and military bungles cost the lives of thousands. Finally Stalin himself (who regarded him as a talentless but devoted fanatic) had demoted him.

'I report to the Central Committee tomorrow,' said Genrikh, so that everyone could hear. 'It's a den of iniquity out here. Adultery. Booze. Corruption. We must restore Bolshevik morals.'

But Satinov was looking at the woman sitting next to Dorov.

'My wife,' said Genrikh, following his gaze. 'Have you met her?'

And *there* was the female doctor in the blue-tabbed uniform of the medical corps with the red cross on her sleeve.

'Dashka Dorova,' she said, offering her hand. Satinov noticed her slightly plump, amber-skinned wrist. 'Yes, we've met before.'

'Of course but . . .'

'But what?' A crooked smile, challenging caramel-brown eyes.

What was he trying to say? That he was surprised that the unattractive pedant Dorov was married to this beautiful doctor?

She leaned towards him. 'Did you know our children are at the same school? My daughter, Minka, knows your sons.'

'School 801? I didn't, but you know, I've never been there. I've been at the front for so long.'

'Where did you meet?' asked Dorov. 'You just said you'd met. I'd like to know.'

'At a little hospital in a village a few days ago,' explained Dashka soothingly. 'A whole unit was poisoned by alcohol . . .'

'Christ! What a waste of manpower,' Dorov said. 'Did you shoot the suppliers for sabotage?'

'No, dear,' Dashka replied. 'I was trying to save their lives.'

'Did we lose any more?' asked Satinov.

'No,' she said. 'Oh, and thank you so much for the mattresses and supplies. I was very surprised when they arrived.'

'You didn't think I'd remember, did you?'

'No,' she said, smiling, her features softening. 'No, I didn't.'

'Would you have bothered with the supplies if she'd been an ugly male doctor?' asked Dorov.

Satinov looked at him coldly. 'How long are you with us, Comrade Dorov?'

But Dorov had turned away.

'Excuse me, comrades, but Comrade Dorov, your plane for Moscow is waiting,' reported one of the aides-de-camp, saluting.

'I'll help you pack,' said Dashka, standing up.

After the Dorovs had gone, there was silence around the table. Genrikh Dorov was as disliked as he was feared. Then Rokossovsky winked, everyone laughed, and the conversation started again.

A few hours later, and the dinner was over. Stalin had telephoned to discuss the offensive and Marshal Rokossovsky had retired. Around Satinov, the other officers and Losha were singing 'Katyusha' beside the fireplace. But he craved a quiet smoke and some cool air. Pulling on his fur-lined greatcoat and wolf-fur hat, he stepped through the doors at the back of the house and out into the night.

It was bitterly cold. The snow glowed on the statuary in the well-kept grounds. Where were the house's owners now? Were they even alive? How quickly fortune could change. Satinov lit a cigarette and sipped at the cognac in his glass.

War was simply a slaughterhouse on wheels, he thought. For

most men, soldiering was tragedy expressed as a profession. And yet he liked this life, the straightforward comradeship of the front, the sense of shared mission, the moral clarity of war against evil.

The orange tip of another cigarette: he wasn't alone.

'Oh, it's you,' he said quietly. 'I thought you'd flown back to Moscow.'

'I'll be here a while yet,' she replied. 'The medical services on this front need reorganization and I can't trust anyone else to do it.' She was wearing, he noticed, that full-length sheepskin greatcoat, which, out here, made her look like a wild animal.

'I prefer to do everything myself too. I didn't realize you were from Moscow.'

'I'm from Lvov originally. Is it so obvious I'm from Galicia?' She laughed with a singing sound, throwing back her head so that he caught a glimpse of her throat.

'No, not at all. You're at the Kremlevka?'

'Yes, I'm its new director. But I'm a cardiologist. What's your speciality?'

'Not hearts,' Satinov said tersely. 'Hearts are the last organs that I consider.'

As they talked, the steam of their breath fused, and when they exhaled, cigarette smoke twisted from their lips and swirled around them like the folds of a grey cloak. He was conscious of her distinct spicy perfume as they walked around the gardens, and then out into the fields beyond the house. The full moon above them had dyed the snow a strange blue so that, as they walked on into the deer park, the blue grass under their feet crunched and sparkled. The snowflakes that gathered in her hair seemed to make it blacker and thicker still.

He stopped to allow Dashka to finish the cognac in his glass.

Ahead was a white colonnade – and now they saw it was a small Grecian temple.

'It's from the Seven Years War,' she said. 'A folly!'

'Let's explore!' Feeling like children, they entered its cold portals, chased by wisps of mist that curled down from little domes and out of alcoves. Suddenly, and without knowing quite why, Satinov was filled with an intense joy. Below them, they could see the gloomy house, surrounded by lines of jeeps, tanks, guns. Smoke from the soldiers' fires rose from the village. In the distance: the sound of a hammer on metal; of engineers mending the tanks; engines revving; volleys of shots; young men singing a love song – was it the Georgian melody 'Tiflis'? A boom and the orange flash of distant howitzers momentarily made the snow itself flare up as if on fire.

Leaning against the wall, he lit another cigarette and told her about his family, of his happiness with Tamara, how the death of his eldest son had fused into the deaths of tens of thousands in the battles where he served, of his pride in his second son, David, his admiration for George's genial mischief (which he envied), of Marlen's successes, and of Mariko, apple of his eye.

'Have you told them all these things?' she asked.

He shook his head.

'But you tell me here? You must tell them; you must tell Tamara.'

He smiled, turning to her, noticing the beauty of her dark eyes, her lips. 'Now, your turn,' he said.

She had one son in the army, a daughter, Minka, who took nothing seriously, and Demian, who took everything seriously, like his father. And then there was her little afterthought: 'My Senka, whom I love so much it makes me grind my teeth.'

'I was like that with my mother,' said Satinov.

'My Senka's quite different from you, Hercules. He's soft and adorable but you – we all know that you're the Iron Commissar. You like to be seen as cold as ice, as silent as the forest.'

'I don't seem very silent tonight.'

'No,' she admitted. 'You've surprised me.'

'I've surprised myself.'

She laughed and he glimpsed her throat again. 'It's my company, of course. I claim credit for your loquacity. I thought you were another silent Bolshevik disciplinarian.'

They had almost avoided the mention of her spouse up to now. It seemed to Satinov to be a significant move in their conversation. 'He's strict at home too?'

'He never lets us forget. He's the puritanical conscience of the Party. But I love him, of course. And you?'

'Probably Tamara would agree. The Soviet man is a product of our harsh times. But I love my Tamara too, and our friends say our marriage is the happiest they know.'

'How wonderful,' she said. 'It's true. I know all the gossip but I've never heard a whisper about *you* being a flirt.'

He threw his cigarette away, a speck of red in the blue snow beyond. 'But what about you, Dashka? Are you famous for your flirtations? You're beautiful enough . . .'

'I like to flirt but it never goes anywhere. I married at nineteen and I've never looked at another man in twenty-one years.'

'And yet . . . ?'

'Nothing,' she said. 'I'm just enjoying this moment.'

He passed her a cigarette and watched her put it between her lips. He leaned in to light it. He closed his eyes for a moment and he could feel how close she was – by the warmth of her face, the scent of her hair and her exotic amber skin, so rare amongst Russians.

He paused, waited for her to move away; then he leaned in closer and, without any decision or reason at all, they were kissing, and he could feel her light, wide lips on his.

Outside the arches and the colonnades, the snow started to fall again, making the night a few degrees warmer. The flakes whirled around them in their little temple. Once they had started to kiss, and once they knew that no one could see them, they could not stop. His hands ran over her fur coat; then he was pushing it open, and then the green tunic and her blouse, delighting in the soft caramel hues of her neck and shoulders.

She was kissing him more hungrily than he had ever been kissed by Tamara. She was biting his mouth, tearing his lips, breathing his breath. For a second, the scientific Communist, the Iron Commissar, returned and Satinov wondered if this was right, normal, and he shrank from her. But as he inhaled her quick breath, tasted the slight bitterness of her cigarettes and the sweetness of the brandy, her passion infected him. She curled herself around him so that he could feel her body, her need for him. He touched her legs above her boots, realizing that he loved their delicious sturdiness. When his hand slid up her American nylons, when it reached the silkiness of her skin, both of them groaned aloud.

Somehow they stopped, and a few minutes later, they were walking back down the hill towards the house.

'Comrade Doctor,' he said in his restored commanding tone, 'we're good Bolsheviks. We both love our spouses. This can *never* happen again.'

'Agreed, Comrade General. Of course.'

'You go in first,' he ordered.

He bent down and scooped up some snow and rubbed it bracingly into his face, onto his lips that still tasted of her. You fool, Satinov, he told himself, after all these years without so much as a glance at another woman, how could you behave like this now?

Yet he felt as if some metaphysical change had taken place inside him. Could one moment like that so change a man? He shook his head. Not Hercules Satinov, surely.

33

The three schoolgirls sat in the Bolshoi box, buzzing with Crimean champagne and excitement because they had never had such a good view of the stage. But Rosa was a little drunk: she was so slight that the bubbles had gone straight to her head. No sooner had they sat down than she closed her eyes and put her hands to her temples. 'Oh my God, I feel dizzy, I feel sick!'

'She can't be sick here!' hissed Minka.

'Imagine if she was sick over the edge onto the orchestra!' replied Serafima. 'I'll take her home.'

'No,' said Minka. 'I'll go. I've shown off my dress, been admired, drunk champagne. I really don't need to see the ballet yet again.'

'Oddly, I'm in the mood now,' Serafima said, waving goodbye as her two friends left.

Alone in her splendid box, she looked out onto the stage, glorying in her isolation until, well into Act Two, a young man in an American uniform joined her. He seemed surprised to find her there, and did not sit next to her but left two seats between them. He placed his cap on one of them.

Serafima looked over at him covertly. He seemed very different from his compatriots she'd met earlier, who were boorish and strapping. In contrast, he was tall and slim, and obviously cultured, for he was watching the ballet intently, his delicate lips smiling as the dancers performed their most challenging steps, sometimes just nodding thoughtfully at the music, with which he seemed familiar, a finger marking the tunes.

When the interval came, he got up and left without glancing at her. She remained in her seat, wondering what to do. She was far too bashful to go to the bar on her own without Minka and Rosa's support, but she felt a bit lonely, sitting in her box as the audience poured out to drink and smoke. So, after a minute, she ventured into the scarlet-carpeted corridor to stretch her legs, and there he was: the slim American, smoking a cigarette. Everyone else must have already bolted for the bar, because they were alone.

'A truly wonderful production,' he said in perfect Russian. 'Lepeshinskaya's the best dancer in the world at the moment.'

'Do you go to the ballet . . . in America?' she asked, speaking English.

He smiled sweetly at her. 'Your English is better than my Russian.' He offered her a cigarette from a silver box and she took it.

'I think Lepeshinskaya's still developing as a dancer,' Serafima said.

'I don't agree,' he said, lighting her cigarette. 'I think she's already reached perfection. My question is: how long can perfection last?'

'Does it matter when it's timeless?'

He seemed delighted with this question and, glancing at the stairs (she guessed he was calculating how long before the crowds would be returning; seconds, she thought), he started to ask tentatively, 'I don't usually ask but . . . I was thinking . . . Would you think me—?'

'No, I wouldn't,' she interrupted him, amazed at her own

brash certainty – and suddenly blushing (how she hated this ridiculous tendency to blush); she had ruined the moment before it had even begun.

'Will you come for a walk afterwards?' he asked shyly, and she was delighted he was not asking her for a drink after all.

'Yes, I'd like that,' she said.

'Meet me fifteen minutes after the ballet in the street behind the theatre.' He stopped, looking uncertain; almost, Serafima thought, as though he was blushing too. 'May I ask you your name?'

She told him.

'Romashkin? Like the writer?'

'My father,' she said, expecting him to say, like everyone else, 'Ahh, you're the film-star's daughter,' but he did not say anything more and she appreciated his tact.

'And yours?' she asked.

'I'm Frank Belman.'

The following afternoon, Satinov was heading out of the Front's staff conference in the library when he bumped into Dr Dorova. They looked at each other, unsure of the right thing to do or say.

'You're still here?' he said curtly. Too curtly, he thought afterwards.

'I'm working,' she said. 'I've been out in the field with our medics since dawn and there's a lot more to do. I'm reporting to the comrade marshal,' and she carried on towards the conference in the library.

Smoke was billowing in the light of low green lamps when Satinov joined them later, and a crowd of officers and adjutants was leaning over the map on the billiard table.

'Comrade Doctor Dorova,' said Marshal Rokossovsky, 'what do you need?'

'A new field hospital needs to be established before the offensive,' replied Dashka.

'Agreed,' said Rokossovsky.

'I therefore need a site easily reachable from the front with the appropriate facilities, space for five hundred beds, and mattresses, and transport.'

'Women are so much more efficient than men,' Rokossovsky said to a chorus of male laughter.

'And that's not all they're good for,' croaked one of the generals. Satinov felt a sudden rush of irritation that he swallowed with some difficulty.

'What more do you need, Comrade Doctor?' he asked.

'I need to look at the site. I must drive out there tonight and check it, so that we can begin setting up at dawn. It's already getting dark.'

Rokossovsky, a cigarette between his teeth, ran one hand through his cropped grey-blond hair and peered at the map again. 'Who can see an appropriate site?'

'I can,' said Satinov, stretching over. 'Here. A shooting lodge. On the main roads. Close to the railway. Just a few kilometres behind the front.'

'Approved!' said Rokossovsky. 'Thank you, Comrade Dorova. Let's move on. Quartermaster, please report!'

Dashka came round to Satinov's side. He had a map pin in his hand. 'Comrade Doctor,' he said, 'here's your site. There! I'll mark it for you.' He pushed the pin into the map.

'I see,' she said, leaning over to put her finger on the spot so that he could smell her spicy scent and see her dimpled wrists.

34

Frank Belman. Captain Frank Belman of the US Army. He looked too young to be a captain. As Serafima waited for him in the small street behind the Bolshoi, close to the dressing rooms, she was impressed by his discretion: he had not said a word to her in front of anyone else; he ignored her in the box after their short chat just as he had before; and she saw that, while the street had been crowded by theatregoers for ten minutes after the ballet had ended, it was now completely deserted. Unlike the boisterous Americans in the bar, he seemed to have an understanding of the Soviet system. Even though it was wartime and so many girls were keen to bag an American, Serafima knew from the comments of her parents' friends in the leadership that already there were signs that this would not be acceptable for much longer.

She looked up, and there he was: a solitary figure, no longer in uniform, but wearing a flat cap and dark blue greatcoat, a cigarette between his lips. He was even taller than her, but with his smooth pink cheeks and wide eyes he resembled a provincial poetry student. He smiled and gave a jaunty two-fingered salute as if to say: Here I am, and, boy, isn't this a blast!

Soon she was at his side. He took her arm and they walked away from the theatre, as if they had done so many times before. First they discussed the ballet rather earnestly until he said, 'I'm being a bit of a phony. I really love the ballet but I'm no expert. I only started to attend here in Moscow. You know much more about it than me.'

'I come all the time,' she said. 'But not so much for the ballet. For us, it's a . . .'

'A breath of the old world?' he suggested.

'Yes. The thirties were so hard and the war's been terrible but now we're winning, it's brought some glamour back to Moscow. Not much . . .'

'But just enough?'

'Well, everything's relative, but for a Muscovite—'

'The Bolshoi's like the aristocratic ball in *War and Peace*?'

'Frank, it seems you're finishing my sentences.'

'Or you're stealing my thoughts, Serafima.'

They both laughed.

'How old are you?'

'I'm twenty-two,' he said.

'I'm still at school,' she said. 'But it's my last year.'

'I know,' he said, looking at her openly for the first time. 'I can tell.'

They were still walking when the blizzard struck, and soon the snow was so dense that they could not see ten metres in front of themselves.

Serafima knew that wartime had intensified life: people lived, loved, died faster than before. But the affinity between her and Frank made her uneasy and suspicious. She had never been in such a situation before, never met a man like this, yet alone one who talked in this manner. She had to wonder: was Frank Belman the sort of man who regularly asked out Russian girls after only two minutes of conversation? How did he know to change out of his American uniform? He may look like a sincere intellectual, she thought, but was he actually a cynical seducer come to drab Moscow to turn the heads of girls eager for the slightest glint of faraway cities? An American spy? Was this a set-up? How could she know? And yet somehow she thought she did.

'How did this happen?' she asked, stopping suddenly and turning to him.

'What do you mean?'

'Well, that I'm here with you now. Did you choose me specifically or was it by chance?'

Frank laughed, and Serafima noticed the way the thick snowflakes were settling on his dark lashes, even longer than hers, she noticed jealously. 'You chose me. First, you were alone in the box, my box; second, you watched the ballet and never me; third, you didn't run to the bar like every other girl but just waited for the next act. So I knew you weren't like the others.'

'How do I know you're not?'

'Do I seem like the others?'

'No. But I don't really know many other men.'

He put a hand on her arm. 'Look, I know what you're getting at because I asked you out so quickly. But I saw that I had just one minute before you left and I'd never see you again. You're wondering if I'm an agent of the capitalist-imperial powers, and I do admit I wondered how a beautiful girl happened to be in my box, alone, on the very evening I decided to come to the ballet.'

She smiled uncertainly. She had not thought of this. 'So you were wondering whether I am a spy?' She paused. 'I don't think I am – unless it's possible to be a spy without knowing it.'

'That's a very Russian idea,' he answered. 'But let me tell you

I'm an attaché, a diplomat in uniform, at the American Embassy. I interpret for the ambassador. But I guess you'd say I'm a real damned capitalist.'

'You're from a rich family?'

'Yes.'

'Do you live in a mansion?'

'My parents do.'

'Do you have repressed Negro servants in white gloves?'

'No gloves, but our butler is black.'

'Does he wear a white coat like in the movies?'

'Yes.'

'So, as a good Communist, I declare you the enemy. I suppose you must be what we call a bloodsucker of the working class?'

He was, he told her, one of those Americans who were as at home in the country houses of England as he was in the mansions of Long Island. His father was Honorius Belman, president of the Southern-Eastern Union Railway Corporation, a Texan born in a log cabin, but he, his son, had been educated at Groton and Harvard, where he'd studied Russian. Frank told her how he played polo with plutocrats like the Rockefellers, that his father was a donor to FDR's campaigns and that he had spent a holiday working in the White House. All of which explained why he had not been impressed by her own famous parents, Serafima realized.

After walking for hours, they were back where they had started. They reached the Metropole Hotel across the square from the Bolshoi. A hotel? He did not seem that sort of man. But perhaps all men were that sort of man, Serafima thought as the doorman in his green braided uniform bowed and the revolving doors spun them into the scarlet lobby.

* * *

Frank bought her two shots of vodka at the Metropole bar but, to Serafima's relief, he didn't mention anything about taking a room. There was a jazz band playing and, on the dance floor, the uniforms of a dozen nations danced the foxtrot. Men's shoulderboards and shiny boots, the bare shoulders and permed tresses of scarlet-lipped girls shimmered around them. They stood watching for a moment as the vodka restored her. She was dreading him asking her to dance. She hated foxtrotting. She had no natural rhythm, and her clumsiness would ruin everything.

'Do you . . . like to d-dance?' Frank asked over the sound of the band. When she came to know him better, she would realize that he stammered slightly when he was nervous.

'If you want to,' she answered, frowning.

'You look cross,' he said. 'You've looked cross ever since we came in here. When you're cross, you lower your eyebrows so you look like an angry swan. More beautiful than ever but quite frightening!'

'Well, the angry swan says sorry. It's because . . . I'm not sure I like being here.'

'But I thought all girls loved to dance,' he said, looking anxious.

'Yes, most do – but not all.'

He cleared his throat a little. 'I have a confession to make. Although I'm told that every man must be able to foxtrot, I can't dance at all. I hate dancing . . . I'm sorry. I'm not much of a date, am I?'

'Oh Frank, I hate dancing too. And I can't foxtrot or anything else. I can only talk and walk.'

So out they went, back into the night, Frank quoting poets that few Westerners knew: Akhmatova, Pasternak, Pushkin,

Blok. They walked across the Stone Bridge opposite the Kremlin. Through the snow, they could hardly even see the towers, gates and stars under its camouflage netting.

Serafima could feel the icy flecks settling on her warm skin and then melting – it was delicious. She stopped as Frank took off his gloves and offered her a cigarette from his silver case. They blew the blue smoke into the grey light where the snowflakes glinted like jewels in the lamplight, and did not speak.

Frank seemed to be thinking hard about something; then he cleared his throat. 'I'm not a playboy. I haven't talked about many of these things with anyone before you. May I . . . m-may I . . . hold your hand?'

She presented her hands to him, and when he unpeeled her gloves, the night became silent and she could see his hands shaking just a little. It was, she thought, truly a moment from the distant past, from a more romantic time.

When he held her hands in his, she turned them to put her fingers through his, and when she squeezed them, he squeezed back; and both of them stood there in the snow, face to face, overcome with the excitement of finding each other. The snow had padded the city so that they could hardly hear anything, see anything. Hours had passed since they met, yet their acquaintance, only as fresh as a night's snowfall, already seemed as if it had lasted for a long, long time. She had never kissed anyone. Never wished to. But she wanted him to kiss her now.

'Serafima, may I . . .'

But she'd already lifted her face to his, and could feel his mouth on hers as the snow fell thickly around them.

35

Satinov crept across the open space between him and the door of an outhouse. The Nazis were only thirty kilometres away, and still fighting for every village. Yet here he was, having given his bodyguards the slip, and about to enter an unknown house and do something that went against every instinct and every rule. He hesitated and then, cursing to himself and cocking his PPSh machine-gun, he opened it, ready for a burst of enemy fire, but welcoming instead the grassy warmth of the stables that reminded him of riding at home, at his dacha. The three horses tethered inside seemed glad to see him and he was even gladder to see them.

Walking quickly through the stables and crossing the yard, he tried the back door of the large house. It was not locked and he slid inside, body tensed and soaked with sweat as he found himself in the capacious kitchen of a *schloss* designed to accommodate legions of servants. Bells were marked with the names of rooms. Holding his PPSh with its round magazine over his forearm, he walked lightly through a green baize door into a corridor that opened into a hall.

He saw the orange eyes first. Two, and then another two. Then pair after pair. He raised the barrel of the machine-gun: does it end here? But no, the heads of a herdsworth of moose, antelopes and bears were mounted up the high walls, reflecting the crimson flicker of a fire crackling in the fireplace. A step further; another step; the floorboards groaned but he was moving fast now.

A movement right in front of him: 'Who is it? Hands up or I'll shoot!' But he knew, of course.

She was tending the fire.

'Do you approve of the new hospital for the First Belorussian Front?' she said, turning to him, her voice with its Galician accent so breathless that the words caught in her throat. 'I've made *chai*. Would you like a cup?'

They sat next to each other, and she poured the tea into china cups and saucers emblazoned with some aristocratic crest. Her hands were trembling, he noticed as the china clinked and she spilled a little. She was as nervous as he was. Her scent, she told him, was L'Origan by Coty, strong and sweet and sharp, reminding him of honey melting in tea and spicy wood burning in a fire. It was getting dark in the room and so she took off her beret and her sheepskin greatcoat, and lit two kerosene lamps on the table.

'I didn't know if you'd come,' she said. 'I didn't know if I was being presumptuous. Or, worse, deluded . . . But I knew I'd come anyway.'

Satinov said nothing. He imagined that two of the animal heads on the walls were talking to him.

'Have you ever wanted a woman so much?' asked the bison with the white glass eyes. 'After the war, Stalin said every soldier deserves a bit of fun.'

But the voice from the lion's head was more censorious and more urgent. 'Think of Stalin. Of Tamriko. Of her husband, Genrikh Dorov. Leave *now*! This is against Bolshevik ethics. Walk out of there right now! You have too much to lose if you stay.'

But it was no good. Satinov shook his head, pulled his great-coat closer and sat down next to her.

'Well, here we are,' said Dashka, leaning against him for a moment, partly, he guessed, out of nerves, partly out of shyness. She produced a bottle of vodka and two little glasses. 'You should have brought the drinks,' she said, 'but I knew you wouldn't think of it. So here.' And she put the glass in his hand.

'I think I need it.'

'God, so do I. Here's to an unlikely and very secret friendship.'

They drank three little toasts and then he kissed her again; he had never kissed anyone who kissed like her.

'Not here!' She took his hand and a kerosene lamp and he followed her up a wide wooden staircase, hung with a gazelle and a zebra. Satinov felt each glassy eye swivel as the two of them passed. They reminded him of his colleagues in the Kremlin.

At the top of the stairs, she led him along the gloomy wood-panelled corridor and opened the door at the end; Satinov was more nervous than he had been on his first wedding night in Georgia in the twenties.

He was so well known for his clean living that Stalin, who gave everyone nicknames, sometimes called him the Choirboy. He could govern the Caucasus, and build a new industrial town in the middle of Siberia; he could dance and shoot wolves and ski; but this . . . what if he was no good at it? What if he failed completely?

'Aren't you going to kiss me?' said Dashka. They were in a bedroom with another giant moose's head over the bed, a fire already lit. The door shut behind him. They were kissing again and Satinov's doubts vanished in that instant. *This*, he decided, was a neighbourhood of paradise. He pushed her against the door.

He pulled the pin out of her hair and her tresses fell around her face. He held a handful, thick and heavy and black, although it turned a lighter chestnut and slightly curled at the ends. 'It's all right,' she said, 'I like having my hair pulled.'

He reached up her skirt, scuffing the thick khaki until he reached the tops of those nylon stockings. 'Oh my God, oh my God,' she was saying. She embraced him, kissing him frantically. Like a schoolboy making love for the first time, Satinov had to keep checking that this was really happening.

They hopped and limped across the floor, his trousers around his ankles, her booted legs and full, bare, brown thighs around his waist, her arms around his neck, her lips on his lips, her hair around him like a web, linked together, and tipped onto the bed.

'I so wanted to feel you. Since last night, I haven't thought of anything else,' she said. 'I didn't sleep and I could hardly eat today. Will you undress me slowly?'

He fumbled with the buttons of her blouse and she helped him, all the time watching him, eyelids heavy, almost closing, the dark edges of her irises seeming to melt. He was astonished by her wantonness.

He hadn't met anyone like this since his boyhood in Tiflis. The boys at the seminary (yes, he had studied for the priesthood at the same Tiflis Seminary as Stalin – but much later) had visited a woman of pleasure, a jet-haired gypsy. 'That one's far too prissy for this,' the woman had said, nodding at Satinov. 'That one really will become a priest.' And she had been right, because a Bolshevik was a sort of armed priest.

'What are we going to do about him?' Dashka said, pointing up at the moosehead above them.

'How about this?' He tossed her blouse up so that it covered the moose's eyes, leaving just the nose peeking out. Then he returned to unbuttoning her skirt.

'Do you think army skirts are designed to be impregnable fortresses for a reason?' she asked. He rolled down her stockings until they were like long socks just below her knees and he started to kiss her knees and up her legs, wrapped as they were in the velvet of her caramel skin. 'It's years since anyone has undressed me like this.'

Satinov started to throw off his clothes too, but: 'Wait,' she said. 'I want to undress you too.' He looked down on her; her body was streaked like a tigress by the orange flickers of the fire and dyed a deeper gold by the lamp. But he could scarcely bear to look for more than a moment before he had to kiss her again, on the lips, on the neck, everywhere; she bit her fingers. They made love again and as they finished, she laughed in a high singsong voice with her head thrown back.

Satinov opened his eyes and saw the dreary room, the plain wooden bed, the heavy Germanic furniture, dimly lit by the fire and the lantern, as if he was seeing everything for the first time – including her.

'Do you know Ovid's poems on love?' she said. 'He wrote that the bedroom is the only place where you can do exactly what you please, and truly be yourself.'

'You're so much more cultured than me,' he said. 'I was expelled for Marxist activities at sixteen.'

'I was raised in a Jewish household filled with books.' She hesitated. 'I feel so shaken up. As if the world has trembled and tilted, so everything, even my sense of time, is in a different place, everything has lost its previous meaning. I'd never have guessed that passion in our forties could be more intense than when we were young.'

'So you've never . . . ?'

'Done this before? Never. Not once in all these years of marriage. I don't know what's come over me. What about you?'

'You really need to ask that question? No, I've never done this before either.'

'I thought all you leaders were womanizers.'

'I've never looked at another woman – and now this.'

'Are you in a panic, Comrade General?'

'Aren't you, Dashka?'

'I should be, but it feels so natural, as if we've known each other since we were young. You know, when I was eighteen, I studied medicine in Odessa and I had a love affair with a student of literature. We smoked opium. I almost got addicted to it – and him. Soon after, I met Genrikh and we got married. With him, I've always known where I belong and that I have a place. That's love too. I need that, you know.'

Satinov looked at his watch and sighed. 'My staff will be missing me. We've got to get back. It's almost midnight.' He dressed quickly, and looked down at her. She was still lying exactly where he'd left her. 'What are you thinking about?'

She gave her slightly crooked smile, her eyes dark. 'I'm thinking of tomorrow. Everyone will see me, and no one will know what I've been doing.'

36

The next morning, Satinov was summoned back to Stavka (which meant Headquarters) by the Supremo (which meant Stalin) to discuss the offensive. Then he was sent on a series of missions, to Bulgaria, to Romania, to see Mao Tse-tung in China . . . but all the time, and throughout the months that followed, he longed to see Dashka again. It was hard to discover where she was: he could not ask his staff to find her, as this would draw attention, and almost certainly someone would tell Beria or Abakumov's minions, and they would start to gather a file against him for debauchery or corruption or something – and it would be stored away until the right moment.

'Who was at Zhukov's headquarters?' he might ask his assistant Chubin.

'Comrade Malenkov was inspecting,' Chubin might respond. 'Oh, and that Dr Dorova was there too . . .'

Then he could call her. 'It's me,' he would say.

'Hello, me,' she always replied.

They could speak on the lines between fronts, freshly laid by the communications staff and therefore probably not yet bugged, but he didn't say her name and she didn't say his, so instead she created another persona, 'Academician Almaz,' an old man who was neither one nor the other of them but both, a hermaphrodite who personified their love.

'I was just calling to enquire about the health of old Academician Almaz?'

'Academician Almaz is exceedingly old.'

'I've so missed Academician Almaz.'

'Almaz is always pleased to hear from you. You should call him more often. He's so elderly, such a hermit these days . . .'

Just to hear her voice with that Galician-Yiddish accent, its rolling 'r's, was a joy to him. When he replayed, as he did constantly, their meetings, he wasn't sure exactly what – out of her various identities – most delighted him: was it her astounding ability to improvise a hospital out of nothing, to save a life calmly, that singsong laughter or her golden thighs? Yet he never ceased loving his Tamriko, the mother of his only daughter, and the centre of his life (without whom his successes would have been impossible). He remembered too how frequently Dashka insisted that she loved Genrikh, adding, 'Besides, if I left him, I'd lose everything.'

Once they met in 'Stone Arse' Molotov's antechamber in the Kremlin. As well as running the army medical corps, she was now Health Minister. When she saw him, she jumped.

'Oh, hello, Comrade Satinov, it's you!'

'Yes, Comrade Doctor, it's me!' They were alone for a few moments in that dreary room waiting for that dreary man neither wanted to see. They talked, in code of course, so closely that he could feel her breath on him. For one moment, he managed to touch her hand and she squeezed his fingers. Ah, he thought later, the madness of those moments!

'How's Academician Almaz? Will you tell him I miss him?'

'Academician Almaz is working so hard, even I hardly get to see him.'

'If you do see the esteemed academician,' he said, 'will you tell the old sage that I think he has the most beautiful mind – and wrists and eyes – I've ever seen! For an octogenarian, of course!'

'The academician has never been more excited to be at a meeting with Comrade Molotov,' she replied. They could not risk a kiss, yet never, he decided, had two sets of eyes so ravished each other, generating enough heat to warm even Stone Arse's drab chambers. Then she said quietly, in that way of hers, barely opening her mouth: 'I think we should stop talking now. Go and sit over there.'

Two generals came in. They'd separated just in time.

'Comrade Satinov!' Molotov – wearing a dark suit, his head as round as a cannonball, his figure as square as a brick – came out of his office. 'Shall we take a walk around the Kremlin?'

'Yes, let's do that,' agreed Satinov. As he talked to Stone Arse, he looked back at her; Dashka was gazing at him with the most loving intensity in her dark eyes – just for a moment, and then she glanced away. Satinov almost gasped with the pleasure. He ached to touch her and kiss her again. As he strolled the Kremlin's courtyards with Molotov, he felt preposterously, dizzily happy.

He saw her and spoke to her so rarely that he had not really thought about what he expected of their fitful relationship. It had no formal future, yet he resolved to enjoy these special moments, which he ascribed to the madness of war and death. Afterwards, however afterwards arrived, he would return to his real nature, his true world.

Yet one evening, when he was alone late at night in his Kremlin office waiting for the driver to take him to dinner with Stalin, he noticed that the phone in the empty neighbouring office was ringing. He'd sent home his aides, so he ran down the corridor to answer it.

'It's Almaz.' He recognized her distinctive voice straightaway.

'Hello. I'm impressed with your cunning,' he said. 'Dear academician!'

'This academician can't talk for long,' she said, 'but I wanted you to know I can't go on with this. I haven't slept for three nights.' He heard her crying and his heart ached for her. 'I'll lose my children, I'll lose everything, and I feel so guilty! I have to give you up. Can you forgive me?'

Satinov clenched the phone, and willed himself to breathe deeply and calmly. He was not, he reminded himself, the Iron Commissar for nothing. 'I understand,' he said finally, putting down the phone.

Perhaps, he thought as he sat in the empty room, his own life as a revolutionary had given him the ability to bear secrets and pressures. He was born for conspiracy. Others, like Dashka, and indeed Tamriko, were not.

He returned to his own office and dialled a number: 'Tamriko?'

'Yes, darling Hercules.'

'I'll be late.'

'Have a good dinner. Did you want anything?'

'Are all the children well?'

'Yes. They're missing you, as I am. Come home soon.'

'I shall,' he said stiffly. But he had never called like that before and he knew it would please her.

An hour later, in the back of the armoured Packard speeding through the silvery woods towards Stalin's Nearby Dacha, he was himself again, the Iron Commissar. Almost.

'After the war,' Frank warned Serafima, 'we think Stalin will crack down. America will be Russia's enemy, so we must be very careful. As a diplomat I'm watched, and with your background you may be too. Our blessing is that we've found each other, but our curse is that we are in a time and place when we can't just live as we're doing now, in the present.'

'I suppose you've thought of using codes?' Serafima asked.

'As a matter of fact, I have. This is how we'll meet. I'll leave a bookmark in the foreign literature section of the House of the Book. If it's in a Galsworthy, we'll meet at the matinée. If it's in Edith Wharton, evening; in Hemingway, ask not for whom the bell tolls, it tolls for us, so come back tomorrow. There will be a ticket under a false name at the Bolshoi for that night's performance.'

'So I will just go to the Bolshoi again and again?'

'You can watch an act or two but when I go out, you go out too, through the fire doors at the back. No one will follow you.'

'And we'll meet in the street.'

'Darling Serafima, I have an apartment. The great thing is that it's not registered as a diplomatic residence. It belonged to a Russian friend who was killed in the war and no one knows about it. It's very simple, but it could be our place. It's near the back of the Bolshoi so when you come out . . . would you l-l-like to meet me there?'

Serafima smiled. She knew this was right – but it amused her that, out of all the girls at school, some of whom seemed so fast, it was going to be *her*, Serafima, who would make love first. She loved Frank and he loved her and it seemed absolutely natural to do it with the man she wanted to spend her life with. She knew the basics, the facts of life, but how it all really worked, she had no proper idea. What if she became pregnant? The scandal would destroy her. Wasn't it the man's job to ensure she didn't? But there was an even bigger problem that ate at her.

'You seem worried,' he said. 'We don't have to do anything at all. Just talk if you like.'

'I'm not sure . . .'

'You want to wait until we're married?'

'It's not that.'

'Then what?'

'I just feel that I'm not . . . perfect. That you'll be disappointed.'

'Nothing could disappoint me about you. Nothing.' Frank's eyes were burning with certainty as he said this.

But it wasn't nothing. It was the snakeskin, the burn on her body. No one except her family had seen it since she had become a teenager, but she'd never forgotten that it was there, beneath her clothes. Her dresses were higher and plainer to protect this indelible stain. She could always feel it, stiffer and rougher than the rest of her. An ugly thing of yellow corrugated skin, it made her feel ugly too. Her only hope was that Frank loved her enough to pretend it was not there.

A lingering dread now haunted her sleep, her classes, her every moment, threatening to destroy her happiness as she had always feared it would. What if Frank was disgusted by her? What if he fell out of love with her? Should she tell him about it first?

They arranged to meet and then she cancelled their date – twice. But in the end, she decided that she must just trust him. If he was the man she thought he was, the Frank she loved, wouldn't he take her snakeskin as an indivisible part of her? She would just have to find out.

37

Satinov did not see Dashka Dorova again until Stalin rewarded him with a special prize: he was to be the Supremo's representative at Marshal Zhukov's headquarters. Three Fronts, 2.5 million Soviet soldiers, 7,500 tanks, were converging on Berlin. But Stalin had chosen Zhukov to take Berlin, and Satinov would go with him.

On 15 April, Satinov reported to Zhukov's headquarters before the Seelow Heights. At dawn the next day, Zhukov's howitzers opened up – the thunder of the barrage shook Satinov to his very innards – and the men went into battle. But the assault didn't go according to plan. Storming those well-defended hills, the Russians suffered 30,000 casualties, and that night, a furious Stalin phoned Satinov.

'Who's responsible for this crime?' he said. 'Find the culprit and we'll shorten him by a head!'

Even Zhukov was demanding new hospitals to handle so many wounded. And so it was that Dr Dorova was summoned urgently, called right from her bed in the middle of the night by Marshal Zhukov himself. Satinov did not see her; he was with Zhukov at the front line, but she was nearby and he found himself constantly looking around for a glimpse of her.

On 19 April, the Seelow Heights finally fell and Zhukov advanced on Berlin, but it took ten days of brutal street-by-street fighting to take the city. It was only after the fall of the Reichstag and the suicide of Hitler that Satinov saw her amongst the Soviet generals in the white stucco hall of the Karlshorst Army Technical Training School. It was 8 May, and Zhukov and the American and British generals were waiting for Feldmarschall Keitel to end the war. Rows of klieg lights beamed a theatrical electric whiteness on the table where the Nazis would sign the surrender. The medals of twenty nations, the oiled hair and rough-hewn skin of the hard-living generals, the powdered foreheads, glazed lips and waved hairdos of aides, typists, drivers and PPZhs were illuminated by the unforgiving zinc light.

She was in her parade uniform, the elegantly coutured (against all regulations) tunic and skirt showing off her curvaceous figure. How the vizored cap of a general of the medical corps, the gold, scarlet, the stars and braid, set off her brown skin and eyes.

Hours passed and the surrender was delayed as the Nazis tried to sue for better terms. Zhukov and Stalin's representative at the negotiations, Vyshinsky, shouted at each other; generals rushed in and rushed out and finally the Nazi generals arrived.

When at last the ceremony was done, Satinov came over to her. 'Dr Dorova.'

'Comrade Satinov.'

'How've you been?'

'I'm fine. What a day!'

'We can tell our grandchildren we were here.'

She looked into his eyes. 'Are you thinking of your son Vanya?' she asked him gently.

'Yes, I am. Today, at last, I can really think of him.' Only a small tic in his cheek revealed how moved he really was, but she saw it.

'We better not talk too much . . .' She glanced over at the egregious Vyshinsky.

'Right, but it's good to see you.'

'And you.'

Zhukov's banquet went on all night. Dish after dish, twenty-five toasts – to Stalin, the Red Army, Soviet women; to Churchill and Truman – but by six a.m., when the dinner ended, Satinov stood beside Zhukov and Vyshinsky to wave goodbye to their drunk Western friends in the blue light of dawn. The war was over. He found her again watching the Americans drive away.

'It's me,' he said from behind.

'Hello, me,' she said.

The skin on her cheeks was pink with excitement, weariness and alcohol. It was the end of a night of toasts and four years of war.

'May I ask . . . Do you ever think of . . .'

'Academician Almaz? Every day.'

'Me too,' said Satinov, turning away from her, from his past. 'Every day.'

38

The matinée at the Bolshoi. All Moscow was already on the streets. The Red Army was in Berlin. The Nazis had signed the surrender the previous night. As soon as the lights went down, Serafima followed Frank's plan.

She came out of the fire exit and then crossed the road. Afterwards she could not quite remember how she found herself in the one-room apartment, with its single chair, white stuffing pouring out of several gashes, and the double bed. There was nothing – no pictures – on the damp, stained walls, except one cheap, water-stained print of Pushkin above the chair.

Frank was waiting. As nervous as she was. When he gave her a cigarette, he was shaking so much he could barely light it and they laughed, which broke the ice a little.

'I think we should have a little drink,' he said, holding a bottle of wine: Telavi 2 from Georgia. 'Your leader's favourite.'

She was so grateful for the wine that she downed the entire glass, and felt a little giddy when he started to kiss her and led her to the bed. She was so aware of her snakeskin that she felt she was wearing it *outside* her clothes. So far he didn't know it even existed and yet it was all *she* could think about.

Then he left her for a moment, drew the curtains, turned off the light and lit two candles that stood on the mantelpiece. She barely dared make a sound; she wanted to whisper something but her heart was beating in her neck like a kettledrum. When he returned, he kissed her mouth and he softly pushed down her dress, planting kisses on her neck. Serafima was flooded with a sensation she did not recognize: a shiver started in her thighs and then crept into her belly, making her lurch with its burning power. For a second she even forgot her snakeskin but then his hand rested on it outside her dress.

'Stop!' she said.

'What is it?'

'You . . . you haven't done anything wrong, but I've got to tell you something . . .'

'I know you haven't done this before,' he said, searching her face. Something else occurred to him. 'Or if you have, it doesn't matter. Either way it doesn't matter.'

'No, no, it's not that. Can we . . . just stop, while I tell you something?'

They awoke in each other's arms. In her room on the top floor of the Tempelhof Geriatic Women's Hospital, which was now full of Soviet wounded. Without powder and lipstick, just her thick hair around her shoulders, her mascara running, she was more lovely than before. This time was so precious that he tried to imprint on his mind every detail of her beauty.

'I dream of walking the streets with you,' she said.

The streets of Berlin were deserted except for Soviet soldiers, tanks, jeeps. All the houses, all the streets, were ruined. The lunar landscape of this obliterated city seemed as unreal as the generals under the klieg lights during the surrender. The tarmac and pavements were cracked, muddy and ingrained with fragments of shrapnel, scraps of material, rotting newspapers, children's shoes, even sometimes a whole man (whose son, whose father?) flattened into cloth and cardboard, crushed into the earth by brutal tank treads.

They were both wearing plain tunics without insignia, and were noticed by no one as they visited the Chancellery, where Hitler had committed suicide, and the Reichstag. Mostly, though, they just wandered through the city. Sometimes when they were alone for a moment he kissed her and she kissed him back, so passionately. She pulled him into a blasted alleyway. He held her by the waist, as her legs came up, and when she cried out, it sounded fierce and almost pagan.

Her need, her desire, her reckless courage enthralled him. Satinov had never done anything so heedlessly carefree. He could have been recognized by any soldier; he could have been reported by any of the thousands of Chekists nosing around Berlin. But after twenty years of disciplined diligence, he could hardly believe how wonderful it felt to be with the woman he suddenly loved in this landscape of destruction.

Slowly, reluctantly, they walked back to headquarters before lunchtime, only to find he had been summoned to Moscow. Their idyll had been far too short.

'Be careful, angel. It will be hard to see each other in Moscow. Almost impossible.'

'I'll think of something,' he said.

'You know how I love Genrikh and my children. I feel safe with him.'

'And you know I'd never leave Tamriko, whom I love too.'

'It's impossible. Unthinkable,' she agreed. Stalin had never allowed any of his leaders to divorce. To do so would not only destroy his career, it could destroy his entire family. Dashka had been right about that.

'Yet I love you too,' he said. 'Is that possible?'

She hesitated and, when they formally said goodbye as he climbed into his car, she saluted and then embraced him *à la russe*. When her lips were closest to his ear, she whispered so quickly, 'I love you, angel,' that he barely caught it. 'More than yesterday. Less than tomorrow.'

'And I you, Dashka,' he whispered it too. 'More than yesterday, less than tomorrow.'

'When I was a little girl, a maid spilled a pan of boiling water and I was burnt. I have a scar on my side that . . . that no one's seen before and . . . I call it my snakeskin. I wanted to tell you so you know what to expect.'

Frank turned to her. They were lying together in Frank's narrow bed, his flank against hers.

'That's why you've been so anxious?'

She nodded.

'Oh darling, I thought something had changed between us.' He kissed her gently on the lips. '*Sladkaya*, my sweet,' he whispered. 'I won't care. It's only you who's worried, and soon you won't be either, I promise.'

'Shall I show you?'

'No need, darling, I'll see you in all your beauty soon enough . . .'

'But I'd prefer to show you so you know. So I can get it over with.'

'If that would make you happier, then show me.' They sat up.

Even though she was anxious, she was still trembling with the excitement. She looked at him. His sweet brown eyes shone with sympathy and love for her; the moisture in them caught the candlelight. He unhooked her dress. Then she faced him again and pulled down the dress slowly, as far as her breasts. She hesitated there and considered running away – out of the door and into the streets. But he shook his head as one does when one admires something beautiful. She reached behind and unhooked her brassiere, faltering there too. She pulled her dress down a little further, covering her breasts with her hands. She closed her eyes in case there was disgust on his face and then gradually she raised her arms and said: 'There!'

'Can I touch you?' he asked, and she could tell from his voice that he was smiling, and she was so relieved. She jumped a little as his hand traced her snakeskin. His fingertips ran over the smooth skin and then across the borderline on to the roughness that extended up from her hip to her breast. 'I think you're so incredibly lovely, and I can't wait much longer.' His fingers retraced the snakeskin lightly, and she shivered.

'Are you sure?'

'More sure than I've been about anything. It can be our shared secret. Let this be the covenant of our love. Always.'

'Our talisman.'

'Yes, our talisman. Do you know Pushkin's poem?' He recited:

'A loving enchantress
Gave me her talisman.
She told me with tenderness:
You must not lose it—'

Serafima interrupted him to finish the verse:

'Its power is infallible,
Love gave it to you.'

She could not believe that she had been so blessed by this kind man who had transformed her fear into a talisman of love. He kissed away the tears on her cheeks.

'Now may I undress you myself? Please?'

The undressing, with all its tension and anxiety, followed by success and relief, had deeply moved her. Now there were red stars before her eyes – was it the wine? – and waves of heat surfed up her body. Now she longed for him to touch her in the places where her body was vibrating with an unknown pleasure that she could neither bear, nor satisfy, nor end. She didn't want to stop even when he reached for a package that she saw was marked 'Trojan.' He covered her eyes, smiling.

'This is much more awkward than . . .' he said, and they laughed out of nerves and she realized he meant her snakeskin, and that both were to be celebrated.

Afterwards, she felt beautiful for the first time in her life. She had sloughed off her ungainliness; yes, she smiled to herself, just as a snake sheds its skin.

39

Dashka Dorova and Hercules Satinov did not see each other again until the first day of term at School 801. It was May, and at the Golden Gates, he could see Dashka and she could see him and sometimes, as they passed one another, she would whisper: 'More than yesterday. Less than tomorrow.' Or just one word: 'Almaz!' But they were constantly watched by spouses, comrades, their own bodyguards and assistants, and both were wary of hurting their families or drawing the attention of the Organs.

When Satinov looked into his heart, he knew he loved Tamriko. He loved Dashka too, but it was a different species of love, and she came second to Tamriko. He saw no contradiction. There were many shades of love, he told himself. Together they made him complete. As for the secrecy, that cost him nothing: he was a Bolshevik.

They had found a way to phone each other. Sometimes the phone rang in the conference room next to his office.

'Hello, it's me!' She would use his words.

'Hello, me.'

'I love you,' she'd say.

'I love you and love being loved by you: it's the most unexpected joy for me, this secret jewel in my life.'

'But where can this go?' she would ask, anxious suddenly.

'For me, it doesn't have to go anywhere. It just is.'

She laughed. 'Is this really you, the Iron Commissar? How has this great romantic survived all these years in the age of ice?'

'I imagine kissing you when we're in our sixties.'

'One day, if we were both on our own, somehow, God forbid, then I know we would be together.'

'What are you wearing?' he would ask. 'What are you doing today?' He hated Genrikh because true possession is to share the fabric of someone else's life, he decided; it's about proximity; love as geography. He longed to know the soft sound of her sleeping and the sleepy smell of her hair in the morning; he wanted to be standing next to her when she brushed her teeth and at the foot of the stairs when she descended them. When she sat down to read, where did she sit?

'It's pure heaven when we talk,' he said to her one evening.

'When we talk, it's as if no one else is in the room,' she agreed. 'I love our calls and I love you. More than yesterday. Less than tomorrow.'

Everything was different for Serafima that term. Before she and Frank had made love, the boys in the school had been intrigued by her squareness, but now it was as if she had been sprinkled with an invisible dust of attraction. Only long afterwards did she realize it was sex.

The boys seemed to sense it, even though they themselves were not sure what it was. They caught her eyes. They watched her, and when she turned suddenly, they looked away. They invited her to join their sports societies, literature clubs, Komsomol camps. George and Minka called her 'the Mystery'; the new boy, Andrei Kurbsky, had a crush on her; and Nikolasha

Blagov was obsessively in love with her. Even Vasily Stalin sensed the difference, that she was already a woman. In class, she was Benya Golden's favourite. And then, out of the blue, Dr Rimm started to write her weird and cloddish love letters.

'It's ridiculous! I'm probably the only girl in the school who's not a virgin. But how can they tell?' she asked Frank.

'There are whistles that only dogs can hear.' He smiled at her, yet she could see the strain in his eyes. It worried him a little. 'Like an oasis in a desert: men might not be able to see the well but they can smell water.'

The truth was that she was enjoying the attention. She wondered which would be worse in the eyes of the school, the Party – the fact that she was making love almost every day (provided she could lose her mother, who always wanted to take her shopping) or that she was in love with an American arch-capitalist. Her entire being was devoted to protecting the treasure that she lived for. It was a dangerous secret, to be sure. Yet it couldn't hurt anyone, could it?

And then came the day of the Victory Parade, and Nikolasha and Rosa's deaths on the bridge. At the Golden Gates the next morning, Dashka managed to grab a moment with Satinov. Checking that no one could hear, and then speaking very fast, she said, 'Hercules, call me today at the clinic conference room.'

Losha drove him through the Kremlin gates and he climbed the steps to his office in the Yellow Palace. At ten a.m., he called her.

'I've got to let you go,' she said. 'This terrible tragedy changes everything. I have to put my children first. I can't do anything that could harm them. I have to make it up to my family.'

'Of course,' he managed to say. 'You're right. I understand.'

'You'll always be part of my life. There's only ever been you and Genrikh and there'll never be anyone else.'

His throat tightened and he could scarcely speak. I'm the Iron Commissar, he told himself, I can't be feeling like this. 'I've never loved like this before,' he said, 'and I'll love you until I die.'

'You can't keep telling me that,' she said. He could tell she was weeping. 'We've got to get over these feelings. But I'll always be here for you.'

'And me for you. Don't forget me, then?'

'How could I forget you? I hope you can forgive me.'

'I will always forgive you, Dashka,' he said. 'Always.' But as he put down the phone, he knew a punch in the stomach could not have hurt him more. When he had given his orders to his aides, he locked the doors and then he fell to his knees. 'How can I live without your love?' he heard himself saying. 'How can I go on?'

When Frank attended the Bolshoi a few days later, and Serafina was not there, he was struck with an awful fear. She had not arranged how to let him know where she was. And no one knew of him so no one could take the message.

He left her secret messages in the House of the Book and attended the Bolshoi every day, hoping he would see her in her usual seat. But no. Night after night passed, and still no Serafima.

He couldn't sleep; he couldn't eat; he imagined the most diabolic things: that she was being raped, or tortured, or that she had already been shot, or despatched to the furthest camps. But while the Satinovs and Dorovs could talk about what was happening, and share the pain with their loved ones, no one in Frank's world knew about Serafima. He hadn't talked about their relationship with the ambassador or his fellow diplomats, and he had never met her family. He fantasized about calling her parents – he had seen so many of her mother's movies – but it was too late for that now.

He would have preferred to see her running into school, safe and happy, even if it meant that she had forsaken him and he would never see her again. But she was not at the school gates on the days he'd stood outside, watching from a distance, desperate for a glimpse of a tall girl with long fair hair.

And then one night at the ballet, he glanced down at the stalls, and there she was. She was back!

Satinov held Tamriko in his arms as she told him about Mariko. 'The greatest privilege of childhood,' she said, 'is to live safely in the present. That's why I became a teacher. I wanted that for Mariko.'

Their daughter's arrest and the agonizing scenes at the Lubianka made him reel. For the first time in his life, he was spinning out of control. He had not wavered when his comrades were being arrested and shot, when his army group was surrounded, even when his eldest son was reported missing and then dead. But now he was struggling to dam up the torrents raging around him – his children in peril, his obsession for a woman who was not his wife.

His special *vertushka* telephone was ringing. He unwound Tamriko's arms and listened to Poskrebyshev's monotone summoning him to dinner at Stalin's. Always a trial, a duty, now it seemed to offer relief of a kind. At least he wouldn't wake at four and lie in sleepless torment till another bruised dawn.

* * *

At the dinner, Stalin was boasting about his exploits in Siberian exile. 'One day I skied twenty kilometres, shot four partridges, fought off a wolf – I shot it right through the head – and then managed to ski back through a blizzard to the village.'

Stalin's exile stories became taller with each telling and Satinov started to think about Dashka. Suddenly she was talking to him: 'You'll always be part of my life, angel, how could I forget you, more than yesterday, less than tomorrow.' Stalin was talking on, almost talking to him, maybe asking his views. But what did Stalin matter when Dashka was kissing him? Concentrate, he told himself, don't lose the thread . . .

Stalin's eyes flashed their yellow glint at him but still he couldn't focus. He was in the cage of a man-eating tiger yet he didn't care if he was eaten. Stalin was pointing at him now. Nineteen forty-five is your peak, he told himself. You saw the storming of the Reichstag, there are towns, streets and factories named after you – but this is nothing compared to losing *her*. For heaven's sake, keep your mind on the job. But he couldn't.

The greenish, blotchy faces of Beria, Khrushchev, Molotov, the wan, sweating Zhdanov were all looking at *him* suddenly. Stalin was waving a finger. Khrushchev, warty, snub-nosed and bald-headed, was waving his hands in the air as the noise around him became distant, and then began to fade completely.

Satinov wanted to tell Stalin that he finally understood that every movie, every popular song, was about the very same dilemma in which he found himself: love lost. He wanted to tell Stalin that now he was just an ordinary man. Nothing more. He had not lost his faith in Marxism-Leninism, but he was indulging in the crassest bourgeois sentimentalism, the very romantic philistinism that had disgusted him in the Children's Case. He remembered how he'd dismissed George, Andrei and their crush on Pushkin. When George said, 'Love is everything,' he had mocked him. Now the white dread of the very same hunger ate at him remorselessly day and night.

Suddenly Beria was elbowing him hard in the side. 'What is this? You're not listening to Josef Vissarionovich? Are you talking to yourself? Wake up, you drunken motherfucker. Comrade Stalin was asking you about Berlin.'

Stalin was looking right at him, peering into his soul. 'Perhaps Comrade Satinov is tired? Well, we all are. What is it, boy? Drink, weariness, war or love?'

The other leaders laughed. 'Drink!' cried Khrushchev.

'Or is it love?' teased Beria.

'Not our Hercules. Surely not,' said Stalin. 'He's far too uxorious! Our Choirboy! Our straight arrow.'

'Either way, you've got to drink a forfeit shot for your rudeness,' Beria said. 'There – now drink that! No heeltaps!'

Satinov drank the vodka in a single scourging gulp, and the next that Beria demanded, but if anything, it made the images of Dashka even more vividly delicious. He fought back the urge to sob uncontrollably.

'What is it, comrade?' asked Stalin, sounding cross and impatient. 'Does Comrade Satinov wish to retire and sort himself out?'

'Absolutely not,' replied Satinov firmly, remembering that in the thirties, Stalin often destroyed those leaders who were no longer competent and hard-working. (Yet even as he reviewed that terrifying prospect, some madness within him, a voice, his own but demented and scarcely recognisable, was saying: Only Dashka matters. I'd die for her.) 'In fact, Josef Vissarionovich, I would be happy to curate more ministries if you trusted me to take on more.'

'Like what, *bicho*?'

'At the front, I learned a bit about medical supplies . . .' Oh my God, he should retract this, but it was too late. 'If you wished it, I'd be happy to supervise the Ministry of Health.'

Stalin narrowed his hazel-specked eyes. His peacocks cried in the gardens outside, a haunting sound. Inside all was silent. 'Good,' he said finally. 'Why not? Health's in a mess like everything else. Sort it out.'

Afterwards, Satinov stood next to Mikoyan at the urinals downstairs. 'Careful, Hercules,' said Mikoyan, an Armenian and the most decent of the leaders. 'Are you mad? Only a suicide dozes off when Stalin's talking to him.'

Satinov hoped dinner would go on all night, and that sometime in the early hours, he would stagger out into Stalin's garden of peacocks and roses – and never wake up.

PART FOUR

Stalin's Game

The true Bolshevik shouldn't and can't have a family because he should devote himself wholly to the Party.

Josef Stalin

40

Dashka was struggling to live. It was as if the air filling her lungs were turning to glue, as if she were wading through setting concrete. With Minka and Senka gone, every moment was dominated by a crushing sadness. If she stopped for a moment, she knew she would collapse, and she wasn't sure she would ever be able to get up. Genrikh's mechanical nature and his fanatical Bolshevism were also beginning to drive her to the edge. Was his obedience to Stalin and his devotion to Chekist justice more important than her, than Senka and Minka? Yet the harsh, strong Genrikh *was* her family; her one concern was her children and they would return only if she were with him.

Now, at the Golden Gates as she walked Demian to the door of the school, she saw Hercules Satinov, magnificent in his general's summer uniform, but as drawn and weary as she. She knew she shouldn't speak to him. Yet she was terrified that he would look into her eyes as she had once looked into his, and they'd remember all that had passed between them.

The very thought of her adorable Senka missing her, crying in his bed, hating the food, literally made her sick – and that was before she even considered his fear during the interrogations; and what if he suffered an asthma attack? These horrors seemed to be swarming over her, within and without. Please God, let them be kind to him and let him come home soon!

She glanced at the parents, bodyguards and teachers surrounding her. It was a typical drop-off, but their lives were ticking over while hers was now utterly still. Nothing was the same for her; everything, even the sunlight and the summer show, was stained a funereal black.

Surely Hercules would know something about Senka? She had to quiz him. Fast. Yet she feared somebody might overhear their anguished conversation, notice the way they leaned towards each other. Any mistake now could cost Senka and Minka dear, and that would make her hate Hercules. When he looked at her, a pulse started on his cheek and she could sense a stormy interior of repressed emotion.

'Good morning. I wonder if the weather will change?' she asked him now. 'The sunshine is . . . blinding me. I don't think I can take much more.'

'Don't look at the sun,' Satinov replied, speaking slowly and carefully. 'It may be blinding you now, but it won't always be so bright.' Was he saying: Let the investigation take its course and your children will be back soon? *What* was he saying? What is this system we've created that treats children in this way? She wanted to scream at Satinov: *What do you know?* But she mustn't scream, she mustn't stare at the sun, she knew she was being tested and she must reveal nothing of her fear and anger. Dissemble, she told herself, but it was almost impossible. It hit her in her belly again and a cramp twisted her insides as if someone were turning a corkscrew in her womb. For a moment, she felt as if she might fall.

'Understood, understood,' she said. 'But will the weather change soon?'

'It is changing,' he said. What did he mean? That the investigation was coming to an end, that Senka and Minka were coming home? 'Dashka,' he said, leaning into her. 'I've heard that there is rain coming . . .'

'Rain?' she asked desperately. 'But the children won't feel the rain because they're inside?'

'Precisely,' said Satinov. 'A few drops may fall on them but *we* are the ones who will get wet.'

'We will?'

'The future of Communism,' he said carefully, 'depends solely on Soviet youth.'

Dashka blinked hard, concentrating on what this meant. Surely he was saying that they were no longer so interested in the children. Her insides relaxed and then tightened like a noose. Or did he mean they were deploying the children against *them*, their parents? Another cramp in her womb made her wince and she pressed her hands on her belly. The deep ache inside her meant she was bleeding. She was not surprised: everyone had an Achilles heel and this was where despair and panic always hit her. But she was wearing a cream-coloured suit, and she was quite unprepared for this. She was late for a meeting at the ministry and now she was bleeding. She had to rush home to change. But then something made her stop: she realized that she had not even asked about Satinov's family. How was Tamara and where was Mariko? Only Marlen was with him. 'I've got to run,' she said. 'Is Mariko here? I didn't see her.'

Satinov's expression softened for a telling instant. 'She can't come to school at the moment,' he said haltingly.

Mariko too? She was only six, four years younger than Senka! What must he and Tamara be going through?

'You too?' she whispered. Sympathy for him and, yes, Tamara welled up in her. She fought the urge to touch him.

Her affection for him rushed through her. If she lingered, it would devour her. But simultaneously disgust, regret, guilt galloped over those feelings and purged her. She shivered at what she had once done.

She suddenly understood that their children were being used against them. What if Senka said something foolish? What about Minka? Would any of them survive this?

41

'There's no need to get rough,' said Benya Golden to Colonel Likhachev. 'Just ask and I'll tell you. I've nothing to hide and you know my secrets better than I.' Benya was a connoisseur of Chekist investigations and he knew how they metamorphosed from one stage to another, just as he knew that while many leaders had the power to initiate and intensify cases, only Stalin could redirect, redesign and resculpt one.

'Let's talk about your life, Prisoner Golden.'

Benya observed his interrogator under the light of the naked bulb that swung low over the table like a censer in an Orthodox church, and noticed how the swollen red pores of his face were evenly spaced, as if by design.

'I honestly can't understand how you ever got a job at that school. In fact I can't understand how you're even amongst the living. Let's see . . .' He consulted his file. 'Born Lvov. In 1939, you were found guilty of terroristic conspiracy. Death sentence commuted to ten years, to be followed by another fifteen, to make a total of twenty-five years in the camps but in September 1941 you were allowed to join one of the shtraf battalions . . .' Likhachev looked at him searchingly with something approaching respect. 'You don't look like a tough guy.'

'I'm not,' Benya admitted.

Likhachev lit a cigarette. 'How on earth did you get to join them?'

Benya shrugged. 'I just don't know.' In the catastrophic retreats of 1941, when Hitler's panzers were racing towards Moscow and millions of soldiers were being encircled and captured, some desperado criminals in the Gulag camps were allowed, as a special favour, to join the penal battalions – the *shtraf*.

Benya Golden was a political prisoner, and 'politicals' were not allowed to join even the *shtrafniki*. But there were a few exceptions: Benya applied because he wanted to defend Russia against the Nazis and because he knew he would perish in the camps anyway. His request was permitted.

'So,' Likhachev said, 'you owe your life to a bureaucratic mistake. We'll look into that.'

The *shtrafniki* were given impossible tasks – do-or-die missions: clearing minefields, defending doomed positions. They were fed one-tenth of the usual rations of a Red Army soldier and, guarded by the secret police, could be shot without explanation or trial for the slightest infraction. If they served well, they could, in the rarest cases of heroic bravery, earn their freedom. But that was almost unheard of. The *shtrafniki* did not live that long.

'How did a puny Yid like you survive?' Likhachev asked.

To his own surprise, Benya had been a savage warrior. His officers recommended him for the Order of Glory (Third Class), but as an ex-political, he could not receive it. Wounded and discharged in 1942, he applied for a teaching job at School 801 and, surprisingly, got the position.

But whatever horrors he had been through, he knew he was still himself, or at least a damaged, cynical, heartbroken version of what he had once been. And a half-man, Benya Golden thought now, is harder to hurt than a whole one. Only his body could be destroyed. That was why he sat calmly in one of the rooms he remembered from six years earlier, and waited for the session to begin.

'From the moment you arrived at School 801, you set out to undermine Marxist-Leninist ideology,' Likhachev was saying.

'No,' Benya replied. 'I wanted to teach literature as I thought it should be taught.'

'What other way is there but the Party's way?'

'I'm not political.'

'You poisoned the minds of the children with romantic philistinism, manifested by the Fatal Romantics' Club.'

'Not at all. I love Pushkin. I had one chance to create a love of literature in young people. In the thirties, I loved a woman. Pushkin was our poet. Our poem, the poem of our true love, was "The Talisman," so when I was close to Pushkin, I was close to *her*.'

'You disgust me, Yid,' snarled Likhachev. 'You wormed your way into that school to corrupt the leaders' children and launch a conspiracy to assassinate Comrade Stalin.'

This answered one of Benya's big questions. When they started to arrest more children, he'd realized that this was no longer just about the deaths of two teenagers. Somehow this had become 'a conspiracy.'

'I was never part of any plot,' he replied, 'unless it was a conspiracy to love *Eugene Onegin*.'

'Was the conspiracy led by "NV"?'

'There was no conspiracy. As for "NV," did that stand for Blagov's name? Nikolai Vadimovich?'

'Do you take us for fools? It's not Blagov.'

'Then I don't know an NV.'

'What does NV mean in *Onegin*?'

'Ah. In *Onegin*, it would be Nina Voronskaya,' Benya said thoughtfully. 'She's the only NV in the poem. I'll recite it for you. Onegin sees Tatiana next to this lovely society hostess:

'She took a seat beside the chair
Of brilliant Nina Voronskaya,
That Cleopatra of the North.'

Benya shut his eyes, taking consolation from the lines.

'Is there a page number for this reference?' Likhachev asked.

'Page? Chapter eight, stanza sixteen, I think.'

Likhachev wrote this down in his childish handwriting. 'And this NV has to stand for a girl, right?'

Benya Golden was tempted to laugh, so simplistic was the implication of Likhachev's question. A conspiracy; an unknown person named after an *Onegin* character? Could the person they were looking for be a girl after all?

'I know my Pushkin,' he said guardedly. 'But I don't know if NV was animal, vegetable, or mineral.'

42

'Good morning, Little Professor. Rise and shine!' said the buxom prison warder whom Senka had nicknamed Blancmange. 'Have you got any new words to teach us?'

Senka noticed her new tone. He was still in the silk striped pyjamas he had been wearing when he was taken; it was past time he changed them. His mother would never let him wear the same pyjamas for so long!

'Did you sleep at all?' asked Blancmange.

'I slept better.'

'Good. You need to rest for what's ahead!'

An hour later, Blancmange brought his breakfast. She smiled at him, ruffled his hair and even presented him with an extra two pieces of Borodinsky bread and a huge triangle of goat's cheese. 'You've lost weight, young man. We need to feed you up. They'll be back in a minute to take you down for your daily chat.'

Chat? Cheese? Senka wondered what was going on. He wondered again when the guards joked as they escorted him, one even swinging his keys like a lantern. Could they have solved the murder case? If these lumpy men were really members of the famous Cheka, Knights of the Revolution, founded by the heroic Comrade Dzerzhinsky, they should have solved it by now. Senka himself could have solved it much faster. Probably there was no ten-year-old in the world who had to consider such serious matters as he did.

He was shown into a different interrogation room, where he found a new interrogator named Colonel Komarov. Where was the Lobster? Tormenting someone else or lying drunk somewhere in a fecal heap, he hoped. Even better, perhaps someone was punching *him*!

The curly-haired new man didn't look like a Chekist at all. He actually smiled at him. Senka dropped his chin and raised his brown eyes in what his mama called his matinée-idol look, but to no avail. When the interrogator lit a cigarette, Senka noticed that he was missing half a finger on his right hand.

'When can I see my mama?' he asked, encouraged by Komarov's apparent friendliness. Mama often said that she needed to cuddle him as much as possible and certainly ten times a day. Poor Mama hadn't cuddled him for weeks. 'Is my mama all right? I fear that she might be missing me. I'm missing her profoundly.'

'You'll see her soon if you're helpful to us,' Komarov replied, crossing his legs so that his boots creaked.

'I've been helpful so far, haven't I?'

'You certainly have.'

Not *too* helpful, thought Senka. Only a simpleton would be too helpful.

'So,' Komarov said, leaning forward, frowning solicitously on his low furrowed brow, pretending to be very interested in Senka, 'I went to a football match yesterday to see Spartak.'

Oh no, thought Senka, this one's going to speak to me as if I'm like all the other little boys. Big mistake, Colonel Komarov.

'I bet you like football, eh? I bet you're a real footballing man.'

'Well . . .' Senka considered whether to humour him or whether to tell him the truth about his attitude to sports. If the Lobster had asked him, he might have lied, but this one seemed kinder. 'Actually, I don't like football.'

'I thought all boys like football?'

'Not all,' replied Senka proudly.

'So I bet you like basketball then? Are you a bit of a basketball kid?'

'No,' said Senka.

'Camping?'

'Are you joking? I hate cold and discomfort.'

'So what do you like?'

'Opera. Ballet. Fiction. Poetry.'

Komarov shook his head, so Senka added, 'I'm serious. I hate all sports.'

'You're very grown up for your age,' Komarov said.

Where was this going? What were they after now? Senka thought. Play along until you find out. 'Not really, but I do prefer to wear a suit at all times.'

Komarov suddenly put out his cigarette. 'Tell me about your papa.'

Prepare all defences, Senka told himself. Man the fortifications. Load the cannons. Sharpen your cutlasses. Something's not right.

'He works very hard on the Central Committee. He doesn't laugh at my jokes like Mama does and he doesn't cuddle me. He's very strict, but Mama says that's because his job is very important.'

'Does he ever talk about politics?'

'Never.'

'What stories does he tell about work?'

'None. He says his work is secret and if I asked him about it, he might smack me. Very hard.'

'Quite right. Does he ever mention Comrade Stalin, for example?'

Senka concentrated hard in order to say the right thing. 'No, except to say, "Today we'll celebrate the Great Stalin's birthday," and, every night, before we eat at dinner, he thanks "the Great Stalin."'

'Do your parents like your apartment?'

'Yes, they love the apartment.'

'How many dachas do you have?'

'Two. Like everyone else.'

'Most people have no dacha at all,' Komarov replied. 'Is two excessive? Does your mother want more dachas?'

'No.' Where was *this* going? 'She's not interested in material things.' Which is a lie, of course, Senka told himself. Mama loves dachas and luxuries from the West.

'Your mother's very well dressed, isn't she?'

'She's the most beautiful mama in the world.' Your love for mama is your *weakness*. Think carefully!

'Does she talk about where she gets her perfumes and clothes?'

'Mama's very hard-working. She's a doctor.'

'But she likes the good things in life, doesn't she? How many fur coats does she have?' Komarov asked.

'I don't know but she looks so beautiful in them.'

'I'd like to hear more about your mother. Will you tell me?'

How strange, Senka thought, that there were no questions about them anymore, the schoolchildren.

'What do you want to know?'

'Do your parents ever talk about politics?' Komarov asked again.

Not in front of us, Senka thought. Only when they whisper in the bathroom (though I sometimes hear things I shouldn't). He was about to say this, and then thought that if they were whispering, it would be because they didn't want anyone to hear, so he decided not to.

'They talk about what's for dinner, what films to see, the weather.'

Komarov reached over and stroked Senka's cheek; then he followed the line of his jaw all the way to his chin, which he tilted up a little with the stump of his finger. Senka sat very still, and tried not to shiver.

'You must help us. If you don't, you won't see your mama. Ever again.'

'I will. I promise,' Senka whispered.

'Now,' said Komarov, straightening up and speaking normally. 'Did you hear your father boasting how his "Genius Boss" used to trust him, but that now he didn't appreciate his talents?'

Senka was instantly alert, adrenalin pumping. His father worshipped Stalin, everyone knew this – but he had once, after Stalin had sacked him early in the war, criticized his master. But how did Komarov know this? It had been in the garden at the dacha. No one had been there except his parents and him. Minka was away. But he remembered now that Demian had been present. Demian had heard it.

'These are just tiny things,' said Komarov affably. 'Nothing really. But you probably remember the occasion? Do you?'

'Criticizing the Head of the Soviet Government would be very out of character for my father,' said Senka.

'Don't fool with me, kid. Don't lie. And there's another little thing. Do you remember the time your mother said, "After all they've been through, our Jewish compatriots round here need some place of their own"? Presumably she meant a Jewish homeland? A Zion in the Soviet Union. She's Jewish, isn't she? Before she was married, wasn't she called Dashka Moiseivna Diamant?'

They had been walking along Granovsky soon after Soviet troops had liberated Babi Yar, where so many Jews had been murdered by the Nazis. Senka remembered how upset his mama had been by this. There had been no one else with them – except Demian. So now he knew that when Demian handed over the Velvet Book to the secret police, he had given them this deadly information too. Senka felt a trickle of fear run down his spine. Demian was a meanie, and Senka knew he was angry all the time because their mother loved Senka more than him. Well, Demian was an imbecile. These two stories could destroy both their parents.

'I'm trying to think,' he said softly.

'Do you know how vast the Soviet Union is? Think of all its tanks, factories, steppes, guns, its people, the Party, the armies and the power of the Organs – and then think of you, Senka Dorov, aged ten. What chance do you have? We could crush you and nothing would be left of you. All we're asking is that you recall two little comments by your parents. Not much to ask, is it?'

'I am thinking but neither sound accurate.'

'I could accept that your brother perhaps made up one of them,' Komarov said reasonably. 'But we think at least *one* of his stories must be true.'

'One of them?'

'Yes, one of them.'

One of the stories was against his father and one was against his mother. Senka knew that neither of them were 'tiny things.' The first: criticism of Stalin himself. The other: Zionist anti-Soviet nationalism. Cut through the codes and put them in Party language and both could be presented as treason. Either could lead to instant arrest and perhaps execution. Yes, Mama, Papa: the eight grams.

Senka's world started to spin. He breathed faster but couldn't get enough air into his lungs. His tummy spasmed.

'He can't have made up both, can he?' Komarov feigned a casual airiness – but then he chewed on the stump of his fourth finger, and Senka realized this tic confirmed the question's importance.

'What do you mean?' asked Senka. His asthma made his lungs feel shallow, and he began to strain for oxygen. He was nauseated; he needed sugar. He remembered the day he couldn't jump over the horse in gym, and how his faked collapse had solved that crisis. He had to do something. How quickly this session had gone from banter to the scaffold.

'Look, it's simple. I've told you two stories, one of which must be true.' Komarov reached out and traced Senka's jawline again. 'Choose one,' he whispered.

Senka felt like a deer in a trap. If he confirmed either story, the Organs would have a case against one of his parents. His papa or mama would be taken away from him and possibly liquidated. Whichever way he took, he would destroy someone he loved. The more he pulled, the tighter the steel jaws would close on his legs. He wanted to offer himself instead of his parents but this wasn't the choice he was being given, and he was feeling so sick that he was swaying in his chair. His mother or his father? Papa or Mama? And why was *he* being given this terrible choice?

'You can't turn down this small request from the Party,' Komarov was saying. 'Choose one or you'll never get out of here.'

'I feel so faint . . . I can't breathe.' And Senka slipped off his chair onto the floor as darkness closed over him.

43

Vlad Titorenko may have been nearly eighteen but he was coping with his interrogations in Lubianka much less well than Senka. Whereas previously he had worshipped his friend Nikolasha Blagov, he now found himself looking up to his interrogators, especially Colonel Likhachev, whose visage of fury and violence he saw as the face of the Soviet State. He would, he thought, do anything for some sign of approval from Likhachev. Instead he had been beaten, but every time Likhachev hit him, Vlad hated Nikolasha a little more. That weird cretin, that traitor, seemed to be mocking him from the grave with his ludicrous plans. Now he would be sent to Siberia and disowned by his parents. Undernourished, sleep-deprived, he babbled about conspiracies, his hands fidgeting, legs jiggling, and he was so jumpy that he was startled by the least sudden movement. His condition even alarmed the warders, who put him on twenty-four-hour suicide watch.

Yes, Vlad said, Nikolasha, that snake, was planning a coup and using the Fatal Romantics' Club as cover. He was an evil counter-revolutionary, a pervert who was in love with Serafima, and yes, sir, all his hyena-friends were in on the conspiracy. Who was the mysterious New Leader? Well, he wasn't sure. The Chekists suggested names and he agreed. Director Medvedeva possibly, maybe Teacher Golden – or how about

Marshal Shako? One time he had seen the Marshal pat Serafima on her behind at the Golden Gates. Yes, *he* could be the one. Or was it Dr Rimm? And so Vlad jabbered on, frantic to please the Organs. Yet nothing seemed to do so.

Until today, when he found the other interrogator, Colonel Komarov, reading the sports pages of the newspaper with his boots on the desk and a cigarette in his mouth. Vlad waited silently, standing at attention. Komarov looked up, waved him into the chair and without a word offered him a cigarette. When Komarov tried to light it for him, Vlad jumped back from his chair, expecting a punch. When he was coaxed back into his seat, his hands were shaking so much that Komarov had to light it for him and then hand it back across the table – as if he were an adult, even a friend.

'You've been very honest with us, Vlad. You'll be going home soon. To see your parents.'

'Oh, thank you, Colonel.' Vlad's eyes filled with tears.

'We don't have to talk about this bullshit anymore. We can talk about anything. Sport. Or home. I'm bored of talking about school pranks.' He paused. 'Where will your parents be at the moment?'

'I don't know . . . They go to the dacha at weekends.'

'Your father is a very capable man, isn't he?'

'Yes.'

'What does he want you to do?'

'He wants me to be an engineer like him. But I'm not doing very well at school. He's disappointed in me.'

'How can that be? I was just saying to Colonel Likhachev that you'll make a perfect Soviet man. You can do anything you want, you're a patriot.'

'Me? Oh, thank you, Colonel.'

'So your father should appreciate you a little more. But perhaps he's too busy with his top job.'

'Yes, and my mother thinks he'll soon be promoted.'

'Really? And why hasn't he been?'

'Well, they think he should be. They think he's been overlooked because everyone's so busy.'

'Who's everyone?'

'Well, the authorities.'

'The Central Committee?'

'Yes, Papa thinks they haven't noticed him, or he'd have a bigger job by now. My father's very clever and hard-working, you know, a good Communist.'

'But he says the Central Committee is to blame? You've heard him say that?'

'Yes, but only to my mother in their room when they're talking at night.'

'She's proud of him?'

'Of course. She says without his planes, we couldn't have won the war.'

'And what did *he* say?'

'He agreed.'

'Have you ever seen the factory at Satinovgrad?'

'Yes, Papa once took us just before the war.'

'Did you hear there were many planes that crashed?'

'Yes, but those weren't the fault of my father.'

'How do you know?'

'He was worried about them but he said the problem was that the designs couldn't be changed.'

'Why not?'

'That wasn't his job.'

'He talked about it with you?'

'Well, yes . . .'

Komarov leaned forward, biting his shortened finger. 'Whose job was it?'

'Papa said it was Marshal Shako's and he spoke to Shako about it, but they agreed they couldn't change the designs.'

'Did Papa say why?'

'No. Just that the designs were approved at the top.'

'The top of what?'

'I'm not sure.'

'You know Comrade Satinov, of course?'

'Yes, he supervises my father's ministry.'

'Perhaps he blamed Comrade Satinov as the "top." He's in the Politburo and the State Defence Council.'

'I think . . .'

'Go on.'

'I think Papa meant above Satinov.'

'Who's above Satinov?'

'Well . . . Comrade Stalin.'

'So your papa says it is the Head of the Soviet Government who approves planes that crash?'

'Yes – well, no . . . yes . . . I'm not sure.' Komarov raised his eyebrows but said nothing and sure enough Vlad filled the vacuum: 'I think he meant that the top people don't understand planes so they sign off designs that make planes crash.'

'Who're they? You mean the Head of the Soviet Government signs the plans?'

'I think he signs everything.'

Vlad noticed that Komarov was writing fast. For a long time, he said nothing, just listened to the nib scratching paper.

'You must sign this statement right now,' Komarov said, pushing the paper over to him.

'Will my parents come to collect me then?' Vlad's stomach clenched and cramped; he felt a burning hole in his chest and a rising fear in his gullet.

'I'm not sure,' said Komarov, sitting back in his chair and crossing his arms. 'After everything you've shared with me, I'm just not sure.'

44

Hercules Satinov had arrived in Germany. The ZiS limousine that collected him from Tempelhof Airport raced and swerved through Berlin's apocalyptic landscape. Lights flickered, illuminating momentary glimpses of figures eking out an existence: a woman carrying a jerrycan of water, packs of dogs, gangs of urchins running, running, a madman dancing around a fire.

Satinov peered out at the red and desperate eyes of humans and animals catching the lights of the convoy as they scurried amongst the burnt-out tank hulks, the mountains of rubble, the shattered shells of buildings. But each shadow, every ruin, reminded him of Dashka, for here he'd held her, there they kissed.

Stalin, who had been at meetings with the American President and British Prime Minister all day, wore the new fawn uniform of a generalissimo with gold shoulderboards and just one medal. Satinov could tell the meetings of the Potsdam Conference had gone well. There was a breezy swagger about him and he had recovered some of his energy.

'*Gamajoba bicho*, happy you could join us,' said Stalin, speaking Georgian. 'We've got the cook from Aragvi with us and I thought you'd enjoy a Georgian *supra*!'

'Thank you, Josef Vissarionovich,' replied Satinov, thinking that Berlin was a long way to fly for some *lobio* beans. He looked around him. Beria, Mikoyan and Genrikh Dorov were there too.

A new line-up, he thought, his experienced mind analysing what it conveyed. Genrikh Dorov was not a good sign: he never came to Stalin's dinners, being more of a retainer than a leader. Stalin deployed him as an attack dog, his presence denoting a witchhunt or an investigation that would have tragic consequences. He thought of Dashka instantly – what must it be like being married to the Uncooked Chicken? He nodded at him in greeting, and Genrikh grinned back at him with menacing geniality. The Dorov children had been arrested too, Satinov thought, but that wasn't why Genrikh was there. He was already slavishly devoted to Stalin, whether his children were in jail or not. No, he was there as a scarecrow. To frighten someone. To frighten me.

'I hope the flight was easy. I hate flying myself. I prefer the train,' said Stalin. 'But I wanted to look at you in the eyes.'

Satinov's six-year-old daughter, Mariko, was in prison with his eighteen-year-old son, George, and Stalin wished to look him in the eyes to check that he was still loyal. It was a rite of passage, and he, Satinov, was not alone. President Kalinin's wife was in prison; Poskrebyshev's pretty young wife, Bronka, had vanished altogether, probably dead. Stalin was telling him that family was a privilege just as living was a privilege, and that both were at the mercy of the Party. And the Party was Stalin. It was an odd system but it was the Bolshevik way, and Satinov was accustomed to it.

They sat down to table, with Satinov on Stalin's right and Beria on his left.

'Have you seen the palace where we're holding the conference?' asked Stalin.

'I have,' replied Satinov, picturing Mariko, screaming, being prised off her mother by brutal warders.

'It's meagre compared with our palaces,' mused Stalin. 'The tsars really knew how to build.'

'They did,' agreed Satinov, hearing Tamriko screaming at him, 'They've taken Mariko! She's six, Hercules. Get her released!' Satinov composed himself, knowing his face must reveal nothing but reverence and fondness for Stalin.

Yet the night seemed endless. He knew, at some point, there would be a clue for him about Mariko and George, providing Stalin was satisfied that he had learned his lesson and harboured no resentment. Soon enough too, he would find out why Genrikh Dorov was here. Such games had perhaps been necessary before the war, but, he wondered, were they necessary now?

'So is everything well in Moscow?' asked Stalin.

'Nothing can be decided without you, but Comrade Molotov and the rest of us are doing our best.'

'You've got to decide things without me,' said Stalin. 'I'm tired.'

'But we need you, Comrade Stalin!' cried Beria.

'The Soviet Union needs your genius, Comrade Generalissimo,' added Dorov.

Stalin waved this away, and his yellow eyes returned to Satinov. 'So Tamriko is well?'

'Very well,' answered Satinov. My wife is distraught, he thought. Our little Mariko is in prison, on your orders, and you look at me knowing this. 'Everyone at home is so proud to see you here at Potsdam, the man who won the war, who led us to Berlin.'

'Yet Tsar Alexander made it all the way to Paris in 1814,' said Stalin. 'Comrade Dorov and I have been discussing you.'

'Me?' Satinov swallowed. This was the warning.

Stalin let the silence draw out. Satinov thought of Tamriko and his children, he thought of Dashka, and he thought: Shoot me, but free my children. Leave Tamara alone.

At last Stalin gave him his satyr's grin. 'Don't worry, Hercules! The Central Committee thinks you and Beria should be promoted to marshal.'

Satinov's first and absurd concern was whether his new rank would impress Dashka. It shouldn't impress her – but he knew it would. He flicked a glance at her husband, who looked away.

'It's an honour and of course I always obey the Party. But I'm not a soldier.'

'Nor is Beria. Far from it!' A disdainful look at Beria. 'But, Hercules, you're a colonel general already,' replied Stalin.

'But I don't have anything like your military knowledge—'

'Or your strategic genius!' interjected Beria.

'I've never commanded so much as a platoon,' insisted Satinov. 'The generals will resent it.'

'That's just the point,' answered Stalin. 'We've voted on it and it's decided.'

'I'm honoured by the Party's trust in me,' said Satinov. The promotion was not reassuring. Stalin often promoted people only to arrest them the next week; Satinov remembered how Kulik had been promoted to marshal two days after his pretty young wife had vanished, never to return. The promotion was to put the generals in their place – like the recent arrest of Marshal Shako. Yet accepting it also meant that he was accepting Mariko's arrest, and conversely, by the rules of their topsy-turvy customs, this would accelerate her release.

But as he said his goodbyes at the end of the evening, Genrikh Dorov offered his moist, limp hand. 'Congratulations, Comrade

Marshal.' But his eyes said: Comrade Stalin once sacked me but now he needs me again. Comrade Stalin wants me to look into *you*.

Satinov pushed by Dorov but when he was in his car, Beria leaned right in through the window.

'I've heard Mariko is fine,' he whispered. 'Silk gloves. Don't worry.'

45

'No, my father would never ever discuss planes with us,' George Satinov insisted.

It was long after midnight in the Lubianka yet the lights burned as always.

'What about your mother?' asked Likhachev.

'I don't know what they discussed.'

'You never overheard?'

'Never. They wouldn't talk about politics or planes. She's not interested in military matters – she says Papa can talk about that with the generals.'

'Which generals?'

'I don't know.'

'Did Shako ever come to the house?'

George noticed with alarm that Likhachev did not describe Shako as 'comrade.' 'I don't think so.'

'Come on, George. The Shakos lived in your building. They never came to the house?'

'Not that I remember.'

'Do your parents ever argue?'

'Everyone argues.'

'About politics?'

'They don't discuss politics.'

'Is your mother a Communist?'

'Yes, very much so.'

'Did you know her father was a bourgeois who travelled frequently to Germany between 1918 and 1921?'

'She never mentioned it.'

'Is she happy with your apartment and the dacha?'

'She never complains.'

'What about your father?'

'My father never complains about anything. He never says anything much at all.'

'Andrei Kurbsky, when you were at the Satinovs' apartment, which rooms did you see?'

'What do you mean?'

'Did you enter the hall, for example?'

'Yes.'

'Describe it.'

'Very grand. Parquet floor. I've never seen such a palace.'

'Then?'

'We went into the kitchen.'

'Who was there?'

'The whole family and the maid.'

'Tell me about Comrade Satinov and his wife.'

'There's nothing to tell. They seemed close.'

'The sons?'

'They're very respectful of him. Afraid of him.'

'What did they talk about?'

'I can't remember.'

'Your mother's at home, but we can always arrest her, you know. Surely you remember something?'

'I think the pilot brother was telling stories about dogfights and aeroplanes.'

'To Comrade Satinov?'

'No, to his mother and Mariko and George and me.'

'Did he mention that the planes were crashing?'

'No.'

'After tea, where did you sit?'

'Me and George went into his father's study. We sat there for a bit, joking around.'

'Were there papers on the desk?'

'Yes, I think so.'

'You didn't look at them?'

'No.'

'But did you notice what they were?'

'No.'

'But they could have been Politburo protocols or aircraft designs?'

'I don't know.'

'Come on, Andrei, concentrate: didn't you see "Top Secret" written on them?'

Andrei shivered. He was cold and tired. He thought about his mother, sitting alone in that paltry room, waiting for him to come home.

'Maybe.'

'Mariko Satinova, how old are you?' asked Colonel Komarov.

'I'm six.'

'Did you see your mama this morning?'

'Yes.'

'You're soon going home but since you're here, I thought we could have a little chat.'

'OK,' said Mariko uncertainly. Komarov could see she was struggling to be brave.

'Is that a little dog?'

'Yes. I have twenty-five little dogs and they go to my school because they're all girl dogs and they do lessons, study things like maths and Marxism, just like everyone does at school.'

'What a fun game, Mariko. Do your mama and papa play?'

'Not Papa. Papa's very busy, but Mama plays.'

'And your brothers?'

'Yes. A bit but George is always out, Marlen is very serious about the Komsomol, and David is always flying planes.'

'Does he tell you about the planes?'

'Yes. They're dangerous.'

'Really? Dangerous because the Germans could shoot them down?'

'Yes, and sometimes they crash.'

'He told this to your papa?'

'I can't quite remember.'

'What did your papa say about that?'

'Say hello to the dog!'

'Hello, dog. What did your papa say about that? Did he blame anyone?'

'I don't know.'

'Did your mother and father talk about it?'

'Is Mama coming soon?'

'You must have heard your mama talking with Papa? About planes? Crashes?'

'I don't know. They whisper sometimes.'

'About what?'

'Important things not for children.'

'Do your dogs ever hear anything?'

Mariko hugged her dog Crumpet, and buried her face in its

fur. 'No, they're far too busy studying Marxism in the Moscow School for Bitches.'

Senka Dorov had spent a few hours recovering from his panic attack in the warm comfort of the sanatorium.

'Is it serious? Is he faking?' Komarov had asked the doctors. 'If he dies here, you'll all pay for it! We need him fit and back here as soon as possible.'

The doctors had taken him to the sanatorium on a stretcher wearing an oxygen mask, and brought him lemonade, bread and jam, tea and sugar. The food had given his mind the fuel it needed, but the steel jaws of this vile trap were sinking deeper into his leg with every moment.

Mama or Papa? How could he destroy either? How had it come to this? It was all thanks to that moron Demian, that weasel!

He considered the choice. Papa was so stern, so humourless. This was Bolshevik justice. Wouldn't Papa understand and say 'The Party is always right,' and 'Better shoot a hundred innocents to catch one enemy'? Papa would say, 'You did the right thing, Senka. If the Party decides I'm guilty, then I am guilty – and I did say that!'

Did Papa even love him? He had never shown it. His mama, on the other hand, did so every day. Yet surely her Jewish comments were less serious, so if he chose her, she wouldn't be arrested? His father's comments criticized Stalin himself, and Papa could lose his head for that.

Choose Mama and both parents would be fine. That must be the right decision. But what if this were a mine in the hidden minefield? What if it were more serious than he realized? Then he would have destroyed his own mother, the person he adored more than anything in the whole wide world and in all human history!

Senka's calculations became colder and sharper. A false choice had been placed before him. He knew whichever parent he chose, the Organs would destroy them both, and the family with them. There must be a way out of the labyrinth.

Now he was sitting in the interrogation room and the courtesies, such as they were, were over.

'Senka, give your testimony,' said Colonel Komarov.

'My brother Demian is more wrong than right,' said Senka. 'The words are right, but he's muddled up the speaker.'

'Just testify, boy, and stop trying to be clever. You may be only ten but on your twelfth birthday you can face the eight grams, the *Vishka*. Don't even think of lying or there'll be nothing left of you for your mother to collect. Did you fake that illness?'

'I would never do that.'

'I hope not. Speak now, boy.'

Senka straightened his back. He had made his choice. Now he had to make sure he got it right.

'It's simple, Colonel,' he said, speaking confidently and lucidly. 'You have the quotations completely the wrong way round. It was my mother who was talking about the "Genius Boss," not my father. My father has never ever spoken of the Head of the Soviet Government. Discretion is a religion with him. Everything that the Great Stalin does is correct. Papa regards himself as no more than a servant of the Party, the Great Stalin, the working class. He never uses the word Boss – *Khozian* – to describe the Head of the Soviet Government.'

'So who complained about the Genius Boss? Who *is* the Genius Boss?'

'My mother complained, and the Genius Boss in our family

is . . . *me*. She was moaning about how spoilt I am. She was being sarcastic.'

Komarov stopped writing and looked up. 'But your mother was promoting Jewish-Zionist nationalism. She's Jewish, isn't she?'

'Demian's confused about that too. I remember it exactly. We were in the dacha and my father – not my mother – my father was complaining about "the Jewish compatriots round here" who need to find a place of their own. But he was talking about our neighbours.'

'What neighbours?'

'The Rozenblats, who are always asking to use our tennis court. In the end my father said, no, that was enough; from now on, the Rozenblats, "our Jewish compatriots round here," needed to get their own place for next year. Papa was tired of sharing with them.'

Komarov ran his truncated fourth finger along his lips. 'But your father's not Jewish?'

'No, my father was raised Russian Orthodox, so *he* couldn't be guilty of Zionist nationalism, could he? Actually, he was if anything being a little anti-Jewish. So I hope, Colonel Komarov, I've answered all your questions. If you want the truth, this is the truth and I swear it before the Party itself. My silly brother told you the right stories but he got them the wrong way round.'

Komarov looked at Senka for a long time. Senka waited, his head throbbing. Would he be hit? Would he ever see his mother again? Then Komarov threw his head back and laughed.

'You're cleverer than I thought. And as it happens I have something for you. It's from your mother.'

'What is it?'

'It's a surprise. A nice one.' He snapped his fingers. 'Go now.'

46

Four a.m. The phone rings in the Satinov apartment. Tamara is not really asleep, and wakes to find she is already standing up, phone to her ear. She has not slept since they took Mariko, and not properly since George's arrest. Every night she skims the surface of sleep, and every morning she feels wretchedly raw. She is not alone: all the parents of the children in the Children's Case are the same. She sees them at the Golden Gates, trying to smile, but bleeding inside, trying to get through the day with this terrible blade swinging over their heads. Who could have created such a diabolic situation, she wonders, in which they are not allowed even to discuss their anxiety, except at night in whispers, and in dreams they try not to remember?

'Is Comrade Satinov there?' The voice on the phone is expressionless.

'I'm not sure. I can go and see,' Tamara says.

'Is that Comrade Satinov's wife?'

'Yes?'

'Be at Lubianka at seven a.m.'

'Oh my God. What are you telling me?'

'You may collect your children.'

Tamara bursts into tears and cries out so wildly that Satinov runs into the room, afraid of an even greater catastrophe. But it's not. It's good news, he assures her, hugging her. They can't go back to sleep now. They must be ready to leave for Lubianka.

It was early morning, and Senka had scarcely slept. He was sure something good was about to happen. What was the surprise Komarov had promised him? Was it his mama? Was she coming to take him home? Had he saved her?

All night his ears had whooshed with the roar of his heartbeat pumping the blood around his body with excitement and longing.

'Wake up, boy!' Blancmange, the warder, called. 'Get dressed!'

'Is there news? Am I going home?' Senka asked.

Blancmange held up her trowel-like hands — it was forbidden to inform prisoners of their fates. 'Put on your best, Little Professor! We've got a surprise for you. Now close your eyes! Ta-da!' And there it was, hanging on a coathanger behind her. Senka's suit, shirt and tie. And his best shoes.

'My suit! I'll be so happy to get out of these pyjamas.'

'Be grateful,' said Blancmange. 'Not all our "guests" are that lucky, I can tell you.'

When he was dressed in his beloved suit and a grown-up shirt and tie, Senka ate his breakfast, noting the addition of an extra sugar lump and slice of black bread. Then two guards escorted him towards the interrogation rooms: Is this the way out? he wondered. Is this the way to Mama?

He imagined Dashka's smile, her opening her arms, her sweet scent.

But the warders opened a door into another interrogation room, where Colonel Likhachev, the Lobster, awaited him.

'But I thought . . .' Senka felt as though he was about to cry.

'I know what you thought,' said the Lobster, sucking on his cigarette. 'But if you want to go home, you have to sign this.'

He pushed a small bundle of papers, held together with a paper-clip, across the desk.

'What is it?' asked Senka.

'It's your confession.'

'My confession? But I already confessed about the notebook.'

'We need another confession.'

Senka forced the rising spasm of weeping back down his throat as he wearily tried to calculate what he should do. He had heard his father tell his mother once, 'There's only one rule: never confess anything.' Now he was faced with this. Dimly, he saw his mother disappear into the distance again.

'It is a record of everything you've told us and all you have to do is sign it,' the Lobster said.

Senka sat down on the hard chair and looked at the papers, suddenly doubting that his mama was there at all. They were tricking him and, for a moment, he let the despair flood through him. Then, gathering his strength once again, he started to read, beginning at the heading 'Protocol of Interrogation of Semyon Genrikhovich Dorov.' Ahead of him lay page after page of dialogue like a stage play with his part marked 'Dorov, SG' on every line. He couldn't remember it all but it sounded right so he returned to the first page, which was in larger type:

> I, Semyon Genrikhovich 'Senka' Dorov (born 1935), confess that I was a member of an anti-Soviet conspiracy. With a faction of other children at School 801 in an anti-Soviet youth organization named the Fatal Romantics' Club, I conspired to overthrow the Soviet State and plot acts of terrorism against members of the Politburo.
>
> Signed: ....

Dated: ....
....

'You want to see your mama?'

'Yes.'

'Then sign it and be done with it.'

'But I was never a member of the club. I was too young. I know I mustn't sign it.'

'You've already signed one confession.'

'I *did* take the notebook. But I *never* plotted against the government. I'm only ten.'

'At twelve you'll be old enough to face the Highest Measure of Punishment.'

Senka flinched.

'Yes, we're talking about death. We could just keep you here for a few more months and then: bang. So sign it!'

'I never plotted and I mustn't sign. I didn't do anything!' Senka could not hold back the tears anymore and started to sob.

Likhachev quivered, infuriated by this howling. It was, he decided, very frustrating working with children. 'Pull yourself together, prisoner,' he shouted. 'Sign it!'

'I won't, I won't! Whatever you do to me, I won't! I know I mustn't!' After all he'd been through, he feared the confession could be used against his father and mother.

'God's breath. Everyone must sign it.'

'Everyone?' Senka looked up at Likhachev. Who else was here? Was Minka nearby? 'Is my sister signing it?'

Likhachev twitched again, stretched in his chair and then bent his own fingers back so they clicked. 'All right, come with me.' He shoved Senka out of the room, down the corridor, opened another door and pushed him inside a room with a glass wall covered by a blind.

'Senka!' It was Minka, still in her smart red dress, looking thinner but very much herself.

'Minka!' They ran towards each other, hugged and kissed through their tears.

'What a sweet pair,' said Likhachev to Colonel Komarov, who was in the room with Minka.

Minka kept her arm around Senka's narrow shoulders. 'Have you signed anything?'she asked him.

'No,' he said, wiping his eyes with his suit's sleeves. 'I didn't think I should.'

'I haven't either,' said Minka.

'But, Minka, you *were* a member of the Fatal Romantics,' whispered Senka.

'Think about Mama and Papa!' she whispered back.

'No whispering!' snarled Likachev. 'Just sign. Both of you.'

'We won't sign,' said Minka.

Komarov chewed on the stump of his finger and then said to his comrade Likhachev, 'Shall we make this easier?'

Likhachev nodded and Komarov walked over to the blind and flicked a switch. 'Who's this, eh?'

Over the tinny speakers, they heard a woman's voice with a distinctively light Galician accent, saying, 'Will they be long, Genrikh? Where are they?' It was their mother.

'Stop, Dashka,' replied their father's voice. 'It's out of our hands. The officials of the Organs are dealing with it according to the rules of Soviet justice. So we wait.'

Komarov flicked the switch again. 'They're next door. Do you want to see them or not?'

'Sign or stay in prison!' added Likhachev.

Minka and Senka held hands.

'We won't sign, will we, Minka?' said Senka, regaining a little professorial authority.

'I'm sorry, Comrade Colonels,' she said. 'We're sure we mustn't sign.'

'We're feeling very brave,' added Senka stoutly. 'We won't do it.'

Komarov glanced at Likhachev, who left the room. Then he unclicked the blind, which flicked up on its roller to reveal a waiting room. Senka and Minka saw their parents sitting awkwardly alongside Irina Titorenka and the Satinovs. No one was saying much.

'Have the others signed?' asked Minka. 'George and Vlad?'

'Of course. Everyone must confess,' said Komarov.

'Then why aren't they out there?'

'Everyone must sign. It's orders from the top!'

'Look!' said Senka, shrill and frightened. 'He's talking to Mama! He's telling them we're never coming out! Should we sign?'

Colonel Likhachev was talking to their parents and their father was rising, looking at the two-way mirror and approaching it. He pointed at them and Komarov clicked the switch on the loudspeaker.

'Children,' said Genrikh Dorov. 'Are you there, Minka? Senka? I can't see you but the colonel says you can hear me. Sign now, and you come home!'

Likhachev re-entered the room, swaggering a little. 'There, you heard it!' he said.

Minka and Senka looked at each other.

'I saw Mama,' Senka said. 'She's in the next room . . .'

Minka put her arms around him and she too was crying.

47

The Satinovs had arrived first, at six a.m. When Tamara saw the room, she staggered and he caught her arm. 'Oh, Hercules, this is the room where I've been meeting Mariko.'

'Patience,' he said, steadying her. This grim grey room, smelling of stale tobacco and sweat, contained four rows of wooden chairs, their seats smoothed by years of nervous waiting families. It was empty but for them. Satinov reflected on his dinner with Stalin: he had been right. Stalin had wanted to look at him before releasing Mariko. But the children were still not home. Was Mariko already looking at them from behind that big mirror on the wall in front of them? How many hundreds of thousands of people had never got this call and had never seen their children, wives, brothers again?

'Are they ever coming?' burst out Tamara. 'Hercules, they're never coming!'

'Hush,' said Satinov. 'We must wait. There is nothing further we can do.'

An hour later, Vlad's mother, Irina Titorenka, arrived, then Andrei's mother, Inessa Kurbskaya – and then the Dorovs. When Satinov saw Dashka, his heart lurched painfully, and he looked away.

Genrikh wore a dark suit and twirled his black fedora round

a finger, a sign of his confidence, which declared: The Great Stalin needs me again! Satinov nodded at him. Then Tamriko rose and greeted Dashka, whose long heavy hair was pulled back in a bun. What tangled lives we lead, he thought as he watched the two women he most loved in the world hugging in Lubianka Prison while they waited for the children they so adored.

A lull; an hour passed; terrible thoughts: What if Mariko got out but Senka didn't, or Vlad did and Andrei didn't?

Tamriko was beside him, her face so loving, so honest. He sighed and took her delicate hand and squeezed it.

Suddenly the door opened. Every parent started – and Vlad Titorenko came in. Crop-haired, bedraggled school uniform, glazed eyes like a zombie. His mother, a jowly, over-rouged woman in a mauve hat like an upside-down chamberpot and a matching coat, exclaimed: 'Vlad!' and dabbed at her tears with a dirty yellow handkerchief.

Vlad cringed and looked around the room, clearly afraid of something. 'Is Papa here?' he asked.

But Mrs Titorenka seemed even more flustered by this question. 'No, no . . . well . . . he's not here. He's gone away.'

That was how Satinov knew that they had arrested his subordinate, Titorenko. For twenty-five years now he, the Iron Commissar, had thrived in this precarious, clandestine world. His children may be coming home, he thought, but his subordinates were being arrested. Not good for him, but not terminal either.

A Chekist came in and talked to Genrikh, who spoke to the mirror, advising Minka and Senka to sign their papers. A few minutes passed. Even Satinov, who had helped storm the Winter Palace in 1917, who had waited in a hushed bunker for the launch of the Stalingrad offensive, was nervous by now, his heart drumming.

Dashka and Genrikh got to their feet. The doors opened and Senka's sweet, high-pitched voice could be heard, talking about seeing his mother again.

'She's a doctor, I hear,' said the Chekist as he held open the door.

'Oh yes, she's the best doctor in the world,' cried Senka. 'She sees all the top people.'

And then there he was. Dashka flew towards her boy and Minka; Genrikh put on his fedora and lingered behind her, his expression seeming to suggest that it was perfectly routine for his children to be arrested and then released.

'Darling Senka!' cried Dashka, opening her arms and bending over to greet him.

Senka threw himself into her embrace and kissed her face. For a moment, Satinov could see only the top of Senka's tousled head as he was enveloped in Dashka's arms. Then she hugged Minka too, and Genrikh touched Dashka's arm: 'Not here. Let's not forget we're Bolsheviks,' he said gruffly.

'Of course,' said Dashka. They headed for the door, and then Dashka looked back and nodded at Tamriko. 'Good luck!' she mouthed. She glanced at him, and then they were gone.

'Oh God, where's Mariko? Where are they?' Tamara started to panic again.

The door opened. They rose to their feet. But no, it was Andrei, pale but otherwise unharmed. He and his mother left.

Satinov and Tamriko were alone again. They held hands, so tense they couldn't speak. A moment later, the door opened again.

'Mamochka!' called a shrill voice. Mariko, followed by George, ran into the room at high speed, holding one of her toy dogs. She ran round the room so fast that Tamriko and Satinov barely had time to get up before she threw herself into Tamriko's arms. Tamriko whirled her round and round.

'Look what I've got for you! Look who's come to meet you!' Tamriko reached into her bag and pulled out a handful of Mariko's toy dogs. 'Old friends and a new one too!'

Mariko squeaked with joy, grabbing the toy dogs, and threw her arms around her mother again.

'Hello, Papa,' said George sheepishly. He was still in his football kit.

'You look OK, George,' said Satinov briskly, 'thinner perhaps. Good to see you!' and he put his hand on the boy's shoulder, an unprecedented act of informality. George looked grateful and Satinov realized his son was scared of his anger.

'Come on,' said Satinov, kissing Mariko on the top of her head. 'It's time to go home.'

They drove back to Granovsky in silence.

'Papa, I'm so sorry. I had to sign,' said George as soon as they were back in their apartment. Father and son both knew that the children's confession could be used against the parents.

Satinov looked at George for a long moment, wishing he could reach across the dark valley of his own reticence. He wanted to tell him how much he loved him, and that he didn't blame him for anything. But he didn't know how to begin.

'I know,' he said briskly. 'You've learned your lesson. The law will take its course. In the meantime you are to finish the term at school. Let's not mention it again.'

'Thank you, Papa,' said George formally.

'Look, Papa, look!' Mariko ran into the room holding a bundle of her dogs. 'My bitches have been in the kennel for being naughty but now they're back at school. I'm so happy.'

* * *

'Prisoner Golden, we know you fornicated with many women and corrupted their Soviet morality.'

'I told you I did not.'

'You seduced your pupils.'

'Never.' Benya looked back at the happiness of his Second Coming, his return from the dead.

'We know from our informer that you met the schoolgirl Serafima Romashkina at the café next to the House of the Book. Did you have intercourse with the schoolgirl Serafima Romashkina?'

'No.' Now Benya was startled that, out of all the children, the case had focused on Serafima. He sensed that she was in grave danger.

'What did you discuss with her?'

'Pushkin. Poetry.'

'Poetry? You suborned her to deviate from Marxism-Leninism with philistine-bourgeois individualism?'

Benya took a quick breath. The interrogator had stumbled on something – but he had not yet made the connections. In the 1930s, Benya had loved a woman who had vanished into the meatgrinder and the Gulags. Now, by pure chance, he had found himself teaching her cousin about literature and love. He and Serafima had met for coffee.

'Do you know my favourite Pushkin poem?' Benya had asked her. 'It's his most romantic poem, and it's special to me. "The Talisman."'

'What a piece of luck,' sighed Serafima, putting her hands together, her eyes shining. She had never looked more beautiful, he thought. 'It's my favourite too. It's our – I mean it's my poem. It's special to me as well.' And Benya had known immediately that she was in love too. For a moment, he turned away from her so she couldn't see his eyes, but she was so happy that she never noticed, and he found himself blessing her in Pushkin's verses to a young girl named Adele, the beloved child of a friend:

> *'Play on, Adele, and know no sadness,*
> *Your springtime youth is calm, clear, smooth.*
> *Surrender to love . . .'*

And she listened with her head on one side . . .

'Prisoner Golden!' The Chekist brought him back to the grim here and now. 'What did you discuss with her? Were you involved with Serafima and her special friend in their anti-Soviet conspiracy?'

'What do you mean?'

'We've worked it all out, Golden, and we know that the Children's Case was a conspiracy inspired from abroad through Serafima, by her secret American lover – a foreign capitalist spy.'

Benya bit his lip. He had been very slow to work this out but now he understood everything: NV, the gorgeous princess, was Nikolasha's code for Serafima. NV and Serafima were interchangeable. Serafima was an inch away from destruction. He realized what he must do. 'You've got that quite wrong,' he said.

Colonel Likhachev scowled. 'Give me your testimony or I'll beat you to a pulp.'

Benya closed his eyes, remembering the elegiac days of that 1930s winter when he was in love. 'I confess that I invented the Fatal Romantics' Club with its bourgeois anti-Leninist philistinism,' he said slowly. 'I dictated the idea of the anti-Soviet conspiracy to Nikolasha Blagov. You asked me earlier who NV was? I am NV. Most Muscovites met some foreigners in wartime and no doubt Serafima Romashkina did too. But let me testify before the Party, before the Great Stalin himself, that Serafima is involved in no foreign conspiracy. I'm the conspirator.'

'You will confess to all this, Prisoner Golden?'

'Yes. Just give me the papers.'

'You understand that this is a terroristic crime according to Article 158, punishable with the Highest Measure of Punishment?'

Benya nodded. Then, as Colonel Likhachev drew up the confession, he just sat back. Graceful images floated into his consciousness. Kissing the woman he'd loved, long ago, outside the Metropole Hotel in a snowstorm. Catching Agrippina's eye as she made tea in the common room. Finding a rare volume in the flea market. And this, his last decent act, protecting a girl who had so much to live for. He imagined he heard the clatter and murmur of the children settling down in the classroom before his Pushkin lessons. There was George. And Andrei. Minka. And at the back, staring out of the window at the cherry trees, no doubt dreaming of her secret love, Serafima.

He clapped his hands and heard his own voice, as if echoing very far away, long ago and in a vanished world: 'Dear friends, beloved romantics, wistful dreamers! Open your books. I hope you'll always remember what we're going to read today. We are about to go on a wonderful journey of discovery.'

48

Early afternoon. The rays of the sun pour through the whirling motes of dust in Frank's apartment to create a golden kaleidoscope on the far wall. Although Serafima doesn't yet know that her friends are about to be released, she senses they will soon be home and all seems right with her world. Frank is there already and there is no need to say anything for a while. He gives her the jaunty two-finger salute that he always gives her, and she can see that he's in high spirits.

She savours the lemony scent of his cologne, the softness of his skin, the texture of his hair (soft as a girl's), his eyes. She kisses his cheek, and then he takes her chin in his hand and starts to kiss her. Her eyes shut and she sighs in the back of her throat.

He starts to undress her and this time she unfastens his shirt herself, her fingers suddenly so agile that they can unbutton at record speed. When he helps her pull her dress over her head, she does not fear the revelation of her snakeskin. On the contrary, she cannot wait to show him that she is still his, all of her, the delicate and the rough. When they are naked, she feels her snakeskin anticipating his touch. The craving is answered as his fingers lightly trace the burnt, parchmenty skin. 'This means you're mine and you'll be mine forever,' he whispers.

'A loving enchantress
Gave me her talisman.'

After they have made love, he holds her in his arms. 'Serafima Constantinovna . . .'

'You're using my patronymic? Why?'

'I have something to ask you.' Serafima feels his body tense next to hers as he gathers himself. 'Will you marry me?'

'Are you joking?'

'No. I'm not much of a jester, am I?'

'I suppose not,' she agrees. 'You're a serious young man.' She pauses, thinks. 'You don't have to do this, you know. I'm not sure they'll let me out of the country, and this could cause so much trouble for you . . .'

'Darling, all I want is to spend the rest of my life with you. Look, I've brought you this.'

He opens a small red box lined in satin. Inside is a gold ring with three diamonds in a row, a large one in the middle. 'I want you to wear this for the rest of your life with me. Please, please, say you will?'

Serafima is so overcome she fears she might faint. Only a few weeks ago, she was in prison. Now she might go from Communist Moscow to New York City in America, from schoolgirl to wife. Suddenly all she wants is to be married to Frank. Yet there is much to fear. Her schoolfriends are still in jail, and she senses the jeopardy in their relationship.

'Are you all right?' Frank asks, concerned. 'You've been through so much recently. There's no need to answer now. I just . . .'

'What?' she asks.

'I just can't face being separated like this again without knowing where you are and how much I love you.'

Slowly she gives him her hand. 'Yes,' she says. 'I will marry you. I want to be with you forever too.'

He slips the ring on her finger and it fits as though she's always worn it.

'What are the chances of that?' he asks. 'It fitted my grandmother and it fits you.' He raises her hand, the one wearing the ring, kisses it, and then her lips. 'Now you're going to be Mrs Frank Belman, we must make our plans carefully.'

The next day at the Golden Gates, a holiday mood. The pollen floats like the flurries of a snowstorm. The air smells of lilac. There's just a week left of term.

'I'm sure I don't need to tell you,' said Satinov to his three children as they walked from Granovsky Street, guards in front and behind them, 'don't discuss anything about the case with each other.'

At the gates, they greeted their friends with three kisses, feeling almost like adults after the nightmare they had been through.

'What's news?' George asked Andrei, like old times. Except after the Children's Case, things were very different.

'Everyone's out of prison,' asked Andrei. 'Thank God.'

'Except our teacher, Benya Golden,' added Minka Dorova, putting her arm through Serafima's. 'But I'm sure he'll be out soon.'

Satinov watched his children going through the school gates. Things may have changed but a fragile normality seemed to have been established, he was thinking as he walked back towards the street, and then stopped.

There was Dashka Dorova on her own, kissing her Senka, her darling Little Professor, as she sent him into school.

She flushed when she saw him. 'Greetings, Comrade Satinov. It's like the start of another term,' she said. 'And congratulations on your promotion!'

The day suddenly seemed dizzily sunny. He longed to explain to her that his promotion wasn't quite what it seemed. Only she would understand, and only telling her would make the thought worth thinking.

'We don't have to discuss the weather today,' he said instead, remembering what she looked like with her thick black hair, now decorously restrained in a bun, loose on her bare shoulders.

'It just got sunnier for me,' she said, smiling in her dazzling, slightly crooked way.

'I wondered . . .'

'What?' she said, a little breathlessly.

'I just wondered about . . . about dear Academician Almaz? How is his gout?'

'He's older and crabbier than ever. And much, much lamer!'

'Should I call him sometime? Am I allowed, do you think?'

She paused, and then stepped towards him so that he could smell her spicy scent. 'I think you might be,' she said. 'Yes, I might even go so far as to say that he is looking forward to it.'

49

It was time for a holiday. Back in his office in the Little Corner after the Potsdam Conference, Stalin felt exhausted and ill.

He was the arbiter of the world. Could he have imagined this when his father, Beso, showed him how to nail a sole onto a boot in his workshop in Gori? When he donned the black surplice with the white collar at the seminary in Tiflis? When he walked across the mountains with a rifle over his shoulder and donkeys bearing the cash from his bank robberies? When he spent those years in Arctic exile fishing with the Eskimos and seducing village schoolgirls? But his mission was never complete. Still no one supported him: wives, friends, comrades – all fools, weaklings or traitors. What tribulations they put him through. Roosevelt, whom he liked and admired, was dead; Truman was a small-time haberdasher, not a statesman. Churchill had lost the election: what kind of system dismissed a man who had just won a war? It made no sense at all, especially when he saw Churchill's replacement: Attlee looked like a provincial stationmaster. Besides, Attlee was a socialist and Stalin despised socialists as liberal saps and milksops, worse than imperialists. A dagger in the back was what they deserved.

The Americans now had their new weapon of astonishing destructive power, the Atomic Bomb, so, just when he, Stalin, was triumphant, he had to put all his energy into catching up with the United States. The oppressive tingling in the back of his neck, the pains in his arms and the weakness in his limbs were getting worse, and the specialists told him he needed to rest. He hadn't had a holiday since 1937, so he'd decided to go down to his villas on the Black Sea. He would have to leave Molotov and Satinov in charge, and they'd screw up, of course. They were too trusting. They couldn't see the enemies. They were like blind kittens. But no matter, his train was already packed. There were just a couple of things he had to do before he left.

He had, he considered, a special talent for movie scripts. He could have been a writer if he'd chosen that path, and remembered his excitement when his teenage poems were published. He now read every movie script and approved every movie filmed at the Mosfilm Studios.

In the little cinema near his office, in fifteen seats covered in burgundy velveteen, the Seven leaders plus the Minister of Cinema, that cretin Bolshakov, sat in rows. They were to be joined by the screenwriter Romashkin to watch some rushes from his movie *Katyusha Part Two*, which was being filmed at that very moment. Stalin recalled that Romashkin's daughter, Serafima, was somehow entangled with Vasily and the Children's Case – but he couldn't quite remember where the case had got to. (That was why he was seeing Abakumov afterwards.)

The film had begun, and Stalin watched the rushes and approved them until the scene where Sophia Zeitlin kissed the actor playing her husband. 'Stop the film! That's vulgar!' he told them. 'The kiss is too long. It's un-Soviet. Look at the way he's holding her. The kiss has to go. What possessed you, Bolshakov, to pass this obscenity?'

'Oh Comrade Stalin, I thought it was OK, but I would never have passed it without showing it to you.'

Stalin enjoyed watching Bolshakov cringe. 'What do you think, comrades? Shall we forgive him or shall we punish him?' Stalin rose and, puffing at his pipe, walked up and down before the screen. 'To forgive? Or not to forgive?'

The only sounds were his puffing and the creak of his leather boots. No one spoke. Bolshakov's face was flushed, and his bald head glistened with sweat. 'Forgive or not to forgive? All right, Bolshakov, we'll forgive. But next time: curb the kissing!'

Next, he gave Romashkin instructions for a new project: he must rewrite *Ivan the Terrible Part Two*. Eisenstein was not to be trusted with the script again. 'Don't just show that Ivan was cruel,' said Stalin. 'Show why he *needed* to be cruel. Understand?'

Romashkin wrote down his instructions but at the end of the meeting he asked if he could create a part for his wife, Sophia Zeitlin.

'Sure,' said Stalin. Well, what's good for the goose is good for the gander, so why not?

Sophia Zeitlin was a beauty, he decided, quite a temptress by all accounts (oh yes, Marshal Shako fancied himself a chivalrous knight, but he'd had a few tales to tell after they'd given him the good beating he deserved). But her looks, those bold black eyes and heavy eyebrows, were Jewish, the name Zeitlin was Yiddish and he wondered if she was *Russian* enough . . . The Jews were everywhere; they wanted to commandeer the war itself, claiming they, not the Russians, had suffered most at the hands of the Nazis. Some of them wanted their own Zionist country in the Crimea, others wanted a new Judaea in Palestine. They were never loyal to anyone. What if they really supported America? Even his darling Svetlana had married a

Jew. Those Jews were worming their way into his own family.

Stalin's head was spinning again, so he had himself driven home to the Nearby Dacha, where he lay on the divan in his office. Abakumov, now promoted to Minister of State Security, was already there, standing to attention. During the next half-hour, he reported on round-ups in Berlin, Ukrainian nationalists to be executed, new intelligence on the American atomic project from the MGB's British agents, the case of a Swedish count arrested in Budapest.

Stalin tried to concentrate but his joints ached as they had ever since his Siberian exiles. Abakumov was a crude policeman, an oaf to be sure, but thank God he was competent.

Now he came to the aeroplane scandal that he called the Aviators' Case. Marshal Shako had been broken, was blaming everyone else, even Satinov, for his faulty planes, and had denounced Marshal Zhukov for exaggerating his role in the victory (Good, thought Stalin, we'll show Zhukov who's boss here). The Children's Case was solved, and before their release the children had confessed to writing anti-Soviet materials.

It transpired that Serafima, Romashkin and Zeitlin's daughter, was not behind the conspiracy after all. Abakumov had uncovered the Enemy who had encouraged the children to embrace anti-Soviet romanticism and play at being leaders: the criminal, who had confessed, was none other than the writer Benya Golden, who had somehow inveigled his way into School 801 as a teacher.

'I thought we'd dealt with him before the war,' Stalin said.

Abakumov was about to explain but Stalin waved him aside. 'Maybe this time, when we've finished with him, he'll be shorter by a head. But we still need to punish the children, don't we?'

'Yes, Comrade Stalin. But I have one additional development

to report. Instead of using French wrestling, I released Serafima early, anticipating that she would lead us to any inappropriate contacts. We knew from an informant at the school that she was meeting someone. We were told that her lover was leaving notes for her in certain foreign books at the House of the Book.'

'Which books?' Stalin was curious. He loved books.

Abakumov consulted his notes while Stalin fidgeted impatiently. 'Novels by Hemingway. Edith Wharton. Galsworthy.'

'Good taste,' said Stalin, noticing Abakumov had clearly not heard of any of them. The uncouth clod.

'Yes, well, naturally we followed her, via the Bolshoi Theatre, and she led us to a love nest. We observed her regularly meeting a young American diplomat. We bugged the apartment. He has proposed marriage to her and she has accepted him.'

'They fuck in this apartment?'

'Yes, Comrade Stalin.'

'She's only eighteen. As a father . . .' Then he remembered that his daughter Svetlana had had an affair with a forty-year-old married screenwriter at sixteen. A Jew. He had slapped her face.

'The American is young too,' continued Abakumov, 'but the whole business is rotten. Since 1941, we've allowed over eight thousand Soviet women who've met Allied servicemen to follow their foreign partners abroad, so I presume we will allow Serafima to go to America with her fiancé, but in view of her prominent family . . .'

Stalin lay back on the divan, inhaled on the cigarette and closed his eyes for a second. The country was devastated, surrounded by enemies, infliltrated by agents, threatened by America. Discipline was essential. But this girl was in love. She was young. She had been in prison. Why shouldn't young people fall in love? he thought. He remembered his wives, his many girlfriends. If only there had been more love in my life, he thought despondently, but we Bolsheviks are a military-religious order like the Knights Templar. The Revolution always came first. I was no husband and now I'm alone. He sighed. Always alone.

'I think we should grant one month more for those wartime love affairs,' Stalin said finally. 'Then the gates close.'

He'd just remembered that Serafima was the daughter of a Jew. Another Jew.

It was Satinov's birthday and before he left the office for home, he noticed that an envelope had appeared in his in-tray typed: 'Com. Satinov. Secret.' When he opened it, all he found was a page ripped from a book of Chekhov's stories. There was nothing else in the envelope so he started to read.

Satinov had read very little literature, yet Stalin often told him that he must read Chekhov to improve himself – 'I'm old but I never stop studying,' Stalin said – but Satinov was always too busy.

Now he read this page from a story called 'The Lady with the Little Dog.' The hero and heroine, both happily married to others, meet at the Yalta resort and begin an affair. He read that they 'loved one another as close intimates, as man and wife, as very dear friends. They thought that fate itself had intended them for each other.' When the lover was on his way to meet her, he mused that:

> . . . not a soul knew about it and . . . probably no one would ever know. He was leading a double life: one was undisguised, plain for all to see and known to everyone

who needed to know, full of conventional truths and conventional deception, identical to the lives of his friends and acquaintances; and another which went on in secret. And by some strange, possibly fortuitous chain of circumstances, everything that was important, interesting and necessary for him, where he behaved sincerely and did not deceive himself and which was the very essence of his life – that was conducted in complete secrecy.

This section was marked. Satinov pressed the bell on his desk. Chubin, his aide, appeared instantly, notebook, pencil and Adam's apple poised.

'Send out someone to the House of the Book to buy Chekhov's stories.'

'Now, comrade?'

'This minute, Chubin. Make sure it contains a story called "The Lady with the Little Dog."'

And when he read the story, he felt he was reading about himself and Dashka. Truly, there was no better present than this.

On the last day of term, the parents of the Children's Case were called in to the school a little before pick-up.

Satinov met Tamriko outside the director's office. She was worried what was coming. 'Suppose,' she whispered, 'suppose they have to go back to prison? Suppose they're arrested again? I just couldn't bear to lose them a second time.'

Satinov kissed her forehead. 'Mariko won't be affected,' he replied. 'Even for George, it won't be as bad as you fear.'

Moments later, Genrikh and Dashka Dorov arrived along with the other parents. Serafima's father, Constantin Romashkin, the screenwriter, was there too; Satinov knew that Sophia was filming. Tamriko stood next to Satinov and she slipped her hand into his and he squeezed it, noticing with a sudden twinge of sadness – or irony – that the Dorovs were doing exactly the same thing. Irina Titorenka and Inessa Kurbskaya were alone.

Director Medvedeva was still suspended so it was the mathematics teacher, old Comrade Noodelman, who opened the door and summoned them in.

'Please be seated and I hand the floor to Comrade Colonel Likhachev who is here to brief you,' said Noodelman.

Colonel Likhachev, in army uniform, greeted Comrades Satinov and Dorov, but merely nodded at the women. What a charmer he was, this torturer! Satinov pushed to the back of his mind the thought that this degenerate had had control over his little Mariko.

Likhachev blinked as if unaccustomed to the wholesome brightness of this school room with its happy posters and jolly geraniums. Unzipping his leather case, he pulled out a beige file marked 'MGB' – Ministry of State Security – and 'Top Secret.' He slipped a single paper out of the folder.

'Comrades and citizens,' he began grandiloquently. 'The children, all pupils at School 801 . . .' He read out their names: George Satinov was the first. Tamriko's grip had tightened on Satinov's hand and he imagined that Dashka's must be clasping Genrikh's fiercely too because both mothers would be thinking of their younger children, fearing prison. Mariko was mentioned. Then there was Minka Dorova. Her mother's face froze as she waited for the next . . . Yes, Senka Dorov. Dashka moaned slightly. Satinov imagined he could hear all their hearts beating in unison, but perhaps it was just his own, for suddenly he found himself suffering not just for one woman and her children but for two.

'All of the above have signed confessions of conspiracy to overthrow the Soviet State and therefore have been liable under Article 158 to be sentenced to between ten and twenty-five years and, for those over twelve years old – that is all of the above criminals except Mariko Satinova, six, and Senka Dorov, ten – to the Highest Measure of Punishment.' Death!

Tamriko gasped, and her hand shook in Satinov's; Dashka's free hand went to her lips.

Likhachev looked up at them and then continued reading. For a moment Satinov questioned his folly in advising Genrikh Dorov to order the children to sign the confessions. Had he made a terrible mistake? Had Abakumov – and behind him Stalin – tricked them all?

'However,' continued Likhachev, 'three judges have decided *not* to proceed on this basis but to suspend formal judgment owing to the youth of the said criminals, who are instead to suffer the following punishment.'

The room was so silent that Satinov thought he could hear the swish of sweepers' brooms in the streets outside.

'We sentence them to one month's exile, if necessary accompanied by tutors or nannies, in Alma Ata, Turkestan. Parental visits allowed weekly.'

Tears ran down Tamriko's cheeks: tears of relief. Four weeks exile with staff was a summer holiday, as good as it could possibly be – even for Mariko, who could go with her beloved nanny Leka.

As they left the director's office, under his breath, Satinov thanked Comrade Stalin for his good sense, his justice. Satinov knew that the Aviators' Case might catch up with him, if Stalin wanted it to do so, but that seemed unlikely. The children were free and both Tamriko and Dashka were safe. That was all that mattered. He watched the two women talking a few steps ahead, admiring them and wondering how on earth he had managed to have both in his life, so he was scarcely listening when he found Genrikh Dorov keeping step with him.

'It's a relief that this case has ended harmlessly,' said the Uncooked Chicken as he peered round to check that no one was listening. 'But I'm afraid, Comrade Satinov, I must warn you, as a friend, that there are many irregularities in the management of the Air Ministry and the Satinovgrad Aeroplane Factory. It will take me a couple of weeks to finalize my report and show it to the Central Committee. When the time comes, we'll have to meet to iron out the problems. But I promise not to keep you for too long.'

50

Serafima, like the others in the Children's Case, had spent a month's exile in Central Asia. She had shared an apartment with Minka and Senka, with the Satinovs right next door (while Andrei, with a smaller budget, stayed in a room across town), and her parents had lent her their maid, so that, apart from the blistering heat, this community of young exiles had actually managed to enjoy the trip. Serafima and Frank had written to each other every day, and sometimes they even managed to book a call at the post office so that, over a clanging line, she could hear his voice as they planned their new life.

On the day she arrived back home in Moscow, her parents were not at home.

'Your mama's on set,' said the driver as the Rolls headed up to the Mosfilm Studios in the Sparrow Hills. Once she had passed the mythically muscular statue of the Worker and Collective Farm Woman outside, she was directed to Studio One.

Every road in that mini-city of cinema seemed to lead to her mother. 'She's down there,' cried a grip, directing her into the huge hanger-like studio. 'That way,' said a guard. 'She's just finishing a scene on the battlefield set,' whispered an actor wearing a Nazi uniform with blood dripping down his face. 'See?'

Sophia Zeitlin, shooting *Katyusha Part Two*, stood next to a grey howitzer on a mud-coloured trench set, lit up with kleig lights that, for all their fluorescence, could not overwhelm her black eyes and crimson lips. She was wearing an unnecessarily tight green tunic and shorter-than-usual khaki skirt (or so it seemed to Serafima). She brandished a PPSh machine-gun and placed a heel on one of the 'dead' Nazi soldiers (some of whom were dummies and others young Russian actors in Wehrmacht uniforms) who lay splayed in suitably death-like poses.

In the script (written, like the first *Katyusha*, by her husband and approved personally by Comrade Stalin), she plays a nurse whose unit has been driven back temporarily. But she fights back, killing what seems to be an entire Nazi army, while also managing to fire a bazooka and take out a Tiger tank. (In the first film, when much the same thing happened, she had fired an entire silo of Katyusha rockets, hence the name of the movie.) Her beloved husband, an ordinary soldier, calls the Kremlin to appeal on her behalf against the bureaucrats who try to stop her, a mere nurse, taking command. And now she is learning the news that Comrade Stalin has backed her—

'Cut!' cried the director through a loudspeaker. 'Bravo, beautiful work, Sophia. That's in the can. Thanks, everyone! Enough for today.'

A boy snapped the clapper and a sweaty grip helped Sophia step over the bodies on the floor while another relieved her of her gun.

'Your daughter's here to see you,' the director called on his loudspeaker.

Everyone looked at Serafima, who shrank back, and then her mother raised a hand to her eyes and peered out through the lights. 'Are you there, Serafimochka?'

'Yes,' she replied.

'Meet me in my dressing room,' Sophia shouted, her voice

echoing around the cavernous studio. She certainly didn't need a loudspeaker, thought Serafima.

In the dressing room, which smelled of tulips, face powder and greasepaint, a flotilla of assistants seemed to be working on different parts of her mother. One was removing make-up, dabbing at Sophia's face with a sponge; a second was pulling off her boots; a third was setting bouquets into vases while Sophia lay back in a chair smoking a cigarette in a holder.

'There you are, Serafima! How was it in Turkestan? As you can see, they're overworking me as usual but it's not easy for actresses of my age. There are always ingénues coming up, willing to do anything to get the parts, and every one of them has a "patron," some boss to pull strings for them . . .'

'Mama, I need to speak to you on your own.'

'Is it something important?'

'Yes, Mama.'

'You can trust my ladies-in-waiting, can't she, girls?'

'Of course!' the assistants trilled.

'No, it's really private,' Serafima insisted. 'And urgent. Would you mind?'

'Oh, all right. Leave us, girls.'

When the room was empty, Serafima told Sophia that she had met an American man and they were engaged to be married.

Sophia looked shocked. 'You don't have to marry him, surely,' she said.

'We're in love, Mama,' Serafima said, 'and we're going to live in America.'

'What?' Sophia seemed stricken. 'You're going to leave me and Papa? You can't do that.'

Serafima smiled. 'You told me often enough to follow your heart, Mama, and that's exactly what I'm doing.'

'And you're engaged? I don't see a ring. Is there a diamond?'

'I tried it on before I went away and it fits me perfectly. But it's so big that I gave it back to him. I'll put it on in America.'

'You gave it back? I've never given back a jewel in my life. Oh Serafimochka! Why an American? Your papa and I will never see you.' Sophia gave a sob and started to cry. Yet to Serafima, even her tears seemed oversized and extravagant.

Suddenly, she dabbed her eyes, the mascara smearing on her cheeks. 'Congratulations, my darling. But . . . when are you planning to go? Surely we can meet him first?'

'Soon, Mama.'

'But you know your timing is terrible for me, darling, don't you?'

'I can't delay going, Mama.'

Sophia put down the cigarette and took Serafima's hands in her own. 'Please delay going abroad. For my sake.'

'I can't. He's waiting for me. He wants to take me to America right away. I want to be with him and when I was in prison—'

'But you're home now. You can go abroad with him anytime. I know an actress who married an English journalist and she went to London with him just a few weeks ago. What difference does it make if you wait just a few weeks?'

Serafima frowned. 'But why?'

'Because I'm up for the most important part of my life. Papa's written a special role for me as the Tsarina in *Ivan the Terrible Part Two,* and your relationship with a foreigner, an American, could spoil everything. How will it look to . . .' Even Sophia never took Stalin's name in vain. '. . . the Central Committee?'

Serafima cursed her mother – her selfishness, her egocentricity – but she loved her too and she wanted her to be happy.

Besides, this involved her father too. Did she want her marriage to start with her mother's unhappiness? Could she build her future on the disappointment of the ones she loved?

'Please, do this for me,' Sophia was saying. 'My life's no bed of roses. Do you think everything's perfect with your father and me? Every day's a Gethsemane! You've attracted attention with your Romantics' Club antics, and I'm alone so much. All I'm asking you to do is wait a few more weeks before you tell people what you're going to do.'

'How long do you need?' Serafima asked.

'Three weeks and the casting will be decided. Shall we say a month?'

What could change in a month? But Serafima felt a grinding uneasiness come over her. It was true that the Children's Case had embarrassed her mother. In fact, it could have ruined her career and she had never once complained. She shook her misgivings away, turned and hugged her.

'Just a month, Mama,' she said. 'Just a month, and then Frank and I are leaving for America.'

51

Six weeks had passed since the children had been sentenced, and although by now they had returned from Central Asia, Hercules Satinov was still there, with his career, his very life, on the edge of a precipice. The strange thing was that, even though his subordinates and some air force generals had been arrested, even though Genrikh Dorov had warned him that there were problems with his ministry, he had not really seen it coming. It had been building for a long time but this was Stalin's style of management – rule by caprice and pressure – and the very fact that he had believed himself to be safe would be a reason in Stalin's eyes to give him a shock.

Now, Satinov sat alone, unshaven – thousands of kilometres from Moscow, from Tamriko, from his family, and the Kremlin – in the primitive kitchen of a small state dacha on the outskirts of Samarkand, smoking a cigarette of rough local tobacco, sipping at a glass of Armenian cognac, and thinking about Dashka Dorova.

A man in blue-tabbed uniform with narrow Uzbek eyes looked in at him from the doorway and vanished again; Satinov ignored him. It was September, and the heat in this red-walled house, built on red soil, was oppressive and he was bare-chested. He was unwell: he was suffering jabs of pain in his chest but he did not know whether it was heartburn or angina.

Heartbreak, he thought, is an agonizing disease that you're delighted to have. How had he lost control? Had he nearly thrown everything away for a woman who had turned his life upside down and almost made it hell? The release of the children had rekindled the passion between them, despite his own reason and her growing misgivings, and this short, last streak had blazed with a special brightness. Yet their quick phone calls and one meeting were worse than nothing at all, for they stirred such pangs of unslaked thirst in him that he didn't know how to quench them. Her last call was almost a relief.

'Once and for all, it's over,' she had said. 'No starting again. With you, I crossed the bridge to the world of passion, but I realize that I'm not cut out for that life and now I've crossed back. We can't risk what is truly precious; we can't make our happiness out of the unhappiness of those we love. These things are easy to start but ending them, that's an art, isn't it? Now, I've got to let you go, angel. I've got to say goodbye.'

And then, later that day, another envelope appeared in his in-tray, typed: 'Com. Satinov. Secret.' He opened it to find a page torn out of a cheap edition of Pushkin's *Onegin*. He had never read it.

'Chubin!'

'Yes, comrade.'

'Run out and get me *Onegin*.'

Poor Chubin, once again bewildered by his boss's sudden literary whims, had done as he was told and Satinov had started to read *Onegin* until he found the page she had sent him. And suddenly there it was. Bending over his desk, he studied it intently. It is a long time after Onegin's duel. After many years of travelling abroad, Onegin meets Tatiana again. By now she is a powerful married lady in St Petersburg – *this cool princess so resplendent* – and Onegin realizes he is passionately in love with her and he writes to tell her. Tatiana is heartbroken – and here was the passage marked by Dashka's pencil:

To me, Onegin, all these splendours,
This weary tinselled life of mine,
This homage that the great world tenders,
My stylish house where princes dine –
Are empty . . .
I love you (why should I dissemble?);
But I am now another's wife,
And I'll be faithful all my life.

Here it was, in the silence of his office with its lifesize portrait of Stalin, and its array of telephones, here was Dashka's answer. He had been furious at his children living in the romantic world, and now secretly, he, Stalin's Iron Commissar, was living it himself. Even though each line flayed him, he read and reread the passage, wondering if he could stand another moment of this emotional rollercoaster that had borne him from misery to exhilaration and back in a matter of days, a circle of joy and despair that had lasted for almost all of their months together.

Now, sweltering in the heat of the red-walled house in Samarkand, he replayed the course of their affair. He told himself he was lucky to have made love to such a woman. 'You're so blessed to love and to be loved,' he said aloud to himself. Then he remembered how once, when he'd reassured her that her figure wasn't too curvaceous, she had replied curtly, 'But you would say that because you're in love with me.' By being so in love, he had lost his power, her respect.

As the Central Asian heat rose around him in waves that distorted his vision, he shook his head. What a contradiction she was: controlled and cool within her own realm yet also capable of this utterly reckless, wanton giddiness that overthrew them both. Sometimes he would amuse – and torture – himself by imagining what time it was in Moscow. What would *she* be doing now, he asked himself? Would she be putting Senka to bed? Undressing at the end of the day? How he hated Genrikh for his intimate proximity to the humdrum secrets of her daily life.

He hated Genrikh too, for his role in Satinov's extended exile in Samarkand, even though he was only the messenger boy for Stalin. Genrikh would do whatever Stalin asked him. A wave of murderous anger passed through Satinov and he dreamed of destroying Genrikh himself – but that would bring down Dashka too, and her family. No, far better that he, Satinov, should face his ordeal alone in Samarkand while the ones he loved – Dashka, his children, Tamriko – were safe far away in Moscow. Perhaps the greatest relief was that Genrikh Dorov suspected nothing of the affair with his wife. No one knew, and hopefully no one would ever know. And if the Organs despatched him with a shot to the head, it would die with him.

So here, in the Samarkand house, he awoke each day with the taste of cinders in his mouth and salt rising in his throat. For, every night, he, Marshal Hercules Satinov, wept in his bed.

52

'Please don't regard me too harshly, Serafima,' said General Abakumov, who was talking to her mother in the sitting room at their apartment. He struggled to his feet, boots creaking, medals a-jingle, his sidearm clinking against the metal in his belt. 'But I wanted to come myself rather than send a subordinate.'

'What is it?' asked Serafima. Abakumov's knobbly forehead and dark brow terrified her, and she stepped back. He reminded her of her time in Lubianka, a time that even now gave her nightmares.

She looked at her mother, and knew something was wrong. 'Tell me, Mama.'

Abakumov cleared his throat: 'Your application to travel abroad with your fiancé has been refused, as has your application to marry him.'

Serafima caught her breath, feeling faint suddenly, only dimly aware of her mother's hand on her arm. 'But everyone gets permission. Many girls have gone abroad . . .'

'I'm sorry,' said Abakumov. 'That's what I wanted to tell you. This is nothing personal and nothing to do with the Children's Case. It's the very fact that so many girls have been marrying foreigners and going abroad that has accelerated the change in the rules.'

'Is there any way you can help us, Comrade General?' asked Sophia, fixing her blazing eyes on him.

'I'm afraid not. I've already looked into that for you. This comes from the Central Committee. Dear girl, take it from me: the road of life is a twisting path and some seeds fall on stony ground. That's the long and short of it.'

Satinov walks into the centre of Samarkand, past the primitive Uzbeks, Kazakhs, Tajiks, walking, squatting, taking *chai* on the wooden platforms of their *chai-khana*s, watching the world turn, far from Moscow, in their robes and embroidered skull-caps. He sits and takes tea in a *chai-khana*. Then he crosses the ruins of the Registan, the old square, and walks between mud-caked walls towards the tomb of Tamurlane; his 'companions,' plain-clothed Uzbek guards, follow him.

Tamurlane, that lame, pitiless conqueror who was the Stalin of his time, lies beneath a ribbed and fluted azure dome like a giant's blue turban. Satinov looks down at the simple jade stone that covers the emperor's tomb and he realizes that his own works, even the world-historical deeds of Stalin himself, may one day be forgotten like this.

It seems unlikely . . . but what if Lenin's state, built on the graves of millions, is one day overturned? he thinks. They might even rename the towns and streets that bear my name. What if all that truly matters is my children, my beloved wife – and *her*, my secret passion.

He bows his head before Tamurlane's simple catafalque. Satinov longs for death, instant, unexpected death, and doesn't fear it. His vision blurs as he gives thanks for this delicious sadness that makes him complete.

* * *

High on a mountain over the Black Sea, an old man in a white linen suit was smoking his pipe, his eyes slits in the bright sunlight, the irises as yellow and speckled with black as a bee stripe, his high, slightly sunburnt cheekbones set with an archipelago of freckles in a range of pockmarks.

'And down here,' he said to his visitors, 'your old host has been weeding the vegetable gardens. Honest labour is good for the soul.'

A gardener, a foxy old man who looked not unlike Stalin himself, was digging, and Stalin nodded at him and said a few words in Georgian. 'He says the tomatoes are not bad,' Stalin explained. 'Would you like some tomatoes and figs to take back to Moscow?'

'It's a beautiful garden,' agreed the American ambassador, Averell Harriman, clad in a cream suit with seams pressed as sharp as razors. 'Generalissimo, I must congratulate you on your tomatoes as well as your other achievements.'

Frank Belman, boyish and slim in his immaculate US Army uniform, translated quickly into fluent Russian. When Stalin laughed, the creases in his face resembled the grin of a tiger, but all Frank could really think about was Serafima. When he saw her after their travel plans had been banned, he feared she would make herself ill with disappointment and heartbreak.

'Well, thank you for coming to see me down here,' said Stalin to the two Americans. 'An old man must rest a little . . .'

The visit was over. Stalin ambled along the path with his bowlegged gait up the steps to the verandah and through the white pillars into the cool villa that smelled of orange blossom and tobacco. Frank noticed that every surface in the house was covered with books: he saw novels by Edith Wharton, Hemingway and Fadayev; biographies of Nadir Shah and the

Duke of Marlborough; heaps of literary journals; an open book marked with Stalin's marginalia in a blue crayon.

Stalin led them through the house and out the other side, where the ambassadorial Buick waited alongside Stalin's limousines. A fat boozy general, probably the chief bodyguard, saluted and tagged along after them down the steps to the driveway. Stalin's seaside villa in Abkhazia was totalitarianism by architecture, Frank thought. The house was an impregnable eyrie atop a steep cliff overlooking the Black Sea, invisible from every angle except from the water, and could only be reached through a single-track tunnel carved into the solid rock of the mountain. Frank concentrated hard to translate every nuance of the ambassador's words but his mind was elsewhere. With Serafima.

'Thank you for seeing us, Generalissimo,' said Harriman. 'I have to tell you we Americans, from the White House to the man in the street, are still amazed and grateful for the heroism and sacrifices of the Red Army under your brilliant command.'

'Please send President Truman my regards,' replied Stalin. 'And I hope you liked the Georgian food and wine.'

'*Didi madlobt!*' said the ambassador in Georgian.

A friend of Frank's father, Harriman was burly and tall, with polo-player's shoulders and heavy eyebrows.

Stalin scanned Harriman benignly. Their conversation seemed to be going horribly slowly, Frank thought, barely able to restrain himself from intervening. He was terrified that Harriman had forgotten about him or, worse, had decided that now was not the appropriate time to make a request.

'Generalissimo, before we leave you to this lovely place and your much-deserved rest, may I ask a personal favour?'

Frank was so nervous that he could scarcely translate this,

yet these were the words that he wanted to translate more than any that had ever been uttered.

'Ask anything. After all these years, we're friends,' said Stalin, looking somewhat moved. 'We've shared some moments as allies.'

'Thank you. My interpreter here, Captain Belman, who has translated at several of our meetings, is engaged to a Russian girl named Serafima Romashkina.'

'Congratulations!' said Stalin. His eyes flicked towards Frank and back. No hint that he knew who she was. 'We believe in love between allies.'

'She's the daughter of the actress Sophia Zeitlin and the screenwriter Constantin Romashkin.'

'You must have good taste,' said Stalin. A grin for a moment, then the inscrutable Oriental mask.

'Yet, probably due to an oversight,' Harriman continued, 'this girl has been refused permission to leave the Soviet Union.'

Stalin glanced sideways at Frank, and Frank tried to look honest and modest and earnest simultaneously.

Stalin sighed. 'Our country is full of yesmen,' he said. 'Lenin called it the Russian disease. Your newspapers call me a dictator, but as you see, I don't control everything. The Politburo has a mind of its own and sometimes I have to be wary not to offend the diehards there.' He waved at the fat general nearby: 'Comrade Vlasik, write down the names.'

The general was already writing in a little notebook. Frank felt the unfathomable glare of Stalin's yellow eyes: 'Don't worry, young man, I'll look into it.'

53

Late afternoon. Six p.m. The phone was ringing. Waiting in the kitchen, Satinov, sporting a prickly grey beard and stained khaki trousers, shirtless, barefoot, picked it up.

'How are you, darling?' Tamara said.

'Good.' Once he had blotted out the momentary disappointment that it was not another voice saying 'It's me,' he was comforted to hear her.

'How's the project?' asked Tamara.

'I'm working hard here,' he lied.

'Is there as much to do as you feared?'

'More. I'm busy from dawn until . . . I just got in.'

'Is the sugar harvest going to fulfil the Plan?'

'I hope so, if we can iron out the problems.'

'Darling, do you know when you'll be back?'

'No, but I think of you all the time. How are the children?'

'Mariko's right here. Would you like to speak to her?'

'Yes.'

'Are you OK, Hercules? You sound a little down.'

'Just tired.'

'Here's Mariko.'

'Hello, Papasha!' A voice as beautiful to him as the nightingale's call. He struggled not to weep.

'Darling Mariko: how are the dogs in their school?'

'They're doing a singing class today.'

'Kiss them from me.' His voice shook. Love, he thought suddenly, is only enough if it can exist in the world one lives in.

'Mariko, I kiss you with all my heart,' said Satinov.

'Bye, Papasha! Here's Mama again.'

'I love you, Hercules,' said Tamriko, sending, he felt, a ray of warmth that seemed too generous to emanate from her small body. It reached him faithfully, as she had meant it to, like an arrow flying through a dense forest to find its mark.

'I love you too, Tamriko.'

'Until tomorrow then,' she said, and hung up.

It hit him then that he might never see Tamriko and Mariko ever again. That he had been so dangerously obsessed with Dashka that he had scarcely cared about his true life. It was only now, as Tamriko put Mariko on the line, that he remembered the interrogation protocols of Marshal Shako. As a Politburo member he had been sent a copy; they contained the following lines:

INTERROGATOR Who is responsible for the criminal sabotage of these planes?

PRISONER SHAKO One man is to be blamed – Satinov.

How much torture had been required to elicit this from his brave friend? But he, Satinov, had read the words like a blind man and had gone about his life as a sleepwalker somehow navigates the familiar stairs and corridors of his life without seeing them.

The next morning, Chubin had come into the office. 'Comrade Molotov wonders respectfully if he might have a word with you and Comrade Dorov in his office?'

Satinov had walked down the long corridors and into the

antechamber, where he found Molotov and Dorov waiting with odd expressions on their faces. Before he could say anything, Colonel Osipov, the head of Molotov's bodyguard, had stepped in between him and them.

'Hello, Comrade Satinov.'

'Greetings, Colonel.'

'This is for you.' He handed him an envelope.

Top Secret

To: Comrade Satinov, E. A.
From: Comrades Stalin, J. V., Molotov, V. M., Zhdanov, A. A., Beria, L. P.
The Politburo agrees that

1. Comrade Satinov has committed grave mistakes in the manufacture of aircraft;
2. That the Security Organs shall check out sabotage and wrecking in Comrade Satinov's departments;
3. We appoint Comrade Genrikh Dorov to investigate Comrade Satinov's conduct;
4. That Comrade Satinov is suspended as a Secretary of the Communist Party and First Deputy Premier;
5. That Comrade Satinov be sent forthwith to investigate sugar harvests in Turkestan.

Signed: Stalin, Molotov, Zhdanov, Beria

He looked for Molotov and Dorov but they had gone.

'When do I go?' Satinov had asked Osipov.

'Have you read it?' Osipov had asked dubiously.

'Of course. Do I leave now?'

'No. First the Organs have arranged a meeting. Follow me.'

And so they'd led him into Comrade Molotov's meeting room. At the table, between two plain-clothed secret policemen, sat a broken man, so thin he barely filled the shabby suit, his shirt collar loose around his bent neck, his face scarred and blistered, his once luxuriant moustaches now meagre. Osipov told Satinov to sit facing this man, and he knew this was a so-called 'confrontation' to elicit a confession from him.

'You recognize this man, Comrade Satinov?'

'Yes.'

'Who is it?'

'Colonel Losha Babanava.'

'Would you accept, Comrade Satinov, that Babanava knows *everything* about you?'

'No, not everything,' replied Satinov. Babanava did not know about Dashka. Or did he? 'But yes, he knows a lot.'

'Babanava resisted us a little. He's a strong man. But now you must tell what you know, Losha.'

'I've told them everything. Everything. I'm sorry, boss.' Losha raised his eyes, and Satinov looked into them searchingly. Had Losha really betrayed their friendship? He wouldn't blame him if he had, but he had to consider what his former bodyguard knew. Could Losha know his only secret: Dashka?

'You see?' said Colonel Osipov. 'So save yourself much pain, Comrade Satinov, and tell us what Losha has already confirmed. Losha?'

A lull. One of the guards tapped Losha's arm, pointing at a typed paper before him. He seemed to awaken.

'I heard you say often that our planes were flying coffins for our pilots and that this was Stalin's fault.'

'Not true. I never said that. Not once.'

Losha seemed to doze off and was again tapped. This time he had difficulty finding his place on the paper, so Colonel Osipov whispered to him. He nodded. 'You were recruited as a spy for the Americans and Zionists.'

'Never,' retorted Satinov. 'I've been a devoted Leninist since I was sixteen.'

'One more thing, Losha,' said Colonel Osipov.

'Yes,' said Losha, 'you corruptly . . .'

Satinov held his breath.

'. . . at the front, when you were at Rokossovsky's headquarters and Berlin, you corruptly sold medical supplies from the Ministry of Health for personal profit.'

Satinov gazed into Losha's soul, aware suddenly that they were close to dismantling his entire life. Just a step from Dashka herself. Prussia. Berlin.

'I know everything,' said Losha, tears running down his face. 'You didn't think I knew of your immoral actions. But I've told them – kerboosh – everything!'

Afterwards, Satinov had been taken straight to the station and put in a reserved compartment with two Chekist guards. Now, two weeks later, he had not yet fallen off the precipice, but he was teetering on the edge of an abyss into which he would inevitably draw Tamriko and the children, and perhaps Dashka and hers. The children of Trotsky had all been liquidated; the lovely daughter of Tukhachevsky sent to the Arctic Circle. So far, he was in limbo, neither alive, nor in heaven, nor hell. He was still so enchanted by Dashka that he was utterly numb.

Satinov's downfall – Genrikh's role in it and Losha's betrayals – was constantly interrupted by a replay of his last meeting with Dashka in the Aragvi private room. It was the climax of their affair, and the end, with all the desperate frenzy of the last hours of a doomed city. Even now, he could taste her, see the flash of her bared teeth as she sat over him, with him deep inside her, demurely covered by her pleated white skirt.

Sex fills just a few hours of our existence, he realized, and yet those precious minutes count more than months and years.

Now he knew that if he didn't extricate himself from his current predicament, he was well on his way to receiving the eight grams in the back of the neck, and sooner rather than later.

54

'This is from me to wish you a long and happy married life,' said Senka, handing over a book entitled *Western Philosophy Since 1900*.

'Darling Senka,' cried Serafima. 'I'll treasure this forever.'

She was standing on the platform of the Belorussian Station in a flowery summer dress holding a little cream leather case as jets of steam blew white and feathery out of the train. All along the grimy platform, people were saying goodbyes in a myriad of permutations. Anyone seeing Serafima and her party would have presumed that they were schoolfriends and family despatching her on a holiday – but she feared that she would never see them or Russia again. And however much she was in love with Frank (who was waiting for her at his new posting in Paris) and looking forward to a new life in the West, she realized that the cliché was true: her soul was Russian and that meant she already missed Moscow, the diamond crystals of ice on her windows, the verses on the poet's plinth in Pushkin Square, the silver birches in the forests, the hidden rushing of water beneath the snows as the thaw came, the ochre and duck-egg blue of old palaces – and that was before she had even looked into the eyes of her friends. The Dorov and Satinov children were all there to see her go. They had shared not just school but the Children's Case too, and so far she had only started to say goodbye to Senka. She was so moved that she could scarcely speak.

'No offence, but your make-up's all running,' said Senka, but he too had started to cry and she took him in her arms, tiny in his Little Professor's suit, and hugged him.

'I know, darling Little Professor,' she said. 'Do I look awful?'

'I'm afraid you do look scary, but I don't care. I will always miss you and think of you as long as I live because you've always been my favourite grown-up, Serafimochka. And I will come and see you,' he said. 'Please reserve me my usual presidential-imperial suite at the Waldorf-Astoria Hotel!'

'Do you promise?' she asked.

'Come on, Senka, you're upsetting her,' said Minka, pulling her brother away. 'Serafimochka, good luck, my dearest friend. Promise to write soon and we'll all have to visit you.' She put her arms around Serafima and held her close. 'To think it all started that day at the Bolshoi and you managed to keep it secret.'

'The big boys always said you were a mystery,' Senka laughed. 'And they were right! I think it's the biggest romance I've ever heard of, greater than all the romances of the medieval troubadours.'

'Quiet, Senka, or you'll make me cry again,' said Serafima.

Her father climbed down from the carriage where he had been stowing her trunk. 'God, that was heavy,' said Romashkin, wiping his brow.

'It's got all her books in it,' said Sophia Zeitlin. She was wearing a purple suit with a white mink collar and a wide-brimmed hat veiled in white chiffon. 'Good luck, my darling.'

'I'm missing you already,' said her father. 'Send us a telegram as soon as you arrive in Paris. Come back and see us soon or we'll visit you too often!' He wiped his eyes and Sophia hugged him as she had not done for years. 'You'd better get in. You leave in five minutes,' he added.

George took Serafima's hand and helped her into her carriage where the best seat had been reserved. A uniformed steward asked if she had any cases to be put above the seat.

Senka jumped into the carriage and put his hand in hers.

'As long as I live,' he said, 'I'll always wish it had been me instead of that American. Am I really too young for you?'

'Oh Senka,' Serafima said, laughing through her tears, 'out you get!'

The train groaned, doors slammed and the carriages creaked and shunted as if they were waking up. Senka and George jumped off the train. A whistle blew. Serafima heard someone calling her name, and looked through the Dorovs and Satinovs to see Andrei Kurbsky running up the platform. She leaned out of the window to say goodbye to him just as the train jerked into movement.

A puff of steam whooshed out as if the train had coughed. And then it was too late for any more farewells as the train moved away, leaving George and the Dorovs and Andrei Kurbsky waving and blowing kisses until she could no longer see them.

Dear Comrade Stalin, honoured father,

I committed grievous errors in my conduct of the aircraft industry. I am sorry that my mistakes and arrogance led to the loss of aircraft and brave pilots. I apologize. As a Bolshevik, I place myself humbly at the feet of the Party and of the Great Leader whose trust I have disappointed and whose wisdom I so need to succeed as a responsible Party worker. On my knees before you, esteemed Josef Vissarionovich, I admit my sins. Please punish me as you will. I am ready to perform any task high or low to help you lead the country and the Communist movement to more victories under your brilliant genius and visionary leadership.

I look to you as a beloved father to teach me. Without this paternal instruction, I am, like all of your assistants, lost and in need of guidance.

Hercules Satinov

It was long after midnight in Samarkand, and the cockroaches in Satinov's red-walled house were manoeuvring as confidently across the floor as tanks in a Red Square parade.

Satinov put down his pen and called the guards. The letter would be despatched at once to wherever Stalin was.

He just hoped it wasn't too late.

55

As the train raced through the rolling emerald meadows and ravaged battlefields of Belorussia, Serafima sat in her luxury compartment watching birches rising slim on silvery parade, ruined villages, blackened tanks and row upon row of skeletal trucks. Sometimes, starving wild-eyed women, more like scarecrows than people, ran alongside the train, their yellow fingers outstretched for a crumb of food.

Serafima lay back in her seat, imagining Frank waiting for her on the platform at the Gare de l'Est in Paris, executing that rakish two-fingered salute that always melted her heart. Would he bring flowers? What do two people about to embark on a new life say to each other? None of it mattered because they loved each other.

She could not imagine what New York would be like. She knew that, after some months at the Foreign Ministers' Conference in Paris, Frank would be taking her back to his townhouse in Manhattan. She closed her eyes and tried to replay images from American movies in her mind, but then she stopped. All that mattered was to see her darling Frank, to kiss him, to hold him, to be his wife. She thought back to the moment they had met at the Bolshoi, the first time they made love, the way he traced the snakeskin on her side and made her feel it was the most beautiful talisman of love the world had ever known. She remembered the shots on the bridge that she had thought marked the end of her romance; her arrest by Abakumov; the prison cell in Lubianka; her mother's insistence that she delay her departure so she could win that part and her own unease as she agreed; the terrible moment her visa was refused; the miracle of how Stalin had looked at Frank and made it all possible.

'Just fifteen minutes to Minsk,' said her steward. 'Would you like *chai*? Lemonade? Juice? Wine? *Champagnski*?'

'Yes. Tea, please.'

The train was already braking for Minsk as he brought in the tea in a china teapot and served it with a napkin on his arm. He gave her the teacup on a saucer as if, Serafima thought, they were in an English duke's drawing room.

She glanced out of the window. She saw the wrecked suburbs of Minsk as she drank the tea and noticed a house missing every one of its walls but still containing all the beds and tables, toys and books of its vanished family. Where is that family now? It was her last thought before the world started to whirl in giddily quickening circles, stealing the strength from her muscles. Dimly, she heard her teacup smashing into smithereens as her head dropped forward, and oblivion descended softly over her like a black velvet hood.

Satinov was sleeping when the telephone started to ring. It was a few hours after midnight, but he picked it up anyway.

'Comrade Satinov?'

'Yes?'

'I have Comrade Stalin for you.'

Vibrations on the line twanged and looped along the wires that crossed steppes and deserts.

'*Bicho!* Boy! Are you busy there?' It was *him*.

'Comrade Stalin, Bolshevik greetings.'

'If I'm not interrupting your work on the sugar harvest, do you have time to talk?'

'Yes, Comrade Stalin.'

'Hercules, you've been re-elected as a Party Secretary and First Deputy Premier.'

A breath of relief. 'Thank you, Comrade Stalin.'

'The Party is always just, Hercules. Comrade Stalin is always fair. Come visit an old man who knows how to grow the best tomatoes in Georgia and we can sing "Suliko" on the verandah at night. Do you remember?'

'Yes, yes, of course.'

'No hard feelings eh?'

'None.'

'Too many informers in this country. Too many yesmen! But everything has to be checked out.'

'Vigilance is our first duty.'

Satinov realized that, although Losha had been tortured, he had not betrayed him. But he *had* known about the affair with Dashka, which was why he had mentioned Prussia and Berlin: to let Satinov know that he knew and would die rather than tell. Satinov swallowed the sudden lump in his throat. He had never had a better friend than Losha. But he knew Losha would never come out alive.

'So to business,' said Stalin. 'Molotov has displayed arrogant insubordination. Go to Moscow. Deliver a harsh reprimand. And one other thing. You curate Health?'

'If you wish it, Comrade Stalin.'

'We need a new minister. That woman doctor didn't work out – they're checking her out. And that husband of hers, what a bungler. There's a plane on its way.'

The phone went dead and Satinov remained half sitting, half crouching, on the edge of the bed, staring into the darkness, absorbing this news. 'That woman doctor . . . checking her out.' The spell cast by Stalin's favour was disturbed by his confused anxiety for Dashka. What had he done?

Skidding tyres and slamming doors; the driveway was illuminated and men in uniforms were turning on the lights in the house. Colonel Osipov, who had informed him of his downfall a few weeks earlier, came into the bedroom.

'Come on, Comrade Satinov,' he said, shaking him as one might wake a child. 'Morning comes early for the fortunate.'

The first day of the winter term at School 801.

Many children had left and Director Kapitolina Medvedeva was proud that most had passed into Moscow University and a few had won places at the élite Institute of Foreign Languages. As she stood at the Golden Gates that September morning, waiting for the parents and children to arrive, she noticed out of the corner of her eye that Innokenty Rimm had, as she had suggested, stationed himself behind her to hurry the children into the school and avoid a long queue.

'Everything's ready, just as you asked, Comrade Director,' said Rimm.

'Very good, Comrade Rimm.' Now she could finally allow herself a little satisfaction that she was back in the job that she loved, while knowing that only one thing had saved her from the unspeakable fate that had befallen her colleague Golden.

After hearing the grave accusations against her at the tribunal at the Education Sector of the Central Committee, she had said: 'Inspectors, comrades. May I speak? This concerns a message from the highest authorities that I think you will find relevant to my case.'

And she had handed them the scrap of paper with its red-crayonned scrawl: *To Teacher Medvedeva. Svetlana certainly knows her history. The Party values good teachers. J. St.*

Yes, Svetlana Stalina had loved history, and one snowy morning in 1938, the little girl with the freckles and the red hair had arrived at class with a note which she had delivered to her favourite teacher.

Kapitolina had told no one about the note, and shown it to no one. Yet this sacred piece of paper had saved her.

The limousines were driving up. And there was Comrade Satinov arriving with his daughter, Mariko. He looked darker and leaner than before, and the lines on his face were more pronounced.

'Good morning, Comrade Satinov,' said Kapitolina Medvedeva. 'Welcome back for another term at School 801.'

PART FIVE

Serafima

She saw it all. In desolation,
The simple girl he'd known before,
Who'd dreamt and loved, was born once more.

Alexander Pushkin, *Eugene Onegin*

56

December 1953

Move closer or you won't see. Move too close and they will see you.

The half-lit Yaroslavsky Station: a freezing hall of flickering lights amidst the darkness of a Muscovite winter through which flit hooded silhouettes and half-faces concealed by the hats, scarves and greatcoats of those who wait. Some of them have been waiting for a very long time for this moment.

The train appears: two needle points of light as it curls and twists its way into the station.

The crowd surges forward. Some people move to the edge of the platform, establishing themselves as official welcomers. Others – who know what to expect or who expect to be disappointed, or those who don't want to be recognized – hang back. No one dares speak louder than a whisper, so that the station with its high baroque roof hisses like a cathedral of spirits. Only their frozen clouds of breath, and the blue-grey of their cigarette smoke, confirms they are speaking at all. All are united by a sense of constricted emotion; all are joyous yet fearful, so that you can sense the muffled heartbeats and quick breaths deep within their fur coats and scarves.

For those who hang back, it is now hard to see anything at all amidst plumes of steam. Now they must strain forward so as not to miss their friends and family who are returning from the infamous Gulag camps of Pechora and Norilsk, in that faraway Arctic Circle of Hades.

Look – here they are! Figures are stepping out of the train, carrying their carpet bags and bundles and battered leather cases. Their faces are yellow and drawn yet they too seem as eager and as afraid as those who have come to meet them. Some embrace; some weep; others search for loved ones who have not survived the long wait, and are not there.

Look, there! There's a familiar face. Is it she? No, it could have been, but . . . Or there?

Two women step down from the train, helping each other: one is older, one younger. Both have aged and yet are preserved as parchment is preserved in the infernal world of the Gulags. Is it she? Yes, unmistakably, there are her dark eyes and crooked mouth, even though her lips seem so much thinner. She is wearing a much-darned, shapeless gabardine coat and a threadbare rabbit-fur hat, and is helping her friend, who is much taller and even more dishevelled, with her little cream suitcase, held together by wispy pieces of rope. And when they turn to peer down the platform to see who might be meeting them . . . yes, it's them. It is Dashka Dorova and Serafima Romashkina come back to live in a world in which so much has changed; in which Stalin is dead and Beria executed; in which some camps are being closed and many prisoners liberated.

Slowly they head down the platform, their faces illuminating and then darkening in the occasional lamps, sometimes vanishing into the steam and re-emerging, wisps of vapour wrapped around them like cloaks, born and reborn again and again. Now they are walking faster, their faces raised, their lips slightly parted, Dashka and Serafima, holding hands for strength.

He moves closer to see who meets them; watches as they

approach a huddled crescent of waiting families, noticing how they slow down, hoping and fearing. Her face is painfully meagre and fallow, its spirit almost extinguished, she who was once so peachy and sumptuous. Her hair is probably grey, he thinks with a stab of pain, remembering its heavy, thick darkness.

She is hugging Serafima – how close they seem – and then Serafima goes one way, Dashka the other.

He follows Dashka. And now she is pointing and dropping her case and opening her arms and her face is losing years and she is smiling, and it is as though dawn has come early and the ochre rays of a rising sun are illuminating and warming the gloom of this frozen station. Without thought, the muscles in his legs bunch for the sprint to reach her first so she will know that she is still loved and has been loved all along. Has she known that? Has she thought of him? All he wants suddenly is to kiss her face, her eyes, her lips, to tell her so many things, to chatter as if no one else were in the room, to hear her stories of the camps, to discover if Academician Almaz is alive, to tell her that he has always loved her.

Do not move a single step closer, he tells himself. Lower your fedora. Step back into the shadows. For now he can see whom she is greeting: the light has caught Genrikh Dorov, but it is a new, scarcely recognizable Genrikh Dorov. He seems fuller in the face, his skin rosy, even his white hair seems thicker. He divorced Dashka when she was arrested in 1945. In the hierarchy of their regimented world, it was the done thing. The alternative was probably death.

Genrikh, banned from visiting Moscow, has come to meet her. He could be arrested just for being here and yet, for the first time in his life, he has broken a Party rule to make her feel loved after all she has been through. Tears gather in his eyes as he watches this. He is grateful that she is being met and cherished as she deserves. That is why he's here, isn't it? But in truth, he is bitterly disappointed; he feels somehow rejected.

Genrikh is holding Dashka in his arms and he can see they are talking. Now she will learn how, on the day of Stalin's death, the leaders had dismissed Genrikh for his 'excesses' and exiled him to the provinces. Power had poisoned him, yet his downfall seems to have rejuvenated him.

What is she saying? 'Where's Senka?' And Genrikh is replying, 'Senka's waiting with the others. He's a young man now. He can't wait to see you. There hasn't been a day when we haven't talked about you . . .'

The crowd pushes forward. Pull your hat down. Melt into the shadows as if you were never here. Go out into the streets and gather yourself; discarding this vision of ghosts, denying this act of quixotic indulgence, return again to Tamriko and the contented, settled home you have made together.

57

It was Dashka who had saved her life. Eight years previously, when she'd boarded the train that would take her to Paris, and to her new life, her future with Frank had seemed like a dream come true.

And then she had woken up to find herself back in the Lubianka as the drugs wore off. Her train journey, her departure, her permission to leave the country – all had been promised to the Americans. Now her sudden sickness meant she could not travel until she was in better health. Later she realized that her personal tragedy was a symptom of Stalin's deteriorating relationship with the Americans, and there would never again be an opportunity to ask for such a favour nor the goodwill to grant it.

Ten years under Article 158 for spying for a foreign power (in other words, consorting with an American, though not for conspiracy to overthrow the Soviet State, for which she would have received a death sentence or twenty-five years): it was only then that she finally began to understand what her interrogation had really been about. Colonel Komarov explained that she was no longer under suspicion for masterminding the Fatal Romantics' conspiracy because her teacher, Benya Golden, had dictated this wicked Jewish-Trotskyite-American conspiracy to the weak-minded Nikolasha Blagov, because he had been in love with her.

'But that's not true,' Serafima had protested.

'You want another ten years for lying to us?' Komarov replied. 'Just confirm his testimony and that's the end of the Children's Case.'

'What will happen to him?'

Komarov drew a line across his neck, and Serafima grasped that Benya Golden had sacrificed himself, not just for her sake, but to liberate all the children he had taught in School 801.

It was a miracle that she survived the train journey to Pechora and Norilsk, unlike the people who died and whose bodies she saw tossed out of the moving carriages, not unlike the slaves she would soon see toiling on timber-felling and railway-building in all weathers, dying in the snows, left frozen stiff in their snowy tombs until they emerged, perfectly preserved, in the spring.

When she arrived in Pechora, she was assigned to the daily logging gangs, but within a few days, the sleepless nights in the barracks, the starvation rations, the exhausting physical strain, prompted a fever so severe it brought her close to death. She lay in her dormitory considering the offers of leering camp guards and tattooed gangster bosses to become their mistress. How else could she survive? But the truth was she didn't want to: she hoped to perish of heartbreak if not malnutrition or fever. What was there to live for? Her death would be her wedding gift to Frank, no less romantic and sacred for his never knowing of it.

Somehow she made it to the sanatorium, a hut with a few bloodstained mattresses and no medicines; there was a corpse lying next to her, a jagged mouth open in a final silent scream. There were no doctors. She passed in and out of consciousness – and then, one day, she opened her eyes.

'You're going to live, Serafimochka,' said a familiar voice. And there was Dashka Dorova smiling down at her, and Serafima wondered if she was in heaven and looking down at the Golden Gates outside School 801 with George and Minka and Senka.

'Dr Dorova, what are you doing here? Were you denounced for something?'

'That's the one thing we *zeks* never discuss up here. But in truth, I simply don't know. Listen, dear, they've asked me to set up a camp hospital – for the guards as well, of course – and' – she leaned over Serafima and whispered – 'I've told them about your nursing training. Understood, angel? I need you.'

And so it was that, over the next few years, Dashka Dorova lobbied the MVD authorities tirelessly to get a few basic medicines and beds, and for any doctors or nurses in the camp to be assigned to her, thus saving her, Serafima, and the lives of many others in the process.

Gradually the two women came to trust each other. Smoking cigarettes, they often talked late into the evenings about the Children's Case; and what it had all meant; and Serafima's own contribution in encouraging the Fatal Romantics' play-acting, in the hope that their make-believe world of poetry and romance would divert her classmates' attention from herself and her secret.

At first, Serafima consoled herself by reciting 'The Talisman,' by looking up at the blue of the sky every day and telling herself she would never stop loving Frank, and that they would be together one day, whatever happened. Over the many hours, years even, that she and Dashka smoked and drank Armenian arak – in the summer, tormented by clouds of mosquitoes on the stope of their hut, in winter around the fire, enshrouded by the perpetual night of the Arctic, days which were dominated by the petty triumphs, vicious feuds and fatal perils of camp life – Dashka talked about her children, and above all of her Senka, whose letters she read and reread and almost memorized. Patiently Dashka listened to Serafima's speeches of love and regret, without telling her what she should do. But she guided her inch by inch to a new realization, a new Serafima. 'Every love story's a requiem,' she told her. One night, Serafima looked at her, her eyes wild.

'He's never coming back,' she said. 'I'm never going to find him again. It was all just a dream that could never have come true. And all these years I've been living this lie.'

She got up, threw open the door of the hut and ran out into the snow. 'Wherever you are, Frank, I release you. Be free!' she shouted up at the rounded blue vault of stars. 'Goodbye, my love!'

'Get back inside, girl,' ordered Dashka from the wooden doorway.

'Does he hear me in America? Do you hear me, Frank? I'm a ghost to you now, and I don't expect an answer. But I want you to live your life, and be happy.'

'Hush! You'll attract the guards and wake up the patients and you're not even wearing a coat, you little fool. Come in!' Dashka ventured out on to the snow in her fur slippers to grab Serafima and pull her back inside.

'Feel better, darling Serafimochka?' she asked her when they were sitting by the fire again. 'You've done the right thing. Now you'll be happier and you'll be stronger to endure this new life of ours.'

Serafima took Dashka's hand. 'Thank you for all your patience.'

'You'll always have the scars,' Dashka said. 'The surgeons can never remove the fragments of shrapnel. They stay in your body forever, almost forgotten until one day, you're jolted and then they'll give you a pang of agony that makes you cry out. But you can live through it, I promise you that.'

Not for the first time, Serafima wondered about Dashka. She respected her as a former minister and doctor, but she was a very private person, an enigma, apparently so tough. Long blinded by Dashka's sunniness, she saw there was shade there too.

'You sound like you have some experience of this yourself?'

Dashka inhaled her cigarette and stared into the fire. 'What's important is not who *you* love but *who* loves you.'

Now, eight years later, Serafima said goodbye to Dashka on Yaroslavsky Station and watched her husband welcome her home. Like so many others, Serafima had not been able to get a message to her parents, but she eagerly sifted through the crowd of faces to see if someone had come to meet her. Some families had been notified; some did not know when their loved ones would be returning. She was just about to head out into the streets to wave down a car to drive her to her parents' apartment when she spotted a familiar face with a diffident smile.

'Andrei? Is that you?' she asked, suddenly delighted to see him.

'Yes,' replied Andrei Kurbsky. He was still handsome in his wholesome way but much shabbier. 'I'm so happy to see you.'

'Who are you here to meet?'

'You, of course.'

'But how did you know I was on this train?'

'I didn't.'

'How lucky we bumped into each other.'

'Not quite luck. I didn't like to think that there'd be no one here when you came home.'

'How did you know that we were being released now?'

'Your mother told me you were in Pechora. I asked a favour so I knew it would be sometime this month.'

'This month? But that means—'

Andrei smiled and adjusted his heavy spectacles, blushing slightly. 'Yes, I've met every train.'

'Every night?'

'Yes. It's not so bad . . . I bring a book and smoke a few cigarettes and sometimes warm up with a jot of vodka. Oh, here, I have some for you.' He gave her a small flask and she took a swig.

The vodka streaked its burning path down her throat.

'Thank you, Andryusha!' She took another shot. 'I don't have anyone else waiting for me. I don't have anywhere to be . . .'

'I know,' he said. 'That's why I'm here.'

It struck her then that he must have always loved her, even when it was not clear she was alive or that she would ever return. She could see too he was not sure how much of this devotion to reveal, afraid that it might frighten her off.

'But you never wrote . . . I never knew,' she said.

'How could I tell you?' he asked. 'I didn't know where to begin.'

She raised her fingers to her face. 'I look truly awful. I was once a little attractive but I must seem like a sort of witch now.'

'Not to me,' Andrei said, speaking in a rush. 'You were always entirely your own person, and now you're even more so. You've probably forgotten that I saw you off on the train that day when you were leaving to be married in the West. I told myself then that I'd meet the train if you ever came back.'

'You did see me off,' Serafima said, remembering his face as the train pulled away. She had not thought about him once in eight years, yet now she was nourished by the feeling he had been with her even then and that somehow she'd known him well a long time. 'It's cold here, isn't it? I'm shivering.'

He picked up her case. 'May I? I suppose you want to go to your parents' place, but' – he searched her face – 'I have a small apartment, and it's warm and full of books and . . .'

As he pushed his way through the crowd into the street where his car was parked, Serafima followed him with tears streaming down her face; she was crying not just out of gratitude for his kindness, but because it was only at this very second that she was really letting go of Frank Belman. This was the end of her old life and the start of a new one with Andrei Kurbsky.

As she passed through the arches of the station, she saw a tall man in the shadows. Through the blur of her tears, she glimpsed a face that reminded her of Hercules Satinov. But it couldn't be him: he was more important than ever now, so what would he be doing here? Pulling down his black fedora, the man disappeared into the night, and when Serafima blinked, he was gone.

Epilogue

1973

The guards called up from the checkpoint on Granovsky: 'The guest is on the way up, Comrade Marshal.'

'Thank you,' said Satinov. Mid-seventies but as lean as a much younger man, he looked at his watch. It was seven in the morning; Tamriko was at the dacha with Mariko, who had never married, and an American delegation was in Moscow to negotiate an arms-limitation treaty, so he, as Defence Minister, had been busy entertaining the Westerners at the Bolshoi and a banquet until the early hours. When he finally got home, the phone was ringing. Satinov had listened carefully.

'All right,' he said. 'Come early in the morning.'

So he was expecting this visit – but he had scarcely slept, imagining what it might mean.

Now he got up and crossed the chandeliered living room, conscious that, in this age of Nixon and Brezhnev, there was no longer a lifesize portrait of Stalin on the wall; instead there was one of himself in marshal's uniform. He walked down the gleaming parquet corridor to the front door, hesitated for a second, opened the door – and gasped in shock.

At her book-lined apartment in the block on Patriarchy Prudy, Serafima Kurbskaya was sitting down.

'I've had a phone call,' she said to her husband, who was standing in the doorway watching her.

'I know.'

'It was from the American Embassy. They want me to meet someone.'

'I thought so.'

'How did you know?'

'I've always expected that call,' said Andrei, 'and I happened to see his name in *Pravda*. He's in charge of the American delegation.'

'I didn't say I'd go.'

'Do you want to?'

'I'm happy not to go. I don't want it to worry you.'

'But do you *want* to see him again?'

'I think I do.'

'Then you must. Serafima?'

'Yes?'

'I owe you this. And if you still have feelings . . .'

'Oh, Andrei. You don't owe me anything. I owe *you* a lot. Twenty happy years. We have our children, our books, poetry, theatre.'

Andrei came over, sat down beside her and took her hand. She noticed how pale he was looking. 'We haven't really spoken about this, but when we were at the school, I . . . I did something that I've always regretted. When I read Nikolasha's Velvet Book, I was worried by his anti-Party views. I felt I had to show my loyalty. I informed the Organs that Nikolasha was propagating anti-Soviet ideas. I was given a controller whom I met in a safe apartment. I wrote reports. I agreed to watch people for the Organs, to protect myself and my mother – a sort of insurance policy after all we'd been through. Even then

I loved you, so I tried to do as little harm as I could, but . . . still . . . When I look back, as I lie beside you at night . . .' Andrei got up, walked over to the far side of the room, cleaned his spectacles, and then came back to sit beside her again. 'It was me who told them about you going to the House of the Book every afternoon, and now I wonder if I played a part in them finding out about you and Frank Belman.'

Serafima put her head on his shoulder. 'I knew you worked for the Organs. I worked it out in my cell in Lubianka. I had a lot of time. And when I came back from the Gulags, you knew which train I'd be on because you asked your KGB controller to tell you.' She paused. 'Dearest Andryusha, I've never held it against you. I know you, like millions of others, had no choice, especially when we were schoolchildren. You *had* to protect your mother. You're a good person. You're mine.'

Andrei sighed; then he put his arms around her. 'Thank you, but I'd still like to drive you to meet him, and I want you to be free to do whatever you want and go wherever you want. I've been so lucky to have you all these years. Now it's my turn to make amends.'

'I'm so sorry,' said Satinov at the open door, wiping his brow. 'For a second, you looked so like . . .'

'My mother?'

'Yes. Forgive me, Professor Dorov, I'm getting old.'

'I suppose she was my age, around forty, when you knew her?'

'Yes.' Satinov turned round and gestured towards his sitting room. 'Please come in.'

When they were both sitting down, Senka Dorov, who had dark eyes and a few freckles across his cheeks, thick dark hair and a full mouth with a slightly crooked grin, looked around at the grand room. The giant portrait of his distinguished host, the fire blazing and the chandelier all reminded him of his childhood, when both his parents were members of the leadership. A maid brought tea.

'What can I do for you?' asked Satinov.

'I'll get straight to the point if I may,' replied Senka. 'My mother died two days ago.'

The news punched Satinov in the solar plexus. 'I'm so sorry.'

'She died of cancer in Pyatogorsk, where my parents retired. She'd been ill for a while.' Senka paused. 'She asked me to deliver a package to you personally.'

'Thank you. As a child you were closest to your mother.'

'We continued to be close. Right until the end. You hadn't actually seen her for a long time, I think?'

'No, not really since 1945. You do look very like her, Senka, just as you did when you were a boy, the Little Professor.'

'But you knew her well.' It was not quite a question.

'In a way.' Satinov had never regretted staying with Tamriko, just as he had never considered leaving her. After his affair with Dashka, he had returned to become the man he had been before – on the surface, at least. The rigid life of the élite continued under Stalin and his successors, and everyone treated him as if he were still his reticent, cold former self. Yet all this time, Dashka had existed in his life like one of those unexploded Luftwaffe bombs they sometimes found, buried deep in someone's garden yet still capable of destroying the entire neighbourhood. Over the years, he had realized that he had made a fool of himself with Dashka – and yet it was a folly that he would treasure all his life.

'Well, this is what she asked me to deliver,' said Senka

awkwardly, proffering a package wrapped in brown paper and crisscrossed with string. 'There! Duty done!'

'Thank you again.' Satinov was aware that his face was expression-free. After all, to hide his feelings was second nature to him.

'Before I go, Comrade Satinov, may I ask you something? My mother's arrest was such a blow to me as a child. But I never quite understood why she *was* arrested. You were in the leadership at the time. I wondered if you knew anything?'

'Even we didn't know everything. We only saw what Stalin wanted us to see.'

'So you know she was arrested for lack of vigilance with state secrets and abetting an Enemy of the People. She was named again in the Doctors' Plot for planning to murder some of the leaders medically and if Stalin hadn't died . . .'

'She'd have been shot.'

'Yes. She thought she'd had a lucky escape. But could it have been something to do with my father?'

'Possibly. Stalin arrested the wives of Molotov, Kalinin and Poskrebyshev.'

'Well, my father's been dead for twenty years now, and I sometimes wonder whether her arrest could have been connected to the Children's Case.'

'Also possible. She helped Benya Golden get the job at the school. Did you know they were at university together in Odessa?'

Senka tilted his head, and Satinov was struck once again by his likeness to Dashka.

'And then there's this,' Senka said. 'Something's always bothered me. Could it have been anything to do with me?'

Satinov thought for a while. 'Tell me,' he said at last. 'Did your mother ever talk about her patients at home?'

'No. Sometimes she whispered to my father, and I heard a couple of names.'

'Such as?'

'Well, there was Zhdanov, but everyone knew about his heart disease.'

Satinov nodded. 'You always knew quite a lot for a youngster, but then you were the Little Professor.'

Senka's answering smile was the very image of his mother's. 'Why do you ask if my mother talked about her patients?'

'Just curiosity. She was so discreet.' Satinov offered him a cigarette and took one himself. 'It must have been quite an experience being arrested during the Children's Case.'

'Your Mariko was even younger.'

'True, but she was only there for a short time. You spent much longer in Lubianka.'

'It was frightening but I concentrated very hard, even though I was so young, on not getting my parents into trouble.'

'You know we executed Komarov and Likhachev with Abakumov in 1954?'

A look of distaste crossed Senka's sensitive face. What does one expect from a liberal intellectual? thought Satinov.

'They were thugs,' he said. 'After Stalin's death, I read your interrogations in the KGB files. I have to say: they set you a terrible trap.'

'They wanted me to incriminate my parents.'

Satinov shook his head. 'Our Organs were full of criminal elements in Stalin's time.'

Senka looked anxious. 'At the time, I thought my solution had worked. But when they arrested my mother, I wasn't so sure. I long to know if I was to blame for what happened to her next.'

Satinov got up and went to his huge chrome safe. He opened

it, brought out a heap of papers, and leafed through them. 'I was looking at these the other day. And here it is, how clever you were. You see here? After your testimony: "Accusations not to be pursued."' He paused. 'I was there when you came out. Do you remember?'

'I do, very clearly.'

'When you saw your mother sitting there in the waiting room, you were so excited. We could hear you talking about her; you were so proud of her!'

Senka threw his head back just like Dashka. 'That's right!'

Satinov clicked his fingers. 'But then you said something else. I can almost hear it. What was it?'

'Well, I said Mama was the best doctor in Russia.'

'What else?'

'That all the top people saw her!'

'Ah – that was it,' said Satinov, thinking back to his days in exile when he had almost wished Dashka ill for making him love her so much. There had been times too when he wondered if he personally had brought about her downfall. Now, finally, Senka had solved things.

What Senka had not known was that just before the Victory Parade in June 1945, Poskrebyshev, Stalin's secretary, had made an appointment to see his mother. He had told her that he himself was not ill. Instead, he had driven her to a dacha where she had examined Stalin, diagnosed arteriosclerosis and a small heart attack, and advised at least three months' rest. Aware that his frailty was the only obstacle to his supremacy, Stalin had never consulted her again. His doctors were the only people on earth who had any power over him, their diagnoses the only threat to his power.

Now Satinov realized that Senka, who had so effectively protected his mama, had announced to a roomful of Chekists:

'Oh yes, she's the best doctor in the world. She sees all the top people.' Reported somehow by word of mouth, this had reached Stalin. *All the top people!* All? Stalin would wonder: Had she spoken about her top patient? This was more than enough to destroy her. Hence the charge: 'Mishandling state secrets.'

Satinov sighed; his arthritis was painful. He had been the only person Dashka had told. She hadn't mishandled state secrets at all.

'It couldn't have been that, could it?' asked Senka, anxious again.

'Not at all. You managed to get out of there without saying a single thing wrong.'

Senka relaxed visibly and his dark eyes glinted. 'What a relief,' he said. 'Thank you. Now I really should be going.'

Satinov stood up and offered his hand. 'Did your mother say anything for me? About the package?'

Senka looked into Satinov's grey eyes for a long moment. 'No. Nothing.'

Satinov understood then that Senka knew about his love for his mother – and he was glad. Their story lived on.

Wearing a blue cap, Andrei was driving a beige Lada up the drive towards an ugly government dacha, a wooden shooting lodge that looked like an oversized Swiss chalet. Four ZiL limousines were parked there, as stately as royal barges. Two bodyguards, specimens of Homo Sovieticus, wearing overtight suits, fat brown ties and combover hairdos, came down the steps with the macho insouciance of KGB men on duty. Andrei showed them their identity cards for the fourth time that hour, and the guards barked into walkie-talkies, returned their IDs and gestured towards Serafima.

Andrei came round to open Serafima's door. He watched her walk up the steps into the chalet. At the top of the steps, she looked back at him and smiled and raised her hand in a slight wave. Then she went inside.

He sat listlessly for a few minutes. Fate had brought him Serafima, and now his marriage hung in the balance. Nikolasha and Rosa had died for the romantic delusion: totalitarian love as reckless melodrama and desperate possession, an orchestra of trumpets and thunderbolts. Now he saw clearly that the real poetry of love was a meandering river, an accumulation of accidents, the momentum of details.

He reached onto the floor of the back seat and grabbed a wad of essays. Holding them against the steering wheel, he started to mark them with a red pen. Just after Stalin's death, Director Medvedeva had hired him to teach Pushkin at School 801, where he was loved by generations of pupils for the flamboyant way he brought *Onegin* to life.

Yes, thought Andrei Kurbsky, he and Serafima owed so much to the clandestine generosity of decent people who had the courage to spread the warmth of kindness even in the age of ice. But they owed most to Benya Golden, and not just a love of poetry. They had named their son Benya, and their daughter Adele, after Pushkin's verse that Benya had recited to Serafima. And Andrei always started his classes with Benya's words: 'Dear friends, beloved romantics, wistful dreamers . . .'

Serafima was escorted through the shooting lodge, into the gardens and to the edge of the birch woods. Dapper and slim, Frank Belman waited for her in a camel-hair coat, a spotted Hermès tie, khaki-coloured slacks and a pair of Gucci loafers. He turned and came towards her, stopping a step away. She did not know what she expected him to do – but he offered her his hand formally.

'I'm so glad you came,' he said. 'I hope you didn't mind that I contacted you . . .'

'No, I wasn't surprised,' said Serafima. 'I knew we'd meet again one day.'

'I'm speaking English because I know you're an English teacher.'

'How well informed you are.'

'Can we walk through the woods? English was your favourite subject, along with Pushkin.'

'You have a good memory.'

'Of course.'

He seemed very assured, this prince of capitalist America, much more confident than the young, faltering Frank she remembered. She was not sure that any part of *her* Frank remained in this suntanned, grey-haired statesman and millionaire. There is nothing for me here, she thought.

'It seems a long time ago,' he went on.

'Yes.' She felt disappointed and yet relieved as she realized she wanted to go home. How could she end this tactfully?

'You know I'm married with four children now?' he said.

'I'm pleased for you.'

'And you?'

'Yes, I'm also married and I have two children.'

He nodded. 'You look wonderful.'

'You seem a real American plutocrat.' She forced a smile. 'One of those villains we read about in our propaganda!' She paused. 'Frank, I'm pleased to have met you again, I really am – but I think I should go now.'

Frank looked most concerned. 'Did I say something wrong? There's so much I want to ask you.'

Serafima stepped back. 'I feel the same way. There's much to say but really there's nothing. So if you don't mind, I'll leave now.'

Satinov closed the doors of his study where so many important events of his life had taken place. At this desk Stalin had called to tell him the Nazis had invaded. Here he'd heard that his son Vanya had been killed. In that Venetian mirror he had seen himself crying about Dashka as he comforted Tamriko after the arrest of their children. Here Mariko had shown him her Moscow School for Bitches the day she came out of prison, Marlen had introduced his parents to his fiancée, and George and his wife had presented their baby son to him. Now he sat in his leather chair and looked at the package that seemed to him to have a faint glow like a lamp deep under the ice.

He cut the string, imagining Dashka, with her short fingers and plump gold-skinned wrists, tying these knots. Later he and Brezhnev would be negotiating the future peace of the world with the Americans. But now he could think of nothing except the woman he'd once loved so deeply. He remembered how, for a long time after Dashka had gone, his life with Tamara and the children had felt like a becalmed ship, and he had wondered if this was death until he realized this hushed serenity was the beginning of his return to happiness . . .

Inside the package was a green uniform, immaculately folded, somewhat faded, a book and some smaller objects. First he looked at the book: Chekhov's *Complete Short Stories*, a cheap edition from 1945. Instinctively he opened it at 'The Lady with the Little Dog' to read the page that she had once sent him, but when he reached the place, the page was missing and there was just a jagged edge. This was the very book she had used to tell him that she loved him – and she had kept it all these years.

Next he drew out the uniform, his hands shaking as much as they had when he had first laid his hands on her body and gradually unwrapped her so that he could touch her glowing skin. He stood up so that he could examine the uniform, and then unfolded it piece by piece on the floor like a body. Here was the tunic with the red cross and medical corps insignia, cinched at the waist, a green blouse, a khaki skirt, its hem turned up a little more than allowed by regulations, a pair of black silk stockings, one pair of plain army boots, a blue beret – and, pinned onto the tunic's lapel, a little Red Cross medical badge. He looked down at each item, utterly bowled over by the thought that had gone into this last present, by the sensuality of the woman who had kept all this, and by the boundless joy of knowing that she had always loved him, all this time.

Suddenly he fell to his knees and lay full length on the uniform. He raised the blouse to his face and recognized her scent, Coty, from all those years ago.

'Hello, it's me!' she said in his ear.

He did not know how long he lay there, struggling for control. But after a while, he got to his feet and brushed himself down, went to the fireplace and fed the material into the flames. He left the tunic until last. He unclipped its medical badge and slipped it into his trouser pocket. As he raised the tunic to his lips for the last time, something heavy fell out of it and he looked down: it was her stethoscope. Old-fashioned, leather. He checked there was nothing left in the fire, but he placed the stethoscope on his desk.

There was a knock on the door: it was his young adjutant.

'Time to leave for the American Embassy in five minutes, Comrade Marshal.'

'Very good,' said Satinov.

'Your wife and daughter are back, Comrade Marshal.'

'Thank you.'

When the door was closed again, he went to the man-sized chrome safe in the corner of his office, unlocked it and brought out the yellowed page, torn long ago from a Chekhov story. Opening the book, he reunited the page with its torn edge, matching each tear on the paper to its other half. Then he closed the tome sharply. He smiled. The page and the book were reunited finally – just as he and the lady with the little dog could never be. He squeezed the book into the shelf next to his desk and his hand was still resting on it when Tamriko came into the study to kiss him.

She noticed the stethoscope immediately: 'That's new,' she said. 'From the war perhaps?'

'Yes,' he said, 'just something from the war. A veteran medic sent it to me.'

'A veteran?' She glanced at him acutely. 'Are you going to keep it?'

'May I?' he asked.

'Yes, of course. You must. What a lovely thing to have. A keepsake.'

'Goodbye, Frank,' said Serafima, offering her hand coldly.

'Goodbye.' He offered his hand too. 'Dear enchantress.' She stood frozen to the earth. 'You know I do remember. Everything,' he said softly.

'Me too.' She broke into a smile. 'Then you will appreciate that I teach Hemingway, Edith Wharton, Galsworthy.'

The names of these authors seemed to strike him as hard as the word 'enchantress' had struck her: he looked away from her and the air between them seemed to change.

'Our code!' His voice had grown husky. 'Serafima, I never forgave myself for your arrest and your time in the camps. It took me years to find out what had happened. Of course I didn't believe that you were really ill on the train, but there was nothing more I could do. We couldn't ask your family without putting them in danger and I felt so guilty that I had ruined your life. It's only now, with *détente,* that I could enquire about you. Thank God you survived, but what I really want to say is . . .' He paused and took her hands. '. . . will you forgive me for what happened?'

Serafima could hardly speak. 'There's nothing to forgive. You were the greatest blessing in my life. You still are. You always will be.' She looked at him, remembering the way he always greeted her with his trademark two-fingered salute, brimming with excitement at seeing her again. 'When did you marry?'

'Nineteen fifty-one. I waited for you for six years.'

'I was still in the Gulags then.' She imagined his diamond engagement ring on the finger of another woman, his wife, the mother of his children. Yet she had released him on that snowy night with Dashka. She, the ghost, had no right to it.

'You know, I still often find myself saying aloud: "Missing you, loving you, wanting you,"' he said.

'So do I,' she whispered. 'I thought of you . . . I thought of you every day in the camps. When I looked at the sun at midday and the northern star at midnight.'

'Not a day passes when I haven't remembered you, Serafimochka.'

'And I you, Frank,' she said. 'But we're both married, and we both have families we love.'

'You're right,' he said, reaching into his pocket as if he was looking for something. 'But shouldn't we keep in contact?'

She thought for a minute, and then shook her head. 'We can't go back, you and I. But you should know: I shall always love you, and nothing will ever change this.'

'I feel the same way,' he said. 'But oh, how I wish it was 1945 again, and we could plan our lives together.'

They walked on through the afternoon sunshine.

'How long were you in the camps?' he asked.

'Eight years.'

'So long. How terrible. How did you survive?'

'I was saved by a dear friend, a doctor – though thinking about you, remembering the time we spent together, helped me survive too.'

Frank closed his eyes for a moment. 'Are your parents alive?'

'Yes. My mother.'

He shook his head. 'If it wasn't for her, we'd be together. Did she get that damned part in the movie?'

'That's the silly thing,' replied Serafima. 'In the end, she didn't get any big parts anymore. Stalin decided she was too Jewish.'

'Your mother felt guilty about you, I guess?'

'For this and for the burn when I was little, but she desperately tried to make up for it and get me freed.'

'What do you mean?'

'I would never tell anyone this, but you. But she bargained with all she had, first with Beria and then with Abakumov, to win my freedom.'

'You mean . . . ? Jesus. Poor woman.'

'Beria just forced himself on her and then it turned out that he no longer ran the Organs, while Abakumov courted her like an old-fashioned knight, but she succumbed too late – just before he was himself sacked and arrested.'

'So she gave herself for nothing? But at the same time she redeemed herself?'

'She didn't need to in my eyes, but yes, I suppose she did.'

'I think we should turn back now,' he said.

'Yes, we must.'

He started to say something, stopped, and then tried again: 'Before we go back, may I do one thing? I've thought about it all these years.'

Serafima took a quick breath as he moved towards her. She nodded. Was he going to kiss her?

He placed his hand on her blouse right over the snakeskin.

'A loving enchantress
Gave me her talisman.
She told me with tenderness . . .'

He recited it in his perfect Russian and Serafima replied:

'. . . You must not lose it.
Its power is infallible,
Love gave it to you.'

'You never did lose it,' she said quietly, feeling a passionate lightness, exactly like she had as a young girl when he first traced the snakeskin and made love to her. She felt her skin answer his touch.

'No,' he answered. 'Because an enchantress gave it to me.'

They walked back holding hands. When they saw the house, he kissed her on the lips and she kissed him back.

'Kissing you is exactly the way it always was,' she said.

She saw he had tears in his eyes, so to let him recover, she walked the last few metres on her own. Up the steps, through the house and out to her car on the other side.

'Where would like me to take you?' asked Andrei when she got into the car. His hands were, she noticed, tapping quickly on the steering wheel.

'Home, of course,' she answered. 'Where else?'

Later that day, after many hours of negotiation, Marshal Hercules Satinov and Ambassador Frank Belman walked through the woods together with the camaraderie and satisfaction that comes with the completion of a project after meticulous and diligent effort. Both were tired; Belman was much younger and noticed that Satinov walked stiffly. After they had talked about the weather, Satinov said, 'I hope, Ambassador, you found what you wanted this morning.'

'Yes, Marshal. I found all I wanted to find.'

A silence except for the birds and their light steps on a carpet of pine needles.

'You can't wish for more than that,' said Satinov. 'To heal the wounds of the past.'

Another pause.

'And you?' Frank asked. 'You said you had received a visit from your past.'

'Yes,' said Satinov, looking out at the woods. His tone was measured. 'It proved satisfactory.'

'You can't wish for more than that,' said Frank – and he

reached into his pocket to touch the diamond ring that he had never given to anyone else, that he had kept all these years, that he had brought for her today.

'When I consider everything,' Satinov said, 'I think we're both lucky men.'

'You're right,' Frank said, holding the ring as if for luck. 'We are the luckiest of all. But I hope you too managed to heal the wounds of the past.'

'There was nothing to heal on my side,' Satinov said gruffly and he walked on ahead, playing with something in his hand. Frank thought it might be worry beads but as he caught up, he saw it was a flimsy medical badge.

A keepsake from the war.

History

FACTS AND FICTION

The chief characters in this novel – Satinov, Dashka, Serafima, Benya and Belman – are entirely invented by me. This is not a novel about power but about private life – above all, love. But it is set amidst the Stalinist Kremlin élite and that means that the familiar dilemmas of family life, the prizes and perils of children, adultery and career, have higher stakes than if the story were set in Hampstead. This novel stands alone, but some of the characters and the families appear in my earlier novel, *Sashenka*.

Obviously some of the Soviet leaders, generals and secret policemen are based on real people and the details of their personalities, sometimes even their words, are accurate. My aim is to make the atmosphere as authentic as I can, but the joy of this is that it is fiction.

For anyone interested in the plausibility of the plot or its inspirations, the novel is very roughly inspired by several true stories.

In 1943, two schoolchildren, both the offspring of high-ranking Soviet officials, died in a shooting on Kammeny Most. In their notebooks, the secret police found joke plans for a government. Their friends, who included many children of the élite, including the sons of Politburo member Anastas Mikoyan, were arrested on suspicion of being members of an anti-Soviet conspiracy. The full story appears in my book *Stalin: The Court of the Red Tsar*, and also in the memoirs of Anastas Mikoyan, *Tak Bylo*, and of his son, *Stepan Anastasovich Mikoyan: An Autobiography: Memoirs of Military Test-flying and Life with the Kremlin's Élite*. I myself interviewed some of the children in question, including Stepan and Sergo Mikoyan and Stalin's own nephew, Stan Redens. The children were in prison for six months and were released only after signing confessions. Their punishment was six months' exile in Central Asia. The Fatal Romantics and the Game are totally invented by me.

In 1944–45, Major Hugh Lunghi of the British Embassy met and fell in love with a Russian girl whom he wished to marry. Lunghi translated for Churchill during meetings with Stalin at the Big Three conferences. When his fiancée tried to leave Russia, she was poisoned on the train and brought back to Moscow. At a personal meeting with Stalin, the British ambassador asked him to allow the girl to leave. He promised to look into it. However, his fiancée was never released. Instead she was arrested for treason and sentenced to the Gulags. Lunghi was not able to make contact with her again until the sixties, when both were happily married to other people.

Stalin was a stickler for showing no favour to the children of leaders, and especially not to his own. He refused to swap his eldest son, Yakov, when he was captured by the Nazis, and was infuriated by the spoilt and decadent escapades of his second son, Vasily. During the war, Vasily took his unit on a fishing expedition during which he and his men used grenades to catch fish. A man was killed and an outraged Stalin had Vasily cashiered and demoted. But such was the reverence shown to the Leader's son (and Stalin's own ambitions for the boy) that he was soon promoted way beyond his limited talents to air force general. On his watch, an air force flypast went catastrophically wrong and ended in a plane crash, and he was demoted again.

In 1945, Stalin was informed at Potsdam by his son Vasily Stalin that Soviet aircraft frequently crashed owing to a manufacturing flaw. Stalin then orchestrated the so-called Aviators' Case against Air Marshal Novikov and other leading military officers as well as Aviation Minister Shakurin. The case was partly aimed at the Politburo member in charge of aircraft, Georgi Malenkov, who was temporarily demoted, but was actually part of a sustained campaign to diminish the power of the Soviet marshals, particularly the ultimate hero, Marshal Georgi Zhukov. Novikov and many other officers were viciously tortured and some were shot. Malenkov was temporarily sent to check the harvest in Central Asia.

Stalin encouraged a rivalry between two secret police chiefs: Beria, long-serving head of the NKVD, and Victor Abakumov, chief of SMERSH, who reported directly to Stalin. Abakumov and Beria were constantly complaining about each other to Stalin. In 1945, Stalin reduced the power of Beria in secret-police matters by sacking him as Interior Minister. Yet Beria remained Stalin's top manager and Deputy Premier, taking charge of the most important project of the era: the creation of the Soviet nuclear bomb. Beria's protégé Merkulov remained State Security Minister until he was sacked in 1946 and replaced by Abakumov. After Stalin's death, Beria, Merkulov and Kobylov were executed in 1953 and Abakumov in 1954.

In 1945, Stalin suffered some sort of coronary attack or minor stroke. He was extremely sensitive about the details of any illnesses which might undermine his political power and suspicious of doctors: hence the Doctors' Plot. His own long-term doctors who diagnosed his arteriosclerosis were arrested. (See below.)

Sexual abuse of female prisoners and ordinary female citizens was the informal prerogative of secret-police bosses, who often used the threat of the arrest of loved ones to blackmail women into giving sexual favours: on his arrest in 1953, Beria's rape and abuse of hundreds if not thousands of women were revealed. His two chief bodyguards, Colonels Sarkisov and Nadaraia, were exposed as pimps and kidnappers of girls whom Beria spotted on the streets of Moscow. It was revealed that Beria had twice caught VD during the war. Abakumov too abused his position. In 1946, Abakumov ordered the arrest of film star Tatiana Okunevskaya after she turned him down; earlier, Beria had drugged and raped her. Stalin turned a blind eye to these cases of favoured potentates but encouraged his henchmen to collect evidence to use against them later.

After 1945, the rise of American superpowerdom and the American support for Zionism that led to the creation of Israel turned Stalin's existing prejudices against Jews into obsessional and deadly anti-Semitism. Stalin created a series of anti-Semitic cases against Soviet Jews, leading first to sackings, then arrests, the killing of Yiddish actor/Jewish leader Solomon Mikhoels in a faked car crash in 1948 and finally the deadly anti-Jewish cases of 1949–50 (in which most of the defendants – Party officials and writers – were executed). In the Doctors' Plot of 1952–53, doctors in the Kremlin Clinic, particularly the cardiologists and the Jews, were accused of murdering and planning to murder Politburo leaders, starting with Andrei Zhdanov, who died of heart disease in 1948.

The wife of Nikolai Bulganin, Politburo member, Armed Forces Minister, Marshal, taught English at one of Moscow's élite secondary schools.

During this period Eisenstein was writing and directing the movie *Ivan the Terrible Part One* and *Part Two*; Stalin supervised the script. The Katyusha was a famous Soviet rocket launcher and there was a popular song called 'Katyusha' – but no movie of that name.

The fictional celebrity couple of writer Constantin Romashkin and the film star Sophia 'Mouche' Zeitlin are inspired partly by the experiences of the real film stars Tatiana Okunevskaya and Valentina Serova. The latter was married to Constantin Simonov, famed poet and Soviet official. As I explained above, Okunevskaya suffered bitterly at the hands of Beria and Abakumov. Serova was luckier but had an affair with Vasily Stalin. Their stories appear in many books, including Simonov's own autobiography, but is told best in Orlando Figes' excellent book *The Whisperers*.

On women in government: one inaccuracy. Stalin distrusted women – and doctors – and never promoted any female to be a full minister, though there were several leaders' wives serving as deputy ministers in his government, including the wives of Politburo members Molotov and Andreyev. Both women were dismissed at least partly for their Jewish origins. Like Dashka Dorova, Polina Molotova was ultimately arrested and divorced by her husband. On her return from prison after Stalin's death, she too returned to her marriage.

The details of daily life, school life and bureaucracy are also accurate, but I have telescoped some of the dates for the purposes of my story. For example, the conversion of People's Commissariats to Ministries – so that the secret police changed from the NKGB to the MGB and the NKVD became the MVD – was a little later in 1946, as was the promotion of Vasily Stalin to general; the granting of military ranks to secret policemen; the sacking of Merkulov as MGB Minister and his replacement by Abakumov; and the real Aviators' Case. The real Children's Case actually took place in 1943. The full story of the history behind this novel can be found in my *Stalin: The Court of the Red Tsar*, but I also recommend Anne Applebaum's *Gulag* and Orlando Figes' *The Whisperers* and *Just Send Me Word*, both of which contain many examples of the sort of stories told in this novel and *Sashenka*.

Acknowledgements

I wish to thank the following friends and sources whose stories have helped inspire this novel with the elixir of passion and the detail of authenticity: Hugh Lunghi, Gela Charkviani, Nestan Charkviani, General Stepan Mikoyan and his daughter Aschen Mikoyan, Sergo Mikoyan, Stanislas Redens, Galina Babkova, Rachel and Marc Polonsky, and Sophie Shulman.

First: Hugh Lunghi. Hugh and I became friends while writing my books on Stalin because he translated for Churchill at some of the Big Three meetings with Stalin. He kindly told me the entire story of his Russian love affair, which inspired Serafima's story. Without him the book could not have been written.

Gela Charkviani, son of Kandide Charkviani, Stalin's First Secretary of Georgia 1938–51, shared his elegant memoirs of élite life, *Memoirs of a Provincial Communist Prince*. Sophie Shulman kindly let me read her fascinating memoirs, *Life Journey of a Secular Humanist*. Gela Charkviani and Sophie Shulman answered my questions about their schooldays in Stalin's Russia. General Stepan Mikoyan, air force pilot, and Sergo Mikoyan, sons of Politburo member Anastas Mikoyan, were both arrested (Sergo was fourteen) in the real Children's Case and both talked to me about their experience, as did Stanislas Redens, Stalin's nephew, who was also arrested.

Thanks to the Polonskys, who had me to stay in Molotov's apartment in the Granovsky building.

I am hugely grateful to my brilliant, tireless and meticulous editor and publisher, Selina Walker, and to the irrepressibly superb Georgina Capel, the best agent in town. Thanks to my parents for editing this.

Above all, thanks to my wife, Santa, for the supreme gifts of serene love and best friendship; and for shrewd advice on this book; and to my adored children, Lily and Sasha, who have inspired the children in both my Russian novels.

SSM